SIGHT UNSEEN

Graham Hurley

This first world edition published 2019
in Great Britain and the USA by
SEVERN HOUSE PUBLISHERS LTD of
Eardley House, 4 Uxbridge Street, London W8 7SY.
Trade paperback edition first published
in Great Britain and the USA 2020 by
SEVERN HOUSE PUBLISHERS LTD.

British Library Cataloguing in Publication Data
A CIP catalogue record for this title is available from the British Library.

ISBN-13: 978-0-7278-8919-5 (cased)
ISBN-13: 978-1-78029-629-6 (trade paper)
ISBN-13: 978-1-4483-0322-9 (e-book)

All Severn House titles are printed on acid-free paper.

Severn House Publishers support the Forest Stewardship Council™ [FSC™],
the leading international forest certification organisation. All our titles that
are printed on FSC certified paper carry the FSC logo.

Typeset by Palimpsest Book Production Ltd.,
Falkirk, Stirlingshire, Scotland.
Printed and bound in Great Britain by
TJ International, Padstow, Cornwall.

To Isobel and Toddy
with love

ONE

It's a hot Friday morning in mid-summer, and I'm in a script conference when my mobile goes off. The opening bars of 'Simply the Best', a download present from H last Christmas.

I glance at the number. We happen to have arrived at an awkward impasse and I'm glad of the interruption. The fact that the call has come from Malo widens my smile. We haven't talked for nearly a week.

'Mum? That you?'

Something's badly wrong. Panic is a word I've never associated with my son.

'What's the matter?'

'It's Clem.'

Clem is family-speak for Clemenza, Malo's girlfriend.

'She's OK?'

'No.'

'What's happened?'

'She's been kidnapped.'

'*Kidnapped?*'

I've just spent two and a half hours with a scriptwriter, a very good friend of mine called Pavel, trying to tease dramatic sense into various fictional possibilities which may, one day, make a great movie. Kidnap sounds as fanciful as some of the wilder ideas we've been kicking around. Just how do you make room for something like this in the real world?

'When?' I manage. 'How?'

Malo is struggling. I play mum, telling him to take a deep breath, telling him that nothing is ever as bad as it first seems. The facts, please. In broadly the right order.

'When did you last see her?'

'Last night. I was staying at her place.'

'And?'

'It was great. Like it always is.'

'That's not what I'm asking. What happened next?'

'We got up as usual. Clem went to work.'

Clem is a top-end moto courier and chauffeuse. She rides a scarlet Harley-Davidson with bass notes to kill for and is the ride of choice for a number of faces you'll recognize from movie posters in any Tube station. She also happens to be the daughter of a very wealthy Colombian business tycoon, a family connection that – just now – is beginning to trouble me. I ask Malo whether they'd been in touch at all since she'd left for work.

'Twice. We were supposed to get together again this afternoon. Womad. Her dad gave us tickets. We were going down there on the Harley.'

Womad is a yearly celebration of global music, art and dance. I know Clem makes the pilgrimage to deepest Wiltshire every summer because she's told me so. Since his return from Sweden last year, Malo has also become a disciple, partly because he knows that Clem – who gigs at various London pubs – is desperate to break into the festival circuit, but mainly because he worships her.

'You said kidnapped.'

'Yeah.'

'How do you know?'

'I got a message with a photo. A couple of hours ago.'

'From?'

'I've no idea. The phone's probably a burner. Untraceable.'

'You've been to the police?'

'No.'

'Why not?'

'Because they said they'd kill her if I did.'

'And what else did this message say?'

'It said they've got Clem. I can have her back for a million. They want it in US dollars. I've got until Monday to find the money.'

'Otherwise?'

There's a silence at the other end. Monday is just three days away. Pavel has his laptop on his knees, his eyes closed, his long fingers gliding over the keyboard. His face is deeply tanned, with signs of UV damage below his hairline. When Malo returns to the phone, I can tell my son is close to tears.

'It was the photo,' he mutters. 'That's all I've got to go on.'

'And?'

'Shit. You don't want to know. Oh, Jesus Christ. Why her, of all people? Why us?'

Pavel looks up the moment Malo brings the conversation to an end. He wants to discuss a scene we have in mind involving our movie's love interest. I tell him it's not possible. Pavel is blind, just one of the reasons he's always attuned to the imminence of disaster. His guide dog, a Labrador, dozes at his feet.

'So what's happened?'

I explain as best I can. Clem. Kidnappers. A photo.

'Have you seen it? This photo?'

'No.'

'So what's so horrible about it?'

Pavel is normally world class at cutting to the chase, but this question sets the bar very high indeed. As the happy recipient of a number of gangster scripts in my time, I can think of countless images that might qualify. Men in balaclavas. Large dogs, always male. A suggestive blade or two. But Malo is close to my heart and I know that all it would take would be the knowledge that Clem was at the mercy of a bunch of strangers. Her face upturned to the camera. Fear in those huge brown eyes. So simple. And so effective.

'I have to phone H,' I say. 'He'll know what to do.'

Pavel isn't sure this is a good idea. Unlike the rest of us, he's never set eyes on Malo's father, but they've been together on a handful of occasions and I've become aware that blindness sharpens every other instinct. Pavel's take on strangers is near faultless. Tiny speech inflections. Body language transmitted through a raspy cough or a shuffle of feet or the impatient clink of coins in a trouser pocket. Even certain brands of aftershave. Minutes after he'd first met H, when we were back in the safety of my battered Peugeot, he'd delivered his verdict.

'Your friend needs to own you,' he'd said. Pavel uses language with the precision of a poet. 'Needs', not 'wants'. A very shrewd distinction.

My 'friend' answers on the third ring. I've ignored Pavel's advice not to make contact until we've settled the debate about going to the police. H, it turns out, has just stepped into Terminal 2 at Heathrow. Malo's news has taken the wind out of me. I dimly remember talk of a business meeting on movie finance with a venture capitalist in Lyon a couple of weeks back. This is a guy with serious money who happens to have taken a shine to a film of mine that did well on the French arthouse circuit. Lunch on a restaurant terrace overlooking the Rhône. A couple of bottles of Krug and a taxi waiting for the return trip to the airport once a handshake deal is in place. Very H.

At first he assumes I'm phoning to wish him luck.

'Piece of piss,' he assures me. 'You around tonight? We need to get the dosh nailed down. The usual place, yeah? Half seven. They don't take dogs, so it's just the two of us. Tell your writer bloke we'll brief him in the morning. Malo OK?'

The writer bloke is Pavel. On the phone to H, I break the news about Clem. For once in the often awkward *pas de deux* that makes do as our relationship, Malo's father is lost for words.

'Say that again,' he manages at last.

I can picture him riding the escalator up to the Departures floor, a small, squat figure with greying curly hair and a hint of a belly beneath the Italian lambskin leather jacket. Since I first stumbled into H's life, largely by accident, he's always struck me as someone for whom life holds few surprises. Until now.

Once again, I spell out what little I know. Malo isn't the kind of boy to make this stuff up.

'He was around when all this happened? Malo?'

'I don't think so. He said they sent him a message.'

'They? Who's fucking "they"?'

'He's no idea.'

'So how do we know they're not dicking him around?'

'There was a photo of Clem, too. Small girl. *Petite*. Very pretty.'

My attempt at irony is lost on H. He's met her a number of times and already regards her as part of our putative family.

'Any proof they hadn't lifted the photo? Was she holding up today's paper, maybe? Today's headline? What you see isn't always what you get. Not these days.'

I stare at my phone and risk a tiny shake of the head. Fake news, I think. Except that my darling boy isn't easily fooled.

'I haven't seen the photo,' I point out. 'But if Malo thinks they mean it, that's good enough for me.'

'You're telling me he's seen this coming? Blokes sniffing around? Following her on that bike of hers? Phone calls, maybe?'

'I've no idea. It wasn't that kind of conversation. Boys need their mothers sometimes, even Malo.'

H grunts. I was right about the escalator. It's delivered him to the Departures level and now he's riding back down again.

'You're at home?'

'I am.'

'Stay there. I can screw the French guy another day.'

TWO

Home is a top-floor flat in a thirties block in Holland Park. The shared spaces – inside and out – are immaculate and recently the management company that looks after the place has taken to putting fresh flowers on every landing and even in the lift. Pavel, who comes here more often than I suspect H would like, says the smell reminds him of one of those boutique hotels favoured by the wealthier production companies. Last night, for the first time, he and the dog stayed over.

Until last year, to my shame, I'd never heard of Pavel Sieger. Then I won the female lead in a radio play for the Beeb, *Going Solo*, authored by Pavel. In some respects it was a comfortably old-fashioned piece, the story of a woman married to a pilot on the Isle of Wight. Together, they build a business around an old manor house and a fully restored P-51 Mustang until the husband is mysteriously killed. To stay both sane and solvent, the woman – me – must learn to fly this World War Two beast of a fighter while trying to understand the real circumstances of her husband's death.

At first glance the script was nicely constructed with tonally perfect dialogue, especially for the female lead. This isn't as easy a trick to master as you might imagine, and it wasn't until after the play was transmitted, to modest critical acclaim, that I had the chance to meet the author. By then I was having to deal with three courses of chemo to attack the return of an aggressive brain tumour that had nearly killed me. Hairless, horribly prone to bruising, and intermittently distraught, I'd accepted the offer of lunch from Pavel with some reluctance.

On the phone, by way of an excuse, I'd mentioned the chemo and told him the nausea had killed my appetite. In response he'd offered his sympathies and told me to expect a tallish guy with a white stick, a lovely dog and a bit of a limp. If I preferred to meet somewhere else I only had to say. Alternatively, I might not want to share lunch with him at all. Shamed, I'd said yes to his original invitation and later that week we found ourselves in a Thai restaurant in Notting Hill Gate.

On reflection, much later, I realized that Pavel had never really explained why he'd asked me to lunch in the first place, but at the time it never really seemed to matter. We actresses spend our entire professional lives pretending to be somebody else and I knew from the moment I'd settled at the table that Pavel perfectly understood this strange multiplicity of selves.

One of the consequences of cheating the Grim Reaper is the discovery that time is a precious commodity. Faced with a middle-aged blind man whose writing I deeply respected, I saw no point in dodging the obvious question. Had he been sightless from birth? Or had something happened more recently?

The frankness of my curiosity seemed to please him. It had happened a couple of years back, he told me, thanks to a condition called GCA. This little acronym (giant cell arteritis) had run amok in the family. His dad was blind, and so was an uncle and a niece. Through his twenties and most of his thirties Pavel thought he'd got away with it, but then came the headaches and a pain in his jaw when he tried to eat. Thirty minutes on Google told him the rest of the story.

'So how long did you have? Before the lights went out?'

'No one would tell me. Sometimes it can happen overnight. Other times the world just gets dimmer and dimmer. Disease is the house guest you'd never wish on anyone. One moment it's kicking over the furniture. The next it's made its excuses and left. At that point you think you're home free, but that's not true either.'

Home free. I remember nodding. The Reaper, I'd thought. And the dreaded knock on the door. By then, we were both tucking into bowls of pad Thai noodles. Pavel sat bolt upright at the table, the way you sometimes see concert pianists at the keyboard. His eyes were closed behind tinted glasses and I watched, fascinated, as he brought the bowl to his mouth and his chopsticks pursued tiny particles of shrimp and chicken nesting beneath the noodles. Over a pair of black jeans he wore a newly pressed shirt of startling whiteness, yet not one fleck of sauce made it out of the bowl.

That lunch was doubly remarkable. When I enquired about the limp, Pavel told me he'd been born with a club foot.

'It's a birth defect,' he explained. 'One foot has a mind of its own. It's turned inward. It won't move. Your chances of getting it are a thousand to one. Once I knew those odds I treated it like a lottery win. Club foot. Lucky old me.'

There wasn't an ounce of self-pity in his voice as he told me this. On the contrary, he seemed pleased – even proud – that he'd dreamed up this little wheeze to cope with his rebel genes. We split a bottle of decent Chablis between us, the Blind Man and the Chemo Queen, and for the first time in weeks I began to feel like a human being. Pavel, it turned out, wasn't his real name at all.

'I was born Paul Stukeley. Pavel is the Slavic cognate of Paul. Under the circumstances, a new name was the least I owed myself.'

'Circumstances?'

'Losing my sight. Blindness I was already imagining as a capsize. The boat I'd taken for granted was sinking. Pavel was my lifejacket, something to keep me afloat in the years that would follow. In my twenties, thank Christ, I made it my business to go and find truly beautiful places I'd remember for ever. Maybe it was an unconscious thing. Probably not. All the warning signs were there, my dad, my uncle, my niece. I was really close to my dad and after he'd gone blind I remember him telling me how he regretted not ever seeing the Grand Canyon. Me? I can live without the Grand Canyon, but I had a list of other places – mainly cities – that I wanted to store away for later in case it ever happened.'

And so a younger Paul Stukeley took cheap flights to sundry corners of Europe. Venice, disfigured by tourists, was a disappointment. Paris he adored already and it never let him down. But the real revelation was Prague.

'It was love at first sight. I went in late October. It was 2015. I'd been in a relationship for a while, several years, but it had come to a very ugly end and I needed to get away. Prague became my new mistress, just like that, and being alone helped enormously. Smoky dusks. The first cold breath of winter. The river the colour of steel as the light began to die. Wet cobblestones in the lamplight. Little bars it was impossible to pass. Until that week I never realized how despair and regret and disappointment and all the rest of it could bleed into something so delicious. I stayed until my money ran out.'

As the light began to die.

In the restaurant, after Pavel had magically summoned the waiter and asked for the bill, I asked him when – exactly – he'd lost his sight. He told me it had happened that same year, 2015, but mercifully after Christmas.

'Why mercifully?'

'Because I went back to Prague. Just to make sure I hadn't imagined it.'

'And?'

'It was beautiful. It was unforgettable. It even snowed. I was still alone but that didn't seem to matter. It was a kind of consummation. That was the moment I became Pavel Sieger.'

'And the blindness?'

'New Year's Eve. I went to bed fully sighted and woke up in darkness. I knew at once what had happened, of course, but the odd thing was that it still took me by surprise. Even with all the clues, all the warnings, you never see blindness coming.'

You never see blindness coming.

That single phrase – so simple, so clever, so *right* – is the very essence of Pavel. He knows how to condense some of life's trickier propositions and put them on the page. This, believe me, is a very rare talent. I sensed it the moment I first read the radio script and I know it now. But this is also a man with a highly developed sense of how life can hurt him. He has the weightlessness of the true nomad. Which is why, this morning in my flat, he doesn't want to hang around and wait for H to arrive. Very sensible.

THREE

Hayden Prentice and I have little in common except our son, Malo. Malo was the result of a drunken night aboard a super yacht in Antibes eighteen years ago. I was a young jobbing actress. 'Saucy', as he was then known, had made a fortune from the wholesale importation of cocaine, laundering the money through a string of canny investments. The yacht belonged to a mate of Saucy's. The following day I took a train down the coast to the Cannes Film Festival and met the man who soon became my husband, and Malo's assumed father. Seventeen years later, my marriage over, a DNA test turned all our worlds upside down.

By this time Hayden Prentice had become 'H' rather than 'Saucy', and he was delighted to discover the son whose existence he'd never once suspected. Malo fell in love with his new dad, with Flixcombe Manor and its hundreds of acres of prime west Dorset, and with the kind of golden life chances that brought him windfalls like Clemenza.

In H's eyes I, too, am cast as a windfall. H is a proud man. On only three occasions has he been drunk or desperate enough to admit that he wants – needs – me full time in his life. A whole floor of my own awaits me at Flixcombe Manor any time I fancy it. H will give me anything that money will buy. Yet at the same time, deep down, he knows that I'm not for sale. Is he in love with me? Yes, a little. Would it ever work out? No, never. This, I know for certain, H will never accept. Hence, perhaps, his sudden interest in movie-making.

He broke the news on the phone three months ago. He'd been paid a visit down at Flixcombe by a young London-based producer looking for locations for a series set in the West Country. H had scented an opening to a world he knew belonged to me and the young man had stayed for dinner. H poured expensive wine down his throat and learned a great deal about the insane economics of movie-making.

Nine out of ten projects are duds. They cost a lot of money and lose even more. But that tenth movie – that golden script that ends up in the right directorial hands – can open the door to a kind of immortality, something beautifully shaped, artfully realized, that will be around as long as people have eyes to see. This phrase, as you might guess, came from Pavel, which is where the trouble began.

On the phone, H sketched out his idea. He'd been doing a little reading and had discovered, to his delight, that a significant number of English stately homes owed their very existence to dodgy money. Smuggling, piracy, tobacco and the slave trade built some of the nation's finest estates, and within a single generation a bunch of hooligans had become pillars of the community. This, in H's parlance, proved that nothing talked louder than serious moolah, a fact that is still incontestable today. So far it was easy to understand H's interest. He, too, was a hooligan. And he, too, had money to burn. What he didn't have was a story. What was this film *about*?

At this point, he seemed to lose his thread. He said he'd found the perfect location. He had in mind all kinds of Tudor mischief. He wanted me to find someone who could mix all the usual ingredients together – greed, violence, sex, loss, death, lots of swash, lots of buckle – and stick it in the oven. Everyone knew that American audiences killed for those fancy olde-England yarns. Find the right story, get the right bloke on the case, and we'd all be rich.

'Richer,' I remember saying.

'Yeah.' He'd chuckled before ringing off. 'Bring it on.'

By now, I'd met Pavel. In the shape of *Going Solo* I knew he was a scriptwriter of real talent with a proven track record. I told him a little about H, enough to know he wouldn't be wasting his time, and in due course I engineered a meeting down in west Dorset. Normally H adores showing off the house and the surrounding estate, but the fact that Pavel is blind robbed him of the opportunity. Instead he had to fall back on statistics – three hundred-plus acres, a multitude of outhouses, a swimming pool, membership of the local hunt, blah, blah – which didn't begin to do the job.

Something else bothered him, too. Like Pavel, H trusts his instincts. He'd taken a hard look at the pair of us and didn't like what he saw. Late that night, once I'd got back to London, he phoned me. Under these circumstances, H sees no merit in any but the bluntest of questions.

'You're at it, aren't you?'

'Who? What?'

'You and the blind bloke. Is he there now?'

'Of course he's not. And even if he was, so what?'

'Put him on. I want a word.'

'I can't. He's not here.'

'Give me a number, then.'

'No.'

This is a word H genuinely hates. When the mood takes me I can be surprisingly stern. I told him he was out of order. I told him my life was my own. The one thing we shared, the one thing we had in common, was Malo, and if Malo ever dared behave like this, I'd give him a slap.

'But I'm his father,' H growled.

'Exactly. So act your age. Pavel happens to be a friend of mine. He also happens to have the talents you need.'

'*We* need.'

'Exactly. So give us a little space. Is that too much to ask?'

H was deeply uncomfortable with this proposition, but the businessman in him knew that I was right. I also suspected that deep down he couldn't imagine yours truly in the sack with a blind man. How wrong could he be?

Last night, Pavel confessed for the first time that he'd asked specifically for me to be auditioned for the lead role in *Going Solo*. Before blindness struck, he'd watched me in a film I made in Nantes called *The Hour of Our Passing*. This was a movie set during the darkest days of the wartime occupation of France. I was much younger then and I think it was the first performance that made me feel I might have a real future as a screen actress, not because I was especially brilliant, but because the film itself was so well conceived and written.

In a scene towards the end, I make love to the male lead whom the audience already know is doomed. It was my first taste of full nudity on set and it went far better than I'd ever imagined. I saw it again last year and marvelled that bits of me were once so firm, so sleek, and – lucky me – so perfectly lit. Curled on the sofa, waiting for Pavel's Uber to arrive, I asked him about that scene.

'You were very natural. That's hard to do.'

'You liked it?'

'Very much. I liked the film, too, if that's your next question.'

It wasn't. Chemo is behind me now and I'm looking forward to an imminent CT scan to see whether it worked or not. A little drunk, I asked Pavel to describe what I looked like in the Nantes movie.

'We're talking your face?'

'If that's what you'd like.'

'Then come here.'

I moved towards him, took his hands in mine. Pavel explored everything through his fingertips. I'd seen him doing it to countless objects over the past few months. Now it was my turn.

His fingers tracked softly across my face. I had my eyes closed. From time to time I heard a soft murmur of appreciation. When I finally opened my eyes, it was obvious that he was getting excited.

'Well?' I asked him. 'Is this the face you remember from that scene at the end?'

'It is. Have you ever walked the South Downs Way?'

'Never.'

'There's a feature called Ditchling Beacon. Back in the day I had a friend who lived in Brighton. In the summer I'd stay with her sometimes. She'd make us a picnic and we'd take the bus inland and climb the hill right up to the summit. On the south side there's a hollow. It's out of the wind. The sun's on your face. You can lie back against the warm turf and see right down to the coast. I was sighted then and I'll never forget that view. Your face reminds me of those afternoons. It feels like touching a memory. Life couldn't have been more perfect.'

'Is that a compliment?'

'It is.'

I smiled. I reached out for his tinted glasses and put them carefully to one side. We both knew this was the first time I'd seen his eyes properly. They were a pale shade of blue, opaque-looking and slightly milky around the edges.

'I feel naked,' he said. 'What do you think?'

His fingers had returned to my face, tracing the curve of my lips. His eyes were closed again, his head tipped slightly back.

'I think we should cancel the Uber,' I said. 'Give me your phone.'

FOUR

Pavel has been gone for more than two hours by the time H arrives.

'A million US,' he tells me the moment he steps into the apartment. 'By fucking Monday. What do these people think we are? Stupid?'

It turns out that he's made a detour en route back from the airport. Ten minutes on the phone to Malo in a tailback on the M4 had taken him to a handsome property in Belgravia where Clem's father, Mateo, had been only too glad to see him. To the best of my knowledge Señor Muñoz is a businessman, fabulously wealthy. H says I'm not wrong.

'Bloke's my size exactly, same build, probably the same background. He's been around a bit. He made a bundle on various deals in Bogotá, mainly property, and spread the winnings around before the last election. He was expecting the embassy in London, because that's where his daughter wanted to be, but it never happened, so he treated himself to a nice address and decided to take a couple of years off. Top man.'

'And Clem? Does Señor Muñoz have any thoughts about his daughter?'

H ignores my question. He's prowling around the kitchen. He says he didn't have time for a proper breakfast this morning. He's starving. I find eggs and a handful of mushrooms and start work on an omelette. Looking for the jar of capers, I ask him whether the kidnappers might be Colombians, maybe some kind of cartel.

'I asked the same.' H has found a packet of Florentines. 'Mateo says not. He already pays off most of the serious criminals back home and the rest have trouble getting up in the morning. No, he thinks this must be a local job. London dealers looking for easy money. She was always a target, that girl. Rich daddy. Out all hours on the bike. Real looker. No wonder they helped themselves.'

'And Malo?'

'All over the fucking place. I told him to get a grip. I told him we'd sort it. I just hope he was listening.'

'Has your new friend been to the police?'

'No way. Mateo got the message, too, and he believes them.'

'So he's paying up? Is that what you're telling me?'

'You have to be joking.' H is peering at the omelette pan. He wants more mushrooms. 'The bloke's like me. Can't stand the thought of dead money.'

Dead money. Not the kindest phrase under these circumstances.

I unearth the last of the mushrooms from the tray at the bottom of the fridge. H is telling me a little more about Clem's father. Back home in Bogotá, he says, kidnaps are ten a penny. Criminal gangs, political crazies, they're all at it, and each one follows the same script. First you keep the police out of it. Then you reject the kidnappers' opening bid and fence off the days to come for some heavy-duty negotiation. Money, H says, got Clemmie into this shit and money will get her out of it.

'But not a million dollars?' I enquire.

'Nothing like. Life's all conversation. Back in Bogotá, Mateo says everyone works on getting these people down to a tiny percentage of the upfront demand. A million US? On a good day that could end up at fifteen grand. Once you start talking, people see sense. Maybe fifteen or twenty was what they wanted in the first place – who fucking knows? All that matters is getting the girl back in one piece. We can save the rest for afters.'

'Afters?'

'These people are out of order. There are things you do and things you don't. Be careful who you piss off, eh?'

H has settled at the kitchen table. The news that I don't have any brown sauce puts a scowl on his face.

I want to know more about Malo. When he's up in London he always stays over at Clem's place, a rather nice Chelsea mews house that was evidently a present from her dad.

'Malo has the key?'

'Yeah.'

'And he's there now?'

'Yeah.' He's staring at the omelette. 'Salt?'

I do his bidding. Where, exactly, did Clem disappear?

'This morning.' H has his mouth full.

'I said where.'

'No one knows. According to Malo, her last job was a pick-up in Maida Vale. She never showed.'

'No word from her after that?'

'None. Mateo has contacts in the comms biz. He says her work phone has been switched off since 11.59 so no one was able to track her. Same with her private phone.'

'No peep at all?'

'Not a dicky.'

I nod. My list of obvious questions is more or less exhausted. I've never auditioned for a part as a private investigator and the real thing is beyond daunting. H will doubtless have ideas of his own about what happens next and that, too, is worrisome. I'm debating whether or not to counsel caution when he wipes the plate clean with a slice of bread and pushes the plate to one side. A coffee, he thinks, would be nice.

I'm about to tell him to make it himself but he grunts something about taking a leak and disappears. With some reluctance, I fill the kettle. This is my apartment, my castle, and I'm uncomfortably aware that Clem's disappearance has given H a fresh opportunity to barge over the drawbridge and into my life.

The coffee is instant. The single mug is starting to cool on the table and there's still no sign of H. I find him standing in the open door of my bedroom, staring in. There's a gurgle from the loo down the hall.

'Company?'

I'm standing beside him. He's gazing at the pinkness of a single Stargazer lily lying on my pillow. Pavel must have smuggled it in there before leaving. He must have plucked it from the vase on the windowsill. He can probably smell flowers like these at a thousand metres. Part bloodhound. Part scriptwriter. Remarkable.

H takes a tiny step back and turns to look me in the eye. In some moods, like now, he can be truly scary. 'Script conference, was it?' He offers me a thin smile. 'Or just research?'

FIVE

ater, early evening, I walk to Clem's place in Chelsea. I have
the address from Malo, whom I've phoned, but I've never
been there. Catastrophes of whatever dimension have a way
of warping your view of the rest of the world. I know this from
my own experience – those numbing hours after I first got the news
that my brain tumour might kill me. Did the skinny young man
handing out free copies of the *Metro* outside the Tube know that
I might be dead by the end of the week? And if not, why not?

I have the same feeling this evening. I want to stop passing
strangers in mid-conversation, tell them about Clem, explain
that she's somewhere deep below the surface of this teeming
city, held against her will, a hostage to opportunity and greed and
maybe bad luck. But every eye I catch, every brief moment of
curiosity or maybe alarm, is quickly gone. The truth is that everyone
else's life is an irrelevance. Spare me, please, your grief.

The mews address is harder to find than I'd anticipated. I
search for the address on my smartphone and try to make sense
of Google maps. The lines are blurred. Nothing relates to the
torrent of traffic down the Fulham Road. Then I remember that
years ago Pavel had a bedsit around here. Those were the days
when he wanted to become a poet, to get his work into print, to
raise his voice above the clamour of the crowd. Blindness had
yet to happen, and so had the showers of serious money that can
come with scriptwriting.

I falter at the next corner and give him a ring. God knows how
but he knows it's me. I give him Clem's address. He knows at
once how to find it. *Carry on down the Fulham Road. Look for a
pub called The Bargeman's Arms. Next right and you're there.*

'You OK?' I say.

'I'm fine. Better than fine. How could I be anything but?'

'I'm glad.' I'm on the move again, looking for the pub. 'And
thanks for the flower.'

*   *   *

Clem's house is at the far end of the mews. Malo takes a while
to get to the door. At first glance, in the fading light, he looks
terrible, and for a heart-stopping moment I'm wondering whether
he's been using again. Last year, when he came back from
Stockholm, his drug of choice was Spice. My poor adolescent
son had become a zombie and it took his ex-drug-baron father,
in a wonderful plot twist, to sort him out.

'Mum?' Uncertain, he lets me in.

The house is bigger than I expected. Bare, sanded floorboards.
Framed posters, some of them Colombian, along the narrow hall.
Fresh flowers exploding from herringbone bud vases. Nice. Malo
ducks my attempt to give him a hug and leads the way to a room
at the back that serves as a kitchen-diner. Photos of Clem and
Malo have been stuck to a whiteboard on the wall above the
breakfast bar. The happy couple posing against the Harley. Mad
souvenirs from some party or other. A joyous shot of Clem on a
tiny stage acknowledging unseen applause. A casting director once
told me that God saved special faces for the camera. Clem, bless
her, has one of those.

Malo appears to be halfway through a bottle of Rioja. In the
absence of an invitation, I find myself a glass from the draining
board, reach for the bottle and settle on the spare stool.

'So what next?'

Malo blinks. His eyes are wet. At first I put it down to what's
happened, but then I realize that he's drunk.

He shrugs, stares down at his glass. He doesn't want to talk
about it.

'I'm afraid you have to. There's no option.'

Lately, I've realized there's a lot of H in my son. Like his
father he hates being told what to do. I reach across to take
his hand. He rocks back on the stool.

'Don't,' he says.

'Why not?'

'Just don't.'

I shrug. I'm hurt but it doesn't pay to show it. I nod at the
wine bottle.

'Is that the first?'

'It doesn't matter.'

'Yes, it does.'

'Why?'

'Because we need to handle this. We need to cope with it. And getting legless doesn't help. I need to know exactly what happened. And I need to see your phone.'

With some reluctance, Malo extracts a phone from his jeans pocket and slides it across to me. I'm still looking at him.

'The message, please. And the photo.'

Malo is looking at his hands. There's a stand-off between us. Above the distant rumble of traffic I can hear the muted howl of an ambulance, the whump-whump of a far-away helicopter, and from next door the chatter of a radio. This is the clamorous heartbeat of a city I know all too well and yet here, in this small moment, I'm more aware of it than ever. We are all of us fragile. Think kidnap. Think cancer. Think Pavel Sieger. We can be taken when we least expect it because darkness, in the end, awaits us all.

Morbid, I think. We have to be brave. We have to be bold. Thank God for H. He'd have none of this.

'Please show me. That's all I ask.'

Finally Malo reaches for the phone. A couple of swipes and I'm looking at the starkest of messages. *Mateo, Malo, we have your girl. She's safe. For now. A million US dollars will get her back. Cash, please. You have until midnight Monday. If you contact the police, you'll never see her whole again. Another message will follow. Start counting the money.*

I look up. *Please* comes as a surprise. *Whole* is chilling.

'And the photo?'

'Scroll down.'

I do Malo's bidding. I find a blue tattoo in the shape of a serrated cross. There are lines within it and a small circular motif in the middle. The surrounding skin, flawless, is a pale tan. The base of her spine, I think, in the small hollow just above her coccyx.

'This belongs to Clem?'

'Yes.'

'What is it?'

'It's called a Chakana. The bit in the middle represents Cusco.'

'What's that?'

'The capital of the Inca empire.'

'She got it done in Colombia?'

'Parsons Green. There's a tattoo studio down there. We went

together a couple of weeks ago.' He lifts the back of his T-shirt
and pulls down an inch or two of jean. I can see a corner of the
tatt but not much else.

'You got one, too?'

Malo nods. For the first time there's a hint of animation in his
voice. He drops the waistband of his 501s a little further until I
can see the whole thing. Malo fingers it the way you might test
wet paint.

'One each – me and Clem,' Malo says. 'The unbreakable bond.'

I nod. The implication is all the sweeter for what's just happened.

'And this next message?'

'I'm still waiting.'

'So what about the money?'

'I've talked to Dad. He's in touch with Mateo. He says there
won't be a problem.'

'A million dollars? By *Monday*?'

'That's what they want.'

His head is down again. He's readjusted his jeans and his T-shirt,
and his whole body has slumped. This, I know, is a message for
me. Shit happens. We have no choice. A million dollars might
even be cheap at the price.

I sit back a moment, shifting my weight on the stool. If I was
still a smoker, this would be the perfect time for a cigarette.

'Have you talked to Mateo yourself?'

'No.'

'Don't you think that might be a good idea?'

Malo says he doesn't know. There's a note of hopelessness, or
perhaps despair, in his voice. He's abandoned the breakfast bar
and is peering into the fridge. He's thinner than his father, with
none of H's chunkiness, but as his face fills out it's impossible
not to recognize the features they share: the set of the chin, the
steadiness of the gaze, and a strange reflexive habit of tipping their
heads back when things get tough, as if inviting people to leave
the room. Just now it's a gesture, of course, and I sense we both
understand that. My poor boy is lost.

Malo is still only eighteen. This last year living down at
Flixcombe with his father has done him a great deal of good, not
least because H has given him real responsibilities. To our mutual
surprise, and some delight, Malo has responded brilliantly to these

challenges, but when I see him like this it's impossible not to remember the way things were.

My then-husband, Berndt Andressen, was a Swedish scriptwriter of rare genius. We married within months of meeting and shared a decade and a half together. At first it was wonderful. Berndt quarried the darkness of his imagination for bizarre twists on familiar tropes and practically invented Scandi noir. I, meanwhile, was dancing up the foothills of minor celebrity, which felt great at the time. Our Malo, on the other hand, was stumbling through early adolescence, bewildered by the frequent absence of a mum and a dad who seemed to be separate stars in their own far-away galaxies, impossibly glamorous, impossibly remote.

We got him out on location as often as we could, mistaking lavish weekends and casual introductions to big-name stars for parenthood when all the poor boy really wanted was the three of us round the table for Sunday lunch. When Berndt and I finally called time on the marriage in an orgy of insult and violence, Malo was nowhere to be seen. By then I'd somehow imagined that he had a tribe of mates he could hang out with but this assumption proved wrong. My darling boy, like his deluded parents, was hopelessly adrift, and I sometimes wonder whether he's ever really forgiven me. Guilt on my part? Of course. By the bucketload. A lingering resentment on his? Who knows?

Malo is back at the breakfast bar with two spoons and an open tin of tuna. This appears to be supper. When I suggest we pop round the corner for something more interesting, he shakes his head. He wants to be here when the next message comes, whenever that is. He's no idea what these people are going to say and he doesn't trust himself in company. Being alone isn't a problem. In fact, just now, he prefers it. Clem, he says, would feel exactly the same.

This is my cue to leave but I linger for a moment or two. One suggestion. Just one.

'You could come home with me,' I tell him. 'I'll leave you alone. We needn't even talk if you'd prefer not to. I just need to know you're . . .' I shrug. 'OK.'

He looks up at me, the faintest smile on his face. There's darkness under his eyes. He looks ill.

'*Your* place?' A slow shake of the head. 'Are you serious?'

SIX

A message awaits me at home. It comes from Pavel. My finger hovers over the reply button on my answerphone. Why hasn't he tried my mobile?

It turns out he wanted to spare my blushes. I've told him enough about my marriage to Berndt, about Malo, and about my son's real father for Pavel to recognize that he's stepped into a minefield. On the phone, in the privacy of my flat, I ask him what that feels like.

'It feels good,' he says. 'We should open the movie right here.'

The concept makes me laugh. Where, in Pavel's world, does fact – in that favourite showbiz phrase – bleed into fiction?

'Everywhere. Nowhere. My kind of truth is subjective, has been for years. If you go blind, life becomes a radio show. You get the hints, the clues, the dialogue, the arc of the story, but the faces, the visual stuff, the stuff that does it for most people, is for you to decide. I've never asked you what H looks like. The same goes for your son. Have you ever wondered why?'

It's true. He hasn't. And neither have I volunteered any real clues.

'So tell me,' I say. 'What does your H look like?'

'He looks like what I want him to look like. Bob Hoskins in *The Long Good Friday* would do nicely.'

'H is a bit taller,' I say at once. 'And better looking. I get it, though. You start with the voice and all the background clues I gave you and whatever else you've picked up and then glue it all together.'

'Exactly. But there's a problem here, as you're about to explain.'

'Really?' I'm staring at the phone. This was supposed to be a conversation, not a seminar. 'So what am I missing?'

'I went blind two and a half years ago. I have a library of mental images but the world moves on.'

'That's called fashion and you're very lucky it passes you by.'

'Thanks.'

'My pleasure.' There's a moment of silence. It feels deeply companionable. Then I ask him about Stargazer lilies.

'I love them. Always have done. And in case you're wondering, I can remember exactly what they look like. I'm also guessing you buy bed linen in dark colours.'

'I do. You're right.'

'Dark blue pillow slips?'

'Yes. This week.'

'And last week?'

'Burgundy red.'

'Excellent. That makes me a lucky man. The pinkness of the lily against the blue of the pillow. Did it work for you?'

'It did. Though I'm not sure about H.'

There's another silence, longer this time. Then Pavel is back on the phone. There's something new in his voice and I can't work out exactly what it is. Caution, maybe.

'He was there in your bedroom?'

'He went looking.'

'Why would he do that?'

'Because he can't cope with someone else in my life.'

'That would be me.'

'It would. And now he knows it.'

'So what happens next?'

'To be frank, I have no idea. He's a jealous man. He wants – needs – all of me. You sensed that. You told me. He can also be violent. If you have a problem with any of this, you only have to say.'

Yet another silence. Then a sound I first misinterpret as interference on the line but it turns out to be a chuckle. Pavel appears to be amused.

'This script is writing itself,' he says. 'I love it.'

For the second time in this conversation I feel the lightest prickle of anxiety at the freedoms this man seems so happy to take. Blindness, especially early on, must be terrifying. You'd feel so lost, so isolated, so vulnerable, so exposed to events. But then comes the compensations – those delicious, fortifying moments when your imagination revs up and becomes, in effect, another pair of eyes. You'd feel utterly liberated. You'd no longer be governed by what was real. You'd live almost entirely in your head. In the true sense of the word, you'd slip the leash and become a nomad. Nice, I thought, shutting my eyes.

Pavel wants to know more about Malo, about the message from the kidnappers, about Clem. Light has a colour temperature, he points out. It has to do with intensity and wavelengths. It's the same with relationships. You know these two people very well. Are Clem and Malo seriously close?

The answer to that has to be a big fat yes. I tell him my son is besotted. I describe the two tattoos, his and hers. Malo wants to shackle himself to this slender, vivid, lovely girl. He wants her for ever and ever and if it takes a million dollars to make that happen, then so be it.

'Shackle himself? Or have her shackled to him?'

'Both. Either. Does it matter?'

'Of course it does. Malo's his father's son. His dad wants you all day every day. Tell me that doesn't make you uncomfortable.'

'You're right. It does.'

'So what's it like for Clem?'

'You think this is her doing?' I'm staring at the phone. 'You think she's gone on the run? Made a bid for freedom? You're telling me this is all some kind of scam on her part?'

'I'm not telling you anything. I'm simply listening.'

Listening. Blind men, I tell myself, rely on their ears as well as their imaginations. Life is all navigation. They need to see in the dark, survive in the dark, thrive in the dark. Pavel is probably half-bat.

I share this thought with him, along with a number of others. I enjoyed last night. A lot. I've always suspected that laughter is the best aphrodisiac but the delicacy of a certain kind of touch – deft, tender, knowing – takes you to some very unexpected places. I'm smiling. I can see the bony whiteness of his body in the throw of light from the candle. I know I should be thinking very hard about getting Clem back in one piece but I have a sudden, overwhelming desire to get very drunk and take Pavel to bed again.

I know more or less where he lives because he's told me but I've never been there. I need the exact address. He gives me a house number in a street off Chiswick High Road.

'There's an all-night Londis on the corner,' he says. 'And there's a lovely Portuguese white on offer at the moment. Ask for the Albariño.' He laughs. 'And don't forget an umbrella.'

I open my eyes at last. The world floods back in. I check my watch. Nearly ten. It's Friday night, for God's sake, and I'll do anything to draw the curtains on an awful day. Two bottles. At least.

'Half an hour,' I tell him. 'Max.'

SEVEN

Milost, Pavel's dog, meets me at the door, which is slightly ajar. She knows my smell by now and we're definitely friends. The name they gave her at the Guide Dog kennels was Grace. *Milost*, Pavel tells me, is Czech for 'grace', another curtsey to the allure of Prague. If you'll never see the city again, at least you can stroke the dog and dream a little. Milost. Malo. Cute.

I take the liberty of stepping in from the rain and Pavel meets me in the hall, a smile on his face. I know he's been living here for more than a decade because he's told me so. That means he was sighted when he made all those little decisions about décor, and colours and wall hangings that help tell other people who we are, and I'm eager to lay hands on some of these clues. The living space downstairs has been knocked through, which would have been very sensible if you were half-expecting to go blind, and I find myself in a big white space dominated by a grand piano in the very middle of the room.

On the walls hang a number of paintings that look original and may have come from the same hand. A couple are portraits, one almost certainly of Pavel. It's been done in oils, the paint thickly textured, the background rendered in ominous shades of the darkest brown. The way Pavel's face is shadowed reminds me of Rembrandt, and the artist has done a fine job in catching the expression Pavel saves for moments when he senses that something – a line of dialogue in a draft script, a mouthful of restaurant food – has taken him by surprise. It's a coming together of delight and curiosity, two blessings that might help him through the eternity of darkness to come.

'She's been a friend of mine for years,' Pavel says. 'The landscapes are more recent. She knows my taste exactly. She describes a stretch of coast or a particular view and if I approve then she goes off and sorts it. She paints to order. I'm a spoiled boy.'

'But you can't see them. Any of them. Apart from the earlier work.'

'You're right. But they're friends in my house. She also favours oils and that makes me doubly lucky.'

'Doubly?'

'Number one that I came across her work in the first place. Number two that I can touch them. Landscapes, if you try hard enough to understand them, have a texture. Here . . .'

He sets course for the biggest of the pictures, a study of a long harbour wall in what looks like the depths of winter. It's a study in greys and murky yellows and dark viscous greens that exactly captures the swirl of water around the granite quay. The weather is unforgiving. A single tiny figure, hooded, faceless, battles the wind.

Pavel has taken my hand. He wants me to shut my eyes, to let the long brush strokes speak for themselves, to trust my imagination.

'But I've seen it already,' I say. 'I know what it looks like.'

'So do I.'

'How can you?'

'She told me about it. She started with a mood. Then came the weather. It's Porthleven, down in Cornwall. She went down there for a week and I went with her . . .' he taps his head, '. . . in here, where it matters. She has perfect recall and she knows how to use language as well as paint. In a different time we'd call that the gift of tongues.'

I nod, still letting my fingers stray across the painting. At first it's a bit like waking up in the middle of the night and not finding whatever you're after on the bedside table, but after a while I think I begin to understand. My fingertips have found the figure on the harbour wall.

'So is this you? Is that what this picture's about? Fortitude? Courage in the face of the elements?'

Pavel's fingers track, unerringly, across the harbour wall until they touch mine.

'It's about getting bloody wet,' he murmurs. 'I liked the picture so much she took me down there for real. September gales. High tide. You could taste the sea, standing on that harbour wall. Fortitude's a wonderful word but it doesn't keep you dry.'

Pavel has the face of a child when he laughs. I give his hand a squeeze. It appears that the pictures have been hung by his artist friend. Has she done a good job? What do I think?

I give the question some thought. There are seven paintings, all different sizes. The lighting is subtle, spots on the wall and recessed downlights in the ceiling, but it doesn't, I tell Pavel, feel like a gallery.

'So how would you describe it? The room as a whole?'

'A cave. Your cave. A trillion years ago I'd have been looking at finger sketches of buffalo. Instead, your clever friend has been more ambitious. What does *she* think?'

'She loves it but she thinks we're running out of space.'

'She's right. You are. You need to move. You need a bigger cave.'

He laughs again, delighted by the thought of a cave, and when I change the subject and ask about the grand piano he limps across and settles on the stool. The dog sprawls on the rug, looking up, giving a tiny wag of her tail.

'You play for Milost?'

'I play for me.'

He reaches for the keyboard, his long, spare frame slightly bent, and begins to play. I recognize the piece at once: Schubert's Impromptu in G. My lawyer and good friend Carlos also happens to be a fine pianist and this is one of his favourites. Pavel's touch at the piano is extraordinary: deft, sensitive, totally sure of itself. At once, from the opening notes, he captures the inexpressible sadness of this piece. It has to be about loss, and perhaps regret, but as the music begins to swell it's also about turning those moments of *tristesse* into something beyond sublime. Never give up, it tells you. Porthleven figured for two hands and a wet night in Chiswick.

At the end of the piece I find myself clapping. It's a spontaneous act of admiration, totally unforced.

Pavel raises a hand in admonishment. 'Don't,' he says. 'You'll upset the dog.'

'You're serious?'

'No. Just flattered.'

'You play beautifully. More than beautifully.' I'm looking at one of those sleek, minimal Bose audio set-ups in the corner. 'You listen to lots of music?'

'All the time.' He gets to his feet. 'A favour? Do you mind?'

He's off again, crossing the open spaces of the room. A TV remote is lying on the sofa. He gives it to me. When I ask him why a blind man needs a TV, he smiles.

'Netflix?' he queries.

'You mean drama? Movies?'

'Of course. In my game – our game – it pays to keep up with the opposition. Dialogue is everything. Who needs eyes?'

I nod. So obvious, I think.

Pavel's bony hand closes on mine. I stare down at it. All that music, all those notes, stored in those dancing fingertips.

'BBC iPlayer,' he says. 'The button in the middle.'

'What am I looking for?'

'Tonight's Proms.'

I find the programme he's after. Grieg's piano concerto with an Estonian orchestra and a Georgian pianist called Khatia Buniatishvili. Khatia is beyond striking: young looking with flawless skin, a tumble of lustrous black hair and full lips layered in scarlet gloss. She has a body most forties' screen actresses would have died for and the low-cut black dress, with its twinkle of sequins, showcases what my Breton mother calls, with some delicacy, her *embonpoint*.

'What can you see?'

'The pianist. Young Khatia.'

'And?'

'She has a very large chest.'

'Ahhh . . .' That smile again.

'You've heard her playing?'

'I have. Last night. All you have to do is listen. All the clues are there.'

I press play and we settle down on the sofa. The conductor mounts the podium and calls the orchestra to attention. The opening bars belong to the pianist. Khatia attacks the keyboard in a sudden flurry of violence, hair everywhere, before the orchestra restores a little order, exploring this first theme, but the camera only has eyes for the pianist. With nothing to do for a moment or two, she sways slowly at the keyboard, head tilted up, eyes half-closed, before taking the conductor's cue again. Her playing, I tell Pavel, is chiaroscuro, light and dark, sunshine and rain. He nods, slightly impatient. He can hear that. He knows that already. What he badly wants is the rest of it. What does she look like? What is she *doing*?

I do my best to oblige. Every physical movement, I tell him, is mannered, thought-out, plotted for maximum screen effect. She takes deep breaths. She seems to sigh a lot. She's the first-class passenger on a ride of her own invention and she loves the fact that she can share it.

'You don't like her.' Statement, not a question.

'I think she's beyond excessive. Most directors I know would throw her off the set.'

We've reached a sudden swoop in the music, a descent into near silence. Khatia, it seems to me, now has the audience exactly where she wants them. Control – essentially timing – is solely hers, and she milks it with a glossy ruthlessness which I find slightly repellent. By now the orchestra has slowed to walking speed to accommodate her vanity. A single chord from her right hand. Silence. Anticipation. Then a note picked up and discarded with a slow toss of the head.

I'm looking at Pavel. He's lying back, his eyes closed. He seems to be enjoying the ride.

'More,' he says. 'Tell me more.'

'There is no more. She's arch. She's way out of line. She belongs in a rock concert. Grieg would have a fit.'

'You think so? You *really* think so?'

'I do.' I take his hand. 'She plays like a porn queen.'

Pavel's bedroom is upstairs at the back of the house. Rain drums lightly at the window and in the smallest hours, after we've made love, Pavel empties his glass, kisses me lightly on the forehead and slips out of bed. Naked, he leaves the room and I follow the soft padding of his footsteps as he goes downstairs. Then comes a moment of silence before I hear the opening bars of the piano entry in the second movement of the Grieg concerto. Oddly enough, this is one passage that Khatia seemed to respect, but Pavel, says little me, absolutely nails it. Not a trace of self-regard, of showing off, of hogging the spotlight. Blindness, it occurs to me, is a shortcut to humility. And thus to grace.

'Well . . .?' Pavel's back at the open door.

'Wonderful.' I extend a hand in the half-darkness. 'Come here.'

EIGHT

S aturday. Hangovers are something I generally try to avoid, especially since my *pas de deux* with the Grim Reaper. Once you've lived with a brain tumour – acknowledged its presence on the scan, understood the impact it makes on more or less everything – a headache of any kind carries the grimmest of warnings. This one is compounded by guilt. My only child's lovely girlfriend is very definitely in harm's way. What was I doing getting drunk?

While Pavel whips up an omelette in his kitchen, reaching for cupboards, rummaging in the fridge, stooping to consign the eggshells to his bin, defying blindness, I unlock the back door and let myself into his courtyard garden. Even out here the walls are painted white, a lovely contrast to the ribbed grey of the slates under my bare feet.

In one corner, facing south, is a reclining deckchair with a built-in foot rest. Here, I think, is where he enjoys the sunshine. Last month, a frequently brutal heatwave descended on London, temperatures soaring into the mid-thirties, but Pavel has often talked about his addiction to this simplest of pleasures. At first I played stern, telling him how dangerous UV light can be, but he waved all my warnings away. 'Sunshine is the mother of light,' he told me. And left it at that.

Malo doesn't answer my call – not at first. I hang up and wait for a minute or two, imagining him beginning to surface with a hangover of his own, then try again. This time I get through. He says he's OK. He says nothing's happened since last night. I know my son very well. He always lies when he's done something he knows will upset me.

'So what's going on?' I ask. 'Just tell me.'

He won't. It's a flat no, disguised as a grunt that becomes an extended yawn. He's knackered. He hasn't slept for most of the night and now I've woken him up. Isn't there someone else I can call at half past eight on a Saturday morning?

'Clem's been kidnapped,' I remind him. 'I just need to be sure we're doing everything to get her back.'

This bid to shame him comes to nothing. There appears to be no sense of urgency, let alone panic. For the latter I'm grateful, but after we've said our goodbyes something is beginning to disturb me. It's Pavel who puts this first flicker of suspicion into words.

'You don't trust him,' he says.

We're finishing his omelette, which he served with lightly grilled tomatoes. With typical precision, he's using a finger of toast to mop up the last of the juices. I resist the temptation to guide him to a pool of neglected leftovers beside his fork, and thank God I did because he's left this mouthful until last.

'Trust's a funny thing,' I say lightly. 'In many ways I trust him completely, but sometimes circumstances can get the better of us all.'

'And that's what's happening?'

'I think so.'

'You think he's not being straight with you? You think he might be hiding something?'

'Yes.'

'Like what?'

'I don't know.'

'But you sense it?'

'I do. And that worries me.'

Pavel looks briefly sympathetic. Magically, he seems to know exactly where my hand is.

'Trust is absolute,' he says. 'No excuses. No exceptions. *D'accord?*'

You agree? This question throws me for a second, then I realize he's talking about us, not my precious son. To date Pavel and I have met perhaps a dozen times, sometimes professionally, sometimes simply for a meal or a drink, but after last night and the night before we're in new territory. He's pushed his plate to one side. I swear he's looking me in the eye. Trust on both sides? Unconditional? Regardless of circumstances?

I mutter assent. Poor Malo, I think.

I get home by lunchtime. Most of the morning I've spent with Pavel. He wants to help with Malo and Clem but for that to happen, he says, he needs to know everything about my marriage, about Berndt, and about anything else that might have shaped my precious son. He wants to be sure of every last detail, year after year, and when I pause to ask why, he bats the enquiry away with a shrug of his shoulders.

Professionally, he says, he wouldn't dream of trusting a story to his characters without knowing them with a deep intimacy. 'Deep intimacy' is a beguiling phrase and I settle down to another blizzard of questions because something similar happens in my own trade. You don't get to make a character live on stage or on-screen without knowing every trait, every wrinkle. First you kid yourself you're someone else. Then you kid the audience.

By noon, exhausted, I make my excuses and leave. Neither of us asks when we might next meet, but I put this down to trust. We both know it will happen very soon. Exactly when doesn't matter.

H is waiting for me outside the apartment block. I recognize his Range Rover the moment I turn the corner. Malo, I think. Has to be.

I'm wrong. H has been to see Mateo again and he has some news he thinks he ought to share. But first he's eyeing me with something close to suspicion.

'Been shopping?' Obviously not. No bag.

'Out,' I say. 'I've been out. It's a girlie thing. Men are the lucky ones. Cabin fever doesn't bother them.'

'An all-nighter?'

'Yes. And before you ask, it's my business, not yours.' I open the passenger door. I don't want him in the apartment.

H eyes me for a moment and then slips the paddle into drive. A second later he's hauling the Range Rover into a tight U-turn and gunning the engine.

'Is this it, then?' I enquire. 'You're kidnapping me?'

He doesn't answer, not even a smile. Only when we get to the first set of traffic lights on Bayswater Road does he volunteer any kind of clue.

'Mateo,' he mutters. 'You two need to meet.'

NINE

Mateo, to my surprise, isn't the man I've been expecting. He lives in a very grand house in Eaton Place. CCTV cameras watch us emerging from the Range Rover and the big, panelled front door opens before we've reached the top step. Mateo is wearing tan slacks and an open-collar white shirt. His handshake is firm but somehow comforting. There's just a hint of Inca blood in the sallowness of his skin and the broadness of his nose but his English is perfect.

He stands aside and invites us into the house, gesturing us up the broad, carpeted staircase to a lounge on the first floor. Unlike most rich men I know he's neither guarded nor boastful. On the contrary, he has exquisite manners and over a truly excellent cup of coffee he quietly congratulates me for a couple of decent parts I had before the Reaper barged into my life. He says he especially liked a role I played in a movie called *Arpeggio*. The fact that this film only appeared in arthouses across Europe simply confirms that H, bless him, has found an ally of real substance in his battle to restore some kind of order to his son's world.

We spend a little time discussing the kind of company Clem and Malo might have been keeping. When Mateo wants to know whether Malo has friends on the drugs scene, I can only shrug. He's certainly been as curious and experimental as every other teenager but after his experience with Spice I'm fairly certain he's cleaned up.

H nods in agreement and Mateo seems to take this assurance at face value. He mentions a text he received early this morning. It was timed at 04.35 and addressed to the same mobile phone of Mateo's the kidnappers have already contacted. The fact that only a tiny handful of Mateo's family and friends are aware of this number he regards as significant.

'The number has to come from Clemenza,' he says gravely. 'There can be no other explanation.'

'And what did it say?'

Mateo exchanges glances with H. H shrugs. *Your call, your information, not mine.*

'They want confirmation that we have the money. They also intend to have a text conversation later today.'

'With you?'

'Yes.'

'About what?'

'The exchange.'

'Your daughter for a million pounds?'

'Yes.'

'So what did you say?'

'I texted back. I said I wanted proof of life. Ideally a video conversation. Failing that I wanted the name of our pet dog.'

'And?'

'Nothing. So far.' He holds my gaze for a long moment. 'There's something else you ought to know. I carry insurance. It's called K&R. Kidnapping and ransom. In Bogotá it's routine, something everyone who might become a target does.' He checks his watch, a chunky Rolex. 'The insurance company retains a firm of response consultants. These are experts in the field. They negotiate all over the world. To be frank this doesn't happen in London very often. That makes us unlucky as well as . . .' he risks a smile, '. . . a little nervous. The consultancy is called Lockdown. I happen to know the person they've assigned to Clemenza. His name is Frank. Frank O'Keefe. He should be here any minute.' He nods at the tray on the low table between myself and H. 'More coffee?'

O'Keefe arrives shortly afterwards. He's a slight man, not tall. I guess his age at late forties, maybe a year or two older. He's wearing a nicely cut suit and a pair of black Guccis and when he extends a hand I briefly glimpse a hint of vanity in a pair of monogrammed cuff links.

Mateo has done the introductions. The two men are obviously friends.

'Ms Andressen?' O'Keefe offers a courtly little nod. 'I understand Clemenza and your son . . .'

'Indeed.'

'Then you have my sympathies. Everything is resolvable. All we need is time and patience.'

I blink. Somehow I thought we were already in the final reel, expecting Clem back by nightfall. Time? Patience? Christ.

O'Keefe parks his briefcase beside the spare chair, accepts a cup of coffee, unbuttons his jacket and sits down. His air of quiet command is palpable. He has no interest in small talk or breaking the ice. In less than a minute he's taken charge of this impromptu meeting.

It appears that Mateo has already told him about the latest text. Now our visitor wants us to know exactly how the next few days, or perhaps weeks, will unfold.

'Number one, Mateo is right. We need proof of life. We need to know she's alive, that she's well, and that she's under their control. Next we never, *never*, meet their first demand. A million US, to be frank, is absurd and our assumption has to be that they're aware of that.'

H knows this already but there's something about O'Keefe that seems to have got under his skin. I don't think he likes being lectured, and he certainly hasn't taken to O'Keefe.

'So what do you put on the table?' H asks.

'We talk, Mr Prentice. We listen. We build a rapport. And then, in due course, we make them an offer.'

'And what if they're not having it? What if they stick at a mill? Make life tough for Clemmie?'

'I suspect that won't happen. These people are criminals, not terrorists. That makes them realists. They're only interested in the money. There's nothing else at stake.'

'Like?'

'Politics or, God help us, religion.' He offers H a thin smile. 'This is London, Mr Prentice, not the Middle East. Money talks louder than anything else and that, believe it or not, is to our advantage. This little episode has to be managed. And that's my job.'

H nods but says nothing. I know he hates conceding control in any situation, but for the time being he has no choice but to listen.

Mateo asks about involving the police. O'Keefe shakes his head. 'In due course, if things turn really ugly, that may become necessary, but not now. In the shape of Clem, the kidnappers have acquired a windfall gain. Quite how much remains to be seen.

Best, therefore, to keep the negotiations tight. No third parties. No police.'

This, for me, is eye-opening stuff. I don't doubt for a moment that O'Keefe has years of experience in these situations, but he seems to be framing the kidnap and its aftermath as just another piece of business. He has two clients. One of them is the kidnappers responsible for Clem's disappearance. The other is the insurance company. His challenge is to bring the two sides together and conjure a happy result. Job done.

I'm thinking of Malo. And of Clem's mother.

'You used the word "ugly",' I say. 'What might that mean?'

'They might make threats. That would form part of the negotiation. They might also put pressure on Clemenza and then video the results. It normally comes in the shape of an appeal directly from the victim. It can be very hard to live with something like that. Raw emotion can put more money on the table.'

This report from the front line, however well intended, is chilling. I'm trying to imagine what it must be like to be Clem just now. What does she dream about – if she ever gets to sleep? How does she feel when she wakes up, not knowing what this bunch of crazies might do next?

Mateo wants to know how he should respond when these people next get in touch.

'You don't. I'll give you a number. Ask them to call me. They'll need to be sure I'm not police. The switch at Lockdown is manned twenty-four-seven. Once they're happy we're not stitching them up we'll be negotiating on another number. If these people are any good, they'll be familiar with the procedures.'

'And if they're not?' H again.

'Then we might have a problem.'

'So what do you think?' I ask H.

We're sitting in the Range Rover, watching O'Keefe saying his goodbyes. Mateo has been joined outside the open front door by a middle-aged woman in designer jeans and a black T-shirt. A heavy gold bracelet catches the sun as she gives O'Keefe a stiff hug and then steps back. The tightness of her brief smile suggests that O'Keefe's assurances about resolving this little issue have fallen on stony ground. Is this Clem's mum? Almost certainly.

'I think I feel bloody sorry for them,' H says.

'You mean Malo? Clem?'

'Of course.'

I nod, wondering whether to share my doubts about our son.

'You think he's being straight with us? Malo?'

'Of course he isn't. He'll tell us what he thinks we need to know. No more, no less.'

'And that doesn't bother you?'

'Not in the slightest. When the time comes, and he's good and ready, he'll tell us everything. Too much pressure now and we'll lose him completely.'

There's an edge of menace in H's voice and I know it's there for my benefit. *Leave this to me*, he seems to be saying. *Everything will work out just fine.*

'You think he's in trouble?'

H simply nods.

'And O'Keefe?' I'm staring out at the street.

'He's like the kidnappers. He's in it for the business.' H gestures round at the properties fronting on to the square. 'Like every other one of these minted fuckers.'

I nod. H, when it comes to the more troubling consequences of the way we live now, is generally right. He has a dark view of human nature, which probably accounts for most of his wealth. Among his many business interests are a couple of insurance companies which, he once assured me, earned him serious money for doing sod all. The fact that Mateo carries kidnap insurance, and that H won't be obliged to contribute to whatever sum Clem finally commands, has clearly pleased him but he's still out on patrol, looking – in his phrase – for the next shit storm.

'Blokes like O'Keefe get paid by the day,' he says.

'How much?'

'A grand? Two grand? There's something else, too. He's probably on a success bonus of some kind. The smaller the ransom he negotiates, the bigger his bung at the end. That's called an incentive. The more money he saves the insurance people, the more he'll walk away with.'

'And?'

'Like the man says, these things take time. Which probably means that Clemmie won't be back for a while.'

'Not Monday, then?'

'No chance.'

H, like me, is watching O'Keefe strolling away down the square. He pauses beside a sleek, new-looking car and then lifts his face to the sun. *All the time in the world*, I think, while the meter ticks on.

'Jaguar XJ,' H grunts. 'Sixty-five grand. At least.'

TEN

I get H to drop me at Clem's place. He says he'd come in with me to see Malo but he's late already and he needs to get back to Flixcombe for a meeting. I knock on Clem's door, wait, knock again. Nothing. I check in case anyone's watching, then squat and yell his name through the letterbox. I can hear a purr from the fridge and the ticking of a clock, but there's still no response. Worried now, I try his number but his phone's switched off. Earlier, during our brief conversation, he was going to make up for a lost night's sleep. Maybe he's still in bed, I think. Maybe the last thing he needs is his mother at his door.

I'm about to head back down to the main road when I remember his car. Malo is still driving a brand-new blue Audi convertible, a present from his grateful father after our clever son had masterminded an ambitious expedition to the Normandy D-Day beaches with a bunch of paying guests. Normally, he keeps the Audi at a parking spot at the top end of the mews. I walk the thirty metres but there's no sign of it. An oldish woman emerges from the last house.

'You're looking for the young lad? The one with the blue car?'

'Yes.'

'You're a friend?'

'I hope so. I'm also his mum.'

She studies me a moment, amused. Maybe there's some family resemblance. The gene pool, as Pavel recently assured me, never lies.

'He went this morning,' she says. 'Around eleven.'

'You saw him?'

'I did. I was in the front there. Rearranging the flowers. He wasn't alone, either, that boy of yours.'

'No?' I'm staring at her.

'No.' She shakes her head. 'Another fella. Older. And black.'

I press her for details. She frowns with the effort of memory. Dreadlocks, she says. And a strange mark on his face.

'What kind of mark?'

'Dark blue. Just here.' She touches her cheek under her right eye. 'It's hard to tell but it looked like a speech mark or maybe a bubble.'

Black. Dreadlocks. And a strange tattoo. I'm back at home in the safety of my flat. To my knowledge, which is far from complete, Malo doesn't know any black people. On the other hand, here is a witness who is telling me different. Maybe this is a friend of Clem's. London is famously multicultural and Clem must run into black people all the time. Either professionally as she zips from delivery to pick-up to delivery, or maybe in the handful of pubs where she often gigs.

Should I start there? Should I somehow compile a list of likely pubs and visit them one by one, a middle-aged actress and mother with a fuzz of hair where my poor mutilated scalp is still fighting the side effects of chemo? Should I offer photos of Clem and enquire about any black companions she might have acquired? Or should I simply await Malo's return and hope that he's in the mood to answer a direct question or two?

You have a missing girlfriend. Her kidnappers want a million pounds. And you're keeping strange company. If you love me, please explain.

Pavel gets in touch in the early evening, a favourite time for him to call. He can sense at once that I'm upset. Without any prompting I explain why. Malo. The missing Audi. And the stranger in the passenger seat. If I'm right to trust Pavel, he'll do his best to help me. If, on the other hand, I've got him wrong the nightmare can only get worse.

'You think this guy is somehow related to what's happened?'

'To be honest, yes.'

'So what did he look like?'

I explain about the dreadlocks. The woman put him in his early thirties. Then I remember the way she described the tattoo. Pavel doesn't respond and for a moment I think he's hung up on me for some reason, but then he's back in my ear, alert and freshly curious.

'Say that again?'

'She said it looked like a speech mark. Or maybe a bubble.'

'You mean an elongated bubble? Like a teardrop?'

'Not me, her. She didn't say teardrop but maybe that's what she meant.' I pause. I'm frowning. 'Why?'

'It doesn't matter.'

'Yes, it bloody does. Just tell me.'

Another silence. Then Pavel announces he's coming over. I'm not altogether sure this is such a good idea. My absolute priority is Malo. Once he's got in touch I need to find him, to be with him, to settle us both down and have a proper chat. No interim distractions. None.

Pavel takes the news badly. For whatever reason I seem to have offended him.

He asks me whether I remember those little swastikas fighter pilots used to paint under their cockpits during the Battle of Britain. I tell him I do. It formed part of *Going Solo*.

'And you know what each of them meant?'

'Of course. They were enemy planes they'd shot down. They were kills.'

'Exactly. These days a teardrop on the cheek does the same job. It's a way of keeping score.'

'It means you've killed someone?'

'I'm afraid it does.'

'Shit.'

'Exactly. Stay there. I'll call a cab.'

Within half an hour, Pavel is at my door. By now I've been thinking far too hard about the implications of what he's told me. Malo appears to have fallen into the worst company imaginable. Maybe that's what he's hiding, why he'll barely talk to me. H is right. The boy's in deep trouble, up to his neck, and this has to be linked to Clem's disappearance. Maybe he's offered himself in her place. Or maybe they've seized them both and it's our turn to receive a ransom demand. Both possibilities, to be frank, are terrifying. H, as far as I know, isn't insured against kidnapping. I suspect he'd scarcely notice a million-dollar dent in his fortune but that wouldn't be the point. No way would he part with a cent on the say-so of – as he'd put it – a bunch of lowlifes.

I tell Pavel we have to go to the police.

'We?'

'Me. I have to go to the police. This is out of control. This is really serious.'

'There may be another way.'

'That's what the guy said this morning.'

'What guy?'

I explain about Frank O'Keefe, the K&R negotiator. Listen to this man for half an hour and there's no reason your blood pressure would rise by even a flicker when the phone began to ring.

'You mean he'd handle it all?'

'Everything. Every last call. Every move on the chess board. He says it all boils down to money and once you understand that, your problems are over.'

'He might be right. Has that occurred to you?'

'Of course it has. And equally he might be talking bullshit. I'm walking into a script I don't much like here. Maybe he's picked up a thing or two about acting, about being Mr Confident, Mr Leave-It-To-Me. Relax, he's telling us. Chill out. Let someone else do the heavy lifting. We'll get her back and that's a promise. You might not like the size of next year's insurance premium but – hey – you're all still in one piece. This is hopeless, Pavel. This is just letting events take over. That's not my way. And it's certainly not H's.'

'So what will you do?'

'I just told you. I'll go to the police. That's what they're for. Last time I checked, kidnapping was a crime. Have I got that bit right?'

Pavel joins me on the sofa. For once, I shrink from his touch, something he senses at once.

'And you really think they'll sort it? Get Clem back? Malo, too, if he's really gone off with someone linked to the kidnapping?'

'I've no idea, but they must know where to start because that's their job. Me? I'm helpless. This is another big fat tumour. In fact, it's worse because it affects other people, people I love. I don't want all this stuff in my life. I've had it with losing control. Anything. I'll do anything to get those kids back.'

'Money would sort it. Do you happen to have a million dollars?'

It's a good question. If we don't want to leave Clem's fate in the hands of O'Keefe and Mateo's insurers then it might be wise to find out.

I get up and find a pad and a pen. I'm doing the sums, angry as well as lost. My divorce from Berndt is still a work in progress. I've generated most of the assets in what used to be our marriage – my apartment, my car, my savings, my investments – but my ex-husband has found a clever lawyer in Stockholm and is fighting for every krona he can get his hands on. My own solicitor keeps assuring me that no court of law would entertain his claims for a moment, but that's not the point. Berndt, if I'm to believe him, has lost more or less everything. Split my estate down the middle, subtract a million dollars, and I'd be living in the street. My mum once told me I was reckless with money. Easy come, she warned me, easy go. Now, looking at the bare figures on the notepad, I realize that she was right.

'A million dollars?' I look up. 'Not a prayer.'

'H?'

'He'd kill these people first. He'd put them down like the animals they are.'

'That's fighting talk.'

'Of course it is. And you know what? I'm not sure I'd blame him.'

'So why go to the police?'

'Good question. This is black and white, isn't it? This is one of those plot points that keep you and me in business. An eye for an eye? Fight fire with fire? Any of that stuff sound familiar?'

'Of course. But who, exactly, are you fighting?'

This, of course, is the crunch. All I have in hard evidence is a thirty-second conversation with Malo's neighbour, a woman I've never met before. There must be a million black guys in London. So just where would we start?

I'm exhausted. I'm close to tears. I feel a headache coming on. I've run out of options and Pavel's presence, for once, is no help. I lie back on the sofa, my eyes closed, fighting to control myself. Then, very dimly, I hear my mobile. Tina fucking Turner. 'Simply the Best'. I'm going to change the ringtone, I tell myself. Something by Bach, maybe.

Pavel passes me the phone. I put it to my ear. For a second or two I think I've stepped into some fantasy script. It sounds like Malo. It sounds like my son.

'Mum?'

'Where are you?'

'Outside. In the car.'

'*Outside?*' I'm crying now, trying to choke back the tears.

'Yeah.' I think I hear him laughing. 'You mind if I come up?'

ELEVEN

M alo has never met Pavel. I'm not at all sure this is the moment to make the introductions but there's no time to get him out of my apartment. More to the point, he has definite views on how I should handle the next couple of minutes.

'Tell him nothing about the black guy,' he tells me. 'Pretend the conversation with the neighbour never happened. Trust me.'

I have a choice, of course I do, but deep down I think I sense his logic. Let Malo do the talking. And see where that takes us.

Seconds later, Malo is at the main entrance, buzzing the video phone to be let in. I take a cautionary look at the tiny screen beside my front door. Anticipating this, he gives me a little wave. Very odd.

I open my front door and wait for him to emerge from the lift. He has a bright smile on his face and bends to give me a hug, which is unexpected and more than welcome. Hard as I look, I can see no visible signs of damage.

'This is Pavel,' I say as we step into the lounge.

The sight of a stranger in my apartment brings him to an abrupt halt.

'You're the blind guy? The writer?'

'I am.'

'Dad told me about you. Schemes and dreams, eh?'

Neither Pavel nor I have any idea what Malo is talking about, but it doesn't seem to matter. He circles the living room as if he wants to check that nothing's gone missing. He has a slightly brittle gleefulness, everything overloud, over-emphatic. Pavel will later liken this to a sports car on full beam careering into corner after corner and he's right. Finally, after I get him to sit down with us, I realize why Malo's here. He wants money.

'Why?' I ask him.

'I'm skint. Something to eat would be good, too. D'you mind, Mum?'

I shake my head. It would be a pleasure to feed my son, but first I need to know why he finds himself so broke. H has given him a generous monthly allowance since way back when he first moved down to Flixcombe. I'm not sure of the exact sum, but I'm fairly certain Malo can rely on more than four thousand a month.

'Is this something between you and your dad?' I ask him.

'Yeah. He's stopped paying me.'

'Since when?'

'Yesterday. I've been drawing on an account of his through ATMs. They won't take my card any more.'

'Have you contacted the bank?'

'Yeah. They say it's confidential between them and the account holder.'

'And H?'

'I can't get hold of him.'

'You've tried?'

'Of course I have. He doesn't pick up. Doesn't return my calls. All I've got is a single text.'

'Saying what?'

For the first time, Malo falters. He's looking at Pavel. Pavel has his eyes closed and his hands are folded in his lap.

'Well?' I ask Malo.

'He wants me back at Flixcombe. I think he wants to bang me up. Keep an eye on me.'

'Why would he want to do that? Just be honest with me.'

'Fuck knows.' He's eyeing the door to the kitchen. 'Have you got any bread? Maybe some bacon?'

I have a couple of rashers in the fridge. In the kitchen, with the door open, I watch Malo preparing a bacon sarnie. When it comes to a top-dressing of tomato sauce he hoses most of it over the work surface.

'Have you been drinking?'

'How would I do that? I've told you, I'm running on empty.'

'Then how come you're so . . .' I frown. 'Hyper?'

'Maybe it's getting to me.'

'What?'

'Everything.' He looks round at me, then nods back towards the lounge. Taking the hint, I close the door.

'You mean Clem?' I ask.

'Of course. I wait and wait for something to go down but nothing ever happens.'

'No one's got in touch?'

'No. I live by the phone. I'm always checking, just in case. You've no idea how that can stress you out. It's being in her place, too. She's everywhere I look. I go to bed and lie there all night and the pillow and everything smells of her but that's just a wind-up because she's not there.'

'There's no one you can talk to? No friend? No mate?' I can't help thinking about his dreadlocked companion, whether he's involved in Clem's disappearance or not.

'No. I want to be around, need to be around, in case anyone phones her landline. You're the only person I've talked to for days. Otherwise it's just me.'

I nod. He's sitting at the table now, wolfing down the sandwich. A curl of tomato sauce has smeared the corner of his chin.

'I came round earlier,' I say quietly. 'Banged on the door. Shouted through the letterbox. The place seemed empty to me.'

'I was in bed.' Malo wipes his chin with the back of his hand, something H would do.

'I thought you said you couldn't sleep.'

'I got there in the end. Fucking wonderful, Mum. Didn't wake up until this afternoon. That's when I tried the ATMs. Nothing worked.' He pushes his plate away and checks his watch. 'Maybe a couple of hundred quid? If you've got it?'

I haven't. My bag's in my bedroom. I manage to rustle up ninety-five in cash and return to the kitchen to give Malo a cheque for the balance. He's still on his feet. I ask him to sit down.

'What is this? Some kind of interview?'

'Please?'

With some reluctance he complies. His right foot is tap-tapping on the lino. He keeps squeezing his eyes. He can't keep still.

I sign the cheque and lay it carefully on the table.

'If you've got anything to tell me,' I say, 'now would be a good time.'

Malo is staring at the cheque. I want him to tell me about his new black friend. I want him to explain exactly why they met and where they went. But I want this to come from him, not me.

'Well . . .?' I ask.

'I don't know what you're talking about.'

'I think you do.'

'Then tell me.'

Our eyes meet for no more than a second before he's on his feet, reaching for the cheque. A cursory kiss lands on my upturned forehead and he tells me he loves me. Then he's gone.

'Cocaine,' Pavel says. 'You can hear it in his voice. The boy's manic. He's also very confused.'

'Frightened?'

'Lost.'

It's hard not to agree. I'm not sure whether Pavel's being diplomatic or not but I prefer 'lost' to any other description. It means, among other things, that I can help him get his bearings.

Pavel and I are together on the sofa. I've broached a bottle of decent Rioja I was saving for a girlie get-together next week. When Pavel asks me what happened in the kitchen I'm happy to tell him. 'My son's lying to me,' I tell him. 'The important question is why.'

Pavel, in the vernacular, likes to play these scenes long. In his view, the pair of them – Clem and Malo – have found themselves in bad company. Her looks and what I agree is my son's reckless overconfidence have swept them out of their depth. One misplaced conversation with the wrong people might have triggered the kidnap and now Malo hasn't a clue what to do about it.

'That's one interpretation,' Pavel says. 'As any screenwriter will tell you, there are, of course, others.'

'Like?'

'Like something more complicit. Anything's possible. Which is rather the point.'

'The point?' I'm getting angry. 'You think Malo's behind all this? You think he helped kidnap his own girlfriend?'

I'm staring at him. Once again I'm finding his sense of apartness just a little hard to take. This is no time for showing off, for treating real people, precious people, people I love, as ciphers in some plot synopsis. Pavel is undoubtedly clever, and witty, and inventive. For a blind person, ironically, he also has the rare gift of insight. On the evidence of his other senses, his judgements about H and Malo have so far been faultless. But these talents come with an almost autistic detachment. He seems wary of soiling himself with the way people really are, of the traps they lay for themselves, of the messier consequences of our many imperfections.

Some of this I try and put into words. Infuriatingly, he understands at once what I'm saying.

'You think I don't care?'

'I think you're used to your own company. I think you trust no one else. In my book that's very sensible. If I was living in the dark I'd probably do the same.'

Pavel looks briefly shocked. Then his face is a mask once again, giving nothing away. At length, he stirs.

'I don't need your approval,' he says quietly. 'Or any kind of excuse. I'm sorry. I'm letting you down here.'

He puts his glass carefully to one side and gets up. So far he hasn't touched a drop. He says he'll call a cab from the sidewalk below.

'Sidewalk? Is this an American script?'

I'm trying to make light of this little exchange. I'm trying to say I'm sorry. It doesn't work. He's already at the door.

I struggle to my feet. A nightmare day has just got darker still. I follow him down the hall, try to catch his hand. He half-turns. He has no dog tonight, no Milost, just the collapsible stick he uses to map his next footfall.

I cup his long face in both hands, ask him to stay, plead with him to stay, but he shakes his head.

'Goodnight.' His eyes are half-closed. 'Take care, eh?'

TWELVE

I wake in the middle of the night. A fitful sleep, punctuated by fragments of dreams I'd prefer not to share, has left me groggy and a little ashamed. None of the relationships that matter in my world are working out. I seem to have developed a real gift for saying the wrong thing at the wrong time. Maybe I should arrange to go blind and then, at the very least, I'd have an excuse.

Pathetic, I tell myself. I roll over and peer at my bedside clock: 02.57. I lie on my back for a moment, listening to the low hum of the city beyond my windows. Then I hear another noise, closer, distinct. Metal on metal, I think. From somewhere down below.

I roll out of bed and reach for my dressing gown, resisting the temptation to turn on the light. The noise is coming from the rear of the building. This is where we park our cars, all sixteen of us, each with our allotted bay. From the lounge window I can peer down on the grid of vehicles on the blackness of the tarmac.

I stand motionless for a full minute. The parking spaces are bathed in that orange sodium glow that comes with life in a big city. My little Peugeot is at the end of the line, almost below my window, and I'm watching a man on his hands and knees beside my boot. One hand is reaching underneath the car. In the other is a tiny flashlight which he uses very sparingly. At last he seems to have finished whatever he's doing. Then he gets to his feet. He's a big man, tall, and he moves into the shadows with the ease of someone who works out. Something, some other noise in the half-darkness, brings him to a sudden halt and as he freezes and looks up I realize that the face beneath the big afro is black.

Seconds later, he's gone. Expecting the cough of an engine and a departing car, I hear nothing. My heart is thudding. I feel the clammy chill of real fear. Has he rigged some kind of bomb? Has he cut my brake lines? Has he helped himself to the Pavel book of plot accelerants in a bid to bring this sad little movie to an end? Is he still out there? Whatever the answer, as my pulse begins to settle, fear gives way to anger. My car, my space, my castle. This must have something to do with Malo, with Clem, but I'm past trying to cope with any of this by myself.

I dial 999 and ask for the police. When the voice at the other end enquires about the nature of the emergency I explain what's happened. Someone's just been interfering with my car. I watched them do it. And now I'd quite like a second opinion on what might happen next.

Moments later, I'm talking to a different voice. He introduces himself as one of the despatchers in the control room. I go through the story again and sense him trying to categorize the urgency of my call. I confirm that I'm alone in my flat on the fourth floor. I give him my mobile number and the exact address. No, there's no one I feel like waking up for support. And yes, I'll be on hand and waiting for help to arrive. The despatcher checks my name again and says he'll arrange for a response car to call by to assess the situation. I tell him I'm grateful and the conversation comes to an end.

Normally, under circumstances like these, I'd take the hint from the despatcher and knock on my neighbour's door for moral support, but Evelyn's in Venice just now and there's no one else I would call on at three o'clock in the morning. After twenty minutes at the window watching for movement – *any* movement – in the shadows below me I give up and make myself a cup of tea. As an afterthought, I cork the Rioja, stow the bottle away and wash up the two glasses. I'm expecting company at any moment. First impressions are all-important.

The response car announces its presence just after four o'clock with a call to my phone. PC Wallace and PC Cleverdon are outside the apartment block. Would I mind coming down and identifying my car?

Not at all. I slip into the trackie bottoms and loose top I used to wear for running round Kensington Gardens and make my way downstairs. The two police officers get out of the car as I emerge from the front door. I lead them round to the rear of the building and point out my little Peugeot.

PC Cleverdon is young. She looks a little like me back in the day when I first realized I might make it in a proper job. She's blonde and watchful, and doesn't give much away. While her colleague circles my car looking, I imagine, for signs of forced entry, she produces a flashlight and disappears down the line of neighbouring vehicles until I can hear nothing but the faint burble of voices on her radio. PC Wallace, meanwhile, is asking where, precisely, the intruder was at work.

I point at the boot. 'Under there.'

'Did you see what he was doing?'

'Not really. It didn't take very long. Maybe a minute at the most. Then he was away.'

PC Wallace is an older man. He has glasses and a neatly trimmed beard and introduces himself as Jerry. He also thinks he recognizes me.

'Actress, right?'

'Right.'

He names a couple of films I made a while back, one with Liam Neeson.

'Top movies,' he says, bending to take a closer look at the boot. 'Loved them both. Netflix? Can't do without it.'

He's on his hands and knees now, the beam of the torch sweeping left and right. Then, abruptly, it stops. I hear a grunt of satisfaction. With his spare hand he pulls something free and stands up. In the pool of light from his torch, I'm looking at an object a little bigger than a bar of soap. It's black and it has two metal discs on the top.

'Magnets,' he says. 'This is a tracker. Talks to someone who wants to know where you're going.' He glances up at me. 'Can we have a chat inside?'

Upstairs in my apartment I make them both tea while Jerry flips his notebook to a fresh page. He scribbles a date and a time and then asks me to describe exactly what I saw. Sadly, my description is far from detailed. Tall. Fit-looking. Jeans and a hoodie and what might have been basketball shoes. Also, he was black, with a big afro.

'A black gentleman?' Jerry looks up. 'You're certain? Age?'

'Hard to work out. Thirties? Forties? Younger? Older? I'd be guessing.'

He nods, doesn't pursue it. I pour the tea and apologize for no biscuits. The female PC, whose name is Dawn, is watching me closely. Jerry wants to know a bit more about me.

'You're married?'

'I was. Once.'

'Divorced now?'

'Nearly.'

'And have you made any other enemies?'

It's a nice line and I oblige with a smile which Jerry – justifiably – takes as applause.

'My ex-husband's Swedish,' I tell him. 'To the best of my knowledge he hasn't been here for months. He's also hopeless with anything practical.'

'You're telling me he's black?'

'No. *Au contraire.* He's very white and very blond. It goes with the passport.'

'But he could have hired someone? Paid them to keep tabs on you? Would that have been possible?'

'It might,' I agree. 'But he's flat broke. Or at least that's what he tells me.'

Jerry nods, makes a note, glances up. 'Anyone else in your life? Anyone married or partnered who might be cheating on their other half?'

I give the question some thought. I'm thinking about Pavel. Might he have a secret consort? Some insanely jealous woman who's hired some heavy to scare off the opposition?

'No,' I say. 'Nothing like that.'

A nod of the head from Jerry and another scribble in his notebook. A voice on his radio has just reported a stabbing on Camden High Street. The victim is deemed critical. Hotel One is already airborne.

'Chopper,' Jerry grunts. 'Busy as you like, those boys.'

We go back to the tracker. While it isn't strictly mine I'll have to sign for the device while attempts are made to trace the point of sale. I'm not to hold my breath at this piece of detective work but it might save a great deal of time if I could come up with a name or two.

'Like who?'

'That's my question, Ms Andressen. Have a bit of a think. Is there anyone or anything that's happened recently that might explain this little incident?'

This, I know, is the killer question. This is the moment when I can spill the beans about Clem, about Malo, about mysterious black strangers with dreadlocks and teardrop tattoos. All of this will doubtless make Jerry's week. Not some lowlife slapping a tracker on the wrong car but a tiny piece of a much sexier jigsaw. I happen to know that kidnap is up there with murder and arson when it comes to proper crime. Despite the kidnappers' warning, is now the moment to break the news about Clem?

I'm still trying to make up my mind when there comes another message on Dawn's radio. A passer-by has reported a B&E in progress at a phone shop in Notting Hill Gate. I know this shop. It's only minutes away. Both Jerry and Dawn are on their feet.

Jerry drops a card on my lap and heads for the door. Dawn has already acknowledged the tasking.

'Bell me tomorrow after two o'clock,' Jerry says over his shoulder. 'I should be up by then.'

'B&E?' I ask. But they've gone.

THIRTEEN

Getting to sleep again, oddly enough, is no problem. Not only have I forcibly addressed the mystery of my unbidden intruder, but luck has also bought me half a day before I have to decide whether or not to come clean about the kidnapping. The proposition about the wrong car seems more than likely. I can live with that. Case closed.

Next morning, early, I phone H. Contrary to what he told me yesterday he's not at Flixcombe at all.

'I'm in Brixton,' he grunts. 'Having breakfast.'

I tell him we need to talk. Has he heard from Mateo at all?

'No.'

'Have you tried to get in touch?'

'No.'

'But something might have happened. Have I got that right?'

'Yeah.'

H is eating and talking at the same time. I also get the feeling he's not alone.

'I had Malo round last night,' I say. 'Why have you stopped his money?'

'Because I had no choice. Talk later, yeah?'

I try to ask when, but he's gone. Angry, I send him a text. *Eating and being offensive at the same time? Here's to multi-tasking.*

He phones back past midday and suggests he buys me lunch. I say yes and within an hour he's outside the apartment. It's been raining all morning and once I'm in the passenger seat I notice two wet patches, one over each knee. He's booked a table at a local restaurant he knows I like. He has to be gone by half two.

Nostimo is an upscale Greek eatery in Notting Hill Gate. The prices are a rip-off, a fortune for each tapas-sized portion, but the food itself is excellent. H sips premium bottled water as he stares at the menu.

'The grilled aubergine is to die for,' I say. 'Why Brixton?'

He won't tell me. Neither is he very keen to explain why he's plunged his newly discovered son into penury.

'I need the boy at Flixcombe to keep an eye on him,' he says at last. 'It's for his sake, not mine.'

'Don't you trust him?'

'No. Since you ask.'

This, at least, has the merit of one of the blunter truths, but for me it's not enough.

'Why? Why don't you trust him? You told me he's in trouble.'

'He is. He's got himself in the shit, big time, and he won't admit it. I can live with stubborn but I've got no time for stupid. He's in it up to here.'

H draws a thick finger across his throat, a gesture that truly chills me.

'Into what, exactly?' I ask.

'You don't want to know.'

'But I do. He's my son, remember?'

'Our son.'

'So tell me.'

'No.'

'Why not?'

H gives me one of his trust-me looks. I know it's meant to be kindly and supportive but it doesn't feel that way. Moments ago I was toying with telling H about the mystery black man with the teardrop tattoo, but I'm not here to be patronized. Information, after all, is power and I, too, can play that game.

'Maybe he's spending too much time alone,' I suggest. 'In these circumstances it doesn't pay to think too hard.' I'm trying to play guileless, the embattled mother still fighting off the after-effects of chemo.

'Alone? Bollocks. What's this?'

I take a look. Spicy tiropita, I explain, is exactly what the menu says it is, a confection of broken filo pastry, leeks and chillies.

'Any good?'

'Delicious.'

'I'll have two.' He's looking for the waitress but I'm determined to get back to Malo.

'You're telling me he's in the shit.' I'm refusing to give up. 'What kind of shit?'

He shakes his head. Once again, he won't tell me. I beckon him closer over the tabletop. H needs to know I'm serious.

'You don't think he's been over at Clem's place?' I ask. 'Waiting and waiting for the phone to ring? Because that's what the boy's telling me.'

'He's lying.'

'How do you know?'

'That doesn't matter. The boy can be a twat. The world's a much nastier place than he thinks it is. He needs protecting. He needs looking after. Maybe that's where you come in.'

'At Flixcombe? Both of us banged up? That's double kidnap.'

'Kidnap, my arse. And that's another thing. We sit and listen to Mr Jaguar at Mateo's place and he'd have us think he's got the whole deal weighed off. That's bullshit. The world's moving on and he should have sussed it. Everything's in play. Everything's changing. In my day, the drugs biz was run by honest guys. It was supply and demand. You spot a hole in the market and you fill the fucker. You try very hard not to hurt anyone, not badly, and you also try very hard to keep your standards up. Decent gear. At a decent price. To people who can pay without robbing other punters blind. That's how I got rich. By playing it straight. By satisfying demand. By keeping people happy. And by making all that moolah *work*.'

'You're telling me this is about drugs?'

'Of course it is. And you're talking to someone who *knows*.'

I nod. I'm sure this is true because people I trust have told me so. Hayden Prentice, one-time drug baron, had a real talent for shrewd investments. In the first place, the money came from cocaine sales. Then, thanks to a small army of bent white-collar professionals – solicitors, accountants, planning consultants, property developers – all that cash funded an ever-growing empire of legitimate businesses from tanning salons and estate agents to care homes and even a security consultancy. Hence Flixcombe Manor, and H's bursting portfolio of legitimate business interests, and all the largesse that Malo has taken for granted.

'You're telling me times have changed? Is that it?'

'Totally. Beyond recognition.'

'And Malo is part of this? Have I got that right?'

'Yeah. Probably by accident. Probably because he didn't look hard enough, didn't *think* hard enough. The drugs biz these days is a swamp. And a swamp is where the real reptiles live. These people are off their heads. Some of them are children, just *kids*. They're tooled up. They probably sleep with knives under their pillows. They'd kill you as soon as look at you. They'd do you for an argument over a couple of quid. The Filth call it county lines. It's basically selling gear over the phone. It's everywhere, all over the fucking country. You think your own little town is safe? You think those sweet kids of yours won't ever get in trouble with drugs? Wrong. And you know why? Because something we all took for granted has gone. Families? Mums? Dads? A proper job? Getting up in the morning? Totally bolloxed. No one has a clue who they are any more, or where they belong, and there isn't a politician in the country who can tell them what to do about it. There's a great phrase I heard the other week. Remember it. Have a bit of a think about it. The end of days, right? Because that's where we fucking are. *At the end of days.* And you know why? Because we never paid enough attention. What happens next?' He spreads his hands wide and shrugs. 'Fuck knows.'

This, from H, has the makings of a speech. The young waitress, visibly frightened, is keeping her distance. Now she pounces, pad in hand. H gives her his order without checking the menu. Pork belly. King prawns. Scallops. And two of those spicy things. I, meanwhile, settle for courgette cakes and fresh calamari. H's little rant has stilled conversation in the courtyard where we're eating and a French family at a neighbouring table are making hasty preparations to leave.

I ask H to tell me more about Malo. Last night, I say, I gave him some money.

'I know. You're crazy. That boy needs money like a hole in the head. He phoned me up. He was laughing. He thought he'd got one over on me. Two hundred quid, am I right?'

'Yes. My money. My decision.'

'And you know what he'll spend it on?'

'Tell me.'

'Cocaine. He was coked-up last night. Totally manic like some teenager off her head.'

'*Her* head?'

'Yeah. Tell you the truth, I'm beginning to wonder.'

'You think Malo's gay?'

'I think he's off his head. And that's at least halfway to gay.' He leans forward. He's sweating slightly, though the last of the really hot weather has gone. 'Something else. The blind guy, your fancy man, was round your place too. Am I right?'

'You are. And for the record he walked out on me.'

'Really?' H can't hide his delight. 'You're telling me you've started saying no? Shit, I'm almost sorry for the bloke.'

I stare at him. I can't believe what he's just said. He's pushed me too far and he knows it. One large hand descends on mine but it's far too late. I reach across the table and slap his face as hard as I can. I feel the sandpaper bristliness of his cheek beneath my palm. He recoils from the blow while the French family gather their kids and head for the door, and then he leans towards me again. I hit him a second time, even harder, and then pick up my bag before making my way back through the restaurant to the street.

For a moment or two, watching the French family hurrying away, I think H might be coming after me, but when I check, the only face I can see belongs to a startled waiter. I turn away from the restaurant and start to walk home. I'm becoming part of the culture, I think. And I'm feeling a whole lot better.

FOURTEEN

H phones me every ten minutes or so for the entire afternoon. Thinking he might try and make an appearance in person, I'm also determined to ignore the video phone. Part of me is tempted to check on Pavel, to risk a conversation, to maybe tender some kind of apology, but that, too, I resist. The palm of my right hand is sore and slightly swollen. A truly wonderful feeling.

Finally, in the early evening, I at last answer the latest of H's calls. He has the grace to say sorry for insulting me and blames, in some unfathomable way, the setting. Posh, he says, always gets him going. What he said was totally out of order and he wants me to know that he's really, really sorry. An apology from H is a first and I even detect signs of something I can only call respect in the way he's handling the conversation. He's businesslike, certainly, but he's also warm. Maybe I've passed some arcane test, I think. Maybe he thinks I might become one of the gang.

'Have you got a pen there?'

I have.

'I'm gonna give you a couple of names. One of them is a girl called Evie. That's not her real name but that's the way they know her on the street. The other is a waster called Bradley. Crap tatts and shit skin. You could read a paper through him. That's our son talking, by the way, not me.'

'Malo knows these people?'

'He does.'

'This is Brixton?'

'Bridport. Malo and Clem have been hanging out there. Start with a pub called the Landfall. The place is full of lowlifes dealing whatever you fancy.'

'They've been using this pub?'

'Yeah.'

'Who says?'

'Malo.'

'Why?' I'm reaching for a pen, remembering the state of my son the first time he met Pavel. 'You think he's buying drugs there?'

'Good question.'

Bridport is a little town in west Dorset I happen to like. It's an easy drive from Flixcombe and one or two of the cafe-bars put Kensington to shame. H is still telling me about the Landfall but by now I'm more than confused. What, exactly, am I supposed to do in a druggy pub in Bridport? What am I after?

'Everything. Anything. Information, especially. Remember what I was saying in the restaurant before you beat me up? About the way things are turning out in this khazi of a country? Keep your eyes open. Take a look around. Have a conversation or two. Mention the boy, and Clemmie as well. Malo says she made a big impact. Find out what they've been up to – anything Malo's not telling us that could explain what's happened to Clem. In your trade that should be an easy gig. Something else, too. Keep tabs on what you spend. Because I'm in the chair.'

'This is some kind of business deal? You're commissioning me? You want receipts?' I'm laughing now.

'Call it research.' H isn't amused. 'Call it what you fucking like. Lowlifes won't talk to me. No way. But it might be different coming from you. Fuck Mr Jaguar. If we want Clemmie back in one piece, this is where we start.'

Bridport, at first glance, is a world away from the kind of town you might associate with hardcore druggies. It's within touching distance of Lyme Regis, surrounded by soft green hills. West Bay, with its pebble beach and busy harbour, is a mile and a half down the road. The town itself once earned a living from rope-making and this is said to have some connection to the width of the main street, though no one's ever explained to me why.

Nowadays, Bridport has become a must-visit for serious foodies and there's a colony of wealthy incomers among those hills, most of whom have swapped the winnings from selling up in London for an acre or two of rural peace. Unless I've been missing something, none of these good folk have much interest in acquiring a crack habit, or arranging meets with a smack dealer.

This is where I need a little help from my son. When I get him on the phone he says he's at Flixcombe and because I can hear

Jess in the background I have no reason to disbelieve him. Jessie, who's a Pompey girl, acts as a kind of housekeeper to H.

'Is this your father's doing?' I ask Malo.

'Yeah.'

'So are you back on the payroll?'

'No chance. Free board and lodging and a fridge full of Stella? Actually it's OK.'

'The Stella?'

'Flixcombe. Dad's right. I need a break.'

'And Clem?'

'Her dad got a video this afternoon, sent direct to his phone. He shared it with me.'

'And?'

'She's talking to camera against a plain white wall. She sends her love, by the way. Asked to be remembered.'

'To me?'

'Yeah. And Dad, too.'

I'm confused again. Malo's making this major breakthrough sound like a video postcard from some vacation spot. The girl's been kidnapped, for God's sake.

'Did she look all right? Sound all right?'

'She sounded nervous. That's not like her.'

'No hint of where she might be? How she might have got there?'

'None. It wasn't that kind of thing. It only lasted a couple of minutes and at the end she held up a copy of this morning's paper. That was a bit weird. She never reads *The Sun*.'

I nod. The headline would authenticate the video, along – presumably – with the date and time on-screen.

'What else did Mateo tell you?'

'He says a guy he knows is talking to the kidnappers.'

'What about?'

'He won't tell me.'

'Is this man's name O'Keefe?'

'Yeah. How do you know?'

'I met him. We both did. Me and your dad.' As lightly as I can, I mention the Landfall in Bridport, saying it figured in a review I was reading in some paper or other. 'It sounds quite nice,' I tell him. It's the thinnest of lies.

'Nice?' The word draws a bark of laughter from my son. 'What else did the paper say?'

I'm staring at the phone. I'm having to invent here and it doubtless shows.

'They said it was authentic,' I mutter. 'I imagine that means real. What do you think?'

'It's OK. Crap sound system. Packed at the weekends. You're telling me you're going there? Making a visit?'

'I might.'

I mumble something about a day out and then change the subject. Whatever happens in Bridport, I'm clearly on my own.

I settle down for the evening and I'm browsing the latest programme offers on iPlayer when I get a call from Pavel's agent. She's been trying to contact him all day without success. He's not picking up and her messages have gone unanswered. This isn't like him at all, she says, and to be frank she's worried. Do I have any idea where he might be?

I like Pavel's agent. I've met her on a couple of occasions, once at a book launch and once at a BAFTA evening where Pavel picked up an award for his work on a costume drama. A place at Pavel's table had come as a surprise, the first present he ever bought me, and given how awful some of these occasions in la-la land can be, it turned out rather well. Misha, half-Polish, is both warm and funny and is immensely proud of her star client. According to Pavel she once accompanied him to an industry get-together in Toulouse and poured a glass of red all over a drunken Russian actor who was being obnoxious.

'Do you want me to go round?' I ask. 'See if I can raise him?'

'You're sure you don't mind?'

'Not at all. My pleasure.'

I turn off the telly and call an Uber, glad to have an excuse to kiss and make up. The traffic is light and the journey down to Chiswick takes no time at all. When I arrive, there's no sign of Pavel. I try the doorbell two, three times and then knock and knock. When I try phoning I can hear nothing that would indicate his mobile ringing inside. Finally a woman emerges from next door and wants to know whether she can help at all. I explain that Pavel's a good friend of mine.

'You were here the other night, right?' She's American. 'I saw you leave next day.'

'That would be me,' I agree.

It turns out that she has a key to the property lodged with her and her partner a couple of years back when they'd both moved in and got to know Pavel.

'Amazing guy,' she says. 'He calls it his just-in-case key. Just in case he locks himself out or gets blind drunk or whatever.' She frowns. 'Blind drunk? That's not good.'

She disappears back into her house and emerges with the key. The fact that he's never had to use it, she says, tells you everything you need to know about their lovely neighbour.

'So deep and, you know, so kinda *brave*.'

She lets us both in. I stand for a moment in the hallway, calling Pavel's name. Nothing. The door to the big room downstairs is a couple of inches ajar and I push it open and step inside. Everything looks exactly the way I remember it, very neat, very tidy, then the woman from next door draws my attention to the TV. It's on freeze frame from the DVD player and the image on the screen is all too familiar. It comes from the scene towards the end of the movie I shot in Nantes all those years ago. The naked woman straddling the doomed Resistance hero is me.

My new friend is staring at it. 'Holy shit,' she says. 'How did he know when to hit the Pause button?'

Good question. I'm back home. A search of Pavel's house revealed no clues to what might have happened. His bed was made. There was fresh pasta in the fridge. The towels in the bathroom were carefully folded. And we could find no sign of a note. All that was missing was the dog. So far so good, but what I can't get out of my mind was that freeze-frame on his TV. Was he expecting me to call round? Manage to gain access? Was it some kind of message? And if so, what did it mean?

Just now I'm phoning every A&E department in an ever-widening circle around Chiswick in search of an injured blind man in his mid-forties with a dog called Milost. No one can help. So far I haven't contacted the police to report him as a missing person because I'm all too aware that I've missed my appointment with PC Wallace. Maybe, if there's still no sign of him over the

coming days, I can dream up some story and get the neighbour
to do it. Maybe.

Ever more worried – first Clem, now Pavel – I retire early. I'm
fast asleep when my phone rings. I roll over, rubbing my eyes,
fumbling for my mobile. Nearly half past midnight.

'Hello,' I mumble. 'Who is this?'

The moment I hear his voice I know it's Pavel. He's lightly
drunk. He says he's been to a concert. Smetana and then a Dvořák
symphony. After that, a meal and a bottle of Macon in a favourite
restaurant. Now he's standing on a bridge trying to imagine the
lights reflected on the pleats of the water. He wants me to know
that the dog is OK, tied securely to a ring on the bridge, and that
he'll always love me.

I'm staring at the phone. I've read enough scripts in my life to
know that this is a suicide call, a moment of fond adieu before
the plunge into oblivion. The Thames after midnight, I think, even
in late August, will be unforgiving and probably terminal.

'Which bridge?' I ask him.

No reply.

'You're nearby? Chiswick Bridge? Hammersmith Bridge?
Somewhere further downstream? Westminster? Lambeth? Waterloo,
maybe?'

There's still no answer but I'm out of bed now, making for the
phone in the lounge. Once I know where he is I can call 999 on
my landline while I try and talk him down.

'Pavel?' I'm pleading now. 'Just give me the name of the fucking
bridge.'

This is the second time in twenty-four hours I've phoned the
emergency services. I'm half-wondering whether the operator
will recognize my voice, or perhaps my number, but it's a woman
this time. Shielding my smartphone, I do my best to describe
what's happening.

'We need a name,' she says. 'And a location.'

Too right. I'm trying my hardest to get Pavel back on the line.

'Pavel,' I whisper to the 999 operator. 'His name's Pavel.'

'And where, exactly, do we find him?'

I'm about to explain the situation all over again when I hear
Pavel's voice. He sounds apologetic. He says he's been attending
to the dog again.

'So where are you?' I ask him. 'Which bridge?'

There's a moment of silence, then I hear a soft chuckle. 'It's the Charles Bridge,' he says. 'In Prague.'

Prague? Shit. I'm about to ask the 999 lady what I do next but Pavel hasn't finished.

'*Ahoj,* my love,' he whispers. 'That's Czech for goodbye.'

The phone goes dead. I swallow hard. The 999 lady wants to know what's happening. I tell her my friend is in Prague and he's probably jumped. She gives me a Foreign and Commonwealth Office number and says it's manned 24/7. They may be able to help. She'll also explore some other options but she thinks a call to the FCO is my best way forward.

I dial the number. It's a male voice this time. He's courteous and sympathetic and he hears me out. Blind man. Tallish. Middle-aged. Dog. Passion for Prague. Charles Bridge.

'And depressed, you think?'

I'm not sure about depression. Just now I'm not sure about anything, but this is no time to speculate about what led Pavel to make the phone call. All I can think about is that image on his TV and the big white spaces of the room he calls home and what it must be like to be seconds away from drowning. Maybe he's been drowning most of his life. Maybe that's it.

'Yes,' I agree. 'Depression probably covers it.'

The FCO man takes some brief personal details. He'll phone the embassy in Prague and ask them to alert the local police. He has a description of my friend and he has a name. God willing, they'll get there in time.

I thank him for his patience and he promises to phone back if there are any developments. In the kitchen I slump at the table and stare numbly at the walls. The word here is guilt. I feel swamped. I feel overwhelmed. Somehow I appear to be responsible for the death of another human being. Worse still, I seem to have killed someone who I'd become really close to.

I try very hard to replay the scene that followed Malo's departure from right here in my flat the other night. Me and Pavel talking on the sofa. His acuity. The sharpness of his instincts. The way he'd read my wayward son. And that splinter of ice at the very middle of him that couldn't – or wouldn't – push the conversation any further.

Were he and H right about Malo using cocaine? Very probably.
But why couldn't Pavel understand how upset I was? Why didn't
he put his arms around me and tell me everything would be OK,
everything would work out, that together we'd plot a route out of
this nightmare?

Plot, I think. The key word, the curse of our trade, the delusion
that real life should for ever resemble the tensions, resolvable or
otherwise, of a good movie script. Berndt, my ex-husband, had
been very good at plots but failed the being-human test and now,
once again, I seem to have fallen into the penumbra of someone
very similar. Except in Pavel's case he had the makings of a decent
excuse. Close your eyes a moment. Let the darkness enfold you.
Imagine being that way for ever. No wonder he took care to keep
his distance.

Took. Past tense. I shiver, suddenly cold. I can see Pavel's body
floating away down the river and I shake my head, part guilt, part
despair, remembering again our conversation after Malo left.
Scriptwriters are there at the Creation. They play God for a living.
They start with the blankness of the PC screen. They invent characters. They cage them in a plot. They put them to the test. And
very often, thanks to the serendipity of a couple of keystrokes,
they decide whether they survive, or whether they die.

I think I've dimly understood this for most of my working
life, especially the God bit, but in the shape of Pavel I know I met
someone who took this strange magic into a different dimension.
That was his talent. That was what made him so magnetic, so
fascinating. He had a gravitational pull I found impossible to resist.
And now he's gone.

When we were talking on the sofa and the conversation was
getting strained he told me that anything – on the page and
perhaps in real life – is possible, and now it turns out he's right. At
the time, in my defence, I failed to pick up the coded message
buried in this simple proposition, so maybe I should have listened
a little harder. And understood.

FIFTEEN

The next morning is Monday. The ransom deadline for Clem is just hours away but now my lovely writer has introduced a new plot twist. Hoping against hope, I hang around the apartment waiting for the phone to ring. If the news from the Foreign Office is good, if the Czechs have managed to lay hands on Pavel, downstream or otherwise, I'll be on my way to the airport in seconds. I have a bag packed. I've been on the internet and found a couple of cheapish flights that would get me to downtown Prague in short order. Quite what might lie beyond this moment of reunion is anyone's guess but in Pavel's world, dark as it is, I'll definitely be back on the side of the angels. And that, believe it or not, matters a great deal.

But there's no word from the FCO. By lunchtime, I'm fighting the temptation to lift the phone. An hour later, I succumb. I expect another voice on the emergency helpline and I'm not disappointed. The woman takes some time to consult the log of overnight calls and then, with just a hint of apology, she regrets that no word has come from the authorities in Prague.

'Is it possible to check?' I ask.

'That might not be appropriate.'

'Then can you give me a number to try myself? Or maybe an email address?'

'I'm afraid not. There's a protocol that governs these enquiries. If anything's happened I'm sure the Czechs would have been in touch.'

This appears to be the end of the conversation. Other phones are ringing in the background. Just another frantic day in Whitehall.

'You'll phone if you get any news?' I'm trying not to sound plaintive.

'Of course.'

'Thank you.'

I check my phone for other messages, just in case, then stand at my window, staring at the greyness of the day. A couple of hours

ago I Googled a map of the Czech Republic. The river that runs
through Prague is the Vltava. According to the best source I could
find, it runs at an average speed of just over two miles per hour.
By now, according to my calculations, that would put Pavel's
body twenty miles downstream. Here, the river runs through a
series of waterside towns and villages. Should I take a flight in
any case? Hire a car? Find a bus? Pay a visit to Kralupy, or Veltrusy,
in search of Pavel's remains? Even the thought of an expedition
like this is slightly grotesque. I don't even know the Czech for
'hello' or 'excuse me', let alone enough of the language to organize
my dead pianist's repatriation. I'm beginning to hallucinate, I
conclude. What I really need is an hour or two of proper sleep.

I awake to Tina Turner. Making a mental note yet again to change
my ringtone, I reach for my phone. To my amazement, it's early
evening. The Foreign Office, I think. Good news at last.

It's H. He wants to know how Bridport is working out.

'It's not. I'm still in London. Working on a new script.'

It's a small lie but oddly close to the truth. It also seems to
keep H in his place.

'You're still up for it, right?'

'I am. Just give me a day or two.'

'Of course. No problem. I've had Mateo on. Just thought you
ought to know.'

'And?'

'He's been talking to that clown O'Keefe. Mateo seems to
think he went in at seven five, maybe ten.'

'Ten what?'

'Grand. I gather they laughed at him. Next thing Mateo knows
he's looking at a text. Two million. They've *doubled* the fucking
price.'

'And what does O'Keefe say?'

'He's pissed off they're in touch with Mateo at all. He says
the whole thing's irregular. He's telling Mateo these people are
amateurs. They haven't a clue what they're doing.'

'So how does that help Clem? And us?'

'It doesn't. O'Keefe can bitch all he likes but in the end these
animals are who they are. We're at the fucking table. You play
the cards you're dealt. O'Keefe doesn't even want us in the room.
He thinks it's his business, no one else's.'

I nod. I think I understand. I could badly use a glass or two of that Rioja Pavel and I started. I head for the kitchen, my phone pressed to my ear.

'So where do we go from here?' I ask H.

'Bridport,' he grunts. 'I'm parked up outside.'

SIXTEEN

We're down in west Dorset by half past nine. The traffic has been evil and I've spent most of the journey brooding about Pavel and half-listening to a Neil Diamond best-of CD, an H favourite. At my insistence he's booked me a single room in a Bridport hotel. Malo, as far as I can gather, has been grounded at Flixcombe until we get to the bottom of whatever's happened to Clem, and I now have a leading role to play in Bridport. The conversations I'm hoping to share at the Landfall will stretch my acting talents to their limits. Adding my son to the mix, living under the same roof, is – for now – an ask too far.

'You're sure you don't want to stay over?'

'No, thank you.'

'You want me to hang around at all? Just in case?'

'No.'

We've left my bag at the hotel and now we're cruising slowly down the main street. This stretch of the town, in the fading light, lives up to its billing. A line of gleaming 4x4s parked at the kerbside. Stylish restaurants, bursting at the seams. We've come to a halt beside one of them, waiting for the traffic lights to change. Three generations are gathered at the same table closest to the window. Tanned, well-fed faces. A grandfather in the rudest of health, jeans and an open-necked sports shirt, shaping some story or other with his big hands. Kids eyeing the last of the rough-cut chips over their iPads. Much laughter.

The lights change and H is looking for a street at the bottom of the town. Here we find the pub. The Landfall, like the restaurant we've just seen, is packed but it's a different clientele: younger, scruffier, poorer. A handful of youth are in a huddle next to the door, sharing a doobie, and heads turn as we roll to a halt. There's something slightly feral in the openness of their curiosity and I'm starting to wonder whether I'll need a tattoo to get past them and into the pub when another car draws up behind us.

H has to move on. He puts a hand on my thigh, gives it a little squeeze.

'It's a shithole.' He slips me a roll of notes. 'Good fucking luck.'

I stuff the money into the back pocket of my jeans, adjust my beret and make my way across the street. H has already gone. I'm on my own. The boys at the door part with some reluctance.

'Nice T-shirt.'

I'm wearing one of Malo's with Albert Einstein on the front. It's been in a drawer in the spare bedroom for months and when I threw it in my bag, just hours ago, it seemed a witty thing to do. Now I'm not so sure. Just what kind of attention do I want to attract?

'Glad you like it,' I murmur, edging sideways through the narrow gap between bodies and stepping into the pub.

The bitter sweetness of the weed has gone. The Landfall smells of spilled ale, the way it should. There's a mix of faces around me, crowding towards the bar. Some are much older than I'd expected. These are outdoor people, maybe builders, maybe fishermen, jowly but fit-looking, heavily tanned. Glassy-eyed, a couple of them must have been here for hours. One of them has a big gold earring. Another has scabs of plaster on his threadbare jeans. He tries to hold my gaze for a second or two and then a huge hand raises his glass in some kind of salute. I nod back and then look elsewhere. An ancient jukebox is playing at full blast. This is no place, thank God, for conversation.

Above the scrum of drinkers is a TV showing a football match. The picture is blurred, blobs of blue chasing blobs of red, and no one's paying the slightest attention. Spotting a gap between three youths in designer tracksuits, I make a lunge for the bar. The barman, I've noted, has been watching me. I've already decided to ask for a glass of wine. It's very obvious I don't belong here so another little stand-out won't go amiss.

The barman wants to know what colour I want.

'Do you have any Shiraz?' I shout.

'What colour's that?'

'Red.'

'We've got red. Big glass? Just you, is it?'

I nod to both questions. He's found a bottle in the fridge. I try to read the label as he pours a generous measure. A glass of chilled Tempranillo on a wet night in Bridport? Why not?

I wrestle H's wad of notes out of my jeans pocket. They're all twenties and I must be looking at two hundred pounds, minimum. The barman is Mr Cool and pretends not to have noticed but the kids at my elbow are seriously excited.

'Fuck me,' says one of them. 'Check that out.'

I do my best to grin. His mate has noticed my T-shirt.

'Who's that?' he wants to know.

'Albert Einstein.'

'Peng,' he says. 'He looks a mad old dog.'

'Peng?'

'Hot. Fit. Who does he play for?'

This, despite the roar of the jukebox, has the makings of a conversation. His mates think the play-for comment is funny. They're drinking something crimson but I don't know what. At some point or other I have to make a start on what I came for and now might be the time.

'I came here to meet my son,' I shout. 'His name's Malo. He sometimes wears a T-shirt like this. Ever seen him?'

The youths exchange glances. They're all thin. Not a teardrop tattoo between them. The barman is handing me my change. The youths all drain their glasses at a single gulp and reach across me to put them on the counter. The message couldn't be clearer.

The barman knows exactly what they're drinking. A nod from me produces three new glasses.

'What's the name again?'

'Malo.'

'What sort of name's that?'

'It's French.'

'How old is he?'

'Your age. His girlfriend's South American. Dark. Small. Really pretty.'

One of the youths is frowning. 'Big bike? Harley? Really cool leather jacket?'

'That's her.' My heart gives a leap. 'You know them?'

'Seen them a couple of times.'

'In here?'

'And around, yeah. Peng bike. Can't miss it. Off the fucking hook.'

On top of the original twenty pounds, the barman wants another £3.55. I haul out the notes again. I'm starting to attract serious attention. One of the youths, the oldest, wants to know whether I'm buying.

'I just did.' I nod at the drinks.

He stares at me a moment, then laughs. The nose piercings don't suit him.

'Maybe you're carrying,' he says. 'What can you do me for a fiver?'

This, it dawns on me, is drug-speak. Bingo.

'Depends,' I say. 'What are you after?'

The youth looks uncertain for a moment. Then I hear a voice very close to my right ear.

'Does your mum know you're here?'

I spin round. A face I've never seen before is looking down at me. He must be in his late thirties, early forties. Underneath the three-day stubble he's handsome and the hint of mischief in his smile tells me he knows it. Black jeans and a Lacoste shirt, with a black leather jacket hooked over his shoulder. Nice.

He bends to my ear again. I can feel the warmth of his breath against my cheek.

'French film star consorting with Dorset lowlife? Am I getting warm here?'

I nod. He tries to put a protective arm around my shoulders and walk me away from the youths. I shake him off, ask him what he thinks he's doing.

'Andy Cassidy?' he says. 'Ring any bells?'

Andy Cassidy is Jessie's partner. They have a cottage in the grounds at Flixcombe and both work for H. I spent weeks last summer fighting him off.

'You know Andy?'

'Yeah. Not a bad bloke for a Villa fan.'

'So how come you recognized me?'

'He's got a couple of your movies on DVD. We watched *The Hour of Our Passing* last weekend. Cracking scene at the end.' He's looking at my beret, which seems to have slipped a little. 'What happened under there?'

'Chemo,' I tell him. 'No gain without pain.'

'Shit happens.' He extends a hand. 'Danny Flannery.'

I'm not sure where this conversation is going, but word of my largesse has spread along the bar and pretty quickly I suspect I'm going to be buying the entire pub a drink. I beckon Danny closer and ask him if there's somewhere quieter we could talk. He says there's another pub down the road that caters for human beings. Better beer, too.

The rain has got heavier. Danny uses his leather jacket to shelter both of us as we half-walk, half-run down the potholed street. The lining of the jacket smells of roll-ups. Only when we're stepping in from the rain and I check in my back pocket for H's roll of notes do I realize they've gone.

'Shit.' I'm checking the other pockets, just in case. What on earth do I tell H?

Danny has one hand on the door. He watches me a moment, a half-smile on his face, then produces the notes.

'Better me than someone else,' he says. 'Carrying that kind of wad in the Fall? You have to be crazy.'

I'm deeply grateful and I say so. I feel about twelve. First drink on me.

'No need.' Danny's smile is wider. 'But since you're offering . . .'

The Baker's Arms is a sanctuary after the Landfall. No music. No crush of sweaty bodies around the bar. Just a sprinkle of lone drinkers, one of whom is bent over *The Times* crossword.

Danny seats me at a table in the corner. I try to insist on buying him a drink but he won't hear of it. He really enjoyed the movie last weekend. A class act deserves something better than rubbish Tempranillo.

'No one's touched that bottle for months,' he says. 'I'd get yourself checked over if I were you.'

He returns from the bar with a large glass of the Shiraz I'd asked for. I taste a drop. Delicious. Danny is drinking beer of some kind. I want to know more about the Landfall.

'Why?'

'It doesn't matter. Not at the moment. Call it a favour. Call it what you like. You go there a lot?'

'Only to score. There's a bloke called Jimmy. You wouldn't know him. Best weed in the county. Always delivers.'

'And he sells other stuff?'

'No, just weed, but the place is a souk. Anything you want and probably stuff that you don't. Andy and I do a couple of lines at weekends if we fancy it. Dial-a-toot gets a delivery to your doorstep but if you're up for a pint or two before you get started, the Fall does nicely.'

'You call it the Fall? The Landfall?'

'Yeah. On really bad nights it's the Landfill but mostly it's the Fall. It used to be a builders' pub back in the day. Go in on a Friday night and you could get a whole house built. Every trade would be drinking there. Plasterers. Brickies. Plumbers. Clap your hands, buy them a drink and you'd have a new address by the end of the month.'

'And you?'

'Carpenter.' He shows me his hands. 'Can't you tell?'

I look at the palms of his hands. I know he wants me to touch them, to admire the ridge of callous where he's sawn timber all his life, but I'll do no such thing.

'So what happened? To the Fall?'

'Business got tough. It's the same wherever you go. Rip-off leases from the brewers. Business rates through the roof. Then Sky wanted silly prices for the live footie licence and people started drinking cheap supermarket booze at home and the game was over. The Fall was never going to be a gastro pub, not with Karl in charge, so he had to find another way. He's been trying re-runs of old footie matches he's recorded but the DVD player's on the blink so he needs something else to pull the punters in.'

'Drugs?'

'Yeah. It attracts the kids, which is a bummer, but it also brings in people like me. We're punters. We buy drinks. On a good night we buy lots of drinks. Karl likes that. We're the only way he survives.'

'And the police?'

'They leave him alone. You're gonna ask me why, aren't you?'

'Yes.'

'Karl scored a deal with the drugs squad. It's all on a handshake. He's got hidden cameras in there and the cops help themselves to the footage. That way they can put faces to names, get a handle on who's doing what, keep everything under control, nice and neat and tidy. In a town like this that matters. Everyone knows everyone. Nothing ever gets out of hand. I thought the cops were

bent at first. I thought some of them were on the take. But I'm
wrong. They're just sensible.'

'You mean it works?'

'Yeah. Until recently.'

'And?'

He studies me a moment and then takes a pull from his glass.
'You never told me what you were doing in the Fall in the first
place.'

'I know. I've got a couple of names for you.' I hold his gaze.
'Do you mind?'

'Go on, then.'

'Kid called Bradley?'

'And?'

'Girl called Evie? I don't think that's her real name but that's
all I've got.'

He nods, says nothing for a moment, then he reaches for a
beer mat and does that trick when you balance it on the edge of
the table. Flip and catch.

'Well?' I ask. He's dropped the mat twice now.

'I know Bradley. I know the family. His dad used to be on the
tools with the water people but he did a runner years back. His
stepdad's a nasty bastard, brick shithouse, likes a drink, once put
the kid in hospital though no one'll say it to his face. You've got
to feel sorry for the boy. Everyone calls him Noodle.'

'Why?'

'There's nothing to him.'

'And he goes to the Fall?'

'Of course.'

'To buy drugs?'

'To sell them. That kid is what happens when the scene starts
getting out of control. Jimmy's old-school. Jimmy's from a
different era. What you get now are kids like Noodle. He's out
of his head most of the time. One day we'll find him dead on the
beach.'

'You mean some kind of overdose? Helping himself to the
merchandise?'

'Yeah, if he's lucky.'

'And if he's not?'

He shakes his head. At last, he catches the beer mat. He says he's heard of Evie but he doesn't know much about her. Only her other street name.

'Which is?'

'Ridgeback. It's a bike. That's the only clue you get.'

'She's on the game?'

'She is. On a bad night fifteen quid buys you a ride. This is all bloke-talk. I've no idea whether it's true but three rides and I'm guessing she'll be knocking on Noodle's door again.'

'For?'

'Crack cocaine. Or maybe smack. Girls like her are going to give this town a bad name. Even Karl admits that.'

'He lets her in the pub?'

'He's barred her twice. Makes no difference. Five pints of IPA and a couple of toots and most blokes get silly. Five minutes round the back of the Methodist Hall. Max.'

'You *know* that?'

'I've heard about it. From blokes I trust.'

'So where do I find her? And where do I find the other kid? Noodle?'

Danny shakes his head. He's said far too much already. He needs to be off. I should talk to Andy, he says. He drains his glass and gets to his feet, slightly unsteady. He's drunk far more than I'd thought.

'I have a son called Malo,' I say.

'I know. Andy talks about him sometimes.'

'He's in trouble. That's why I'm here.'

'What sort of trouble?'

'Trouble that takes me to the Landfall.' I nod at his empty glass. 'Another?'

SEVENTEEN

In the end I take Danny for a Thai. I was planning for us to get a table in the restaurant but he insists on a takeaway we can eat in his van. The passenger seat is a nest of paperwork, jotted notes, empty KFC boxes and sundry tools. Neither of the interior spots seem to work and in the spill of light from the street I make a space for myself while he unpacks the food. This is the kind of meal that Pavel adores. With a pang of guilt, I realize I haven't thought about him once since arriving in Bridport.

'Stella?'

Danny has a four-pack stored in the darkness behind his seat. When I tell him I'll split one, he just laughs.

'Not in this town, you won't.' He passes me a tinnie.

The moment I start digging into the Thai green curry, I realize I'm famished. Neither of us say anything for minutes on end. The van is parked up on waste ground beside what seems to be a row of industrial units. A peaceable drunk who looks far too old to be out this late weaves past and then stops to relieve himself against the wall.

'Harry McGuire.' Danny laughs softly. 'My dad went to school with him. Dodgy prostate these days.'

The old man moves on, stained trousers and a limp. Danny has finished his pad Thai rice noodles. He produces a pouch and a couple of skins and rolls a doobie, crumbling the dark resin on to the tobacco. He does this one-handed while taking the odd pull of Stella from what's left in his can. This, in semi-darkness, is impressive.

'You mind?' He moistens the paper with the tip of his tongue.

'Yes.' I nod. 'I do. It's the same with cigarettes. I hate the smoke.'

He shoots me a look and then puts the doobie away for later. For a moment or two we both stare out at the row of units. The old man has disappeared.

'What's it like?' he says at last. 'All those movies? Being famous?'

'That was a while ago. I think I was probably a different person then.'

'Wilder? Less uptight?'

'Younger. It's probably the same thing. Uptight's wrong, by the way. If you really want to smoke just open the window.'

He smiles. He says I haven't answered his question.

'You're talking about getting myself noticed? Becoming a bit of a celeb?'

'Yeah.'

'It's odd. Weird. You push your luck, or other people push it for you, and at the start it feels like a game but then you realize it's for real and that's when it can get a bit of a pain.'

'You're kidding. You're rich. You're in the papers, in the magazines. People can't get enough of you. You're telling me that's a pain?'

'I am. Try it sometime. That kind of fame's supposed to liberate you but it turns out it's not like that at all. You can't buy freedom. In fact, it's quite the reverse. Celebrity's the place they bang you up in. Remember Garbo? The dark glasses? She ended up wanting to be someone else but by that time it was too late.'

'And that happened to you?'

'I got sick, very sick. In fact, I nearly died. That changes everything and, believe it or not, I'm glad it happened.'

'But you're better now? Cured?'

'Probably not. And that's a good thing, too. I know it's a cliché but you've no idea how wonderful it is to wake up in the morning.'

Danny nods. He says that makes me lucky. He wants to know about Malo. Andy says he came from a one-nighter with Prentice.

'You know Hayden?' I ask.

'Yeah. I met him a couple of times round Andy's place.'

'And?'

'Gangster. Definitely. Much nicer bloke than he seems at first sight, but credit to the guy. He made his money and now he's home safe. How many people these days can say that?'

Much nicer bloke than he seems at first sight. Perfect.

Danny says I haven't answered his question. He still wants to know about Malo. A one-nighter or something different?

'A one-nighter, definitely. I was on a shoot in Antibes. He was with a bunch of mates on one of those huge motor yachts. Far too much money and absolutely no taste.'

'So how did it happen?'

'He poured margaritas down my throat. He also made me laugh. The next day I went down the coast to Cannes and met the guy who became my husband. He was a lunatic, too, but it took me the best part of seventeen years to find out. Malo happened nine months after we met. The DNA test was another surprise.'

'And now?'

'Now Malo has a proper dad and we're all glad about that.'

'And you?'

'I'm Malo's mum. Not an easy gig.'

'And Prentice?'

'We're friends. We get along. In some situations he's a godsend. In others a total nightmare. What he wants is Antibes again, but he knows that will never happen.'

'You've remarried?'

'No.'

'But there's someone there?'

'Yes.'

I've always found something lightly erotic in straying into territory like this with a virtual stranger. It was the same with Berndt, all those years ago, and with Pavel, more recently. In a sense you've nothing to lose because these people don't know you and what they take away from the conversation, what you've lightly scribbled on their blank sheets of paper, doesn't really matter. Unless, of course, they become your husband or your lover. There's also a wistfulness about Danny I find both attractive and intriguing. Like most men, he's a bit lost, but unusually he doesn't mind showing it. Is this candour or a negotiating tactic? Probably the latter but I live in hope.

'How old are you?' I ask him.

'Forty-one.'

'My age. More or less. What do you most regret?'

The question seems to pain him. He tells me he's got a generally shit life but no worse than most blokes he knows. He's good at his job, and that brings the money in. He does the best cut roofs in the town but you're out in all weathers on the building sites, up and down the ladder with the timber, and he's starting to feel it. Until a couple of years back, he says, he was a decent footballer, semi-pro in his youth, but the knees are going and once you start worrying about hospital tackles you know it's time to jack it in.

I've no idea about cut roofs but I can picture a hospital tackle.

'So you miss the football?'

'I do. I watch the Bees most weekends when they're playing at home but it's not the same.'

'The Bees?'

'The local team. Down St Mary's. Western Premier League.'

'So why go along? If it makes you unhappy?'

'For my lad, Scott. He's like me at that age. Football crazy. Totally off the planet. If it wasn't for the Bees I probably wouldn't see him at all.'

'You're married?'

'Used to be.'

'And now?'

'I'm seeing someone but she's got three kids of her own and even getting her out for a drink is a joke.' He glances across. 'Don't fancy a spot of babysitting, do you?'

'How old are they?'

'Nine, eleven and twelve, all girls. She's mother hen. Worried sick about them. Even at that age.'

'Why?'

I get another look, part disbelief, and then he shakes his head. 'You never told me why you were in the Fall tonight.'

'You're right. I didn't.'

'It's the lad, isn't it? Your Malo?'

'Yes.'

'He's got a problem?'

'Yes.'

'The marching powder? Something heavy? Crack cocaine? Smack?'

'I don't know. Not for sure. There's something else that's happened, too.'

'Like?'

I shake my head. I won't tell him. Not yet.

'I don't get it,' he says at last. 'The kid's got everything. He couldn't have it more cushty. He lives out on that huge country estate. According to Andy he drives a brand-new Audi. He's money on legs. So what's he doing in that shithole of a pub?'

'I'm assuming he went to score. H won't have drugs in the house. Ironic, *n'est-ce pas?*'

'H?'

'Hayden. Hayden Prentice. HP. His mates used to call him Saucy. When he finally grew up he shortened it to H. It suits him perfectly. You get what you see. H. No messing.' I want to get back to Danny's private life. 'Your girlfriend's got three daughters. What's her worst fear? Noodle? Evie?'

'Of course. You won't believe what goes down now.'

'Here?'

'Everywhere. This last year or two everything's changed. Gear used to come in from Bristol, sometimes Manchester or Liverpool. You had to go to Dorchester to score, maybe even Bournemouth. The dealers would train it down. Deliveries on a Thursday, round the back of the station, ready for the weekend. Mates would pay and collect and we'd all have a toot on the Friday night. I was never into anything heavier, and neither were most blokes I know, but you could get that too if you were really desperate, though it would cost. Now it's all London and you don't have to drive anywhere because they come to you.'

'They?'

'Kids. Kids so young you'd never believe it. Kids even younger than Noodle. They're animals, these kids, and they're clever. They pick people off. You've got some kind of problem. You're on the sick or you're handicapped or you're a loony and the council have given you somewhere to live and one day there's a knock at your door and there are three kids you've never seen in your life and they come barging in and they take the place over and they'll chin you if you even raise an eyebrow. They're out there day and night, taster giveaways, good gear, really cheap. They're on the phones. They've got a client list. They're banging out the special offers. They want to sell to you, and your best mate, and your mate's best mate, and pretty soon they've got most of the estate on their books, and the likes of Suze has chained her kids to the sofa because these kids don't know where to stop. They've got a business model and it's really simple. Great gear. Great prices. But never do me on the money.'

This has to be county lines. I try the phrase on Danny.

'You know about that stuff? County lines?'

'Yes.'

'How?'

'H told me. He said it was the new hard sell, kids on phones all the time, oblivion made easy.'

'Is that what he called it? Oblivion made easy?'

'No, that's my phrase.'

'It's great. It's perfect.' He doesn't bother to hide his admiration, which makes me blush. Time to change the subject.

'So who's Suze?' I ask.

'She's the woman I mentioned earlier with the three daughters. So far she's OK drug-wise but that's because they never go out.'

'And your boy?'

'Scott plays football. He's got a brain in his head.'

'Lucky you.'

'Lucky him. His mum's a cow, as well. That's another reason he'll stay clean. He's terrified of her.'

I laugh. Danny tells me it's true. He never got properly divorced, he says, because he was too frightened to turn up for the court hearing. She's kipping with a mate of his now and she's turned a bloke who'd stop at nothing into a hamster.

'She's got him tied to the wheel.' It's Danny's turn to laugh. 'I bumped into him at Morrisons the other day. She's even got him doing the shopping now.'

He at last gets round to lighting the doobie. The sweetness of the weed is filling the van. I wind the window down.

We sit in silence for a while. The wind has got up and I think I can hear the distant roar of the surf from some faraway beach.

'Where do I find these kids?' I ask him.

'Don't bother. They won't talk to you unless you're buying and even then it's going to be a short conversation. You get new faces all the time and some of them are black. Did I mention that?'

'No.'

'That matters round here. Not that they care a toss. These are Somali kids from London. They're wild. They know no fear. It's just business, man. County lines. Here's a tenth. Give us thirty. Enjoy.' Danny sucks in a lungful of smoke and tips his head back.

'Noodle?' I suggest. 'Evie?'

'Noodle sometimes kips in a tatty old tent down on the beach in West Bay. Ask anyone.'

'And Evie?'

'Evie's shacked up with an evil bastard called Brett Dooley. Nice enough when it suits him, but basically a psycho. He's thick as well as violent and the state of the woman tells you everything you need to know. Dooley trades her to settle drug debts and beats her up the rest of the time. Has done for ever. A mate told me Evie tried to run away once. Dooley went to Dorchester and found her at her sister's. Gave them both a hiding before bringing Evie back on the bus. Poor bloody woman.'

'They still live together?'

'Of course.'

'Where?'

Danny turns to look at me. He's astonished.

'You're serious? You want to talk to her?'

'I want to know where she lives.' I'm checking my watch. 'That may not be the same thing.'

EIGHTEEN

D anny drops me off at the hotel. He's given me an address for Evie and a health warning about the kind of welcome I can expect from the man in her life. He's also scribbled a phone number in case I need to be rescued from any other pub. When I give him a hug and thank him for his time I can sense that he'd like our conversation to continue. For someone with so many friends, so many roots buried so deep in this little town, I can only conclude that he's lonely. This he appears to confirm with his parting shot, an open invitation extended across the front passenger seat as I stand on the pavement and prepare to shut the door. 'I'll cook for you any time,' he says. 'As long as you're not a bloody vegetarian.'

The Bull Hotel is on the town's main street. I met the girl at reception earlier. She fetches my bag, gives me a key and points out the lift. For some reason I've been upgraded to a deluxe king room. This includes a four-poster bed and a freestanding bath in the en suite, and when I take a proper look at the flowers taste-fully arranged on the table in the window I realize they're from H. *You're a star already*, goes the message. *How many other women would be seen dead in a pub like that?*

I'm tempted to phone him and say thank you but there's something about this evening that stays my hand. I've done this by myself. I've come up with a result of sorts. Thanks to my lonesome carpenter, I think I'm beginning to understand this little town, the way it works and the opportunities it might offer to a bunch of incoming kids with an eye to business and nothing to lose. On the way to the hotel, ever-helpful, Danny had warned me to be careful. 'Nothing frightens these little bastards,' he told me. 'Streetwise doesn't begin to cover it. They think they're immortal. Just remember that.'

Evie. Noodle. Tomorrow, I think. I pull the curtains and settle on the bed to check my phone. It's been a while now since I had that last conversation with Pavel and just a part of me still expects

some word from Prague. Maybe his body has been recovered.
Maybe he's still alive and has been traced to some hotel or other.
Either way, I need to know. I scroll through a day's missed calls,
texts and emails.

Confirmation from Amazon of a book order I'd been expecting.
A cheerful update from my Breton mum on the third week of
heatwave at Perros-Guirec. Word from my agent about the
possibility of a leading role in a French cop drama set, of all
places, in Nantes. Might I be available for what she calls 'conversations' in Paris late next week? She's talked to the producer
and she thinks the part is mine for the asking. If that's the case,
shooting is scheduled to start after Christmas.

I gaze at Rosa's message. January, next year. What might have
happened by then? To Clem? To Mateo and his wife? To Malo?
To Pavel? And to the inside of my head?

I fire off a reply to Rosa. In principle, I tell her, Paris sounds
fine. If she can give me an exact date, I'll confirm ASAP. In the
meantime – a long shot – has she heard from Pavel at all? Rosa
is a night bird. Pavel is one of her favourite men, largely because
she's never quite figured out how a blind person can be so much
more perceptive than the rest of us. Back comes the reply. *Thanx
for Paris. Got a postcard from Pavel this morning. The Orkneys
in this heat? Lucky man.*

The Orkneys? I'm staring at my smartphone. To the best of my
knowledge the Orkneys are north of Scotland. Just to be sure, I
do a Google search and confirm it. I'm right. Stromness. The cliffs
of Hoy. Twenty-four-hour daylight in the middle of summer.
Squadrons of killer midges. I phone Rosa, apologizing at once for
bothering her. She's listening to Aretha Franklin. The goddess of
soul has passed away and Rosa is having a teary night with her
huge collection of LPs.

She wants to know if I'm all right.

'I'm fine,' I lie. 'I just want to check something out. It's about
Pavel. What was the date on the postmark?'

There's a longish silence while Rosa goes looking for the postcard. Then she's back.

'Yesterday. It came first class.'

'And what does he actually say?'

'On the postcard, you mean?'

'Yes.'

'He says he just got back from a dive in Scapa Flow. He says he touched a battleship.'

'What's Scapa Flow?'

'I've no idea, my precious. I thought you two were close?'

'We are.'

'Then why the call? Am I allowed to ask?'

I mumble something about local difficulties, apologize again for the lateness of the hour and end the conversation.

Back on Google, I'm looking for clues about Scapa Flow. It turns out to be a huge body of water that served as a naval anchorage. The German High Fleet scuttled itself there at the end of the Great War and twenty years later a German U-boat stole back and sank a Royal Navy battleship, HMS *Royal Oak*.

Dimly I half-remember a conversation with Pavel over a meal several months ago. We'd both had a lot to drink and he was telling me about an idea he'd had for a movie. It seemed to feature a son obsessed by his father's death. His grandfather had been a high-ranking officer aboard a German battleship. His belief in the Kaiser and in victory had shaped his entire life and after the German surrender he'd spent seven months sitting on that same battleship in Scapa Flow trying to come to terms with defeat.

During that period he'd written an extensive diary which somehow survived the scuttling and now the grandson, a successful businessman and keen scuba diver, has returned to Scapa Flow to explore the German wrecks. This coincides with the capsize of his own marriage, and the way Pavel told it in the restaurant, the movie would try and interweave both disasters.

I remember thinking at the time that this challenge had Pavel's special magic all over it – a plaiting of military history and something infinitely more personal – and the fact that Pavel himself has now dived on the wreck comes as no surprise. The image of him using his fingertips to explore a long-ago tragedy is altogether wonderful. Except that he's not supposed to be in bloody Scotland at all. He's supposed to be in Prague. Dead.

I shower and towel myself dry, overwhelmed by both relief and something more visceral that might well be anger. The best stories, as Pavel always insists, detach you from real life. You float away down the river of fiction, lie back, and enjoy the view.

The storyteller's challenge is to cast a spell, and the longer that spell lasts, the better. The journey down the river goes on and on. Night falls. You maybe doze a little. But when the sun appears again the river is still there, meandering on, bend after sleepy bend, and you lie back, assured that one day you will arrive at a destination worthy of its name. That, at least, is the way that Pavel likes to put it.

I step back into the bedroom and let the coolness of the cotton sheets enfold me. On the phone, Pavel lied. He lied about Prague and he did nothing to prevent me from concluding that he'd thrown himself into the water and ended it all. That's what he'd wanted me to believe. That was the whole point of the call. But why? Did he go to these lengths because I'd gotten too close? Because I'd asked him for more than he could possibly give? Because I'd become some kind of emotional burden? Or was the whole baroque lie another virtuoso demonstration that real life was there to be manipulated into whatever shape he fancied? Another twirl on the trapeze of his wildest imaginings?

Whatever the truth, he appears to be alive and for the time being I'm very happy to settle for that. Anything as mundane as an explanation, I tell myself, can wait.

NINETEEN

Breakfast, according to the guest notes beside my bed, is served in the hotel's dining room. I'm down there a minute or two after eight o'clock. I've written down the address that Danny gave me for Evie and I plan to call a cab once I've done justice to a plate of scrambled eggs and bacon from the buffet. It's only when I'm returning to my table that I recognize the figure bent over a cup of coffee in the corner. H.

'Like them?' He's slipped into the other chair at my table.

'Like what?'

'The flowers.'

'The flowers are lovely. Sweet. I'm touched.'

'So how did it go?'

In the broadest terms, I tell him what happened. The Landfall, in a phrase I treasure, is indeed a souk. People tell me you can buy anything there and I've no reason to disbelieve them. This wild west Dorset explosion of the freest enterprise is tolerated by the drugs squad for reasons of their own and while the pub is overrun with youth, Karl the landlord is doing his best to hang on to his old hard-drinking clientele. More troubling, I suggest, are the larger consequences of what's happening. The Fall sounds all too prescient.

'Malo?'

'They know him there. They recognized the T-shirt. And they knew about Clem, too.'

'Was he a punter? Was he buying?'

'That wasn't clear.'

'Why else would he be there?'

'I've no idea.'

H grunts and helps himself to a slice of my toast. This morning, he said, he'd had a conversation with Jessie in the kitchen. Andy had taken a call from a mate of his late last night.

'Bloke called Danny? Ring any bells?'

I duck my head, load my fork with scrambled egg. Rule one: never underestimate this man.

'Danny's a carpenter,' I say. 'He's been using the pub for ever. He knows the town backwards. Interesting guy.'

'And?'

I tell H about the debris washed up by the tide of drugs, about Noodle and Evie, and about the platoons of young London-based Somali dealers moving from squat to squat.

'Cuckoos,' H grunts. 'They nest with the numpties.'

'You know this already?'

'It's nationwide. It's the business model I told you about. County lines. Travelling salesmen have been doing it for ever. It's all about territory.' He reaches for the little pot of marmalade. 'And violence.'

Mention of violence takes me neatly to Evie. I offer a little sketch of Brett Dooley.

'He pimps her out?'

'He does, according to Danny. That way she helps to pay his drug debts.'

'So he's in the swim, this Dooley? Got his finger on the pulse? Knows where the bodies are buried?'

'Yes.'

'Runs with the London boys?'

'I've no idea.'

'But he'd know them, yeah? A town this size, that can't be hard. And if he knows the London boys, that might take us to Clemmie.'

I nod. I agree. When I remind H that the kidnapper's midnight deadline is fast approaching he tells me not to worry. Deadlines, he says, are just a negotiating tactic. What matters just now is Brett Dooley. H says we need an address. I've written it down. I have it in my bag. I slide it across the table. H stares at it.

'This is where he lives?'

'It is.'

'Fuck.' He looks up. 'You don't need the day job. Stick with me.'

I leave my bag upstairs and step outside. Under a cloudless sky the temperature is already heading for the mid-twenties. H leads the way across the road to the Range Rover. A figure in the front passenger seat gets out and stands in the road. He's tall, fit-looking, early forties at least. He's wearing jeans and a white singlet that testifies to a serious gym addiction. He's also black with a bushy afro and his basketball shoes look brand new.

'Meet Wes. Wes, this is Enora, Malo's mum.'

I've heard the name before. H mentioned him a couple of times last year in conversations about his beloved Pompey. I know exactly who this is.

'You're Wesley Kane? From Portsmouth?'

He nods, smiles. He has the whitest teeth.

'So what were you doing under my car the other night? Tracking device? Am I right?'

Wes glances across at H. He has the grace to look briefly troubled. H tries to shrug it off.

'Needs must,' he mutters.

'Needs must what?' I turn on H. 'I don't understand. You were trying to follow me? Find out where I was going? All of that?'

'Yeah.'

'Why? You don't trust me? You thought I might go to the police about Clem?'

'Yeah. And that's exactly what you did because the fucking tracker was gone when I checked and that can only be the Filth.'

I frown. Then I remember H picking me up in the rain outside my apartment. The wet patches on his knees, I think. He'd been checking for the tracker.

'It *was* the police,' I say hotly. 'What else was I supposed to do? It might have been a bomb for all I knew. Why not use the phone? Why not ask me where I was going? Why try and be so bloody *devious*?'

H has no answer. Wes enquires whether this is the full domestic and if so whether we'd like to batter each other in the privacy of the car. It's a nice line but I haven't finished with H yet.

'Of course I rang the police.' I'm getting very angry. 'That's what they're there for, in case you were wondering. And yes, they came round. And yes, they found the tracker. But no, I never mentioned Clem. Not once. Not then and not since. Is this music for your ears? Do you trust me? If the answer's no, I'm going back to the hotel. A cab will take me to Dorchester. It's an excellent train service. I can be back in London in time for lunch. So just one favour, eh? Do you trust me or not? A yes or no will do fine. And please don't swear in public.'

'Of course I fucking trust you.'

He turns to Wes, who opens the rear door. Moments later, with H at the wheel and Wes feeding the address into the sat-nav, we're on the move. I shake my head, thinking suddenly of Pavel and his long white fingers exploring the remains of the sunken battleship. Madness, I think. Everywhere.

The address I've been given turns out to be a minute's drive south of the main street. This, I suspect, was once a council estate. We're looking for Larkrise Crescent. The houses are semi-detached and most of them are a credit to their owners – bright paintwork, borders filled with shrubs – but number thirteen at the end of the road is the orphan in the family. An old mattress and a sagging armchair have been abandoned in one corner of the front garden and scabs of dog mess form an untidy semicircle inside the rotting gate. A wheelie bin at the side of the property is overflowing with pizza boxes and empty plastic bottles of something called Frosty Jacks.

Wes has noticed my interest. 'Cider,' he says. 'Seven and a half per cent fight juice. Three pounds fifty for three litres in Iceland.'

I nod. In the upstairs window I think I see a woman's pale face behind the fall of curtain. The moment she catches my gaze, she's gone.

H is already standing at the front door. He raps three times and takes a tiny step back. In his suit and tie he looks like a bailiff I once had to answer the door to in a movie we shot in Middlesbrough. On-screen, I was silly enough to answer the summons. In this sun-kissed corner of Bridport, they know better.

H tries again. Nothing. Wes has disappeared around the back.

I join H at the door. 'There's someone upstairs,' I tell him. 'I saw her.'

The bell push beside the door doesn't seem to work. H raps on the door for a third time.

Again, no response. Wes has reappeared. He says there's a dog locked in a coal bunker in the back garden. There's also a door into the back of the property. Someone's had a go at the lock recently and it'll be a piece of piss getting in.

'Neighbours?' H grunts.

'No one I can see.'

H nods. Wes leads the way round the back. He doesn't even have to give the door a push because it's open already. I'm standing in the sunshine gazing at a length of orange rope hanging from the branch of what looks like an apple tree. At the end of the rope is an old tyre.

'It's for the dog, love.' Wes again. 'Probably a pit bull. They clamp on and hang for ever. Old Pompey trick. Warms the dog up for the real thing.'

He lopes across to the tree and produces a sizeable flick knife. Seconds later he's cut the rope and now he's coiling it around his raised arm.

Back at the house, H is standing in the open doorway. Even from where I'm standing, it's difficult to put the smell into words. Blocked drains? Rancid cooking oil? Curdled milk? More dog mess? More weed? Take your pick.

We're in the kitchen now. I'm looking at a drift of takeout cartons that never made it into the bin and a fresh curl of dog turd at the foot of the fridge. One of the taps over the kitchen sink appears to have broken and no one's washed up for days.

H is shouting for Dooley. When nothing happens, Wes dumps the coil of rope on the kitchen table and checks the two rooms downstairs. Then I spot a pair of legs descending from the floor above. I meet her in the hall. This is the face in the window. She looks middle-aged but she's probably younger. She's stick-thin. She has an urchin haircut dyed bright green with mysterious bald patches. Her nails on both hands are bitten to the quick and she's wearing a single plastic thumb ring, the deepest black. Her rolled-up jeans are filthy and the Levellers T-shirt has definitely seen better days. There are traces of old bruising beneath her left eye and when she opens her mouth there are more gaps than teeth.

'Evie?'

'Yeah. What of it?' She's looking at H. She doesn't seem the slightest bit surprised to find strangers in her house.

H wants to know about Dooley. 'Where is he?'

'Dunno.'

'Just tell us, love. Don't fuck about.'

'I said I don't know. That's the truth.'

H takes her into the front room. There's no carpet, no furniture, no ornamentation of any kind. Just a couple of deckchairs and a widescreen TV.

H can't believe it. He's asking about the deckchairs. WDDC is stencilled on each frame.

'Nicked them off the beach,' Evie explains. In the brightness of the light through the front window I can better see the traces of old bruising beneath her left eye. Her feet are bare. A single toe ring in that same black plastic.

Wes has appeared in the open doorway. H gestures up at the ceiling and Wes nods. I listen to the soft pad of his footsteps as he mounts the stairs. For a big man he moves like a ghost.

H is asking when Evie last saw Dooley. She starts to tell some story about a mate of theirs with a problem baby but then she loses interest in the lie and chews at a reddened finger. Moments later comes a grunt and then a thud from upstairs before a commotion on the landing and a volley of oaths.

'That's him.' Evie yawns. 'Must have come back early.'

Wes is wrestling Dooley down the stairs. H and I join him in the hall. Dooley is a big man, running to fat. He's naked apart from a pair of Calvin Kleins and there's a parrot tattoo on the side of his neck where the whiteness of his torso gives way to a summer tan. His face is scarlet, probably the Frosty Jack, and like Evie he's obviously given up on dentists.

'Who the fuck are you lot?' he wants to know.

H doesn't bother with a reply. Instead, he tells Wes to take him into the kitchen and make him nice and comfortable.

I think it's occurred to Evie that this little episode might not end well. She wants to know what the fuck's going on. I'm in no position to tell her and H has never been much interested in explanations.

'Take her for a walk, yeah?' H is looking at me. 'Half an hour should sort it.'

Evie doesn't want to go for a walk and says so. She wants to stay here. She wants access to the fridge and afterwards she wants a bit of peace and quiet. H ignores her. We follow him into the kitchen where Wes has just finished trussing Dooley to the single chair. The orange of the rope is perfect against the blue of the CKs and Dooley has already given up struggling.

'Whatever you want,' Dooley says, 'just fucking take it.'

This seems to amuse H. He tells Wes to look in the fridge. The fridge is empty except for half a litre of milk, a single miniature Mars bar and a small object wrapped in cling film. Wes takes the latter out and gives it to H. H unwraps the crystal, gives it a sniff, and then opens up the dripping tap and sluices it down the sink.

Evie, watching, can't believe her eyes. 'Cunt!' she yells. 'That was fucking mine.'

H ignores her. Once again, he says he wants me to get her out of the house. Then he turns to Dooley and gives him a wink. 'Put the kettle on, Wes,' he says.

TWENTY

Evie and I make a leisurely tour of the estate. Evie is still barefoot and whenever we come across other pedestrians I notice that they'll cross the road rather than get anywhere near her. At first, she doesn't want to talk. Whatever I ask her, however hard I try, she refuses to even acknowledge me. Only when I tell her we might be police does she show a first flicker of interest.

'You're not Filth,' she says. 'You're too fucking clever for that.'

'Clever how?' I try and push this a little harder but she isn't having it.

We walk on in silence. Then she suddenly pulls me to a halt. 'What about my Brett, then? What's going on back there?'

I tell her I have no idea. It happens to be the truth but she doesn't believe me.

'You're gonna fucking hurt him, aren't you? Is this to do with last week?'

'What happened last week, Evie?'

'You're telling me you don't know that, neither?'

'I know nothing. Except that Brett can get violent.'

'You mean we fight? That's true. We're as bad as each other. On the Jack he can be an arsehole. Me too, when the mood takes me.'

'And he pimps you out? Have I got that right?'

'Yeah. But it's fucking easy, isn't it? I know most of these men. They're knobs, all of them. Men are slaves to their fucking dicks. Shut your eyes and it's over. Job fucking done.'

'Is that Brett talking or you?'

'Me. Brett hasn't got a brain cell left. Without me he'd be wetting himself. Nursemaid, me. Full-time carer. You fucking make sure that man doesn't get hurt. If he does, right, it's down to you.'

'And?'

'You don't want to know.' She frowns, as if the question's only just occurred to her. 'So who the fuck are you, anyway?'

I'm wondering whether this is the time to mention my son in a bid for more information, but decide against it. There's something utterly wasted about this woman's life and I find that truly scary. The single Mars bar in the fridge. The bruises. The blackened stumps that were once teeth. The toe ring. The smell. This is Bridport, for God's sake. This little town is the aspirational proof that there's life beyond Brexit, beyond the yawning gaps between rich and poor, that you can surround yourself with interesting shops and wonderful food and cheerful strangers that will wish you a very good morning and mean it. Yet here we are, one of us barefoot, en route back to the wreckage of two lives and doubtless countless others.

We round the corner. We've been gone for more than half an hour. Number nine is in sight at the end of the road. One of H's phrases has been haunting me all day. 'Tell me about county lines,' I say.

Once again she stops. I get the impression that smiling doesn't come easy. 'Fuck me,' she says. 'You *are* Filth.'

We can hear the gasps of pain from outside the kitchen door. Evie kicks it open with her bare feet. Dooley is doubled over, his hands cupped over his sodden CKs, and steam is still rising from his lap. He must half-hear the door because his head comes up. His nose has been pulped and there's blood everywhere. Tears are pouring down his cheeks and bubbles of pink saliva have appeared at the corner of his mouth. The last time I saw anguish like this was a crucifixion fresco in the coolness of a Venetian church. Nails through the palm and a crown of thorns, I suspect, might have been a kindness compared to this. Wes, I will later learn from H, has been kettling again. I feel physically ill.

'More, boss?' Wes glances up at H.

H shakes his head. He's adopted the bedside manner of a hospital consultant. He thinks the treatment is working nicely. Time to bring matters to a halt. 'That's fine, Wes. I don't think we need to bother Mr Dooley any further.'

'You want me to untie him?'

H nods. He's taken off his jacket and for the first time I notice the blood on his knuckles.

The moment Dooley slumps free of the rope, Evie is on her

knees in front of the chair, her arms around him. Not for a moment do I question Danny's account of this relationship – the ceaseless violence, the drink, the drugs, the sheer brutality of the man – yet it's incontestable that poor, wasted Evie still holds a candle for this monster. It's there in front of me. She's trying to kiss him, to comfort him, to soothe him, to make all the pain go away. She'll phone for an ambulance, get him to A&E, let them sort him out. She won't leave his bedside. Not tonight, not ever. I turn my head away, ashamed to be a witness at so intimate and yet so grotesque a moment. Venice again, I think. *Una vera pieta.* Christ.

TWENTY-ONE

We return to the hotel. I'm still trying to come to terms with what I've just seen in Dooley's kitchen. This is way, way beyond anything I've ever imagined. Some of the scripts I've read have made room for stagey helpings of violence, and some of H's friends have hinted that Malo's dad is unsentimental when it comes to settling debts, but this is flesh and blood, not fiction or hearsay, and it turns my stomach. Dooley is no angel but no one deserves what happened in that kitchen.

Not that H appears the least bit bothered. Wes fancies a spot of lunch and H treats him to an all-day breakfast at the local Wetherspoons. Dooley, I learn, has got himself on the wrong side of the new masters of the Bridport drugs scene and had been expecting a visit for a while. His old dealer, who never let him down, had been chased out of town a while back, leaving Dooley and a number of other regulars at the mercy of a bunch of Somali kids from London.

At first, the news was good. Incredible gear. Incredible prices. But then the ask for both crack and heroin went up and up and Dooley found himself looking at a sizeable debt. Worse still, the London kids weren't interested in his offers of Evie in part-settlement. At this point, says H, Dooley made the mistake of not taking the kids seriously. When they threatened to torch his house, he laughed in their face.

'They said that? Said they'd burn the place down?'

'They did, according to Dooley. He was getting a bit cagey by this time but Wes had the kettle on. You start at the knees and head north. Most blokes, they've worked out what happens next and a splash is normally enough.'

This is repugnant, largely because H appears to take it for granted that everyone accepts the rules of engagement. So how did Mr Dooley feel?

'He wasn't keen at all and it took longer than it should for me to suss why. The kids were having problems all over. Unpaid debts.

Thousands of quid. And punters going missing. They needed someone to grass these people up, find out where they were.'

'And that was Dooley?'

'Big time. They gave him freebies in return, but Dooley knew that one day these mates of his would realize what he was up to and come looking.'

'And he thought that was us?'

'No chance. He'd no idea who we were but that's not the point. The point is he has names, phone numbers, texts.'

'We're talking about the kids?'

'We are. And by the time Wes had emptied the kettle, we had the lot.'

H pushes his plate aside and puts an iPhone on the table. I know he's showing off, and I hate what he's done, but I can't resist a peek. The phone, it turns out, belongs to Dooley.

'Here. Look.'

H has brought up a text from one of the London kids. *Morning, my people. Wake and bake. New flavas in Stardog import (3.5 for £40). Big bitz available. Buddy cheesecake (3.5 for £40).*

I read the text a second time. I'm clueless about Stardog and Buddy cheesecake but I recognize textbook marketing when I see it. They might be flogging holidays or DIY special offers. There's something else, too, even more disturbing. *My people.* So simple. So hundred per cent confident. And so scary. No wonder Danny's Suze keeps her kids chained to the sofa. Better give them long days of crap television than risk them out on the streets.

'What about the kids themselves? Who *are* they?'

H bends to the phone again. Lately I've noticed that his keyboard skills are nearly as slick as his son's.

'These kids are the infantry. Dooley stored them in a file of their own.'

H opens the file and swipes through the names. Humpty. Rooster. Tick Tock. Shagro. No photos. No more clues. Just the names and a number. Very county lines, I think. According to H, these are the kids who deal the drugs on the street, grow the market, make sure no one ever goes short. He says they used to do something similar in Pompey back in the day but never had the proper technology. For a moment I think I'm detecting a note of faint regret but then he swipes again and perks up.

'So who's Larry Fab?' I'm peering at the names on the screen.

'He's the boss man on the ground here.'

'Who says?'

'Dooley. Larry Fab's the enforcer. He happens to be white. Dooley thinks he's down from London. This is the guy you never want to mess with. He's also the one you go through to get to the Plug.'

'The Plug?'

'The main supplier. You never see him. You never meet him. Dooley says he stays in London, lives on the phone, pulls all the strings. This little town would be an outpost in his empire. You'd have to go along the coast for the real killing. Weymouth. Bournemouth.' He offers me a tight smile. 'Pompey.'

I nod, sit back. Wes has doubtless heard all this before but I'm impressed.

'So where does Malo fit in? Or Clem? You're telling me they've been buying drugs off these people? Is that the way it worked?'

'Dooley doesn't know but he recognized both the names. He said the kids talked about them sometimes, especially Clem. She made a big impact, her and the bike. They called her the Inca Queen. Dooley says that's serious fucking respect.'

'But they were punters?'

'He's no idea. All he knows is that she was rich. That's what the Somali kids talked about. All the time. Colombia. Rich daddy. Oodles of the laughing powder. You know how these things work. All she's got to mention is the word Bogotá, or maybe just Colombia, and the kids are off and running. She should have kept her mouth shut. Malo, too. Even this place is a jungle.' He taps the phone. 'These kids can smell money at a thousand yards. She's in a clearing. She's unprotected. She's staked herself out and waited for the hyenas to arrive. The rest of the script writes itself. Ransom demand on Malo's phone? A million dollars cash? Piece of piss.'

A bunch of hyenas is a powerful image and I suspect it's probably close to the truth. These people are predatory. Clem and Malo were theirs for the taking. The pair of them roar down on the Harley for a night in leafy Bridport and after that it all goes badly wrong. Wrong pub. Wrong company. The wrong word. In the wrong ear. Easy.

'You think they set her up, the Somalis?'

'I think they may have done. Mateo's mate, O'Keefe, goes on

about these people not knowing their arse from their elbow, but that's code for him bumping into something a bit new, something he's not quite sure about. These kids fit the bill. They wouldn't normally bother with kidnapping. Unless they want to give someone a slapping and then make a grand or two when they give him back, they don't have to. The money's out there on the streets. They're minted already.'

'So why bother with Clem?'

'Because she was irresistible. There's a phrase Dooley used just now. He said the Somalis love to strut their stuff. It's all front, all ego. A million US? *No problema, amigo.* This is what we can do. Just watch.'

I nod. I think I understand. There's an obvious question here and it's been bothering me since we walked out of that house.

'What next?' I ask.

H drops Wes and me at the station in Dorchester after Wes has finished his treacle pudding. H says he has a couple of issues to raise with his son and if I was Malo I suspect I'd be heading for the hills. The train is nearly empty. Wes will be getting off at Southampton en route to Pompey while I continue to London.

We're clattering through the New Forest. So far Wes has been catching up with emails while I read a copy of the *Guardian* someone has left on the adjoining table. Last year, under difficult circumstances, I got to know a freelance journalist called Mitch Culligan and this morning's edition includes a piece he's done on the collapse of local government. No one would accuse Mitch of putting a smile on the nation's face but he cares deeply about issues that pass most people by and he has a gift for calling out politicians who should know better. I'm finding out why it doesn't pay to be a child in care in Northampton when Wes draws my attention to something out of the window.

I look up. In the middle distance, among the parched grassland, a gaggle of ponies are foraging for something to eat. Wes thinks the smallest one's really sweet. Seconds later, suddenly curtained by trees, they've gone.

I've decided I like Wes. He has a slightly dreamy air, as if he's not quite ready to leave adolescence, and his attention to the smaller courtesies of life seems completely unforced. He holds doors open for me. He readied a chair at the table in Wetherspoons. And he insisted on carrying my bag when we got to the station and joined the queue for a ticket. He's also extremely good looking and when – for the second time – he apologized for giving me a fright the night he fitted the tracking device I told him it didn't matter. 'Not your fault,' I said. 'I'm blaming H.'

Now I want to know what Malo's father might have in store for Bridport's new drug lords. I've asked H himself but he said he'd yet to decide. That, I know for certain, is a lie. You don't get as rich and successful as H by procrastination.

'From here on?' Wes has been making notes from his emails and now he sits back and starts to twiddle the pen between his fingers, a trick I've never quite mastered. The way Wes does it seems unconscious, instinctive, and thus super-cool.

He glances out of the window again, looking for more wildlife. 'Well?'

'I'm guessing we start with Larry Fab. He seems to boss the Bridport end and he'd be the one to take us further up the food chain. There has to be a main supplier.'

'You mean the Plug?'

'Yeah.'

'In London?'

'Yeah, probably. I'm not saying the Plug's down for the kidnapping. H is probably right about the Somalis going freelance. But I'm guessing London's where we'll find the girl.'

'So what happens? How do you do it?'

'We ask Mr Larry Fab some serious questions. Get his entire attention.'

'And how do you do that?'

'We probably kidnap him. That way we keep it nice and tidy. Give ourselves time to get the details right.'

Kidnap him. I should have guessed. An eye for an eye. Luckless Clem for Larry Fab.

'And you're comfortable with that?'

'Kidnapping him?'

'Hurting him.'

'Of course. It's ways and means. We could try writing him a letter but he probably can't read.'

I nod, say nothing. One of the reasons this morning has shaken me so badly is more than obvious: it's the first time I've seen H in action. Not once has he tried to disguise how he made his fortune. He sold drugs, lots of drugs, to lots of people. He made squillions of pounds, invested it wisely, and has been living off the proceeds ever since. He never boasts about his wealth but it's there in bricks and mortar, in the view that he owns, and in the quiet despatch of sizeable cheques to old mates in trouble. Incontestably, that makes him a decent man, but the fact remains that the drugs scene – in one of Mitch Culligan's phrases – is free enterprise gone bonkers, and Wes's party trick in that hideous kitchen is the evidence that it can get very dark indeed.

'Does it ever bother you? Any of this?' I ask Wes.

'Any of what?'

'What happened this morning. Pouring boiling water all over a man's lap?'

Wes gives the question some thought. Finally he points out that Dooley always had a choice. 'He could have copped to the questions right off,' he says. 'We could have been civilized about it. Had a conversation.'

'And did you try?'

'To be honest, no. Not really.'

'Why not?'

'Because he wasn't that kind of bloke. I've been in this game a while. Believe it or not, I know what I'm doing. People like Dooley just lie. They'll tell you any old shit just to get you out the door. They'll swear on their kids' lives that it's the truth but you know all along it's really bollocks. We went there to get names and that, in the end, is what he gave us. It's a shame we had to hurt him but with scum like him there's no other way. You saw the state of that woman. You think that was some kind of accident? You think she got a face like that by falling down the stairs? You should have seen the state of their bedroom. There were great clumps of her hair on the floor. That has to be his doing. That's when he sets about her, drags her around by her hair roots. Maybe next time he'll think twice, eh?'

'You believe that?'

'No. Never. Scum stays scum. So she's well and truly fucked.' He looks out of the window again and his face brightens. 'Look at that one . . .' We're still in the New Forest and he's found another pony. 'Sweet or what?'

TWENTY-TWO

I'm back home by mid-afternoon, after a detour to an exhibition of German romantic art. An hour's exposure to the sublime despair of Caspar David Friedrich has done me the world of good. Whatever happens next, I'm never going to be the monk gazing at the darkness of that terrifying seascape.

My apartment feels safe and cave-like after the events of the past day or so. I lock the door, put the chain on and decide to take a nap. Next week I'm due another scan to check out the status of my tumour. *Inshallah*, the X-rays and the chemo should have chased most of it away, but in the meantime the medical consensus – my consultant, my GP, and the practice nurse – is to take it easy. My consultant says he's on speaking terms with the Grim Reaper, and nothing keeps you more alive than a good night's sleep.

When my mobile begins to chirp, I ignore it. I've swapped Tina Turner for the opening chords of a Bach Toccata and Fugue, a favourite of Pavel's, and it's much easier on the ear. I'm on the sofa drifting off to sleep when the phone goes again. And again.

It's Rosa, my agent. At first I think this has to do with the imminent get-together in Paris to discuss the Nantes project. I give her the date of the hospital appointment and tell her we'll have to work around it. She says she's still waiting to hear back.

'I'm not calling about the French people at all,' she says. 'It's Pavel.'

Pavel? My heart sinks. This can only be bad news. And it is.

'He's in hospital,' she says. 'In Glasgow.'

'How do you know?'

'How do I *know*? He phoned up and told me. Are you all right, precious? Have you been drinking?'

'I'm fine. Never better. Did you talk to anyone else? In the hospital?'

'Of course I didn't. I just told you, it was Pavel on the phone. He made the call and it wasn't the longest conversation in the world.'

For a moment I toy with letting her into my Prague secret but decide against it. The fact is that Pavel was never in Prague, certainly not recently, and possibly not ever.

'So what's happened?'

'He's had some kind of accident. He was a bit woolly but I gather it involved the wrong end of a swimming pool. He's in a special unit. He thinks he might be paralysed for a while.'

'Shit.'

'That's exactly what I said. Tell me something, precious. Are you angry with him?'

'Yes, a little.'

'Care to tell me why?'

'Not really. Why do you want to know?'

'Because he asked me to make this call. He said he would have done it himself but he wasn't quite sure about his status.'

'His *status*? What does that mean?'

'I've no idea. Have you got a pen, precious? Something to write on? You have to phone the hospital. Ask for the spinal injuries unit. They'll have to get someone to his bedside because he can't hold the phone himself. Does that make any sense?'

'It does,' I tell her. 'At least it means he's bloody there.'

I'm making the phone call within seconds. The woman on the switchboard has a Scottish accent. OK, so far. Moments later, I'm talking to another woman. I begin to explain the situation but she hasn't got time for the small print.

'You're after Mr Sieger,' she says. 'And you are . . .?'

I give her my name. That's all she wants. I wait for a while at the window, watching our gardener trying to rescue a stand of hostas from terminal drought, then there's a new voice on the line. It certainly sounds like Pavel but he's very faint, as though he's trying to have the conversation through a sheet or two.

'It's me,' I say. 'Are you OK?'

'Fine. Good. Excellent. Never better. Actually, not.'

'So what's happened?'

He won't tell me, not on the phone. Might I have time to pop up?

Pop up? My grasp of geography isn't everything it might be but last time I checked, Glasgow wasn't on the Underground map.

'How long are you in for?'

'I don't know.'

'Are you in pain? Does it hurt?'

'That's the strange thing. Nothing hurts. Most odd.'

'Can you move anything?'

'Not much. Only my head.'

'And will it get better?'

'No one seems to know.'

'Shit.'

'Quite. And that's another thing.'

'Don't.' I check my watch. Eighteen thirty-two. Heathrow is down the road and there must be planes to Glasgow. Drama is infectious. I'd sensed it in Rosa's voice and now I'm at it, too. 'Hang on in there,' I say. 'I'll be with you as soon as I can.'

'That's kind.' Pavel sounds exhausted. 'Under the circumstances.'

The flight north is the last of the day. I sit beside an American oil executive with a laptop and a long story about the wife in Houston who doesn't even try to understand him. We share a couple of gin and tonics and agree that life sucks. Only when we're on the ramp and the queue in the aisle is shuffling towards the exit door does he enquire about my own reason for paying Glasgow a visit.

'A friend of mine's just got himself paralysed,' I tell him. 'Call it moral support.'

The hospital is a twenty-pound cab fare away. At half past ten in the evening I don't fancy my chances of getting into the spinal injuries unit, and when I ask at the hospital's front desk it turns out I'm right.

'Come back tomorrow morning,' the woman says. 'If you're after accommodation, there's a Premier Inn down by the Quay.'

I call another taxi and settle down to wait. Ever since my last conversation with Pavel came to an end, I've been pondering his final words. Should I treat *under the circumstances* as some kind of apology for his Prague fantasy? Should I delete that little episode from my hard disk and pretend it never happened? Or has the time come to look reality in the face and admit that I'm somehow involved with a man, at best a dreamer, at worst a serial liar, who's slipped his moorings?

The taxi arrives and takes me to the Premier Inn. The room is

functional and baking hot. It's also on the top floor. I open the
window as wide as I can. There's no mini bar and the sight of
the kettle rekindles images I can do without. I pour myself a glass
of water and tell myself it's good for me.

I'm in bed, nursing the last of the water, when the phone goes.
This time it's H. He's been hearing reports of thunderstorms and
flash floods in London. Am I all right?

I'm oddly touched by his concern. One moment he's bloodying
his knuckles on a total stranger. The next he's worried that I might
have been hit by lightning.

'I'm fine,' I tell him. 'I'm in Glasgow.'

'That's in fucking Scotland.'

'You're right. The rumour's true.' I try to mime the accent
but I need something stronger than lukewarm water to do a
proper job.

When H enquires further I tell him about Pavel. The news that
this new man in my life is lying in a spinal unit seems to cheer
him up no end, and from his point of view I can see the logic. If
you're paralysed from the chin down, the scope for hanky-panky
is seriously limited.

'You've seen him?'

'Not yet. Tomorrow morning.'

'Find out how that script of ours is going, yeah? He'll have lots
of time, flat on his back. Getting that script done might even be
therapeutic.'

I'm tempted to tell him that Pavel has cooled on H's original
idea and come up with some alternative starting points but H is
already telling me that the French blokes from Lyon, the ones with
the serious dosh, have been on to him again and that he needs to
keep them sweet.

'I'm sending the boy down there,' he says. 'Tomorrow.'

'You mean Malo?'

'Yeah. I've given him the brief, the bones of what we all agreed,
and I'm sure he'll play a blinder. For one thing it'll keep him out
of fucking trouble. And for another, he speaks the lingo. They'll
love him. Everyone does. That's why we're in the shit with
Clemmie. Total strangers, couple of beers, and the boy's telling
them his life story. That's the way it happened down in Bridport.
Swear to God.'

The ransom demand has now expired. I ask H whether he's been in touch with Mateo. Or O'Keefe.

'The K&R King? No fucking point. Number one, the guy never listens because he knows it all already. Number two, there has to be a better way.'

'And you've found it?'

'Of course I fucking have. Wes get you home OK?'

'Wes got me as far as Southampton. Nice man.'

'Wes? Top guy. A word to the wise. Just watch yourself. He acts the adolescent but don't be fooled. He rates you. He's probably fallen in love with you. And when that happens he gets very silly. Any nonsense, give me a bell and I'll sort it. Good luck tomorrow, eh? And give the patient my best.'

The line goes dead and I'm still wondering how on earth Malo will cope with negotiating any kind of movie budget when I catch the first rumble of thunder. Within minutes the storm is on top of us. The heavens have opened and I'm fighting to get the window closed against the wind before I'm flooded out. Back in bed, towelled but still damp, I wonder about phoning H with the latest on the weather but decide against it. Forked lightning, the sudden white-hot brilliance against the night sky, has always been a very special pleasure. Pavel, I think, might remember moments like these.

TWENTY-THREE

The spinal injuries unit at the Queen Elizabeth University Hospital is a brick-built single-storey building that forms part of the larger hospital complex. All the beds are occupied by bodies, all male, with various degrees of inertness. Eyes follow me down the ward as I make for the bed at the end. Walking beside me is a youngish nurse who appears to know a great deal about Pavel's prognosis. The fact that he's blind, she says, makes him doubly unlucky but it's the consultant's belief that he might stand a slim chance of making at least a partial recovery.

'Meaning?'

'Control and sensation. It's not my place to say this but at the moment he's pretty helpless. The X-rays are quite promising. We think we've minimized the swelling. He was in good hands up in Orkney. They did a fine job.'

'And he knows this?' We've paused short of Pavel's bed but I'm sure he's listening. 'Ears of a bat,' I whisper. 'Be careful what you say.'

The nurse smiles and goes quiet on me. I think I might have frightened her a little. It's not every day she'll find herself nursing a blind man and if Pavel stays here for any length of time she might find herself having to cope with other surprises.

'You're a relative?' she asks at last.

'A close friend.'

'You've known him long?'

'Not really, but long enough, yes. Some people are really gifted. He's one of them. Did you ever see that TV series set in Sarajevo?'

'I did, yes.'

'Pavel wrote it.'

She nods. She's impressed. The consultant, she says, won't be doing his rounds until late afternoon. She's told me pretty much everything they know to date and I'm welcome to stay as long as I like. The coffee machine's in the corridor, plus a choice of sandwiches. I tiptoe to Pavel's bedside. I'm right. He's heard every word.

'You could be my agent,' he says softly. 'Would you like that?'
'No.' I fetch a chair and settle carefully beside the bed. 'How
are you?'
'A little frightened, if you want the truth.'
'The nurse says you'll probably get better.'
'I know. I heard her. Just now it doesn't feel that way. Blindness
I can cope with. Sending out messages and getting nothing back
is very, very scary.'
'Can you feel this?' I touch his hand.
'No.'
'This?' I move my finger slowly up his arm.
'No. I can feel nothing.'
'This?' I kiss him softly on the lips.
He manages a nod and the beginnings of a smile. They've taken
his glasses away and he lies flat on his back, his eyes open but
sightless. He says he wants his hands to cup my face but the
messenger he despatched has somehow gone missing.
I'm looking at the bed. A single tube trails from under the sheet
to a plastic bottle on the floor. Pavel's head has been encased in
a hoop of stainless steel, presumably to prevent movement. The
contraption looks like something out of the Spanish Inquisition,
though the real torture would be the condition itself. Not being
able to physically respond to a kiss? Unimaginable.
'So what happened?'
He's trying to swallow but he obviously finds it difficult. There's
a plastic cup beside the bed with a bendy straw. I ask him whether
he wants a drink and he says yes. I do my best but most of the
water slops over his chin and then trickles down his chest. When
I find a tissue and start to clean him up he tells me not to bother.
Below his neck, he can't feel a thing.
'Spa hotel,' he whispers.
'What?'
'Spa hotel. Brand new. Lovely swimming pool.'
His eyes flick towards me and I finally realize what he wants
to tell me. This is how the accident happened. This is why he's
ended up here, his brain disconnected from the rest of his body.
The story takes a while to unfold, chiefly because he can only
manage a sentence or two at a time.
He'd flown to Orkney at the invitation of a German TV company

who'd been impressed and intrigued by his movie project. They'd booked him into a brand-new spa hotel outside Stromness and hired a couple of local divers to accompany him on a series of descents on an ancient German battleship. This idea, in the first place, had come from Pavel himself. A blind man sees through his fingertips. What better way to explore the rusting evidence of Germany's long-ago humiliation?

'Had you dived before?'

'Never.'

'What was it like?'

'Wonderful. You become a bird. No gravity. No limits. Underwater, you're flying.'

Weightless, I think. Pavel's default setting. The footage from the dives, Pavel gathered, was excellent. The German director was more than pleased. Once the dives were over, Pavel did a lengthy interview, explaining the parallel between the protagonist's marital anguish and the German fleet's larger catastrophe. I'm still not entirely clear how one relates to the other but Germans often have the weirdest ideas when it comes to avant-garde movies and the director, according to Pavel, declared the interview a masterpiece of creative daring.

That night, the shoot over, they all celebrated. At two in the morning, still drunk, Pavel decided to go for a swim in the hotel's new pool. He needed, he said, to be underwater again. He needed to feel *free*.

'And?'

'The pool was very close to my room. You could smell it, the chlorine, once you were out in the corridor. I was naked, just a towel.' He tries to frown. 'I must have dived in the wrong end.'

'You mean the shallow end?'

'Yes. My fault.'

He remembers his head hitting the bottom of the pool, everything going suddenly numb, no real pain, then his head breaking the surface of the water. Somehow he managed to turn on to his back. CCTV cameras were already bringing a security guard to the pool. It took three men to get him out.

I stay at Pavel's bedside all day. Given the circumstances, there's no way I'm even going to mention Prague, or my anguished calls to the police and the Foreign Office. Whatever hurt he'd been nursing from our last conversation is now ancient history. Poor bloody man.

We talk fitfully. I try not to strain him. Much of the time he appears to be asleep, his eyes closed, his thin chest barely moving beneath the whiteness of the sheet. I stroke his hand from time to time, more comfort for me than him, and when the consultant arrives late in the afternoon I stand aside while he conducts a brief examination.

We talk afterwards in a small, bare side office. The consultant is a little more guarded than the nurse I met earlier. He's older than most of the staff I've seen and he has a gauntness that suggests regular exercise. Prognoses for spinal injury, he explains, can be a nightmare, largely because the nerve tissue doesn't repair itself. Pavel, technically, has broken his neck but the good news is that pressure on the spinal cord itself might ease a little. Soon, if he's lucky, he may feel the first signs of returning sensation. Best case, he might regain the use of his hands and arms.

'I understand he's some kind of writer? Is that true?'

I nod. News travels fast. I explain briefly about his work for TV and radio. Feature movies, too.

'You obviously know him well.'

'I do.'

'Is there anything you'd recommend? Assuming we can get him into a wheelchair before too long?'

'Sunshine. He loves sunshine. Do you have a terrace here? Some kind of patio?'

The consultant nods. It seems there's a little garden patients can use. Then he pauses.

'He's out in the sun a lot, isn't he? I noticed the lesions on his face, up by the hairline. Solar keratosis can be a little unsightly. Maybe the garden's not such a great idea.'

I hold his gaze. Medics, no matter how caring, sometimes drive me nuts.

'Pavel's blind,' I point out. 'And now he's paralysed as well. I doubt he'll be losing any sleep about UV damage.'

I stay in Glasgow for another long day. By the time I say goodbye to Pavel he thinks he might be able to feel just a flicker of sensation in his arms. He's wary of celebrating too early, of trying

to trap this songbird in case it flies away, but I can sense his relief.
I kiss his fingertips and promise to come back as soon as I can.
He tells me that the consultant is already talking about a move to
another unit further south and that would obviously make things
much easier.

I'm about to leave for the airport when Pavel asks me about
Cotehele. Cotehele is a fabulous Tudor mansion H has chosen for
the movie he wants Pavel to script. It's tucked away in the depths
of the Tamar Valley on the Devon/Cornwall border and I happen
to know it well. Pavel is aware of this, and although we've kicked
around a number of story options we've never really discussed the
depths of my private passion for the building and the estate. Now,
though, he seems suddenly keen.

'I want to go there,' he says. 'And I want you to take me.'

TWENTY-FOUR

arrive back in London to find the lights on in my apartment. There's only one person in my life who has a key and that's Malo. He's sprawled on the sofa watching *The Blair Witch Project*.

'You're supposed to be in France,' I tell him.

'I went yesterday. Came back this afternoon.'

'And?'

'They're really, really keen.'

'On Cotehele?'

'On the idea. I was selling an outline, nothing more.'

'So what does "keen" mean?'

'Dad reckons twenty million, ball park.'

'Dollars?'

'Euros. If we get the script right, they don't think that will be a problem.'

I nod. Ball park. Twenty million euros. Part of my son's charm is the way he can slip unannounced into other people's worlds, pick up a phrase or two, and busk his way to a result. I've watched him pull this trick on a number of occasions now and it never fails to impress me. He can only have got that kind of confidence from H because I certainly don't have it. Actors need a script. Malo makes it up as he goes along.

'So what were they like, these people?'

'Sharp. Quite funny. Great restaurant, right on the river. Best steak ever.'

'And you did the whole thing in French?'

'*Bien sûr.*'

'And were they impressed?'

'Relieved. They speak OK English but I think they had trouble following Dad.'

'*Aucune surprise.* I often have the same problem.'

Malo shoots me a look. Given everything that could so easily go wrong in our little *ménage* we all get along surprisingly well, but I'm always aware of my son's loyalty to his natural father.

From the moment, back last year, when he first set eyes on Hayden Prentice, Malo has been glued to his dad in a way that only shared genes can explain. Not that H gives anyone an easy ride.

'Your father was in Bridport the other day,' I say carefully.

'I know. And you were there too. So what went down?'

'He didn't tell you?'

'He gave me a bollocking for drinking too much and chatting to the wrong people. As if I had a choice.'

'I don't understand.'

'It's Clem. Men just go nuts about her. That can be a pain, believe me.'

'And that happened in Bridport?'

'It happens everywhere.'

'Your dad seems to think that has to do with . . . you know . . .' I shrug. I'm beginning to hate the word 'kidnap'.

'Her getting lifted?'

'Yes.'

'He's wrong. Bridport's a doze. Nothing happens. Clem's up here somewhere.'

'You *know* that?'

He won't answer me. We've got to an especially scary bit of the *Blair Witch* movie where the kids have discovered the derelict cottage in the woods. They're out of their depth. They're helpless. They can feel the presence of evil and they haven't a clue what to do. Very apposite.

'Great movie, Mum.' Malo is glued to the screen. 'I've seen it three times already and it still scares me shitless. You know how much it cost to make? Sixty thousand US.'

Really? I don't want to talk about movie budgets and *Blair Witch*. I want to talk about Clem.

'You've never told me exactly what happened.' I reach for the remote and mute the sound. 'Now might be the time.'

Malo lunges for the remote. He's outraged. He might be fifteen again. Or ten. I push him away and then find the off button.

'Mum!'

'You can pick it up later. It won't go away.'

'That's not the point.'

'No?' I'm trying to get him to look me in the eye. 'You're telling me *Blair Witch* is more important than Clem?'

'You know about Clem. I've told you everything.'

'You've told me nothing. You said you were together at her place the previous night. You said everything was fine. You told me about the Womad tickets her Dad had bought. Then you got the message on your phone. That's all I know.'

'But that's what happened.'

'OK. This was the Friday last week. Am I right?'

'Yes.'

'So let's go back to Thursday night. You told me everything was fine.'

For the first time, he falters. This moment of hesitation tells me I'm getting warm. Pavel, bless him, was right. There's much, much more to this story than meets the eye.

'Well? You *were* with her?'

'It's complicated.'

'I like complications. They've never frightened me.' I pause. 'You were at her place? Both of you?'

'Yes.'

'And?'

He won't say. I'm still trying to work out whether he's embarrassed to tell me, or he's desperately trying to concoct some other story when he tells me I wouldn't understand.

'Why not?'

'You just wouldn't.'

'Try me.'

He shrugs, a gesture I know he wants me to interpret as resignation. His acting skills aren't quite as good as his mum's. Not yet.

'We had a row,' he mutters. 'And then she walked out on me.'

'What was the row about?'

'That's not your business.'

'Malo, it absolutely is. Whether it matters to you or not, Clem going missing has got us all in a bit of a state. Me. Your dad. Clem's parents. Everyone.'

'I can handle it,' he says at once. 'Just leave me out of it.'

'*What* did you say?'

'Leave me alone.'

'Malo, this isn't about you, it's about Clem. We're all assuming she's gone. We're all taking these messages at face value. Someone's locked her away. Someone might do her a great deal of harm unless we come up with a great deal of money. Isn't that the way it is? Or are you telling me something different?'

Malo turns his head away, won't respond. I'm good with body language. I sense he's starting to panic.

'Well?'

'I told you. We had a ruck.'

'But why? That's what I'm asking. *Why?*'

He shakes his head, won't say.

'Had she met someone else?'

'No way.'

'Have you?'

'No.'

'Then why? Why did she walk out on you? Why did she leave that night?'

Silence. Malo has picked up the remote but he makes no attempt to put the TV on.

'Did you try to follow her?'

'I couldn't. She was on the bike.'

'You have a car.'

'I'd been drinking. She was working until late. By the time she got back I was pissed. That didn't help, either.'

I nod. Clem, to the best of my knowledge, is teetotal, never touches a drop. She also goes to Mass every Sunday, often with her mother.

'Help me, Malo.' I'm trying to nail down the pieces of this jigsaw. 'You've spent all evening drinking alone. She comes back from work. You have a row. You won't say why, or what the row was about. Maybe it's because she saw the state of you. Maybe not. Either way she walks out. I'm guessing you tried to call her. Would that be right?'

'Of course I tried to call her.'

'On her work phone?'

'On her own number.'

'And?'

'She wouldn't pick up. She was blanking me. She does that sometimes when she's really annoyed.'

'But I expect you tried again.'

'Yeah.'

'And again.'

'Yeah. Same result. In the end I went to bed.'

'Drunk?'

'Very.'

'Did she come back that night?'

'No.'

'And next day? The Friday?'

'Next day I woke up and got on with stuff. I thought it would all blow over and I was right. We talked on the phone. She had the tickets for Womad. She was cool about everything. We fixed to meet in the afternoon before going down there. It was going to be a great weekend.'

'Did you ask where she'd been? Where she'd slept that previous night?'

'No.'

'Why not?'

'Because it didn't matter. Shit happens. She's got lots of mates. I was packing stuff for Womad. You just get on with it. Then I got the message with the photo. The rest you know.'

'Did you contact these mates she might have stayed with? Did you ask around?'

'No.'

'Why on earth not?'

'Because these people were threatening to kill her. I had to keep it tight. A million US and everything would be cool.'

'And you believed that?'

'Of course I did. What fucking choice did I have?'

The question is a challenge. My persistence has upset him and it shows.

I check my watch, tell him it's been a long day.

'That's it?' He's still staring at me.

'Yes.' I offer him a thin smile. 'For now.'

I have a restless night. I haven't bothered to make any sleeping arrangements for Malo because he's perfectly capable of finding the spare bedroom by himself. From time to time, jerking awake between broken dreams, I think I can hear the TV in the living room but I'm not certain. I get up early, ten past six, and find Malo fully clothed on the sofa, his knees tucked up to his chin, his hands thrust deep between his thighs. I contemplate him for

minutes on end, ghosting back and forth to the kitchen. In my
heart I know he's lying to me about Clem. But why?

A couple of hours later I leave the apartment. My favourite
wholefood cafe is a ten-minute walk away on the Bayswater Road.
A table at the back gives me the privacy I need. I order poached
eggs with avocado mash plus a baked carrot and turmeric fritter
and then make the call to Mateo, Clem's father. As soon as he
realizes it's me he's hungry for news.

'What's happened?'

I apologize for phoning so early and ask whether it's true that
he has contacts within the Vodafone organization. He says yes.
He helped them get to the right people in Bogotá when they were
setting up the network there. Favours like that, he says, never go
amiss.

'You can get hold of phone billings?'

'Yes.'

'Like Clem's?'

'Of course.'

'Both her work phone and her personal phone?'

'Yes.'

'And have you done that?'

Mateo hesitates, then he wants to know exactly what I'm
after.

'That night before she disappeared,' I say. 'Did she take any
calls from Malo? On her personal phone?'

There's a moment's silence. For a moment I think he's hung
up on me but I'm wrong.

'Why do you need to know?' he says at last. 'You mind me
asking?'

'Not at all. Give me the answer and then I'll tell you why.'

'OK.' Another silence, longer this time. Finally he tells me that
Malo placed three calls that night.

'To Clem?'

'Yes.'

'Late?'

'After midnight.'

'And did Clem answer them?'

'Yes, every time.'

'And they talked?'

'The first time for thirteen minutes. The other two conversations were shorter.'

'And did she talk to anyone else?'

'Yes.'

'And do you have that number?'

'Yes. It was pay as you go and it hasn't been active since.'

A burner, I think. Malo's phrase. Someone in the drugs biz.

'One last question,' I mutter. 'The day she went missing. The Friday. Did she phone Malo at all?'

'She made no calls that morning,' he says. 'Her phone was off.'

I've closed my eyes. I'm conscious of rocking slowly back and forth at my table in the cafe. Mateo wants to know my own role in this. I steady myself and then ask him why he hasn't shared this little bit of news about the after-midnight calls earlier.

'O'Keefe made me promise not to.'

'So he knows, too?'

'Obviously.'

I nod. This, at least, makes some kind of sense. Mateo is still waiting for word from me. I must deliver my side of the bargain.

'Malo is lying to his mother,' I tell him. 'And now I must find out why.'

Mateo's laugh is mirthless. He says he's sorry and wishes me good luck. I thank him for helping me out.

'You'll keep me in the loop?' he asks.

'Of course.'

I thank him again and hang up. The waitress is en route across the cafe with my breakfast but I'm already on my feet. I tell her I've lost my appetite and leave a twenty-pound note on her tray beside the poached eggs.

I'm back outside my apartment block in less than seven minutes, a world record, but when I check for Malo's Audi in the car park there's no sign of it. Upstairs in the kitchen I find a note on the back of my gas bill.

Love you, Mum, Malo has scribbled. *Laters, yeah?*

TWENTY-FIVE

L aters? The word dogs me for hours on end, so casual, so dismissive, so dishonest. He was awake when I left. He was awake on the sofa and the moment he was sure I'd gone he'd fled. Last night I'd got far too close to whatever secret my son is trying to hide. *Laters*, if Malo has anything to do with it, will be as far into his probably uncertain future as possible.

Mid-morning, expecting the delivery from Amazon, I'm looking for small change for a tip. I keep my stash of coins and the odd fiver in a cupboard in the kitchen but when I look, it's gone. I know it was there a couple of days ago because I raided it for parking-meter money. Thinking I might have stored it somewhere else, I start opening other cupboard doors. Only when I spot the jar lying on the floor by the swing bin do I realize what's happened. It's empty.

Malo again. H has withdrawn our son's allowance. Without Clem to bail him out, he's probably flat broke. I do a rapid mental sum, trying to tot up how much he might have got from the jam jar. Maybe forty pounds, if he's lucky. This, as Pavel might say, is beyond pathos.

I search further. I never keep any kind of record of the food I've got in stock but the closer I inspect the shelves the more bare they look. The clincher is Marmite. Malo adores the stuff and I know I've only just started on a new jar. For whatever reason, probably habit, I keep it in the fridge. And I'm right. The Marmite, too, has gone.

By lunchtime I know exactly what I need to do. Malo, as H doubtless intended, has only one choice if he's to avoid the nightmare option of getting himself a job. Flixcombe Manor is where he calls home. My forty quid will pay for the petrol. That, I suspect, is where I'll find him.

I've no great desire for yet another conversation with H and so I phone Jessie, his housekeeper. Jessie and I have always had a rather guarded relationship but I think she's finally accepted that

I have no designs on her partner, Andy, and so lately things have
got a little easier.

I ask about Malo.

'He arrived an hour or so ago.'

'How was he?'

'Foul, if you want the truth. Andy says he's stressing about
Clemmie but that sounds like an excuse to me. Someone needs to
take that young man in hand.'

'His father?'

'That's someone else who's lost his sense of humour. Maybe it
runs in the family.'

'H is in residence?'

'Very much so. The rest you don't want to know.'

I press her for more but she won't elaborate. Then I suggest
we might have a proper chat later.

'You're coming down?' She sounds alarmed. 'Are you sure
that's a good idea?'

I'm still angry about last night's lies, about my son stooping to
common theft, about feeling helpless in a mess of someone else's
making. I no longer care about the kind of reception that might
await me at Flixcombe. As soon as I've checked up on a friend,
I tell Jessie, I'm driving down.

Pavel, when I finally make contact on the phone, sounds a whole
lot better. When I ask him whether he's got any feeling back, any
control, he says no, but he also assures me that he's had a long
conversation with this unwanted guest in his house and he has a
feeling the demon will shortly be stepping back into the darkness
where he belongs.

By 'demon' I imagine he means paralysis but the good news,
the very best news, is that Pavel is back on form. He loves personi-
fication and it's only now that I suspect it must be one of the ways
he's able to cope. If life deals you a rubbish hand, look it in the
eye and never blink. That's an artless metaphor if you happen to
be blind but I'm sure that Pavel, if he ever gets to download and
listen to this, will get my drift.

I leave London in the early afternoon. By tea time I'm turning in
through Flixcombe's imposing gates and making my way up half

a mile of drive. After the experience of Bridport's dirtier secrets I realize that this is H's castle: solid, easily defended, and comfortably removed from the Humpties and Roosters of this world. More to the point, if the barely concealed CCTV cameras are any guide, they'd never get within shouting distance of the main house.

The manor itself is within sight now, glimpses of bone-white pillars through the trees, and as I slow for the final turn at the far end of the drive I remember only too well how the sheer size of this estate excited Malo the first time he laid eyes on it. That was the moment, in retrospect, that I probably lost him, though several months earlier he'd voted with his feet and joined my estranged husband and his new partner in Stockholm. At the time that had hurt me deeply but Berndt will always be Berndt and I think at some unconscious level I always knew that Malo would be back. That, as it turned out, was exactly the way it happened but when it came to the most important person in his life, H has no competition. On both sides it was love at first sight and, barring the current tiff, I imagine it always will be.

I'm close, now, to the house. To be wholly objective, and thus fair to H, it's a delight: Georgian in origin, perfect proportions inside and out. In the late afternoon the windows at the front of the house are ablaze with reflected sunshine and as I glide to a halt I have just a moment of envy for my son's unthinking inheritance of such a handsome pile. The engine off, I'm still gazing at a pair of peacocks that H must have acquired from somewhere when I hear a soft tap on the front passenger window.

I glance across. It's Andy, Jessie's partner. I lower the window.

'Mind if I hop in?' Without waiting for an answer, he opens the door. 'Best drive round behind our place.'

'Why?'

'We need to talk.'

With some reluctance I do his bidding. His hair is wet and he smells of shower gel. Since I last saw him, weeks and weeks ago, he's also lost weight.

'Diet or exercise?' I ask him.

'Bit of both. Jess took a good look at me last month when we were on the beach and said I was turning into a fat bastard. That woman never lies. What choice did I have?'

Andy is a natural charmer. Like Danny, he has the looks and

he knows it: well-shaped face, light blue eyes and a winsome thatch of unruly blond hair. His real ambition, he once told me, was to become an actor. Hence his constant pestering in the early days: how to break into showbusiness, who to impress, what passages to learn by heart if an audition ever came his way. I told him to take a look at a couple of Willy Loman's longer speeches in *Death of a Salesman*, but I'm not sure he ever did.

We've arrived at the tiny patch of gravel behind the cottage that he and Jessie share.

'It's H,' he says. 'I think he's losing it.'

'How come?'

'I dunno. Jess says it's the Clem thing, people helping themselves, dissing his family, but me . . .' He shrugs. 'I dunno.'

'Symptoms?'

'He's manic, all the time. He never lets up. Malo came back just now and H got him into the kitchen within seconds. "Where've you fucking been? What the fuck's going on?" You know the routine.'

I do. But I want to know what else is happening.

'He's called some kind of pow-wow. Jess heard him raving on the phone. He's got a bunch of guys coming up from Pompey. They'll be here tonight. Jess says this is like something out of *The Sopranos*. He's going to war.'

'Against?'

'You tell me. I'm guessing the kidnappers. I just hope the poor bastards know what's coming.'

'Any idea who these people might be?'

'None.'

'And H?'

'I think he has a name or two. You know the black guy? From Pompey?'

'Wes. Wesley Kane.'

'Yeah. He's been here a couple of days now. He and H were away most of yesterday. Jess saw them when they came back. Looked like H had been in some kind of fight.'

'He's hurt?'

'Jess says not. Couple of bruises on his face. Swollen knuckles. Judge for yourself.'

I'm thinking about Larry Fab, the dealer at the very top of the

Bridport dung heap. H had promised himself a couple of hours with the guy, just him and Wes, and H isn't the kind of man to let patience get in the way of what he'd call a result.

'You've no idea what happened?'

'None. All I know is I've just spent all morning turning the barn into a shooting range.'

'*Shooting* range? Are you serious?'

'Yeah. Jess says the Pompey guys are probably bringing the guns.'

'*Guns?*' I'm appalled. 'Fuck. He *has* lost it.'

'Exactly. Call me old fashioned, but I'm not at all sure H knows what he's getting into here. Tony Soprano's the business but he's make-believe.' He grins. 'Danny sends his best, by the way.'

'Danny Flannery? Your mate?'

'Yep. He said he really enjoyed your little chat the other night. I told him he had no chance but I'm not sure he believed me.'

I can't work out whether H is pleased to see me or not. I've found him in the library at the front of the house, the hideaway he likes to use when he needs time and space to think. He's sitting at a table in the window with a copy of the *Daily Mail* on his lap. By now it's Friday, way beyond the ransom deadline, but H doesn't seem to be unduly bothered. Andy's right about his face. Not just bruised but swollen.

'What happened?'

'You don't want to know.'

'I do. Just tell me.'

Something in my voice gets H's attention. My expedition to the Landfall, I realize, has at last given me a foothold in his world.

'We had a conversation with Larry Fab,' he says.

'We?'

'Me and Wes. We got an address from one of the lowlifes. Kids that colour are hard to miss in Bridport. Wes tells me he's gone back to his mum in London.'

'You hurt him?'

'We got the address.'

'And then what?'

'We lifted the guy. Knocked on his door and offered him out.'

Offered him out, I think. Very Pompey.

'He told you what you needed to know?'

'Yes. After a while. A London address. Might be useful. Worth a shot.'

'Useful how?'

'We don't know yet.'

'And did any of this involve boiling water?'

'No chance. We were in the back of Wes's van. He had a go with a vacuum flask a couple of years back, but Wes says it's not the same. It's all anticipation, isn't it? Give the bloke the sight of a boiling kettle, give him time to have a bit of a think and you'll be amazed what people tell you. No, Mr Larry was good. Respect to the man. Made it hard for us. In the end it's a numbers game, two against one, but it was a decent ruck.'

'So what made him talk?'

'Wes. He promised to kill him and the bloke knew he meant it.'

I'm trying very hard to picture Wes's face. I don't remember a teardrop tattoo but I might be wrong.

'Does it ever get to you, any of this?' I ask H. 'Be honest.'

'Never. Wes tells me it got to you, though.'

'He's right. I thought what you did to Dooley was horrible. If you want the truth, it disgusted me.'

'You don't think shit like that happens all the time?'

'Not in my world it doesn't. And I hope not in Malo's.'

'Ahh . . .' H tips his head back. There are crumbs on the newspaper from the plate of biscuits he's demolished. 'Is that what this is about?'

'Partly, yes. Malo's lying. We both know that. The question is why.'

H looked at me for a long moment. He hates sharing information when he doesn't have to, but I'm right about my little performance in the Landfall. He seems to want to trust me.

'Wes put a tracker on the Audi after Clemmie went missing. The boy swears he never left her place the following couple of days but that's bollocks.'

'Where did he go?'

'Brixton.'

'You followed him?'

'We tried but we lost him. We had the GPS from the tracker but by the time we got to the address he was on the move again.'

'And this address?'

'Ties up nicely now we've had a word with Mr Fab.'

'You mean they're the same?'

'Yeah.'

'You're telling me Malo's been talking to the kidnappers?'

'That's what it looks like. The question is why.'

I take a deep breath. I've been toying with sharing Malo's dalliance with the dreadlocks guy, the one with the teardrop tattoo, but this latest news has put my own piece of sleuthing in the shadows. Our son's precious girlfriend is at the mercy of a bunch of lunatics. And Malo has paid them a visit.

'So what does he say? Malo?'

'Nothing. I haven't had it out with him yet.'

'Why not?'

'Because that's exactly what he's waiting for. Attack the enemy when he is unprepared. Sun Tzu. *The Art of War.*'

'Enemy? You mean Malo?'

'The boy's out of his fucking depth. Wes says it's like a cult thing. He's stopped thinking for himself and that makes him a liability.'

'Is that why you've cut him off?'

'Yeah. At the fucking knees. What else could I do?'

'You could have a conversation. Talk to him. That sometimes works.'

'He'll blank me. He'll lie. He'll come up with a thousand reasons he wasn't where he knows he was. Trust me. He's my son. I was exactly the same. Black's black? You call it white and see what happens.'

'That's denial.'

'Of course it fucking is, and that's where we are. Tonight we're having a bit of a sesh in the barn. Lots of Stella. Lots of loud bangs. The boy's in charge of changing the targets. Any luck, it might bring him to his senses.'

TWENTY-SIX

The Pompey contingent start arriving in the early evening. These are faces I've seen before, back last year when H threw a party to celebrate the discovery of the son he'd never dreamed existed, but now the mood has changed. There must be a dozen of them in all and one glance at the vehicles parked untidily outside gives you a clue to the way time has dealt each one a hand. Two BMWs, one of them brand new. A gross 4x4. A rusting van belonging to a plasterer. And the rest a selection of pick-up trucks with names like Barbarian and Warrior. This isn't subtle. As Andy quietly observes, if you want to advertise a state of mind you might as well drive a Chieftain tank to work.

The mood, if anything, is gruff, even sullen. H has called these men to the colours and they've been loyal enough to turn up, but in one or two muttered conversations I get just a hint of resentment. The all-nighter last year was richly lubricated, with a brilliant sound system, lots of Tina Turner, plus a gaggle of Thai lovelies who were turning tricks in a van outside. This evening, by contrast, has the feel of a bill falling due for all that glorious mayhem and some of these ex-hooligans can't help noticing their surroundings. Wealth has bought H an eye-watering slice of rural England. This, Andy points out, is a trillion miles from Fratton Park.

But the cases of Stella work their usual magic and the smells from Jessie's kitchen suggest a decent curry in the offing, and by the time H calls his guests to order in the big main room down-stairs the mood has lifted. Some of these men – and they're all men – are wearing combat boots and camo trousers. Several could do themselves a favour and talk to Andy about diet and exercise but their eyes are hard and there's a definite feeling of anticipation. I notice Malo on the sidelines. He can't take his eyes off the display of weaponry Wes has carefully arranged on the Regency mahogany table.

H thanks everyone for coming along. I've already suggested

he might be sensibly coy about the details of Clem's disappearance and it turns out he listened. Indeed, there's no mention of her at all. Instead he hints at some larger insult, undefined and undescribed, that has led to a bust-up with a bunch of infant lowlifes in a nice little town down the road. Quite how this might justify the pile of guns on the table is anyone's guess, but H has never bothered to justify his wilder initiatives and now isn't the time to start.

'These animals need sorting out,' he growls. 'Take it from me.'

There's a stir in the room. A guy in the front, wearing a Pompey shirt, asks whether H is selling the white powder again.

'Not at all. No fucking need.' He gestures round.

'So this isn't about turf?'

'No. It's about fucking manners. These people have taken a very big liberty. They've helped themselves to something they shouldn't and it's gonna be our job to get it back.'

'So what is it?'

H dismisses the question. For the time being, he says, he's not going into details. What he plans to mount is an expedition to concentrate one or two minds.

'Where?'

'London. These people think we're twats. We live in the country. We're there for the taking. They couldn't be more wrong and it's gonna be our job to make them see the error of their fucking ways.'

I'm looking hard at Malo. I've no idea whether or not this is a bluff on his father's part but it's certainly making an impact. My boy has been spending far too much time indoors these last few days, but now he's even paler. And he still can't take his eyes off the guns.

Another of H's soldiers is interested in what might go wrong.

'We're gonna be killing people here? Only last time I checked, the Filth aren't going to be fucking impressed.'

'No one's gonna be killed. No one will die. We'll be there to make a point, get under their fucking skins, maybe take a hostage or two. Don't fuck with us. Then we'll be off.'

'So whereabouts in London?'

'Brixton. We've done the recce. We know the address. It'll be a pizza delivery. With guns.'

Malo again. He's scratching himself. He can't keep still. At the first opportunity, I think, he's gonna be on the phone. Has H thought about this? Has he factored it in?

Jessie appears at the door. She semaphores something to H, who doesn't get her drift.

'Louder,' he says. 'Talk to me.'

'When do you want me to serve the food?'

H frowns. Then he checks his watch before looking up at Jessie again.

'Laters,' he says.

We troop across to the barn. H normally stores gardening equipment here but Andy's done a good job on getting everything out. At the far end, lit by flanking lights on metal stands, is the target area with a backing of hay bales. H is starting the evening's entertainment with an uneven line of tethered balloons filled with helium. This gives the evening the feel of a kids' party, which isn't altogether inappropriate, but H has gone for black balloons with crude daubs in white Pentel. Eyes. Button noses. Unsmiling mouths. The kids' party has become the Black and White Minstrel Show. Pompey humour again. Vile.

H asks for volunteers for the first round of balloons. Hands go up.

H turns to Malo. 'Son? You're in charge. Choose six blokes. One magazine each. You know how they go in? Anyone here will show you.'

Malo does his father's bidding. Andy distributes the hand guns, all automatics, and gives Malo a stack of magazines. I watch Andy teaching him how to slip the magazines into the butt of the guns, then load and ready the weapons. This time last year, Andy was teaching my son how to ride a trials bike. Now, he's teaching him how to kill someone.

'You're ready, son? Blokes all tooled up?'

Malo's nod of assent lacks conviction. H wants him to be sure.

'Check the guns, son. Do it fucking properly, yeah?'

Malo goes from face to face, checking each weapon. I feel very, very sorry for him and yet I'm beginning to sense what H is up to here. Every general should take infinite care in preparing the battlefield, in this case that stretch of swampy ground around our son. If Sun Tzu didn't say that, he should have done.

'OK, son? Done the biz? Happy?'

Malo nods again. His voice appears to have failed him. Then he visibly stiffens, gets a grip, and arranges the shooters in a line.

'When I tell you,' H says. 'One balloon each, yeah?'

The shooters exchange glances, then nod. One of them is licking his lips. Another permits himself the faintest smile.

'Do it!' The order comes from Malo.

There's a deafening crackle of explosions, partly ammunition, partly balloons. The air is suddenly blue with smoke and something acrid catches in the back of my throat. Andy has taken care to pull the barn door shut but I imagine heads lifting from dinner tables four fields away. Fireworks? When it's not even dark?

Most of the balloons are history. Three remain and the same shooter despatches them all, one after the other. Bang. Bang. Bang. This draws a round of applause from H who seems delighted. The shooter's name is Wayne. H promises him pole position when it comes to putting the shits up the Brixton numpties. Wayne reloads again and says it will be an honour.

Malo helps Andy raise another line of balloons from beneath a net in the corner. This time all the balloons are despatched at once. The smell of cordite in this confined space is overpowering. Even H is trying to mask a cough.

Andy has produced a scarecrow figure knocked up from broom handles, binder twine, a ragged pair of trousers and an old denim jacket I suspect once belonged to Malo. A huge pumpkin, an obscene shade of orange, serves as the head and Andy has topped this grotesque figure with a straw hat.

Malo can't take his eyes off the jacket. Everything H does always has a purpose and if he's set out to get our son's undivided attention it's certainly worked.

H wants the assembled company to pretend they're part of a firing squad. He wants them to take five steps back and then – again on Malo's command – drop the target. 'Think Brixton,' he says. 'Think heavy traffic. Think people everywhere. Think the getaway cars at the kerb. I know you can do this. Just prove it to me.'

Heads have turned. One of the shooters has a question. 'Back in the house, you said we weren't gonna kill anyone.'

'Yeah?' H is smiling. 'I really said that?'

'You did.'

'OK.' He's looking at Malo now. 'Then maybe I was wrong.'

TWENTY-SEVEN

B y midnight, most of H's Pompey troopers have climbed into their vehicles, grunted their goodbyes and disappeared into the darkness. A hard core, two of them including Wes, have decided to stay the night and are watching a DVD of *Darkest Hour* I gave H for his birthday. H himself, who has now seen the movie three times, slips out of the den and joins me in the kitchen.

'Where's the boy?'

I've no idea. Jessie and I are sharing a second nightcap – cocoa with two shots of Armagnac. Jessie thinks he might be down at the cottage with Andy. H tells her to phone and find out.

Jessie's right. H takes the phone and asks Andy to send Malo up to the barn. Jessie and I exchange glances. H has been in a foul mood all evening. This very definitely isn't party time.

I walk over to the barn with H, partly because he's asked me to, and partly to defend Malo's interests. I'm as keen as H to get to the bottom of what's going on but I've seen Malo's dad at work now and I know the kind of damage he can inflict.

Malo, it turns out, has been drinking. The moment he walks into the barn, it's obvious: his eyes are wet and he walks with the kind of exaggerated confidence that suggests a tinnie too far. H has seen it too and it seems to enrage him even more. He's re-arranged the metal stands so a single pool of light falls on what's left of the scarecrow. The pumpkin head lies on one side, a thin, yellowish liquid still oozing from dozens of bullet holes. The broomstick frame has been splintered and when Malo finally comes to an uneasy halt he can't take his eyes off the denim jacket. It, too, is full of holes and one of them has half-destroyed a smiley badge I gave him a while back.

'Well?' H grunts.

'Well what?'

'Don't get fucking clever with me, son. This is your dad talking and in case you'd forgotten, this is your mum. We're family. We don't keep secrets. Nothing sneaky. Not in our house. All we want, the both of us, is a bit of respect and a bit of honesty. Clemmie's a cracking girl. We all love her. You're lucky to have met her, lucky to have got her attention. So just one question. Where the fuck is she?'

Malo shakes his head. He won't meet our eyes. He says he doesn't know. H steps closer and for the briefest moment I'm certain he's going to hit him. Instead he extends a hand to lift Malo's chin, pulls him closer and gives him a long, hard look. Malo is terrified. I can see it in his face. He's biting his lip. He's totally out of his depth. There isn't enough Stella in the world to cope with a scene like this.

H turns to me. 'You try,' he says. 'Fuck knows, he won't listen to me.'

I ask H to step away. I do my best to assure Malo that we have everything, including ourselves, under control. No one will get hurt as long as we're honest with each other. All we want is the truth.

'You told me yesterday what happened after Clem walked out that night, the night she went missing.'

'Yeah?'

'Yes. You said you tried to call her private number. You told me she didn't pick up. That turns out to be a lie.'

'Lie' is a big word. Malo flinches. 'Who says?'

'I talked to Clem's dad. He has a contact at Vodafone. According to their records, you made three calls and had three conversations. The longest was the first one. Do you want the exact times?'

'The record's wrong.'

'I don't think so.'

'He's looking at the wrong phone.'

'He isn't. He knows Clem's number. And he knows yours, too. If you want to tell lies, Malo, you should make allowances for other people. We're not stupid. And we only want the best for both of you. So why don't you tell us exactly what went on that night?'

There's a very long silence. Malo is still staring at his denim jacket. H is somehow managing to contain himself.

'Well . . .?' I ask.

'I told you last night.' Malo is biting his lip. 'We had a huge row.'

'About?'

'Me. Us.'

'How huge? Remind me.'

'Horrible. It was horrible. She had a whole list of things I'd not done, things I'd said I'd do.'

'And was she right?'

'Yeah. She's always right.'

'And that was enough to take her wherever she was going?'

'Yeah.'

'So where was she going?'

'She's got mates. I told you. Places she can crash.'

'But where? You'd have asked her. Even the amount you'd drunk, you'd still ask her. So where was she going?'

Malo shakes his head. He says she wouldn't tell him.

'These mates. You knew them too?'

'Some of them.'

I steal a glance at H. After my last conversation with our son this is old territory for me, but I'm repeating myself for H's benefit.

'So did you phone any of these people later? Did you have a ring around to try and lay hands on her? Make sure she was OK?'

Malo is about to nod, to agree, to say yes, anything to put him in a better light, but then he remembers Mateo's contact at Vodafone and has second thoughts.

'I went to bed,' he says. 'I told you. I finished the bottle and went upstairs. I was wasted. Gone.'

I glance sideways at H. He's inscrutable. He doesn't want this to stop.

'Carry on,' he tells me. 'There's got to be more.'

There is. At last, I describe my conversation with Clem's neighbour at the end of the mews. The moment Malo left in his Audi with the mystery passenger.

'What passenger?'

'Black guy. Dreadlocks. And a little teardrop tattoo.' I touch my cheek beneath my eye. 'Here.'

Mention of the tattoo gets H's full attention. This time he can't help himself. 'This bloke got a name, son?'

'I don't know what you're talking about. What bloke?'

It won't do. The denial is tissue-thin. Even Malo doesn't believe it. I go through the details again. 'This is the company you're keeping,' I point out. 'So given the circumstances, don't you think we're right to be disturbed?'

'Who is he, son?' H this time. 'Just fucking tell us.'

Malo shakes his head. Says he can't. Won't.

'Can't? Won't? That's language we don't use, son. Not here. Not now. These people are evil. Tatts like that don't happen by accident. You're in deep shit. Just tell us how it happened and what you were doing with this tosser. The rest we can sort.'

'How?' Malo's question is beyond blunt and should tell us exactly why this son of ours is loath to go much further. He's probably frightened of a squillion things just now, but the two of them that matter most are his father and the man with the dreadlocks and the teardrop tattoo. Malo has become the meat in someone else's sandwich and is terrified to imagine what might happen next.

'How?' Malo asks again. 'What are you going to do?'

It's H's turn to be coy. He won't answer the question but I, too, have a stake in H's next move.

'Your little army is going up to London?' I ask H.

'Might be.'

'And then what? You kill someone? Pour hot water all over them? Make everything better again? Just how does all this work?'

H ignores me. He's staring at Malo. 'I want this man's name, son. I'm guessing you have an address, too. Does that sound reasonable?'

Malo shakes his head. No, he mutters. No, no, no way.

'Why the fuck not?'

'Because . . .'

'Because what?'

'Just because.' He shuts his eyes and shakes his head as if something's come loose inside and he wants to get rid of it. Then, once again, I watch him make some kind of unspoken inner decision. He blinks a couple of times, staring at nothing, then rubs his eyes.

'Tomorrow,' he mumbles. 'I promise.'

'Tomorrow what?'

'Tomorrow I'll tell you everything.'

'Wrong. You'll tell us now. Here. Both of us.'

'No, Dad. Just give me a break, yeah?'

He steps to one side and heads for the door. H moves to inter-
cept him but I manage to pull him back. Malo has disappeared.

H turns on me. 'You're crazy.' He pinches his finger and thumb
together. 'We were that fucking close.'

'I know, but you've got to give the boy space. He's been drinking
again. That's something else we have to sort.'

I hear the front door of the main house open and then close.
Malo has a wonderful suite of rooms on the second floor beside
H's office, last year's bait to lure him down here to Flixcombe,
and it worked. He's been in residence ever since.

I'm looking at H. He's trying to make the best of the situation,
reluctantly agreeing it might be better to talk to the boy once he's
sobered up.

'You're right,' I say. 'We owe him that.'

There's a brief silence between us. H looks exhausted. He
had a bad crash last year on a trials bike, ending up in hospital
for weeks, and I know there are moments when the pain of all
those injuries comes back to haunt him. Now is just such a time.
He's shifting his weight from one foot to the other, trying not
to wince. I step a little closer. There's something I want to share
with him.

'The guy with the dreadlocks,' I murmur. 'You think he might
be the Plug?'

'You mean as far as Bridport is concerned? The county lines
thing?' H is staring at me.

'Yes.'

'Controlling the Somalis down there? And the white kids?'

'Yes.'

H doesn't answer for a moment or two. His eyes are the deepest
black. I'm half-expecting him to blank me, to tell me – as ever
– to leave the business end of this saga to him, but finally he has
the grace to nod.

'Yeah,' he says. 'I do.'

I spend the night in one of the guest rooms at the back of the
house. H has pushed off to bed with barely a word of farewell,
gruff again, and towards dawn I lie awake, listening to the stir of
the wind in the trees beyond the walled garden. Conflicted is too
small a word to describe my feelings about Malo. I haven't the

slightest doubt that he's been lying, certainly to me, but I know he's wounded in all kinds of ways and that gets me close to forgiving him. *If only*, I think. If only he'd trust us. If only he'd let us into his world. And if only I could ease his father's desperate grip on the life he's left behind. Pompey. Retribution. Grown men pouring bullets into a scarecrow. And that poor bloody Dooley bent over his steaming groin, howling like an animal.

I get up early and pad down to the kitchen in the dressing gown I keep on the back of the door. I'm sitting barefoot at the kitchen table when H appears. A night's sleep seems to have done nothing for his mood. He spoons coffee granules from the jar and re-boils the kettle. I close my eyes, turn my head away.

'The boy's gone.' H has settled at the table.

'What?' I ask.

'Gone. Done a runner. I should have known, should have sussed it. That's a problem isn't it? Kith and kin? Your own blood? *Our* own blood? And yet it takes nothing for him to stitch us up.'

I nod. I'm trying to digest this latest bombshell. 'It's hardly nothing,' I say finally. 'You're right. But if it's any consolation, he's gone in all kinds of ways. The boy's adrift. He's totally lost it.'

H nods. He says he won't get far. The Audi's disappeared but Malo has no more money for petrol and H has acquired his phone.

'I'll go out for a look later,' he says. 'Then we'll have a proper conversation.'

I close my eyes again. I don't want to think about a proper conversation. Moments later, I hear the kitchen door open. It's Wes.

'Checked them, H.'

'And?'

'One missing. The Glock.'

Glock? I'm staring at H.

'I asked Wes to check the guns. We had thirteen last night.' H turns to Wes. 'Ammunition?'

'Three magazines. All for the Glock.'

'And?'

'They've gone, too.'

TWENTY-EIGHT

'm back in my room, lying on the bed, when my phone rings. Thinking that my precious son might have acquired a pay-as-you-go phone, I answer the call.

'Malo?' I'm half-sitting up now.

It's Pavel. I dab at the wetness on my cheeks. Even from Scotland, he probably knows that I've been crying. He's got something important to tell me. To be more precise, two things. His voice is much stronger. He sounds confident, even happy.

'Are you sitting down?' he asks.

'Sort of.'

'I'm talking to you by myself. Picking up the phone? Scrolling to the directory? Punching the number? All my own work.'

This is his Neil Armstrong moment. One small step, I think.

'And the other thing?'

'They're sending me home.'

'You mean home home?' I'm amazed.

'England. There's a special unit in London. The verb they keep using is "monitor". They want to track my recovery day by day. I get the feeling I've become some kind of guinea pig. There's probably a TV series in it. Life beyond paralysis. Blind diver reconnects. Be honest, do you think my agent can handle this?'

Despite everything, I realize I'm laughing. 'Make sure you get a release clause,' I tell him. 'You don't want to be in hospital for ever.'

It's his turn to laugh. Then he asks about Clem.

'Still gone.'

'Nothing happening?'

'Lots. All of it terrible.' I tell him about last night, about the gathering of the Pompey faithful, about the shooting range that had once been the barn, and about our cack-handed bid to ambush our son and squeeze the truth out of him.

'You'll frighten the boy,' Pavel warns. 'And then he'll go.'

'Too late. You're ahead of the game. He's gone.' I'm crying again. I can't help it.

Pavel offers his sympathies. We need, he says, to talk face-to-face. This is strange coming from a blind man but I think I know what he means. He's talking the language of comfort, of physical presence, of smell and touch, everything – in short – that I'll never get from the other men in my life. This kind of rapport, of mutual reaching out, demands a degree of surrender, a concept which has zero appeal to either H or Malo.

'Nice idea,' I agree, 'but when?'

'A couple of days. Maybe even tomorrow. They're polishing the ambulance as I speak.'

If only. H is out all morning in the Range Rover, searching lane after lane for signs of Malo's Audi. By the time he returns, he's convinced the boy must have laid hands on money from somewhere. A full tank, he says, would take him anywhere in the UK. All he needs is a hundred quid or so and he can survive for days.

'I'm thinking the money might have come from you. Am I right?'

I don't even bother to answer him. A shake of the head is all I can manage. Our son has got a gun. Thanks to last night, he knows how to load it, point it, pull the trigger. Desperation and late adolescence go hand in hand. We should have left him alone last night. Now, literally anything might happen.

'Like what?'

'Like he starts holding up banks, corner stores, old ladies on park benches, whatever it takes. We've driven him away when we needed him here. How clever was that?'

The thought of Malo embarking on a life of crime seems to amuse H.

'It's a nice idea,' he admits. 'But he wouldn't have the fucking bottle.'

'Then why take the gun in the first place?'

'You tell me.'

'You thinking he might have gone back to London?'

'Yeah, I do.'

'To get Clem back?'

H nods. He's given this proposition some thought already. He's now convinced that Malo has been in touch with the kidnappers. Hence his visit to Brixton with Mr Dreadlocks. When Wes last checked the underside of the Audi, the tracker had been removed, more proof – in H's eyes – that his son has fallen into shit company.

'These people know exactly what they're about,' he says. 'They check everything, every last detail, and that's because they can't afford not to. Each of these county lines operations nets around a hundred K a week. That kind of money, you take no risks. Malo's a choirboy. Glock or no Glock, they'll eat him alive.'

'And Clem?'

'She's the wildcard, and the way they've doubled the ask tells me everything I need to know. These people are arrogant. The top guys are in the fucking blue yonder. I'm now betting the Somali kids on the ground for the heavy lifting, Larry Fab as the enforcer, Mr Dreadlocks as the Plug and some guy at the very top to boss the whole operation. Wes says the Somalis are off the scale and I believe him. No manners at all. Kill you. Eat you. Rape your mother and leave her upside down in a wheelie bin. You think kettling's horrible? The Somalis wouldn't even plug the fucking thing in. They'd cut to the chase. Take your head off and mail it to someone you love. That's why God invented those really big Jiffy bags.'

'You *know* all this? For sure?'

'Yeah.'

'And you think you can really take these people on?'

'No chance.'

'Then what was last night about?'

H gazes at me for a moment. I sense he's trying to work out whether I'm taking the piss.

'Tell me,' I say again. 'Pretend I'm even more stupid than you thought.'

'It was about the boy, about Malo.'

'You really wanted to frighten him?'

'Of course I fucking did.'

I gaze at him. I shake my head. Pavel had it right all along.

'Brilliant,' I mutter. 'So guess where that leaves us now.'

H and Wes depart in the Range Rover after lunch. H doesn't tell me where he's going but my guess is London. Wes, apparently, is a genius when it comes to picking locks. There isn't a door in the kingdom, H once told me, that can resist the attentions of Wesley Kane. Clem's place, I tell myself. A whole night ripping the place apart.

There's no way I'm going to join them. London is an enormous city but I can visualize only too well the moment when the pair of them appear in my car park with yet more bad news from the front line. Some document they've found at Clem's place. Or maybe another phone. Or a list of names, some of whom need frightening. For the time being, I'm better off here, doing whatever I can to understand the chain of events that led to Clem's disappearance.

Late afternoon, I pay Jess and Andy a visit. Jess, according to Andy, is asleep upstairs. Andy makes me a cup of extremely thin coffee. I want to know more about Danny Flannery.

Andy says there's not much to tell. Decent chippie. Makes respectable money, especially for this neck of the woods. Lives alone. Chases demons. All-round good bloke.

'Demons?'

'He jacked his marriage in. His missus is a bit of a nightmare, got a real mouth on her, and there came a point when he'd had enough. Since then you'd think he'd never look back, but that isn't true, either. I think in some weird way he misses her. Weed's fine in small doses but he's smoking far too much. He got it on with another woman recently, Suze, but she's got problems of her own.'

'I know. He told me.'

'And did he tell you about her kids? They're off the planet, all of them, and the oldest isn't even a teenager yet.'

'So what happened to the father?'

'Fathers. Plural. They fucked off.'

'Both of them?'

'All three of them. Don't let Bridport fool you. They talk a great game round here – foodie heaven, fancy shopping, property prices through the roof – but blow the dust off and it's as fucked-up as everywhere else. If you fancy getting seriously depressed I'm sure Danny would do the business. In fact, I know he would.'

I nod. I enjoyed talking to Danny the other evening, and I was grateful for him getting me out of the Landfall in one piece, but it wasn't hard to sense the *tristesse* behind the witty one-liners and the easy smile. Now, thanks to Andy, I'm a little wiser about what it takes to keep your head above water in blissed-out west Dorset.

'So you don't think it's a good idea me seeing Danny again?'

'Depends what you're after. If you want a good night out he'd be happy to oblige. Like I say, he's a nice bloke, heart of gold.'

'That's not it. I want to find out what happened to Clem.'

'Then Danny can only take you so far.' He pauses. 'This thing is out of control. You know that, don't you?'

'What thing?'

'Clem. Malo. Most of all, H. I've seen him like this before, years back, after a bloke called Bazza Mackenzie got killed. That was in Pompey and H was the heir apparent. He loved Bazza. They were that close. And when the Filth took him down he wouldn't leave it alone. He had names, blokes in uniform, blokes in CID. He wanted to set the record straight. He wanted revenge, restitution, blood. For weeks, until other people made him see sense, he lost it completely. This is very similar. As you saw last night. And unless we're careful, he's going to blow it again.'

'Blow what?'

'This.' Andy gestures vaguely at the window, at the looming shadow of Flixcombe Manor and the untold acres beyond. 'We've been here for a while now and we take all this for granted. We shouldn't. No one's bulletproof. Not even H.'

I nod. It's not hard to see what Andy and Jess have to lose here. At the same time, there's someone else at stake.

'Clem,' I remind him. 'You're thinking we just forget about her?'

'Malo told me about her dad and the K&R guy.'

'O'Keefe?'

'Yes. In life, just sometimes, it pays to defer to the professionals. That was never H's style but in this case it might be the sweetest way to get the woman back. Make contact, open negotiations, strike a deal. That's a red rag to the likes of H because he hates losing control. But that can make him his own worst enemy.'

'Says you.'

'Says me.' Andy is watching me carefully. 'So what's your take?'

'Mine?' I shrug. 'I think there's more to it than meets the eye.'

'Care to tell me why?'

'Not really.'

'But this is more than a hunch? You've got evidence?'

'Yes.'

'And is this about Malo?'

I hold his gaze and shake my head. I'm not saying. Andy nods, as if he understands, and then I look round, suddenly aware of another presence in the room. It's Jessie. Her hair is tousled and she's rubbing the sleep from her eyes. She must have got up and stolen down the stairs. Now she's standing in the open doorway and I'm guessing she's been privy to most of our conversation.

Andy makes room for her on the sofa. 'Tell Enora about your bloke in the swimming pool,' he says. 'And see where it takes us.'

TWENTY-NINE

Jessie, it turns out, is a keen swimmer. She drives down to the Bridport Leisure Centre three times a week and tackles the seventy lengths that clock up her personal mile. She's been doing this since Christmas, one reason she's in such good shape. Gradually, over the months, she's come to know a handful of the other regulars that churn up and down but recently all of them have had to make space for a new face in the pool. This is someone much younger and – more to the point – very, very good.

'Good, how?'

'Style. Stamina. Speed. This boy must have been born a fish. He leaves all of us for dead.'

'Age?'

'I'm guessing. Maybe eighteen? Nineteen? He's definitely started shaving but that's not the point. This lad isn't from Bridport at all.'

Malo's age, I think. Interesting. I want to know more.

'We think he's probably down from London.'

'How do you know?'

'One of the guys talked to him in the showers. I don't think it was the easiest conversation but he's definitely not local.'

'Some kind of work placement?'

Jessie laughs. Nice idea, she says, and probably not a million miles from the truth.

I tell her I don't understand. Is he with a local firm?

'He's a drug dealer.' This from Andy.

'How do you know?'

'Jess has seen him in the rugby club car park next door to the leisure centre. He drives a nearly new BMW. Badge of office. It's even the right colour.'

I'm assuming black and it turns out I'm right. Andy nods. How many kids can afford a motor like that?

Jessie picks up the story again. From time to time she's had brief eye contact with this youth. 'You know the way it goes. You start by nodding if you meet at the end of a length. Then you might get a grunt of apology if you get in each other's way. We're not best buddies. We've never even had the beginnings of a chat, but there's the makings of a connection there.'

'How come?'

'I had a problem with the car the other day. It turned out to be the battery but I didn't know that at the time. I was under the bonnet for a while, poking this and that, and the Beemer was nearby. During that time he had three customers. All boys. All young. It was very slick. The dosh. The handover. Done.'

'We're talking a couple of bags?'

'More. In old brown envelopes.'

'No CCTV?'

'One camera but the Beemer is invisible behind a hedge. It's always busy at the leisure centre, people coming and going, kids in the holidays and at weekends.'

'Is he black, this boy?'

'No, white.'

'And does he have a name?'

'The guys in the pool call him The Machine. That's to do with his swimming. I think it's a compliment.'

'And they know he's dealing?'

'No. I've kept what I just said to myself. I still can't be a hundred per cent certain but without the flat battery I'd never have sussed him. Me? I'm a Pompey girl. You get a nose for stuff like this.'

'He helped you with the battery?'

'He did, and that was nice of him. He even offered to run me round to a garage he knows to buy a new one.'

'And?'

'I took him up, of course I did. I blew lots of smoke up his arse, told him what a fantastic swimmer he was, star of the pool, but when it came to any kind of conversation, proper conversation, he didn't want to know.'

'Accent?'

'Neutral. Could be London.'

'But you think he's living in Bridport?'

Jessie shrugs, then glances at Andy.

'That would have to be a yes,' Andy says. 'You're feeding the market and this is the biggest place around. These guys make base camp, recruit local dealers, spread the word, and then wait for the punters to arrive. My guess is he's running a team of kids and they rock up to the car park for re-supply.'

'Are any of these kids black?' I ask him.

'Yes.'

'Somalis?'

'Yes. And scary, some of them.'

Jessie's nodding in agreement. There's one other thing. 'This boy has a friend,' she says. 'A really pretty woman. Dark. Mad hair.'

'She swims, too?'

'Never. But she often comes to watch. I've seen her in the Beemer, too. When she thinks no one's watching she's all over him.'

'Age?'

'Older. Maybe late-twenties.' She's smiling. 'To tell you the truth, I'm not sure I blame her.'

I nod, say I'm grateful for all these leads. She says it's no problem.

'You want to borrow a cozzie?' she asks. 'I've got one going spare.'

I'm not a great swimmer. I enjoy Mediterranean beaches and the odd frolic in the shallows to cool down but in my mum's judgement, as a Breton girl growing up in a house overlooking a beach, I was always a bit of a *poule mouillée*, which means 'pussy' or 'wuss'. Bracing dips in La Manche, the moment early spring arrived in Perros-Guirec, were never my style.

Jessie, bless her, offers to accompany me to the pool next day. The Bridport Leisure Centre lies to the south of the town and we're parking up in Jessie's car before eight o'clock in the morning. Jessie points out the black BMW behind a hedge in the adjacent rugby club car park. She's going for a swim and I'm welcome to join her but I elect to stay at the poolside. For the umpteenth day in this wonderful summer, the weather is near-perfect.

The moment I tug on my plastic bootees and step inside the pool area I recognize The Machine. He's swimming crawl. Every stroke seems effortless, head tucked under his rising arm, mouth half open, and he glides through the water with barely a splash. The pool looks new, six lanes, twenty-five metres long.

Early-morning regulars are thrashing up and down but The Machine carves a path through the bodies with never a glance left or right. When he comes to the end of a length he somersaults under water before pushing off again with his legs, resuming that mesmeric rhythm.

Jessie appears within minutes, tugging on her swimming cap, and she pauses at poolside to nod at the blur in lane five before diving in. Her breast stroke is more than accomplished but The Machine laps her and everyone else for length after length.

He's out of the pool by half past eight. He has a swimmer's body: powerful shoulders, broad chest, narrow waist, skimpy Speedo briefs. He peels off his goggles and runs his fingers through his sodden black curls. I've checked everywhere for the rumoured girlfriend but there's no sign.

Jessie has given me the keys to her car. I make myself comfortable behind the wheel and wait for The Machine to appear. He emerges from the leisure centre within minutes, picking his way through the other parked vehicles, making for the nearby entrance to the rugby club car park, a mobile pressed to his ear. He's wearing designer jeans, flip-flops and what looks like a brand-new white T-shirt. No trackie bottoms, no hoodie. Beside the BMW he lingers to finish the conversation before getting in. This morning of all mornings he may elect to drive off but mercifully he doesn't. I have a clear view across the car park. He's on the phone again.

I wait, debating what to do. I trust Jessie completely. I believe her story about the deals going down. If I don't take the initiative and seize this moment, I tell myself, then the rest of the morning will have been pointless. At length, a black youth I judge to be in his mid-teens appears beside the BMW and bends to the driver's window. In return for what looks like a fattish roll of notes he gets a brown envelope. Then, just as Jessie described last night, he's gone. Five seconds, absolute tops. Glance down to check my own mobile, I think, and I'd never have laid eyes on him.

Minutes go by. Then another figure turns up, male again but white this time, in torn jeans and a Liverpool football shirt. More notes. Another envelope. Gone. The Machine's on the phone again. He's gesturing with his left hand, a splay of fingers, short jabbing movements. Is he angry? Excited? Is trade especially lively on a

Sunday morning? I've no idea. Is it the mystery girlfriend at the other end? Pass.

The call over, he relaxes back against the seat and then seems to be fiddling with the radio. What does he listen to? What kind of music fuels a drug dealer in late adolescence who swims like a fish?

I get out of Jessie's car. Now, I've decided, is the moment to find out. Before another supplicant arrives. Before he's had enough and fires up the BMW and roars away. Before I exhaust my own small stock of courage.

I tap on his window. He turns his head. He still has reddish rings around his eyes from the goggles but the eyes themselves are the brightest blue. Coloured lenses, I think at once. He's put himself together the way actors do before they make their entrance on set. The two-day stubble. The black curls gelled just so. The single silver piercing at the very top of his ear. The faintest hint of a smile.

'Yeah?' He's looking up at me. There's no warmth in the question, quite the contrary, but I'm ready for this.

'May I?' I'm nodding at the passenger seat.

'May you what?'

'Get in?'

'Why? What do you want?'

The accent, as Jessie has warned me, is neutral but what comes as a surprise is just the hint of a lisp. I tell him I want to buy two rocks of Bad. Bad, I understand from Andy, is street talk for crack cocaine.

'Are you Filth, or what?' The word 'Bad' seems to amuse him.

'I'm no one. I'm me. Enora. Enora Andressen.'

It's awkward trying to shake hands through an open car window and he makes no effort to be part of this pantomime. Something about me seems to have caught his attention.

'You were in the pool, weren't you? Just now?' he touches his own head. 'Red beret.'

'I was.'

'You were watching me?'

'Yes.'

'Why? Why would you want to do that?'

I nod at the empty seat again. 'Let me in and I'll tell you.'

I know he's in two minds now. Sensibly, he wants nothing to do with me. On the other hand, I seem to have intrigued him.

'Take it off,' he says. 'No one wears a beret in weather like this.'

I do what I'm told. My hair is beginning to grow back again but only just.

'Chemo?' he asks.

'Yes.'

'Where?'

'I had a brain tumour. A glioblastoma. You know about any of this stuff?'

'My mum died last year. Lung cancer. Fags. Forty a day for years on end will kill you but she never listened.'

'And is that why you swim?'

'No. I swim for me.'

I nod. I'm thinking about Pavel. 'I've got a good friend,' I tell him. 'Dived in the wrong end of the pool. Broke his neck. He's in a hospital in Glasgow just now, paralysed from the neck down.'

'Yeah?'

'Yes. So be careful in there.' I nod towards the leisure centre.

I think I'm detecting the faintest smile on his face. He leans across and opens the passenger door. 'Get in,' he says. 'Five minutes, then I'm out of here.'

I walk round the bonnet and slip into the front seat. He's been listening to Ed Sheeran, not the gangsta rap I half-expected. The car smells of a perfume I know very well indeed. My lovely neighbour Evelyn bought me some for Christmas.

'Chanel Number Five,' I say with a hint of approval. 'Nice.'

I've wrong-footed him at last. 'A girlfriend,' he mutters. 'You're not buying at all, are you?'

'No.'

'So you *are* Filth. You have to be.'

'Sadly not.'

I have several photos of Malo and Clem on my Samsung. He takes the phone. Big hands. Bitten nails. A single silver thumb ring. He's looking at a selfie of the happy couple aboard Clem's Harley, helmets in their laps, gurning for the camera.

'You know these two?' I ask. 'Ever seen them?'

He won't answer me, not at first. Then he wants to know why I'm asking.

'The boy is my son. His name is Malo. His girlfriend is called Clemenza.'

'You say.'

'I say.'

'And?'

'They've both disappeared. First Clem. And now Malo, my son. They bought drugs down here. Probably in the Landfall.'

'It's a khazi.'

'You're right.'

'You've *been* there?'

'Yes.'

He nods and I detect just a flicker of respect before his eyes return to the phone. 'Prove to me you're not Filth,' he says.

I've anticipated this question. I recently co-starred in an art movie called *Arpeggio*. It didn't do at all well on limited release and it's now available, free, on YouTube. I take the phone back. A series of keystrokes takes me to the opening sequence. A woman is making a phone call at the zoo in Regent's Park. The background, slightly out of focus, is full of chimpanzees.

'You've got proper hair,' he says.

'That was a couple of years ago, before the operation and the chemo. I was also a kilo or two heavier.'

He's hit the play button. He seems fascinated.

I look up and then put a hand on his arm. 'Police,' I say quietly. 'A patrol car.'

'Shit.' He's already firing up the engine. 'What the fuck is this?'

'Trust me.' I retrieve my phone. 'Just drive out. I'm an actress, not a cop.'

We're on the move across the car park. Our route takes us past the patrol car which has stopped outside the main entrance to the leisure centre. Neither cop, one male, the other a girl barely out of her teens, spares us even a glance.

'She must be your age,' I say lightly. 'Didn't go to school with her by any chance?'

'Down here?' For the first time there's a hint of warmth in his voice. 'You have to be joking.'

We drive out on to the bypass and then take a road signposted to West Bay. Minutes later we're in another car park, this time with a view over the harbour. A gaggle of boats stir uneasily on gusts of wind from the sea. Fat seagulls forage for scraps among the piles of harbourside fishing nets. A family with a couple of kids clamber out of a 4x4. Moments later, we watch them making for the beach with armfuls of wet suits and a blow-up dinghy.

'They call you The Machine.'

'Who?'

'The people you swim with in the pool. You're the talk of the changing rooms. My girlfriend's a real fan.'

Silence. He's ignoring the compliments. Then he asks me what I really want.

'I want Clem safe.' I'm still holding my phone. 'And I want my son back.'

'So what's any of this got to do with me?'

'I think . . .' I shake my head. 'I *know* my son's got himself in serious shit.'

'Really? How?'

'It has to be drugs. And it probably started here.'

'Why here?'

'Because he lives quite close by, with his father. Do you know a young lad they call Noodle?'

'Yeah, I do.' He nods towards the beach. 'He spends most nights kipping in a tent out on the beach, under the sea wall. He's totally wasted. Sad, sad little bloke.'

'Because of drugs?'

'Partly, yeah. And one or two other things. Being gay down here doesn't help.'

'These are your drugs?'

'I don't do drugs.'

'That wasn't my question. You certainly sell drugs. I watched you. About half an hour ago.'

'You did?'

'I did.'

He nods, says nothing. Then he turns and he looks at me. The sudden grin feels spontaneous enough to be genuine. 'I know people who would kill you for saying something like that,' he says. 'You should be more careful.'

*   *   *

We talk for perhaps another half an hour. I'm very conscious that I've got Jessie's car keys in my pocket but I sense I'll never get an opportunity like this again. For whatever reason, The Machine likes me, or – at the very least – has taken pity on the post-chemo actress in the red beret. For my sake, and perhaps Malo and Clem's, he needs to mark my card.

'You have to stop thinking drugs,' he says. 'This is pizza with a bigger mark-up.'

'So I gather.'

'I'm serious. You never heard this from me but there are people in this business you'd never want to cross. They've moved into Bridport the way they've moved into a hundred other little towns. It's purely business, supply and demand. Figure out the distribution and you get very rich, very quickly. Kids in this town want a slice of that pizza and they think it's money for nothing, but that's because they know fuck all about anything. You set them up in someone's house, someone who won't answer back. You give them a couple of grand's worth of ten-quid bags and wait until they've done the business and then you pay someone to roll them late one night when they're least expecting it. Next day they're a couple of grand in the hole and that's when they start working for you for ever, just to repay the debt.'

'But you've got the money back already.'

'Of course. That's the whole point but the kids don't know that. It's all about control, exploitation, dog eat dog. That's how business works – any business. It could be anything, any commodity. This just happens to be food.'

'Food?'

'Drugs.'

I nod. So simple, I think. I hold his gaze. Those amazing eyes. 'So does you mean *you*? You're controlling these kids? Dishing out the drugs. Taking in the money?'

'No way. I'm a swimmer. You know that. You've watched me.'

'You never use yourself? Dabble? Sample the merchandise?'

'Never.'

'So who do you work for? Who do I need to talk to at the top of the chain?'

He won't answer. He's reaching for the ignition keys to start the engine. Then he has second thoughts and asks me for a pen and something to write on. He wants my contact details and an email address. When I ask why, he shakes his head.

'You have to trust me,' he says. 'Otherwise someone's going to get seriously hurt.'

THIRTY

Seriously hurt? In some ways it's a tribute to the last year or so that this phrase carries less menace than perhaps it should. Living with the magnetic pull of H, and increasingly Malo, I've become aware that daily life can be a great deal more bothersome than I'd ever imagined. Add the brain tumour that has so nearly killed me, and you probably get the picture. We live from day to day. Life is all verbs. Salvation lies in the imperative mood. Enjoy!

Back at Flixcombe Manor I retire to the library and eye the phone, wondering whether to share The Machine with H. Instead, I call Pavel. He's pleased to hear me. He has lots to report. He says his appetite has returned and at the risk of overloading me with details he's happy to confirm that his digestive tract is back in full working order. Better still, he's hearing rumours that his catheter's days are numbered. In what he terms one of life's more painful ironies, he tells me that feeling and sensation below the waist have returned with a vengeance. It's nice to be in charge again, he says, but having a tube stuck up your penis is bloody uncomfortable.

'Think tomorrow,' I tell him. 'They'll whip it out and after that, you'll feel a whole lot better.'

He thanks me for my concern. He wants to know how things are going. I tell him about my visit to the leisure centre, about The Machine, and I riff for a minute or two about the way the local drugs scene is slowly slipping into focus. Thanks to Danny and Andy, and now The Machine, I'm beginning to understand how it all works. When Pavel presses me for a headline, that single phrase that might excite the working dramatist, I realize that it's hard to better The Machine's take on the teeming souk that is the contemporary drug scene.

'Think pizza with a fatter mark-up,' I say. 'That pretty much nails it.'

Pavel is impressed. He tells me he's trying to visualize this

young man. I give him a few clues – age, body shape, hair colour
– and when it's obvious he's starting to struggle a bit I go for the
lazy shortcut.

'Think Theo James in *The Divergent Series*,' I say.

'That's after my time. I've never had the pleasure.'

Of course not, foolish woman. I pluck another name from my
memory, someone Pavel might have laid eyes on before he went
blind.

'A young Paul Newman but taller,' I suggest. '*Cat on a Hot
Tin Roof*? Playing against Elizabeth Taylor? Getting the picture
here?'

'Perfect. And for the record, I was a huge fan. That performance
in *The Hustler* made me wonder whether I hadn't been gay all
my life and never noticed.' He's laughing at the memory. It's a
lovely sound. Then he's back with the image of the pizza. 'This
is a reef for all of us, am I right? Invisible at all states of the tide
but no less deadly?'

'Far from invisible,' I tell him. 'But I suspect you've got the
rest right.'

I mean it. Full immersion in Bridport's nascent drugs scene
carries a number of dangers and one of them is the temptation to
overplay what I've witnessed. But the last few days have given
me a number of images I don't seem able to consign to the recycle
bin: the Landfall at full throttle, Danny's late-night musings on
the way it all works, Brett Dooley's agony in the kitchen and now
the chilling efficiency of The Machine's retail operation. Pile each
of these glimpses one on top of the other and it's hard to resist
the conclusion that we're collectively screwed.

'Forget terrorism,' I say. 'Forget paedophiles. Think kids. It's
all about getting off your head. One day, this stuff might fall into
the hands of people who really understand business. And you know
what? It's happened already.'

I can hear Pavel chuckling. Like most writers, I know he's
addicted to catastrophe. Not bad luck. Not the odd accident. But
a full-blown disaster.

'You think it's that bad?'

'I do. From where I'm sitting, these guys – The Machine and
his little crew – have got us all in lockdown. Social media nearly
did it. Shit telly nearly did it. But this is the real deal. We've

stopped thinking for ourselves because that's where the drug
scene takes you. Total dependence. Full-on surrender. You heard
it here first.'

'You sound angry.'

'I am angry.'

'And helpless?'

'Far from it.'

'So what next?'

Good question. The Machine has my contact details. I can
wait for a call, or a text, or even an email but that – just
here and just now – feels far too passive. This morning I was
brave enough to seize the initiative and take a risk or two. Given
everything else in my life, not least my next brain scan, that needs
to continue.

'There's a local junkie who might be a key part of all this,'
I tell Pavel. 'His street name's Noodle and I think I know where
to find him.'

THIRTY-ONE

I don't leave Flixcombe until nearly midnight. Earlier, I'd raided H's brimming cellar and helped myself to a bottle of Chateau Lafite. I go down to the cottage and present Jessie with the wine as a thank you. I have just a sneaking suspicion that she's guessed its provenance but that doesn't matter because I'll replace it later. I also ask her for the loan of a torch, telling her that there's a problem with my bedside lamp. Andy offers his services at once but a look from Jessie shuts him up. She gives me an LCD torch she picked up from a garage and tells me to keep it. She doesn't believe the bedside lamp story for a moment.

'Where are you off to?' She's walking me to the door.

'Nowhere special.'

'You want company? Moral support?'

I stop, one hand on the door handle. It's a sweet offer. I'm genuinely touched. 'No, thanks,' I say. 'I'm sure it'll work out.'

Traffic at this hour in the depths of west Dorset is minimal. Within less than half an hour, I'm in Bridport. I take the bypass south and follow the signs to West Bay. The car park where I and The Machine had our little chat is virtually empty. I get out and lock my car. The way to the beach takes me around the harbour and out towards the low growl of the waves on the shingle.

Passing rows of locked harbourside food shacks, I'm thinking of something Pavel once told me about Chesil Beach, the long ribbon of foreshore that – in Pavel's phrase – parcels Lyme Bay. At the easterly end, the stones are big and round but every mile you walk west they get smaller and smaller until here in West Bay they're mere pebbles. In the darkness of a winter night, he told me, sailors offshore could tell exactly where they were by simply listening to the draw of the retreating waves. The bigger stones produced a certain note. The smaller pebbles sounded very different. At the time, sighted, Pavel had found this fascinating. Now, like a sailor condemned to an eternity of nights, it would matter infinitely more, yet another clue to the way a blind man has to map the world around him.

I'm on the seafront now. A tall, modern-looking block guards the entrance to the harbour. From four storeys of apartments, not a single light. West Bay, even at the height of the holiday season, is obviously asleep by half past one in the morning.

I pause beside the sea wall. The wind off the sea is cool on my face and the crescent of pebbles and sand recedes into the darkness. Try as I might, I can see no sign of a tent.

I peer seawards, fighting the temptation to ring Pavel, to point my smartphone at the ocean and ask him to guess where I've ended up, but then I picture the ward up in Glasgow, equally quiet, every patient probably asleep, and tell myself to concentrate on the business in hand. A tent. And a sad little chancer called Noodle.

I follow the promenade past a seafront shelter. The shelter is empty, a drift of discarded fish and chip wraps white in the half-darkness. Further on is a flight of steps that descends to the shingle. From the top step I can see the whole of the beach. Tucked into a nearby corner, hard against the sea wall, is the low shape of a tent.

I stare at it for a long moment. The little tent, invisible to anyone on the promenade above, has been artfully sited. Noodle, I think, must steal down here under cover of darkness. He's become an animal, semi-feral. He knows how to hide from predators, from people who might want to hurt him, and by dawn he's probably packed up and gone.

I glance round. The seafront is empty, no sign of life. The tide is low, the line of breaking waves the faintest white in the darkness. From the harbour comes the slap-slap of halyards against metal masts. Overhead, unseen, a swirl of noisy gulls.

I pull my anorak a little tighter. The promenade comes to an end just metres away and in the moonlight I can make out the thread of the cliff path climbing away to the west. There are houses on the bluff that overlooks the town, window after window curtained against the eerie brightness of the moonlight.

Now or never, I think. Step by step, I make my way down to the beach and inch along towards the tent. I try to mask the throw of light from Jessie's torch with my other hand but it's already obvious

that Noodle needs to work on his pitching skills. The tent sags badly
to one side. There are scorch marks at the front where the front
panel meets the rumpled arch of the roof, and one of the guy ropes
has come loose from its metal peg. The front flap is open and unse-
cured, the ties dangling in the wind, and an oblong of cardboard
protrudes from the tent, licking at the pebbles like some mute tongue.

I shine the torch briefly on to the cardboard. Once, it must have
been a box. *Cooking oil*, it says. *This side up*. Noodle probably
retrieved it from the back of a restaurant, or perhaps a waste bin.
Flattened, it now serves as insulation against the dampness of the
pebbles. Noodle, I think, will never get closer to fitted carpet than
this. Motionless, I stare down at the tent. If I'm after a metaphor
for a life in ruins, for a clinching sign of these benighted times,
I need look no further.

I kneel quickly beside the open flap, letting my eyes adjust to
the darkness inside. The smell of sweat and neglect is overpowering
but there's something else I recognize – the sweetness of a joss
stick or two, evidence that someone is still fighting the tide.

Beyond the cry of the gulls I can hear the rasp of the waves
on the pebble beach but as the seconds tick by I become aware
of another sound, just as rhythmic but much closer. Someone's in
there, huddled down on the cardboard. I can hear them, the lightest
intake of breath, a pause and then a gummy little grunt as they
breathe out again. Noodle, I think. Asleep. Has to be.

This is the moment I have a decision to make. Simplest, sanest
and probably kindest would be to turn my back on this claustro-
phobic little tomb and tiptoe away. Nothing disturbed, no one
roused, no one frightened. I hesitate for a moment and then shake
my head. Malo, I think. And Clem.

I turn on the torch again, shielding the beam. Then, through a
spread of fingers, I shine it into the tent. Not one body, but two.
They're lying side by side on the flattened cardboard. Both are
male, both young, both thin, both fully clothed. They have their
arms round each other, probably for warmth, and the closest of
the two figures, the bigger of the two, is wearing a knitted woollen
beanie with RNLI on the front.

I stare at this tableau for far longer than I should. It's full of
pathos, of an unspoken vulnerability, two barely grown men
huddled together to ward off armies of ghosts. It reminds me of

some of the refugee footage I've seen recently on TV, whole families sleeping under plastic sheets, fleeing the near-certainty of an ugly death. A burned-out joss stick stands in a jar on the cardboard. Also a candle in a dirty saucer and a Bic lighter. There are coils of vermicelli pasta in a single takeout carton and the puddle of sauce has already congealed. Noodle, I think. Eating out again.

One of the bodies, the nearest, is stirring. I'm tempted to turn the torch off but I don't. His face is very young and very pale against the surrounding darkness and when his eyes open, his first instinct is to raise his thin arms to ward off the inevitable blow. I crouch quickly beside him.

'Noodle?' It's a ridiculous name.

The face grunts. Then comes a volley of oaths and the youth is struggling to his feet, pushing me aside before I can react. Flat on my back on the pebbles, I hear another curse as he trips before recovering his balance and making off towards the steps. The patter of footsteps on the promenade slowly recedes.

I get slowly to my feet, adjust my anorak, brush myself down. Then I bend to the open flap.

'Noodle?' I say again, this time much more softly.

In the throw of the torch, the other youth appears to be still asleep. Once, I'm guessing, he'd been some lucky mother's pride and joy. There are still hints of choirboy in the dimpled cheeks and once-blond curls, but life has been less than kind to him lately. The jeans are way too big and the tatty grey T-shirt badly needs a wash. At last he begins to stir. One eye flicks open but the other, swollen and purpled, stays shut. There's another bruise, older, high on his temple and at least two of his lower teeth are missing. An old actor friend I treasured from my days in northern rep once told me that nothing ages a man more quickly, and more permanently, than disappointment. And here, in a scavenged festival tent in west Dorset, is the living proof.

'Who are you?'

It's an utterly reasonable question. I give him my name and apologize for waking him up. I'm not here to hurt him, I say. And I have absolutely nothing to do with the police.

'Where's Jake?' He nods down at the empty space on the mattress.

'He's gone. My fault. Sorry.'

He nods, trying to take it all in. Then he starts to scratch himself and half-rolls over. The beam of my torch follows him, revealing a nest of debris piled against the wall of the tent. I glimpse a couple of dessert spoons, a syringe, a twist of grubby paper and what looks like an old inhaler. Noodle's fingers have found the inhaler. He begs me not to turn the torch off. I nod. All I can do is watch. He's found a fragment of tin foil. He holds it up to the beam of the torch. He wants me inside the tent. And he wants me to close the flap.

I have no time for misgivings. This is Noodle's life, not mine. Inside the tent, there's barely room for two of us. Cosy doesn't begin to do it justice.

Noodle says he needs the needle.

'Needle?'

'Down there. Soon as you like.'

I spot the needle beside the remains of the joss stick. Picking it up isn't easy.

'Give it me. Please.' He sounds like a child.

I pass him the needle and watch him puncture the tin foil. In the twist of paper are a couple of crystals. Bad, I think. Crack cocaine. Has to be. Noodle selects the biggest crystal, holds it for a moment between his fingertips. The inhaler, I realize, has been crudely refashioned as a pipe.

'That was yours? The inhaler?'

He stares up at me, shakes his head. 'I found it. Out there on the beach. It does OK.'

He slips the tiny pebble of cocaine into the bowl and seals it with the foil. Then he reaches into the semi-darkness at my feet and finds the lighter. Moments later, a tiny flame is beginning to heat the crystal. My torch has settled on the inhaler. I can hear a tiny cracking noise. Noodle's face looms over the pool of light. He's waiting for something, his good eye bright at last. I see a curl of bluish smoke and his head goes down and he starts to inhale the fumes before he rocks briefly back, the sudden jolt of relief contorting his face. *Wake and bake*, I think, remembering one of the dealer messages on Dooley's phone.

Should I stop this? Should I play mother, step in, confiscate this makeshift pipe, tell him to get a grip? Too late. His head's down again and he's sucking the fumes deep into his lungs. I watch, fascinated on one level, ashamed on another. This is complicity, I tell myself. Or, even worse, a form of voyeurism. I'm doing nothing when I should be intervening.

I reach for the inhaler, but the second I move, Noodle turns his back to keep me at arm's length. This is the way an animal would react, I tell myself. What suddenly matters more than anything else in the world is that tiny, shrinking crystal. And so I leave him to it, saying nothing, doing nothing.

After a while, the crystal has gone. He stretches out on the cardboard, propping himself on one arm, buzzing, wanting to talk.

I ask him how I can help.

'Help how?'

'Help you.' I gesture around. 'This is no way to live. This is pathetic.'

'You've got money?'

'Yes.'

'Can you give me money?'

'How much would you want?'

'As much as you're carrying.'

I do the sums. I have my purse with me. Last time I looked, it contained half a dozen notes. Say fifty pounds. Maybe more.

'Say I said yes. Say I gave you money. What would you do with it?'

I already know what the answer is. If this child is honest he'll tell me he'll buy more drugs. I'm wrong.

'I'd start to settle my debts,' he says.

'Not buy drugs? You're serious?'

'I've got all the drugs I'll ever need. This stuff. Smack. Whatever. And that's because I sell the stuff. Gear is easy. I help myself. But in the end I need to pay the man's bill.'

'So who's the man?'

He shakes his head. No way is he going to tell me. He says he's tried begging in the street. On market days, especially, he might make a quid or two.

'Is that enough?'

'No.'

'So what happens?'

One hand touches his swollen eye. In the throw of light from the torch it's a gesture I'll never forget. With the pleasure, he seems to be telling me, comes the pain. Not simply of withdrawal but of punishment. That's the price he has to pay, as sure as day follows night.

'So why don't you chuck it in? Find help? Clean yourself up?'

'Because I can't.'

'Won't.'

'You're right.' He nods. 'Won't.'

'You *like* a life like this?'

'It's what happens.' He shrugs, beginning to scratch again. 'You're nice. You listen. I like you.'

'Thanks.'

I have no idea where this conversation might go next. I get out my phone and scroll through my photos until I find one of Malo and Clem together. Noodle barely spares it a glance.

'I've heard about you,' he says. 'I know who you are. You were in the Fall, right? The other night? With a big roll of notes?'

'I was.'

'Looking for a kid with a funny name, right?'

'Malo. He's my son.' I show him the phone again. 'That's him with his girlfriend. Her name's Clemenza.'

'Beautiful.' Noodle ignores the phone. 'She was beautiful.'

'Clem?'

'Yeah.'

'You met her?'

'Yeah. Your boy wanted to score. She didn't. They had a bit of a domestic. Right there on the street. Down from the Fall.'

'And who won?'

'She did. And I did, too.'

'How?'

'We had a bit of a chat. Your boy had gone. Just walked off. She wanted to know all sorts of things, that girl.'

'About?'

'Me. You get used to it after a while. You're at it, too. I'm sure you mean well, and it's nice that someone takes an interest, but . . .' He shrugs. 'You do what you do, yeah?'

You do what you do.

I want to know how the conversation with Clem ended. Did Malo come back? Did the row in the street start all over again? Did Noodle finally manage to make a sale?

'No need.'

'Why not?'

'She gave me seventy quid. Told me to keep it. When I asked why, she wouldn't say. If you want the truth, I think she was sorry for me.'

'And then you parted?'

'Yeah.'

'Just said goodbye?'

'Yeah.' He manages a smile. 'And thank you.'

He's scratching again. I suspect the tiny pebble of Bad is wearing off and it turns out I'm right. Noodle rolls over and begins to fumble around where the side of the tent meets bare pebbles. The torch reveals a small plastic sachet. The powder inside looks brown.

'Jake normally helps.' Noodle is offering me the syringe. 'D'you mind?'

I take the syringe. A smear of blood has caked on the plastic barrel. Noodle needs the light from the torch. With some care he tips some of the brown powder into the spoon, then asks me for water.

'Plastic bottle. Over your side.'

I haven't noticed the bottle before. He got it off the beach again, I think. Recycling with a twist.

Noodle asks me to pour a little of the water into the spoon. He stirs it up with his finger then begs another favour.

'The lighter?'

I'm beginning to get the picture here. I coax a flame from the lighter and hold it under the spoon until the powder has dissolved. Still holding the spoon, Noodle talks me through filling the syringe with the warm liquid. When I've finished, he abandons the spoon and asks for the syringe. Holding it up against the beam of the torch he expels the last of the air and then lays it carefully on the floor. A cheap plastic belt secures his jeans. He slips it off and then offers me a bare arm.

'Just there by the elbow,' he says. 'As tight as you like.'

I'm staring at his skinny little arm. For the first time I notice the track marks criss-crossing the paleness of the flesh. I wind the belt around his arm. Way beyond the normal line of holes, he's fashioned some more. I tighten the belt and secure it with the buckle. Very slowly, a vein begins to fatten. Noodle watches it for a moment, then reaches for the syringe.

'That's heroin? Am I right?'

'Yes.'

'To do what?'

'To take the pain away. To make me sleep. Don't go yet. Not yet, please.'

This is way beyond complicity, but I know I have to see this through to the end. In the dark, with me gone, he might miss. Or overdose. Or whatever else. His pain is everything. But just now, for the trillionth time, he knows exactly what to do.

I watch him steadying the needle against the vein, just letting it lie there. Foreplay, I think. The overture before the main event. Then he eases the needle into the vein and there's a moment's pause before his grubby little thumb settles on the plunger and the barrel of the syringe begins to empty.

Once he's done, he lies back, his good eye closing, the hint of a smile on his face. I want to cover him with blankets, but there are none. I want to read him a story, get him off to sleep, but there's no need. His breathing has slowed and he seems at peace.

The syringe still dangles from his forearm. I reach forward, remove it as gently as I can, and then unwind the belt. He doesn't react. I watch him for a moment longer before turning the torch off and backing softly out of the tent.

Darkness again, I think.

THIRTY-TWO

For a long time, I sit in my car just staring out at the blurry pools of light in the nearby docks. Once, another vehicle arrives and makes a slow circuit around the car park passing very close but I pay it no attention. What I've just seen, witnessed, is more shocking in its way than anything Wesley Kane can conjure from a kettle and a length of rope.

The guilt I felt earlier has gone. I need to study this new world of mine just the way I'd study any other script on-screen or on stage, and I hug this rationale, this excuse, tight in the awareness that it gives me comfort. I've truly no idea what happens next but I want, very badly, to get a great deal off my chest. I know exactly who's going to be on the receiving end but I know as well that I can't make the call until the start of the working day.

When I finally get back to Flixcombe, it's gone half past four in the morning. I creep upstairs to the bedroom I'm using and try to talk myself into going to sleep but my body – or more precisely my brain – isn't listening. All those little neural pathways are fizzing with names and faces and half-remembered fragments of conversation. Noodle. Danny. The Landfall. Andy. The Machine. Broken shards of the mirror that used to be rural England.

In the end I do manage to get to sleep, waking fully clothed to a tap at the door. It's Jessie. She wants to know whether I'm OK and – far more importantly – she's brought me tea. I struggle upright and take the proffered cup.

'I'm fine,' I tell her.

'Andy says it was light when you got back.'

'He's right. I'm sorry I woke him up.'

'Don't be. He's always up early.' She wants to linger. 'Get what you wanted?'

'Yes.'

'Am I being nosy?'

'Yes.' I offer her a rueful grin. 'The older I get the more life surprises me. Do you ever find that?'

'Never. In fact, quite the reverse.' She frowns. 'Should I be envious?'

'No.' I can't stop thinking of the syringe dangling from Noodle's forearm. 'Quite the reverse.'

In the end, to my relief, she leaves me in peace. According to my mobile, it's mid-morning. I finish the tea and rummage in my bag for the number of the Glasgow hospital. By now, if they haven't already shipped him south, Pavel should be in the mood for a longish conversation. I dial the main switchboard number and ask to be put through to the spinal injuries unit. After a while, a nurse answers. I recognize her voice at once. We met when I was up there.

'It's Enora,' I tell her. 'Enora Andressen. Pavel's friend.'

'Ah . . . right. I'm afraid he's asleep just now. Do you want to phone back later?'

I tell her that won't be a problem. Then I ask whether they have a date for the transfer south.

'The transfer where?'

'South.'

'Why would we do that?'

I'm staring at the phone. Something very cold is clutching at my heart. Not again. Oh, please God, not again.

'How is he?' I ask.

'Much the same, I'm afraid.'

'Still on the catheter?'

'Of course.'

'Any sign of . . .' I close my eyes. 'Is he getting any kind of feeling back? Maybe his arms? Legs? Feet?'

'Not that he's told us.'

I nod. I'm hearing everything she's telling me but I have to be certain. 'So no progress at all?'

'I'm afraid not. We were more optimistic a couple of days ago but a break that high, C4, no one should be holding their breath.'

'Is it worth me talking to the consultant?'

'Of course. Don't take any of this stuff from me.'

She advises me to phone just before lunch and gives me the number for his direct line. She also says that she can see Pavel from the nursing station and thinks he might be awake now.

'You still want to talk to him?'

'No, thanks,' I say. 'I think I'll wait.'

By the time I talk to the consultant, I've decided there's no point hiding the truth. Pavel is a fantasist. That's probably what makes him such an original talent. That's probably what's brought him the respect of pretty much everyone I know in the industry. This is the man who has pushed blindness aside and delivered scripts of rare brilliance. His dialogue, in particular, is the envy of other scriptwriters. He's learned to imagine total strangers by their speech patterns, by their little linguistic tics, by the silences they leave between words. His ears and his brain paint the pictures his eyes can't see.

'Pavel,' the consultant says. 'You're naturally after an update.'

I shake my head. I tell him no. Then I describe the news I got from Pavel himself, how much better he's feeling, how sensation has returned to most of his body, how excited he is by the prospect of a transfer south. This makes me feel worse than disloyal, and I've taken the precaution of swearing the consultant to silence on the subject, but once I've finished ratting my lovely Pavel out, the consultant tells me I've done the right thing.

'This is denial, of course. You probably don't want to hear this, but spinal patients pretending everything's going to be fine are all too common. I'm afraid the neuropathy is against Pavel. We may be able to coax a little sensation back into his hands and arms but there's absolutely no guarantee. We've done our best to explain that but you'll forgive him for choosing not to believe us.'

'I will. Of course I will. Pavel's problem is credibility. He has an amazing talent for making the most unlikely things live on the page. I shouldn't be confusing fact with fiction. I should learn from my mistakes.'

'Meaning?'

'I should make allowances. All I've got to deal with is my own gullibility. He's got to cope with a great deal more than that.'

'You're telling me he's fooled you?'

'All the time. Sometimes it matters. Sometimes it doesn't. Just now I think I need a little time to adjust.'

'You want to talk to him? Now?'

I give the proposition some thought. Then I shake my head. 'No, thanks,' I say. 'Maybe tomorrow.'

THIRTY-THREE

'm downstairs in the kitchen when I get the call. Jessie is outside with a pair of scissors raiding the herb garden for mint and rosemary. I'm looking at my smartphone. *Number withheld.*

'Hello?'

It's a woman's voice I don't recognize. Faint hint of an American accent. She asks whether I'm Enora Andressen.

'Yes,' I say. 'Who is this?'

'We need to meet. You know Lockett's Copse? Off the Beaminster road? I'm there now. As soon as you can. And don't bring anyone else.'

'I'm sorry,' I say, 'I didn't catch your name. Who are you?'

I wait for an answer but nothing happens. She's gone. I slip my phone into my jeans pocket and abandon laying the table. I've been up to Lockett's Copse with Malo. He'd discovered it on an outing with the trail bikes with Andy and he wanted to show me the view. You get there on a series of country lanes that narrow and narrow until they end in a turning circle of loose dirt and gravel. Park up, walk the fifty metres through the trees to the top of the rise, and the Flixcombe estate lies before you, stretching away towards Bridport and the sea. H loves the place. He says it makes him feel baronial.

I check my watch. It's nearly midday. We're heading for lunch and Jessie has readied a bowl of new potatoes. She's back in the kitchen with a fistful of herbs. When she checks what time I'd like to eat, I tell her I have to go out.

'Now?'

'I'm afraid so.'

'Can't it wait till after we've eaten?'

'No.'

I'm tempted to offer an explanation, not least in case I get myself into some kind of trouble, but I know this will raise too many other questions. Just now, I'm on my own.

It takes less than ten minutes to get to the copse. The weather, after weeks of Mediterranean heat, has begun to break and rags of cloud shadow the parched yellows and browns of the surrounding hills. At the end of the lane I pull on to the springy turf and park. There's no sign of any other vehicle.

I get out and stand for a moment in the fitful sunshine. Up here, just for one moment, I can taste autumn in the wind. I look round, wondering what's supposed to happen next. Will this woman be alone? Is she out there, among the trees, watching me? I wait, feeling slightly ridiculous, an actress without a script or stage directions.

When nothing happens, I start to make my way up towards the crest of the hill, under the gaze of a gaggle of crows high in a beech tree. Then, abruptly, the crows have lifted and gone and I'm aware of another figure, tall, striding down towards me. She's wearing jeans and a fleece over a collarless patterned shirt. She's dark, with an explosion of wild black curls, and the closer she gets the more certain I am that I've seen her before. Her face is unforgettable: high cheekbones, flawless olive skin, and a full mouth that curls easily into the widest smile. To my surprise, she seems pleased to see me.

'Thanks for showing up,' she says. That American accent again.

'No problem.' I gesture round. 'So what's this about?'

'It's to do with my guy.'

'Your guy?'

'His name's Brodie. You met him yesterday.'

'The swimmer? At the pool?'

'Sure. Me? I'm the messenger here. You're ready? You're listening? 'Cos sure as hell I ain't gonna say this twice.'

I can't take my eyes off her face. This has to be the woman Jessie mentioned, the woman at the pool. All the clues are there: her complexion, her beauty, her age. Brodie is a very lucky boy, I think. And I'm more certain than ever that I've seen her before.

'You're an actress,' I suggest. 'Am I right?'

Her smile fades. She has very distinctive brown eyes, the colour of amber. I take her silence for assent.

'Takes one to know one,' I say lightly. 'Where would I have seen you last?'

She won't tell me. This conversation isn't about her, she says, or even me. It's about Brodie.

'Really?'

'Yep. Here's what you need to know. You two never met, never talked. As far as you're concerned, he doesn't exist.'

'But he does. And for a drug dealer he was very helpful.'

Mention of drug-dealing draws an emphatic shake of her head. Brodie has nothing to do with drugs. Brodie is the cleanest guy she's ever met. End of. Period.

'So why is he selling?'

'It's a business thing. I'm sure that's what he told you and here's something else about the man: he never lies.'

I study her for a long moment. 'You're his agent?'

'I'm his very best friend.'

'And he's frightened I might speak out of turn?'

'Frightened isn't a word we recognize, ma'am. Brodie doesn't do fear. Never has. Never will. Brodie is ice. Brodie is a dream. We need to protect him here, you and me. Me because I take care of my men. And you because we think alike.'

'Meaning?'

'People you love? People who matter to you? No one wants them hurt. Stay cool here and no one comes to any harm.'

I'm staring at her. The menace behind the smile couldn't be any clearer. The wind is starting to ruffle that amazing hair and the dialogue belongs in a soap but I'm beginning to get the picture.

'You mean Malo? Clem?'

She nods. She's meeting my eyes without a trace of a smile. 'We agree about my Brodie?'

'Of course.'

'Good. Then everyone stays safe.' She takes a step further and – with a curious formality – extends a hand. 'I loved what you did with *Arpeggio*,' she says. 'Some of those reviewers were way out of line.'

I carry the memory of her face back to Flixcombe. By the time I'm turning in through the gates at the bottom of the drive I've realized exactly when I saw her last. One of Pavel's favourite shows is *EastEnders*, a soap he describes as bespoke drama for serial depressives. He tunes in to every episode and treats it like a series on the radio. Recently, the storyline called for an American love interest and I'm near-certain that the actress the producers brought in was Brodie's admirer.

I'm still working out the quickest way of putting a name to that remarkable face when I slow to make room for an approaching car. It turns out to be Andy. He signals for me to stop and pulls over on to the grass. Moments later, he's opened my passenger door and climbed in.

'Something to show you.' He swipes his phone screen. 'This was posted a couple of hours ago. Facebook's bound to take it down but Danny says it's gone viral already. He thought you might be interested.'

He finds the image he's after and hands me the phone. I think I'm looking at a body lit by the harshness of a flashlight. Receding into the darkness beyond, I can make out the curve of a pebble beach and on the right of the picture the dim shape of what I take to be a tent, but that's not the point. In the middle of the shot, sprawled face down on the wet pebbles, is a thin figure. Torn jeans and a scruffy grey T-shirt. Bare feet. One thin arm flung forward, fingers outstretched. The face is turned to the brightness of the light, one eye still closed, the other open but unseeing.

'You know him?'

I don't answer. Noodle, I think. Poor, broken Noodle. Danny, a couple of nights back, had warned me that one day this man would end up dead on some beach or other and here he is, the prophesy fulfilled. The shot is full of pathos and reminds me of a similar photo of a dead child on a beach on a Greek island, washed ashore after drowning at sea. The same inert accusation. *The world failed me. And look what happened.*

'Here. Take it.'

Andy has found a tissue from somewhere. I dab at my eyes. Tears, I tell myself, are the least I owe an image like this. I blow my nose. When Andy asks for the phone back I won't let him have it.

'Who took this shot?'

'I've no idea. The Facebook page was created specially. That's all I know.'

'He's dead?'

'Very.'

'Killed?'

'Danny thinks drowned. He's got a mate who's a lifeguard. He helped recover the bloke just now. They put him in a body bag and shipped him across to the harbour.'

'No injuries?'

'I've no idea. Danny didn't say.'

I nod. I'm still staring at the phone, at the face, at the patches of pale skin beneath the torn jeans. Noodle would never have gone swimming, I tell myself, not in the state I left him. Someone paid him a visit. Someone carried him out of that draughty tomb of a tent and dumped him in the sea.

'And the police?' I glance at Andy.

'They're all over it. Danny's doing a roof nearby. Turns out he's got a grandstand seat. The Bill have taped off the beach and last time we talked there were blokes on their hands and knees in grey suits crawling all over the pebbles. It's *Crimewatch*, he says. For real.'

I've seen more than my fair share of TV crime shows and I'm thinking very hard about the treasure of forensic clues I must have left last night. My fingerprints on the inhaler, on the spoon, even on the bloody syringe. Fragments of my DNA plastered over other surfaces. Not to mention the probability of CCTV at the car park. Game, set and match, I think. If they're looking for a prime suspect, it may well be me.

'You know this guy?' Andy asks again. 'Was that why you borrowed the torch last night?'

'I needed the torch to see in the dark.' I nod at the shot on the phone. 'Which has nothing to do with that.'

Andy doesn't begin to believe me. I can see it in his eyes, in the way he retrieves his phone with a tiny shrug of his shoulders, in the final backward glance he spares me as he gets into his car. But by now I don't care about Andy. What's far more important is what the contents of the new Facebook page tell me about Brodie. I was summoned to Lockett's Copse because The Machine knew only too well that the first port of call for Bridport's finest was likely to be me. And the last place he wants his name to be mentioned is in any statement that I might chose to make.

I need Pavel again. Badly. This has all the makings of a prime-time script. Am I wrong in thinking that Brodie, aka The Machine, somehow knew that I'd paid a visit to the beach last night? And that Noodle might have been a little too loose-lipped for his own good? Is that why he'd been silenced? Carried bodily out of the tent, dragged into the sea and put to death? And is that why the body on the beach is doubtless appearing on smartphones across Bridport? A terrible warning to anyone else who might step out of line?

Shit. The car park, I think. The headlights that suddenly appeared after I'd made my way back from the beach hut, after I'd abandoned Noodle to what turned out to be a death sentence. One circuit of the car park. One glimpse of the woman behind the wheel. That's all it would have taken. And after that, the boy had barely minutes left to live.

I know now what real guilt feels like. Not the shame of helping someone into a stupor but the far larger charge of ignoring the probable consequences. Stuck behind the wheel in that car park, I'd been engulfed by what I'd just witnessed. I'd let down my defences and poor Noodle had paid the price. I should have been cannier, I tell myself. I should – at the very least – have gone back and watched over him. That's what he needed. That's the least he deserved.

From nowhere comes the blast of a horn. It makes me physically jump and the moment my eyes find the rear-view mirror I realize I'm doing it again, compounding one moment of inattention with another. Behind me, filling the rear window, is the bonnet of a black Range Rover. H, I think, back from London. Perfect bloody timing.

THIRTY-FOUR

Jessie, bless her, has stayed lunch until we both turn up. H has driven down alone. Wes has taken the train back to Pompey. With Jess at the table, our conversation is limited to small talk. The iniquities of the A303. The curse of the congestion charge. How hard it is to meet anyone English in central London in high summer.

Lamb chops and new potatoes, plus a glass or two of chilled Sauvignon, give the meal an almost festive feel. We're rich. We're successful. We're living the rural dream. Only when Jessie has cleared the table and retired to the cottage do we crash land where, days ago, we were last together.

'Well?' H enquires. 'What's gone down?'

'Gone down' is a phrase I know he's picked up from Malo. I want to know where he is. I need to know what's happened to our son.

'You first,' H grunts.

I tell him everything's been fine. I've seen a bit of Jess. I've taken a stroll or two. I'm halfway through a good book. I've done a bit of shopping.

'You make it sound like a holiday.'

'Really? How about you? Last time we talked you were about to let Wes loose on Clem's front door. Any luck?'

'We got in.'

'And?'

'We had a look round, gave the place a going over. Tell me something – why do women need so many pairs of shoes? Wes counted more than seventy. That girl needs locking up.'

'Very funny. Any sign of our son there?'

'Plenty. That boy needs to learn how to wash up, make a bed and all the other stuff you should have taught him. The place was a khazi.'

I ask yet again about Malo. Was he there in person?

'Christ, no. The closest we got was the hair in the shower pan and the roaches down the side of the sofa. I'm telling you, the boy's a dosser.'

'I'm sure you're right. Was there any sign of the gun, by any chance?'

'No.'

'So where is he?'

H ignores the question. Then he tells me something I hadn't expected. Mateo, he says, has had a run-in with the K&R King.

'You mean O'Keefe?'

'Yeah. It turns out Mateo has been taking a leaf out of our book. He doesn't believe O'Keefe has a clue what he's up against and he's decided to talk to these people himself.'

'What people?'

'The jungle bunnies who lifted Clemmie.'

'And?'

'He won't tell me, not yet, but you get a nose for these things. Number one, we're definitely dealing with a bunch of Somalis, mad bastards, all of them. These guys do the heavy lifting. They're street level. They're in it for the money and the pose. A handful are down in Bridport and they work with some guy called Brodie and answer to Larry Fab. Number two, like you thought, Mr Dreadlocks is the Plug. He gets the stuff down to Brodie and Larry Fab. Sitting above Mr Dreads is the top management, probably a white guy, but Mateo thinks the Somalis have declared UDI, told the management to fuck off. This is a shop-floor rebellion. The Somalis obviously want a bigger slice of the action – more say, more dosh, more control – and though Mateo won't admit it, he thinks the key might be Clemmie. Two million US would fund a hostile takeover bid. And from where I'm sitting, that sounds more than plausible.'

'You're telling me that Mateo is talking to these people? These Somali kids?'

'One way or the other, yes. Either the Somalis or Mr Dreads, or the top management. My guess is that Mateo has walked into the jungle here. Major turf war. No one really in charge. None of this will be easy. Texts? Phone calls? Face-to-face? I've no fucking idea but Mateo's certainly an improvement on the K&R King.'

'You think Mateo's in some kind of negotiation?'

'Yeah.'

'And he'll pay the money?'

H doesn't answer. There's someone knocking at the front door. With Jessie gone, he gets up to investigate. I'm still sitting at the table, nursing the last of my wine, listening to the rap-rap of his heels on the polished marble floor. After he opens the door, I hear a murmured conversation. Then he's back in the kitchen with two strangers in tow. Both of them are uniformed.

'Filth,' H grunts. 'Asking for you.'

I've never been arrested in my life, nor taken into custody, though I've played this scene on a number of occasions. On-screen, it often calls for panic, hysteria and occasionally physical violence, roughly in that order, but I'm surprised to find that the real thing is a great deal more civilized. The sergeant in charge is polite, even solicitous. He asks for ID, checks that I have no one vulnerable to look after, and then invites me to accompany him and his fellow officer to Bridport police station where detectives are waiting to interview me.

'In connection with what?' H has been listening.

'A young man has been found dead, sir. This morning. We think Ms Andressen might be able to help with our enquiries.'

'Yeah?' H is looking at me.

I shrug. Short of making a scene there's very little I can do. I try to step towards the hall but H is standing in my way. 'So what's this about?' His face is inches from mine.

'I've no idea.'

'You need a proper brief. Say nothing. I'll bell Tony, right?'

Tony Morse is H's favourite lawyer, a suave Pompey veteran whom I met when H threw the party for Malo. According to H, Tony always does the business. He has immense presence both inside and outside the courtroom and I certainly felt a little of that when we shared a midnight conversation at the party last year.

'Fine,' I say. 'I'll wait for Tony.'

We drive to Bridport. Twice I ask why I've been detained like this but conversation is limited to the weather and the policing challenges of the imminent Bridport Food Festival. I find it difficult to envisage a public order breakdown over fresh tomato salsa and portions of apple spelt and say so. This makes the uniformed sergeant laugh, which I find oddly comforting.

At the police station, I'm booked in by someone called the

custody sergeant. I don't much like the first word in his job description but I give him my full details and hand over the contents of my bag. A female officer appears and shepherds me to a nearby suite where she takes a DNA swab from my mouth. Watching her bag and label it, I can think of nothing but the moment Noodle slipped the needle of the syringe into his broken vein. Bits of me were all over that syringe. The match will be perfect.

'We need photographs. Over here, please.'

I follow the PC to a neighbouring wall and stand immobile while she prepares to take the shots. I've done camera tests all my life but this is very different. Unhappy with the first results, she asks me to keep my mouth shut while she takes another set.

'It's just like a passport shot,' she says. 'Try not to smile.'

As if, I think. A pair of swing doors takes us to a corridor and an office at the end where I meet a middle-aged man sitting in his shirt sleeves at a bare desk. He has a brutal haircut and the kind of tan that sailors get, and when we walk in he's studying the contents of a thin file.

He introduces himself as DC Chaulk. When I raise the issue of legal representation he immediately offers me the services of the duty solicitor. I decline as gracefully as I can and say I prefer Tony Morse.

'Where do we find him?'

'Portsmouth, as far as I know.'

'And he'll attend?'

'Of course. I'm sure he'll be delighted.'

The detective checks his watch. Even with what he calls 'a following wind', waiting for Mr Morse could cost us at least three hours. This, he implies, would be less than helpful in the current circumstances.

'No one's told me what I'm doing here,' I say. 'Might that be a good place to start?'

He shoots me a look. I'm doing my best to be polite and low-key, something that seems to irritate him even further.

'A body was found on the beach down at West Bay,' he says. 'A young lad already known to us. I'm afraid I can't give you any more details at the moment. You have a number for Mr Morse?'

As it turns out, H has already made contact with Tony. He's abandoned an afternoon with his kids and he's now en route down from Pompey. He arrives a minute or two before six o'clock, by which time I've read two editions of *Dorset Life*. Twice.

Tony has been assigned to a small, bare office reserved for defence solicitors to conference with their clients. He's beautifully dressed – exquisite suit, plus a mane of greying hair – and he smells divine. He gives me a long hug, which is nice, and asks me how I'm bearing up.

'I'm fine,' I say. 'Better than that poor lad on the beach.'

Tony has already got the bones of the story from the detective inspector leading the investigation. Young junkie. Local lad. No signs of physical violence apart from facial bruising, which may turn out to be days old. Exact cause of death yet to be determined by a post-mortem but currently assumed to be drowning.

'So where's the crime?' I ask.

'Very good question. For the time being they're treating it as a suss death and that's because they have to.'

'Suss?'

'Suspicious. With respect to your lovely self, they want to know what you were doing in a nearby car park in the middle of the night, and what the forensics might tell them once they've finished with the scene.'

'Scene?'

'A tent on the beach where they assume the boy was kipping.' He smiles at me. 'Any thoughts?'

I've been anticipating this question for the last three hours. I'm unschooled in exactly how much trust you should vest in your defending solicitor, especially when he's become a friend. How much has H told him about the last week or so? Has he even mentioned Clem?

'I've been worried about Malo,' I say carefully. 'I think he's been doing drugs again.'

'Again?'

'He had a Spice habit when he came back from Stockholm last year. It was horrible.'

'And now?'

'We think cocaine. I'm assuming he buys the stuff down here because he lives nearby. These last few days I've been asking around because that's what mums do. If you want the posh word, I've been on a bit of a journey.'

I tell him about the Landfall, about Danny Flannery, and about Wes kettling Dooley. The latter comes as no surprise to Tony, who's known Wes for years, but I appreciate his concern on my part.

'The man can be an animal,' he says. 'And that's on a good day. What else have you got for me?'

I tell him nothing about my expedition to the swimming pool and the conversation with Brodie that followed. Neither do I trouble him with this morning's encounter at Lockett's Copse.

'So where's Malo in all this?'

'I've no idea. He seems to have disappeared.'

'*Disappeared?*'

'Yes.'

'But you've put it to him, surely, about the cocaine?'

'Of course.'

'And?'

'He denies everything. He's all over the place. His brain's gone, and now him with it. A lot of this stuff I try and keep from H. It just upsets him.'

Tony nods. He's produced a rather elegant notebook, embossed black leather, and he scribbles himself a line or two before looking up.

'And the boy on the beach?'

So far, I only know him as Noodle. His real name, according to Tony, is Bradley Sawyer. I explain again about Danny Flannery. He was the one who told me about the tent.

'The kid lives there?'

'Most of the time, yes.'

'And you're telling me you were with him? Last night?'

'I was.'

Tony pulls a face. He doesn't want to hear this. 'Why?' he asks. 'Why do a thing like that?'

I do my best to offer a coherent explanation. I badly needed to join up all my Bridport dots and I thought Noodle might be the one to help me.

'And was he?'

'Yes, in a way he was. He'd met Malo. I showed him a photo. He remembered the face.'

'And he sold to Malo?'

'Yes.'

'Cocaine?'

'Yes.'

Tony scribbles another note. Then he wants to go back to last night. I paid my son's dealer a visit. Then what happened?

'There was another man there. He was off the moment the torch woke him up. Noodle was out of it.'

I describe exactly what happened. I have Tony's full attention.

'You helped him smoke crack?'

'I did.'

'And you were there when he shot up afterwards?'

'I was. He needed help again. The state of the boy . . .' I shake my head.

'But why? Why did you get so involved?'

'Because I felt sorry for him. Maybe I shouldn't have done what I did. Maybe I shouldn't have been there at all. Maybe I'm just soft in the head. Does the law allow for that? For trying to *help*?'

For the first time I recognize a flicker of anger deep in my soul. For the life of me, I can't work out what I've done wrong.

'The lad's dead,' Tony points out.

'And you think I did that?'

'No, that's not what I'm saying, but you may have been the last person to see him alive, and that marks any detective's card.'

'You think he committed suicide? Just walked into the ocean and filled his lungs?'

'I'm suggesting nothing. I'm doing what the police are doing. I'm marshalling the facts into the likeliest order and wondering what they tell me. There's CCTV proof you were in the car park. The footage has you away from the car for nearly an hour. They're boshing the scene as we speak. The forensics will put you in that tent. By your own account you were playing nurse. That's where the interview will take them. As long as you stick to this story of yours.'

'You believe me? Or you think I'm making it up?'

'I believe you. I believe what you've told me. It won't be the whole truth because everyone always keeps a little something back but that needn't trouble us for the time being. No . . .' He pushes his notebook away and leans back in the chair. 'It's nice.

It's neat. It's tidy. It paints you in a good light. You're looking out for your son. And you're playing mum with Mr Noodle, as well. Let's just hope they don't find anything embarrassing back home.'

'At Flixcombe, you mean?'

'Yes. They're doing the full search as we speak and my guess is they'll bosh the cars as well. Some people would say they're being over the top, even vindictive, and I'd be tempted to agree. From time to time they get the urge to send everyone a message and this might be one of those occasions.'

A full search of Flixcombe Manor? Looking for the white powder floor by floor? Room by room? I'm appalled by the chaos I've unleashed.

'And H?' I enquire.

Tony studies me for a moment. That same pained expression. 'Pissed-off won't cover it.' He smiles. 'I'd suggest incandescent.'

THIRTY-FIVE

Tony sits beside me as the interview begins. DC Chaulk has been joined by a younger female detective he introduces as DC Carrie Martin. Carrie has an innocence about her that reminds me slightly of Clem. She's a good-looking girl with a neat blonde crop and the subtlest line of mascara under her eyes. She's wearing a low-neck black T-shirt under a two-piece suit and has a habit of studying her perfect nails while DC Chaulk makes the running. In any other setting I'd put her down as a bit of an adornment. This proves to be a woeful miscalculation.

Chaulk starts the recording machine, announces the date and time, and repeats the caution under which I was arrested. He then introduces the faces around the table and asks for a full account of my movements last night. I oblige as best I can, aware of Carrie Martin making notes as I speak. Only when I crawl into the tent, disturbing the other figure inside, does her biro pause.

'You saw this man?' she asks.

'Not really.'

'So how do you know it was a man?'

'He needed a shave.'

'Can you describe him? Age, for instance?'

'I'd be guessing.' I frown. I'm thinking of my brief glimpse of the two figures intertwined. 'Young, probably. Maybe Noodle's age.'

'You mean Bradley Sawyer?'

'I mean Noodle.'

She nods, says nothing, ducks her head, makes another note. Chaulk tells me to carry on. I describe what happened between myself and Noodle. This episode ends with the boy unconscious again, a beatific smile on his face, a thin trickle of blood seeping from the puncture wound in his skinny forearm.

'And that's it?' Chaulk hasn't taken his eyes off me.

'That's it. I went back to the car park. The rest you know.'

Chaulk glances sideways at Carrie. This appears to be some kind of invitation. Get in there and help yourself.

Carrie studies me for a moment or two. Her gaze is unblinking. I was wrong about her innocence.

'You went there to score drugs, didn't you?' she says.

'No, I didn't.'

'Then what were you after?'

'I've just told you. Nothing.'

'Then why bother the lad? At that time of night?'

I start to explain about Malo, my wayward son, and my journey through the netherworld of Bridport, but then I feel the lightest pressure on my forearm. It's Tony. He wants me to stop.

'This line of questioning is oppressive,' he says to DC Chaulk. 'You asked for an open account. That's exactly what you've got. I suggest my client has nothing to add. When she left that tent, Mr Sawyer was alive. That's all you need to know.'

Chaulk mumbles something about these being early days in the investigation and the importance of keeping an open mind but Carrie hasn't finished. She produces a laptop from a bag beside her chair and makes an announcement for the benefit of the recording machine.

'19.47,' she says. 'DC Martin introduces CCTV evidence.'

She opens the laptop. A couple of keystrokes take her to a video file. Then she angles the screen so we can all take a look. Both Tony and I lean forward. I'm expecting to see a well-lit car park in the middle of the night. Instead, I'm gazing at the interior of a crowded pub. It's the Landfall. I recognize the jukebox in the corner. Already highlighted is a middle-aged woman standing beside the bar. She's wearing a red beret and she has a roll of notes in her hand.

Carrie is watching me carefully. 'Would that be you?' she asks.

'It would.'

'We've done some work around that hand of yours, blown up the image. We estimate around two hundred pounds. Would that be fair?'

'Yes,' I agree. 'It would.'

'So what are you doing in a pub like that with two hundred quid? Everyone knows that's where you go to score. You were buying, weren't you?'

'Yes.' I nod. 'Three glasses of something red for the lads you can see beside me.' I nod at the screen. 'That's the barman who served me a minute or so earlier. I'm sure it's all there in the footage.'

'Twenty quid? Twenty-five? What about the rest? What did that get you? Cocaine, was it? Smack? A meet round the corner when you left the pub? Cut us just a bit of slack, Ms Andressen. Pretend we're not quite as thick as everyone thinks we are.'

'I went in there to try and find out about my son.'

'This is Malo? The boy you mentioned to Sawyer?'

'Yes.'

'And what did these youths at the bar tell you, Ms Andressen?' Chaulk this time.

'Not much. I suspect they'll tell you anything if you're buying the drinks.'

'So it was a waste of money? Is that what you're saying?'

'I'm saying that I came down to the pub that night to ask some questions, to make some enquiries. In the end those enquiries led to Noodle. There's a man you'll see in that footage. He's got a leather jacket. He takes me out of the pub. Afterwards we talked and he mentioned someone called Noodle, someone who sold drugs, and he told me where this character often spent the night.'

'So you went to find him?' Carrie Martin again.

'Yes.'

'Last night?'

'Yes.'

'To buy drugs?'

'I couldn't. I had no money on me.'

'Then maybe it was a barter deal. Some of the guys on the street love that. In fact, they prefer it to money.'

'Barter what?' I'm staring at her.

'Sex. A blow job, was it? Or the main course?'

I'm staring at her. I want to tell her to wash her mouth out, to have just an ounce of respect. Is she serious? Or is she simply trying to shock me into some indiscretion or other, some tiny mistake that will, under pressure, bring my little house crashing down?

Tony is lodging another protest. DC Martin's line of questioning, he tells Chaulk, is misconceived, deeply offensive and entirely inappropriate. Her suggestion that his client would be offering sexual favours in exchange for drugs she never uses is frankly grotesque. He condemns the interview as a fishing expedition. Unless the line of questioning changes tack, he will counsel his client to keep her silence. In other words, go 'no comment'.

Chaulk shrugs. 'That's your right, Ms Andressen,' he says. 'A court of law, of course, would draw its own conclusions.'

Court of law? I blink. This is getting out of control. My eyes return to the laptop. If only I'd never gone to the bloody Landfall in the first place. If only, as my neighbour Evelyn might say, I'd stuck to my knitting, concentrated on my career, crossed my fingers for the next brain scan and got on with real life. Malo has a great deal to answer for.

'Is this your son, Ms Andressen?' DC Chaulk has accessed another file on the laptop. I'm looking at Malo, head and shoulders, photographed against a plain white wall I recognize only too well.

'You've arrested him?' I can't believe it.

'This is a couple of months back. He was arrested by our colleagues in Reading at a gig for possession of cannabis. He was lucky. He got off with a caution.'

I nod. I'm numb. Malo never said a word. DC Martin wants to know more about my son.

'You say you've been trying to find him. Am I right?'

'Yes.'

'But that makes him a missing person, does it not?'

'Yes.'

'Then why haven't you reported it? We call these people mispers. We take them very seriously. You don't just mislay people, not if you love them, not if they're close to you, not if they're your son or daughter.' She pauses. 'Do you have any comment to make?'

I have a great deal to get off my chest. I was foolish enough to walk into this airless little office in the expectation that I'd be treated with just a modicum of respect. Instead, in short order, I've been accused first of prostitution and now of parental neglect. I'm about to tell this woman exactly what it feels like to lose a son and a possible daughter-in-law to a bunch of marauding Somali gangsters when Tony, once again, steps in.

He's asking for a pause in proceedings. He needs a moment or

two in private with his client. Chaulk's finger hovers over the stop
button on the recording machine. He announces a brief adjourn-
ment. Then, after an exchange of glances, he and Carrie Martin
get to their feet. Tony watches them leave the interview room. The
moment the door closes, I realize just how angry he is.

'This is a car crash,' he says. 'What are you holding back?
What haven't you told me?'

'Is it that obvious?'

'I'm afraid so. You're supposed to be an actress, for fuck's sake.
If this was an audition, it wouldn't matter, but that woman is
walking all over you. She knows you're hiding something, which
is why she's being so fucking unpleasant. Do us a favour here . . .
just give me a clue?'

I sit down. I don't know what to say. This isn't good.

'Well?' Tony is tapping his watch.

'H never told you?'

'Told me what?'

'Told you about Clem?'

'Clem? Never heard of her.'

'She's Malo's girlfriend. And about a week ago she got
kidnapped.'

'*Kidnapped?* You're serious?'

'I am.'

'And the police? Do they know?'

'No.' I shake my head. 'I'm afraid they don't.'

THIRTY-SIX

T ony insists I go 'no comment' for the rest of the interview.
He plainly doesn't trust me at the hands of these professionals and as the two detectives begin to crowd me across
the desk, pecking away at this story of mine, I find a strange
sense of satisfaction in parrying their every question with the
same response.

I know, in Tony's eyes, that I have a great deal of ground to
make up, and as the interview gets longer and more disjointed I
begin to toy with differences of inflection. In response to some
questions, the most innocuous, I'm downcast and a little *sotto
voce*. 'No comment,' I murmur. To others, when Carrie Martin is
being especially aggressive, I play it full-on, max *allegretto*, an
up-beat, almost joyful 'No comment' that I know gets under her
skin. This little phrase, my own solicitor once told me, is a killer
in any conversation and so it proves.

DC Chaulk ends the interview at just gone ten o'clock and
retires to conference with the detective inspector in charge of the
investigation. The conversation evidently takes far longer than
it should, which is not, in Tony's view, a good sign. DC Chaulk
returns to the interview room and then walks me down to the
custody sergeant. I'm not, as yet, to be formally charged with
the preparation of a controlled drug for injection but the detective inspector, an officer we now call the SIO, is insisting on police
bail, which apparently means I must resign myself to an eternity
of reporting regularly to this same police station in a bid to stop
me fleeing the country.

It's gone midnight. We're in Tony's BMW, driving back to
Flixcombe. Lost in a thicket of legal terms I don't begin to understand, I'm trying to guess what might happen next.

'They'll carry on looking.' Tony has succumbed to a small, thin
cigar. 'They have confession evidence that you helped our little
friend with crack cocaine and then heroin, but they think there's

more in your pot. Had they charged you, they couldn't put any more questions. Doing it this way, they can.'

'More interviews?'

'Very possibly. It depends. The one thing in our favour is that the men in blue are running on empty. Their budgets have been slashed and slashed and we should know how that feels because the Home Office has done the same to us. Johnny Plod has run out of budget. He's very thin on the ground. People are beginning to notice and that makes them very nervous. The county lines thing is the perfect storm. It's where the rubber no longer meets the road. The truth is that the police have lost it, lost the battle on the streets, but you're high profile. If they can get a headline or two out of you, so much the better. Sadly that's not in our favour. If they can put you in court, they will.'

I nod. I think I'm following the logic here. 'And if that happens? If they charge me? Drag me in front of a magistrate? A jury? What then?'

'Don't ask.'

'But I just did.'

Tony nods. I sense he's trying to protect me but just now I'd like him to be frank.

I reach across and put a hand on his thigh. 'Just tell me,' I say.

'OK.' He nods, then expels a thin plume of blue smoke. 'Crack cocaine? Smack? Both Class A substances? Possession – you're looking at up to seven years. Supply and production? Life. There's something else, too. They'll do a PM.'

'PM?'

'Post-mortem. If the tox says paralysis due to Class A ingestion they'll arrest you again.'

'What for?'

'Manslaughter.'

Manslaughter? A life sentence for supply? Christ. It isn't Noodle who's died, it's me. Tony has been quick to qualify the sentencing tariffs with all kinds of extenuating circumstances but he doesn't hide the seriousness of the situation I've made for myself. In all kinds of ways, he repeats, I couldn't have chosen a worse moment to put my fading celebrity on the line. No matter how genuine my motives might have been in that sad little tent, I'm offering the media and the politicians a loaded gun. *Actress in drug-death mystery. Murder or assisted suicide?* The headlines write themselves.

H, to my huge relief, offers nothing but sympathy. Jessie opens the door to Tony's knock and H is waiting up for our return in the library. Sprawled in his favourite armchair, a huge balloon of brandy at his elbow, he struggles to his feet and puts his arms around me. Two search teams have spent most of the afternoon and the evening going through the house. Both cars, his and mine, have been taken away for detailed examination. But so far, he says, the Filth have come up with nothing and far more importantly he knows they never will.

'All that white powder bollocks is history as far as I'm concerned,' he tells me. 'It did us very nicely back in the day but enough is enough. Thank fuck for booze.'

He sends Jessie out to the kitchen for more glasses and then pours huge measures of Armagnac for us all. Andy, Jess confirms, has buried a week's supply of weed where no one will ever find it. H proposes the usual toast – death to the Filth – and we all settle down. I'm waiting for Tony to break the news about the charge I may well be facing. So far he hasn't said a word but H is watching him closely. The two of them, to my knowledge, go back decades. Tony Morse is one of the few people H will ever listen to.

'Well?' This from H.

Tony does more than justice to the evening's developments. Yours truly, in his view, has done something very bold and very silly. He's full of admiration for my motherly instincts but he fears they're wasted on the men in blue. Last night has left me a sitting duck for the guys in power trying to protect their arse. If I go down for drugs offences, or for complicity in someone's death, then it will buy the chief constables and the senior honchos in the Home Office just an ounce of self-respect because a sentence like that, widely reported, will be proof that the battle for the streets, and for the nation's kids, isn't quite lost.

I smile, then get up and take a bow. 'Not my finest hour,' I murmur, *'mais je ne regrette rien.'*

Tony supplies the translation. H applauds. He tells me he's proud of me. Paying a couple of junkies a visit at one in the morning isn't something any man would do lightly, let alone a woman. It's just a shame, he said, to waste all this effort on someone like Malo.

'You've talked to him?'

'He's upstairs.'

'*Upstairs?*'

'Yeah. The boy came crawling back this evening. Brassic. We had a little chat.'

'About Clem? He told you what he's been up to?'

'No. He still won't budge.'

'And the gun? He's still got it?'

'Yeah. I took it off him. His gangster days are fucking over. There's something else you should know.'

'What?'

'It turns out the trip to Lyon to see the French guys was a car crash. They're not interested any more. He would have told me earlier but he said he was frightened.'

'Of what?'

'Me.' H shrugs. 'He'll be fine by tomorrow. Once he starts growing up.'

My temptation is to head for the door, run up to Malo's little suite of rooms and check he's still intact, but I manage to resist it. Tony wants to know about Clem.

'You've told him about Clemmie?' H is staring at me.

Tony intervenes. 'She had no choice,' he tells H. 'You never send a soldier into battle without bullets. This was worse. Enora was being torn apart by a very clever detective. This woman knew she was looking at the mother lode but couldn't work out what it contained. Enora was on the verge of coughing the lot but I managed to call a break. After that, I could load my gun and see them off.'

'She went no comment?'

'She did. But no thanks to you, my friend. Manslaughter isn't something we should take lightly. The Class A tariff is a nightmare. Pervert the course of justice and you could be looking at something even worse.'

'You think that's what we're doing?'

'Not me. Them. Kidnap's up there with homicide and arson. If you're going to get this Clem lady back it needs to be done quickly.'

'Else?'

'They'll build the case against Enora and take her to court. Clem home safe and sound will be the sweetest mitigation ever.' Tony's hand settles on mine as he turns to look at me. 'You were out of your head with worry. You put yourself in harm's way to get her back. The video's already out there. We've seen it. The pub? The bloody car park? The tent? The kid's body on the beach? Play it right and it could be the movie of your dreams.'

H is grinning. Jessie, too. Looking at Tony, I'm full of admiration. A speech like that in court would play very nicely indeed. Only one problem, I think.

Clem.

THIRTY-SEVEN

It's Tuesday, more than a week beyond the ransom deadline, and breakfast at Flixcombe Manor quickly develops into a council of war. Tony has already made a call to his office back in Pompey and rearranged his diary. One of the other partners, he says, will cover him in the magistrates' court and he can catch up with everything else later. Watching him watching H, I sense he doesn't entirely trust either us or our judgement and on the evidence of the last few days, I don't blame him.

Jessie is ferrying plates of eggs and bacon to the table. She brings a moment of light relief when she describes a member of yesterday's search team finding a stash of spent ammunition in the barn. H, she said, blamed an infestation of killer hamsters and when that didn't raise a laugh he changed his plea to rats.

'They're still trying to work it out,' H grunts. 'Never waste a joke on the Filth.'

This happens to be the moment when Malo joins us in the kitchen. He looks terrible and when I cross the room and offer a hug, he backs away. Jess's suggestion of scrambled egg on toast draws a shake of the head. He says he feels like shit. He'd spent his last few quid on tablets that were meant to help him sleep but they haven't worked. All he wants is to close his eyes and find Clem in the bed upstairs. It's a pathetic little speech, delivered in a toneless mumble, and does him no justice. H doesn't even spare him a glance. That bad.

Malo's gone and Tony wants to know the plan. All eyes turn to H. He's looking at Tony.

'So we don't go to the police, right?'

'Right. And I'm not part of this. I never knew.'

'You never did. That happens to be true. Because I never fucking told you.'

'Good. But this has to be quick. Speed matters. So where do you think she is?'

This is the killer question and H knows it. In every conversation he has to be top dog. He has to wee on every lamp post. He has to own everything, know everything. But on this occasion he's clueless. Literally.

'London,' he says. 'It has to be London.'

Tony is underwhelmed and it shows. London, he points out, is a big place. Just where might H start?

H says he has an address for the Somalis. He and Wes went there only a couple of nights ago. This is the doss in Brixton where Malo paid a visit. The address Larry Fab gave them.

'And?'

'They saw us off. Big time.'

'How?'

'We talked our way in. That wasn't a problem. The smell, *stench*, was unbelievable. Mr Dreads was there and we were trying to have a quiet word but then a huge Somali guy off his head on fuck knows what arrives. Just appears from nowhere. Naked apart from a pair of kecks. With a *machete*? And the animals behind him? Working out which bits of us to eat first? You have to be joking. There are times and places and that wasn't one of them.'

'You left?'

'We did. Even Wes was glad to be out of there. And for the record, I'm thinking Mateo is right. You don't mess with these guys. They think the world's there for the taking and I can't see anyone stopping them. That's why the Somalis make such great pirates. They never know their place.'

I can sense a sneaking admiration in H's voice and Tony's caught it, too. It's not just O'Keefe who's been overtaken by the giddy pace of change in the criminal *milieu*. It's H, as well.

'You think Clem might have been in that house? Flat? Whatever it was?' I ask H.

'I've no idea. But Mateo's certain they're the key.'

I explain Mateo to Tony Morse. Clem's dad. Very big interests in Bogotá. Currently camping in a squillion-pound-a-month rental in Eaton Square. Very civilized and probably very clever.

H smiles. 'Top bloke,' he says.

Tony's nodding. I get the feeling he's glimpsed a flicker of light in the darkness. Someone sane. Someone wealthy. Someone with the biggest stake of all in his daughter's safe return. The only problem is that Mateo, as H readily admits, is a bit of a loner. H is looking at me. It's my liberty potentially at stake here and he needs to know how to bring this affair to a happy end without months of negotiation.

I'm thinking hard about the woman I met yesterday, the figure who ghosted out of the trees at Lockett's Copse and warned me off any mistake on my part that might implicate The Machine. Last night, I made sure Brodie's name never surfaced, not once, and in that one single instance I played a blinder and kept my word. The Machine will probably know that, because no one's come knocking at his door.

An actress, I think. Who recently guested on *EastEnders*.

'Give me ten minutes.' I'm looking at H. 'Then I'll be back.'

I phone my agent, Rosa, from the privacy of my bedroom. Her assistant, Fran, says she's really busy with the accountant but I manage to get her to put me through.

'Bloody VAT,' Rosa says at once. 'Who needs it?'

I tell her I'm after a name and ideally an address. Failing that, getting to this woman's agent might be useful.

'What woman?'

I give Rosa the clues, which I admit are sparse. Mention of her height and her colour and above all her hair, coupled with her recent outing in *EastEnders*, trigger a memory or two. Rosa has never met this woman herself but she knows who to call.

'Very bad girl,' she laughs. 'If you were married you'd never let her past the gate. If I've got the right woman, men who should know better can't keep their hands off her.'

This sounds not just promising but slightly ironic. According to Jessie, it's The Machine who gets molested.

'You'll phone me back?'

'I will, precious. You're sounding, if I may say so, slightly anxious. Is everything OK?'

'No, far from it.'

I know Rosa thrives on gossip and would like nothing better than a longer break from the VAT return but when she gently presses me for more details I ask her to be patient.

'One day I'll tell you everything,' I promise, 'but just now it's bloody impossible. The woman's name, please. Quick as you can.'

She phones back within the hour. I'm at the sink with Jessie in the kitchen, half-listening to H earbashing Tony Morse. He thinks it's time Malo got a grip on himself. He's given the boy lots of opportunities and most of the time he's more than risen to the challenge. Lately, though, he's gone back to being a moody adolescent and H has had enough.

Now H is wondering whether a spell of work experience with Tony's lot might do the trick. Tony spends most of his professional life dealing with the wreckage of Pompey's underclass – feral kids who have fallen through every conceivable safety net – and maybe Malo needs to see what happens when lives come off the rails. It needn't cost Tony a cent. H, as Dad, will foot the bills. Just tie the boy down. And show him a bit of real life.

Tony is non-committal and I don't blame him. He's suggesting that Malo might benefit from a spell with one of the Third World charities when my phone rings. I dry my hands. Rosa, I think.

'Ready, precious? Got a pen there?'

Tony produces a sleek Montblanc ballpoint. I borrow H's copy of the *Daily Mail*. It's open at one of the sports pages at the back. In the space above a piece predicting Mourinho's downfall at Old Trafford, I write a name. *Baptiste Woodruffe*. I stare at it a moment, then check with Rosa that I've got it right. This is really what the woman calls herself?

'This week, precious? For sure. That's what I'm told. My source is impeccable and you're going to owe her a very large drink because there's more.'

She gives me a mobile number. I want to know where she lives.

'I gather that depends.'

'On what?'

'On her private life. There's lots of it, lots and lots. Just now she's spending time in the West Country but my lovely friend says she's also got a place in town. You want to hear something really funny? She spent three days on the *EastEnders* set and caused such chaos they had to write her out after her first appearance. That set is a boot camp. They don't put up with any nonsense. The lovely Baptiste? She trampled them underfoot. Good luck, precious. Take care.'

About to ring off, she tells me that my interview with the French producers in Paris has been postponed a couple of weeks. Their fault, not ours. *No problema.* Then she's gone.

H and Tony have been watching me on the phone. H wants to know what's going on. I tell him I've been talking to my agent. He taps the name I've carefully written on his newspaper.

'*Baptiste Woodruffe?*' he says. 'This is some kind of movie?'

'Yes.' I offer him a smile. Lying's becoming a way of life. 'They're in pre-production at the moment. Rosa thinks there might be a role for me. I've got to phone the casting director, have a chat, find out more.'

H nods. His eye returns to the paper and he carefully tears off the top strip where I've made my notes.

'Great title.' He gives me the curl of newsprint. 'Can't fail.'

THIRTY-EIGHT

t's mid-morning before I get the chance to make the call. The
number rings and rings until finally someone picks up. To my
surprise, it's a male voice. Definitely not The Machine. Much older.
I ask to talk to Baptiste.

'Who is this?'

'My name's Enora. Enora Andressen.'

'Can I tell her what it's about?'

'I'm afraid not. It's personal.'

There's a beat or two of silence. Then I hear a mumbled conversation in the background before I have another voice in my ear.
This is very definitely the woman I met at the top of the hill. The
same slightly breathless American inflection. The same playful
determination to get to the point.

'Hi,' she says. 'So how come you know my name?'

I say nothing. She must be walking now. I can hear the *clack-
clack* of heels on a solid floor. Somewhere big, I think. Somewhere
full of echoes. I catch a door closing.

'I asked you a question, right?' She sounds slightly out of breath.

'You did. I saw you in *EastEnders*. The iPlayer's wonderful.
Second time round you were still great.'

'Well, thank you.'

'My pleasure. You're OK to talk?'

'Go ahead.'

'I've been interviewed by the police. You probably know that.
Their idea, not mine.'

'Right.'

'You want to know any more?'

'Sure we do.'

I smile. *We*, not *I*. 'He's there? Your Brodie?'

'No.'

'But you're still in touch?'

'Of course.'

'Then tell him I said nothing. Absolutely nothing.'

'And the police? Did they mention him at all? We need to know.'

'His name never came up. Not from my point of view and not from theirs.'

'This was a long conversation?'

'Three hours.'

'You're kidding me.'

'I'm not. I'm on police bail at the moment but my solicitor is telling me to expect arrest and a charge.'

'For what?'

'We're talking Class A drugs and a body on the beach at West Bay. At some point, probably very soon, I'm going to be re-interviewed but you might tell Brodie I had nothing to do with that boy's death. I expect you can work the rest out.'

'I can?' She laughs. 'I'll take that as a compliment.'

'You're very welcome. Might I ask a favour?'

'Sure.'

'Tell your Brodie he owes me. I'd appreciate another meeting. This number will find me day and night. You might tell him something else, too. Time waits for no man, least of all him.'

I end the conversation at this point without saying goodbye. I hope I've seeded enough clues for Jessie's favourite swimmer to work out that it might be in his interests for us to have another conversation. So far I've kept my word to Brodie but if Tony is right and I'm looking at a lengthy prison sentence then all bets might be off.

I wait in vain for a call back, doing what I can to help Jessie around the house. After a couple of hours, when nothing happens, I go upstairs. Malo is lying fully clothed on his bed, pretending to be asleep. I know he's pretending because he's inherited none of my acting skills and hopelessly overdoes everything he associates with having a nap. The breathing is far too deep, his head is far too immobile, and he foolishly indulges in stagey little add-ons like a faux twitch under his left eye.

'Malo . . .' I settle on the bed. 'Are you in there? Are you listening?'

He tries to bluff me for a couple of seconds longer and then gives up. The left eye opens.

'Yeah?' he mumbles. 'What is it?'

I ask how he is. He says he's OK. He's not up for any kind of conversation and it's obvious he wants me gone. This suits me just fine.

'I'm after a favour,' I say. 'Just one. I'm thinking you'll have Mateo's phone number. I seem to have lost it.'

'Why do you want it?' H's son, I think. Trust nobody, least of all your own mother.

'I need to give him a ring. There's something he might be able to help me with.'

'Is it to do with Clem?'

'Not really.'

'*Not really?* What's that supposed to mean?'

'It means that it's personal. I know this might be hard to believe that it has nothing to do with you.'

Malo nods, reaches for his mobile. He scrolls through his directory and finds Mateo's name.

'I'll send you a text,' he says.

'Fine.' I'm still beside him on the bed. 'Do it now.'

I mean to phone Mateo once I'm back downstairs but Tony Morse is about to leave for Pompey. He's already said his goodbyes to H and now it's my turn. On the asphalt circle in front of the house, he gives me a kiss on the lips and another long hug and then writes his personal mobile number on the back of his business card in case I need his services again.

'You really think that'll be necessary?'

'Yes, I'm afraid I do.'

'And you don't mind?'

On the point of opening his car door, he pauses. 'Is that a serious question?'

'It is.'

'I see,' he frowns. 'Two hours on the road? Crap plod coffee? That nice DC Martin?' He smiles up at me. 'Bring it on.'

I watch him make himself comfortable in the BMW and then head for the long curve of drive that will take him down to the main gate. Back in the day, according to H, he'd burned through a series of sports cars the way he'd exhausted a series of wives. Only after his third divorce had nearly cleaned him out had he taken a vow of chastity and acquired a second-hand BMW saloon.

Nice man, I think. And, despite his best efforts, still very much in the game.

H is down in the barn with Andy. Last night's rain has gone and there's a freshness in the wind that hints of early autumn. The sun is out again and I walk across to the orchard where Andy has recently installed a wooden bench. The bench is new and a plaque on the back records the passing of Jessie's all-time favourite dog, a hyperactive Jack Russell with absolutely no social skills. For reasons I never understood, the dog was called Emmet and spent most of its life terrorizing the local cat population. H adored it and insisted on paying for both the bench and the plaque. You're getting soft in the head, I told him when I found out. And that's nice.

Mateo answers my call on the second ring. He says he's pleased to hear from me again. When I ask how he and his family are coping, he admits it's especially hard on his wife. She and Clemenza always had a very close relationship and she's finding it extremely difficult to come to terms with what's happened. In a way, he says, it's worse than a death. Had their daughter fallen under a bus, at least there would have been some kind of certainty, and perhaps closure, but as it is the pair of them spend far too much time trying to fend off what he calls the blacker thoughts. Nights are the worst, he says. We kid each other that we're asleep but all the time we both know otherwise.

I offer my sympathies and when he makes a guarded enquiry about Malo I tell him that the boy is bearing up and that, in the end, both H and I are sure that Clem will be returned. At this point, I'm tempted to ask him about O'Keefe, H's least favourite K&R expert, and about Mateo's own attempts to open negotiations with whoever is holding Clem, but there's something in Mateo's manner that tells me a question like this would be far from welcome.

Instead, I ask him about his friend in Vodafone, the one who could access call logs. Is his access limited to Vodafone alone?

'By no means. My friend, too, has friends. Call data is readily available. You have a particular number in mind?'

'I do. I have the exact time. And I'm guessing you might be able to access the location.'

'You're right. We might.'

I give him Baptiste's number. He reads it back to me and then promises to be in touch again when and if his friend gets a result.

'This might take a while?' I ask.

'Not at all. I have your number. This afternoon, I hope. It's been a pleasure to talk to you.'

I'm taking a leaf out of Malo's book and having a nap upstairs when my phone goes. I've pulled the bedroom curtain against the brightness of the afternoon light and I fumble in the half-darkness for my phone. I'm expecting a call back from Mateo. Instead I find myself talking to Pavel's consultant up in Glasgow.

He apologizes for calling me out of the blue but thinks a conversation might be in order.

'Why? What's happened?' I'm up on one elbow, rubbing the sleep from my eyes. This is a different kind of guilt. Pavel, unlike poor little Noodle, is a very close friend of mine, but not once over the last twenty-four hours have I spared him more than a passing thought. Locked in a body that won't work any more he deserves, at the very least, a conversation.

The consultant clearly regrets being the bearer of bad news. Only days ago, with all the usual caveats, he'd been offering modest hopes for perhaps the partial return of sensation and control. Now, alas, that ever-fainter hope has vanished. The latest tests have confirmed a serious lesion in the upper reaches of Pavel's spinal cord. The tissue of the central nervous system, once damaged, cannot repair itself. Pavel himself understands this only too well and all the indications are that he's had enough.

'Enough? I'm afraid I don't understand.'

'He's suffering from serious depression. He's a brave man, and he's resourceful, too. He has a remarkable imagination. That may be a result of his blindness, we simply don't know, but whatever the reason we all have tremendous admiration for him.'

'But?'

'But it's not enough.'

'Your admiration?'

'His ability to live in his head. A week ago he had a body he could rely on. Now he's somewhere very different and I think it's dawned on him that this is for keeps.'

'But that's always the case, isn't it? With all your patients?'

'Of course, you're right, but Pavel is unusual. This morning he told me that someone had locked his door and thrown away the key. His hearing is fine. He can still taste, still swallow, but that's about it. Nothing but darkness, he said. For ever.'

Nothing but darkness. It's hard not to imagine myself into that head of his and shudder at the implications. The endless ward routines, day after day. Unseen hands spooning food into your mouth. The awareness, or perhaps the assumption, that someone must be attending to your lower half, emptying your bowels, adjusting your catheter, monitoring your urine flow. Weird, I think, to find yourself so entirely at the mercy of other people. Not just for now. Not just for tomorrow. But, in Pavel's own despairing phrase, for ever.

'What can I do to help?' I ask. The consultant has obviously given this question some thought. He thinks it might be an idea if I came up and paid Pavel another visit, not least because I obviously know him so well. That way, he and the nursing staff and the support team might be able to arrive at a plan for coaxing Pavel out of his depression. 'You really think there is a plan? Options? Given what he now has to put up with?'

'I'm sure there is,' the consultant says at once. 'I could introduce you to hundreds of patients we've treated over the years and most of them have gone on to lead perfectly worthwhile lives. I tried to get that over to Pavel this morning. I told him the darkest hour always comes before dawn. Not a happy choice of phrase for a blind man, I'm afraid, but belief is all-important. That's what keeps these people going. At Pavel's stage, it's all they have.'

The darkest hour. I can picture Pavel's face only too well the moment the phrase shaped itself on the consultant's lips. The slightest flicker of distress, the tiny hint of a grimace. Pavel is a connoisseur when it comes to language. He's cherished its power and its beauty all his working life and he knows equally how easy it is to abuse. The darkest hour? He'd see through this benign little fib before the consultant had even finished the sentence and I suspect his patience, or that deep well of courage he's drawn on since he went blind, is running out. There's something unspoken here between me and the consultant and before I volunteer to head north again, I know Pavel would want me to voice it.

'I'm sure you're right in everything you say,' I tell him, 'but the fact is that Pavel has run out of options. And that, believe me, will matter more than anything else.'

'Meaning?'

'Meaning you're right. The man's probably had enough. And in his situation, I'm guessing that you and I might feel exactly the same way.'

When I go downstairs again, I find H alone in the kitchen. I'm not a moody person by nature. My lovely mum never had a moment's patience for a strop or a sulk and I learned very early to keep my feelings to myself. H knows this and I suspect it's one of the reasons – once he got himself beyond my minor celebrity – that he wants more of me in his life. Now, the look on my face tells him something's seriously wrong. He reaches across the table and puts one large hand over mine. 'Don't worry. Tony will sort everything out.'

'It's got nothing to do with Tony. Or the kid on the beach. Or Clem. Or even Malo.'

'It's about me?' He looks appalled. 'What the fuck have I done?'

'It's not you.' I give his hand a squeeze. 'It's Pavel, my writer friend, *our* writer friend.'

I tell him about the conversation I've just had with the consultant. H, as ever, is deeply practical. 'We've got to get you up there,' he says at once. 'Poor fucker. You wouldn't wish that on anyone.'

'You're right, you wouldn't. But you know what's worse? What must be beyond even Pavel's imagination? How to bring it all to an end. You're blind. You're helpless. And worse still you're surrounded by people determined to keep you ticking over. That won't end. That goes on for ever until you can sweet-talk or bribe someone to see it your way. To be frank, I can't think of anything worse, and more to the point I'm sure that goes for Pavel as well. The long goodbye? The longest goodbye? The never-ending goodbye? Take your choice. They're all grotesque.'

My little speech draws a grunt of agreement from H. For once, he's lost for words. I'm trying very hard not to break down completely. I still have his hand in mine.

'You know something?' I mutter. 'I believe Tony. When he says they might bang me up, I'm sure it's more than possible. In fact, they might bang me up for a very long time. But none of that, not a single second, would compare to what that poor man must be going through. Someone's turned his lights off, and bound him hand and foot, and locked his door, and thrown the key away. Even the thought of that must be unbearable.'

H, bless him, spends the next hour or so making phone calls. By suppertime, he's in touch with a private pilot called Buster Clegg. Cleggie, as he prefers to call himself, flies something called a Cessna from an airfield over the county border in Devon. He's very happy to take me to Glasgow tomorrow and if I can get myself to Dunkeswell by eight in the morning we should be in Scotland in time for lunch.

'If you want to stay over a couple of days, no problem. This guy says he loves Glasgow.' H is beaming. 'How does that sound?'

It sounds great. I don't have to report to the police for another three days. An excursion to Glasgow will do nothing to get me any closer to Brodie or Baptiste but that's not the point. Pavel, I think. So completely alone.

'That's more than generous.' I give H a hug. 'But wouldn't it be cheaper to go Flybe? This must be costing you a fortune.'

'Forget the money.' H shoots me a grin. 'Cleggie comes highly recommended. And tell your mate he still owes me a script.'

At H's insistence, we eat *en famille*. Jess and Andy come up from the cottage and H presents us with his take on *coq au vin*. I know this is for me, a gentle reminder that Malo's dad knows a thing or two about French cuisine, and even Malo himself has the grace to make short work of the helping H piles on his plate.

'Great, Dad.' He seizes a crust of bread to mop up the juices exactly the way his father's just done. 'Top work.'

H is beaming again. He's done apple crumble for dessert, using our own Bramleys from the orchard, and he's attacking the lumps in his custard when my mobile begins to ring. It's Mateo. I make my excuses and step into the hall, closing the door behind me.

Mateo has been talking to his friend. Not only does he have a location for Baptiste's phone but he thinks he's found the address.

There's a pad and ballpoint pen on the occasional table beside the hat stand, and I grab them.

'Beaufort House,' he says. 'The nearest village is Broadhembury.'

'Where's that?'

'Devon. My wife's favourite county. Clemenza loved it, too.'

I nod and make another note. Mateo's use of the past tense is disturbing. 'No news?'

'Not much. Not yet.'

'Anything you might share?'

'I'm afraid not.'

I'm still looking at the address. How come Mateo's friend could be so precise? The question draws a chuckle from Mateo.

'It's the only building around there.' He gives me a postcode. 'Check it out on Google Earth.'

I return to the kitchen. Malo wants to know who was on the phone and what was so important I had to leave the table.

'It was Pavel,' I tell him. 'About tomorrow. He needed to know I'm really coming.'

There's a silence around the table. H is still at the stove, stirring and stirring. 'Making other plans, was he?' He glances over his shoulder. 'Or is that in bad taste?'

We retire early that night. In the privacy of my bedroom I go to Google Earth, type in the postcode for Beaufort House and await the result. Within seconds, I'm looking at a country pile that reminds me immediately of Flixcombe. The same rich sense of entitlement. The same spread of handsome Georgian windows. I even spot a pergola in the walled garden that I know H has just ordered from an ad in *Country Life*.

I'm sitting on the bed with my back to the door. Unaware that I have company, I'm taking a 360-degree tour of the property when I sense a presence behind me. It's Malo. He says he's come to say goodnight. He can't take his eyes off my iPad.

'Where's that?'

I bluster for a second or two and then tell him I'm checking out a possible location.

'This is for the Pavel movie?'

'Could easily be.'

'Then why didn't you mention it earlier?'

'I couldn't. I've only just found it.'

He doesn't believe me for a second. Taking a final look, he gives me a peck on the cheek. Only when he's back beside the door does he nod at the iPad. 'You should be careful, Mum. It'll be porn next.'

THIRTY-NINE

Next morning, between them, I get the full treatment from Malo and H. My son appears at my bedroom door shortly after six o'clock with a mug of tea. Thirty minutes later, down in the kitchen, H has readied my favourite breakfast. For reasons I can't fathom, I'm starving hungry. I demolish the fruit and muesli and empty the yoghurt pot while H plots a cross-country route to Dunkeswell. The drive seems to take no time at all. Nearly half an hour early, we surprise Buster Clegg who's parking his Porsche beside a smallish white aircraft. It has two engines and a rather fetching scarlet stripe that runs the length of the fuselage.

H tells me to wait while he walks across and introduces himself. I watch the two men shake hands. The conversation seems to take a while and once or twice H gestures back towards the Range Rover. Cleggie is older than I'd expected, mid-fifties at least. His sandy hair is beginning to thin and a pair of glasses dangle from a lanyard around his neck. He's powerfully built, enormous hands, and he towers over H. He wears a black flying suit, which looks even older than he does, but it fits him perfectly.

H finally summons me over. Cleggie's handshake is on the firm side. I've brought an overnight bag, just in case, and when I ask him where I can stow it in the aircraft he turns his head and taps his right ear. 'That one's best,' he says. 'Ask me again.'

We're taxiing out to take-off within minutes. On the far side of the grass runway I can see a line of gliders parked untidily on the springy turf. They have the look of abandoned toys and apart from us there's no sign of activity on the airfield. As we lift off, I spot a tiny figure that must be H. He gives us a wave. I raise my right hand in a rather regal *adieu* and seconds later my phone begins to ring.

'Behave yourself,' H says. 'Cleggie was in the Red Arrows.'

It's true. Within the hour we're passing a vast brown smudge that Cleggie tells me is Manchester. He seems to fly by his finger-tips alone, tiny movements on the control column, strangely delicate for such a big man. We've talked most of the way and by now I know a great deal about close formation aerobatics and the alarming consequences if you get a manoeuvre called the Eagle Roll badly wrong. Red Arrows pre-season training, says Cleggie, normally happened in Cyprus where you could pretty much guarantee the vis. 'Vis' turns out to be visibility, clean air, and the point of the story is that nothing prepares you for the real thing. Back in the UK for the start of the display season, you could never guarantee anything weather-wise and Cleggie says he's lost count of the occasions in the middle of the night when he's awoken in a cold sweat, reliving the moments when his wingman had suddenly vanished in low cloud.

'It sounds lunatic, and if you haven't done the prep it'll kill you. A thousand feet? Five hundred and fifty knots on the dial? We knew we were good because we survived.'

I sense there's a life lesson in there somewhere, a reminder that catastrophe, wherever possible, should never take you by surprise, but I don't push it. Half an hour later we're deep in Scottish airspace and Cleggie is rhapsodizing about a film of mine his wife hated but he adored. He's forgotten the title but that doesn't matter. More important, he says, is the way I took no shit from the pervy college lecturer who was trying to get into my knickers.

'You had the balls to see him off,' he says with a nod of approval. 'And then you stitched him up with that other woman of his. I loved that sequence so much I got it on DVD and watched it again.'

We're within touching distance of Glasgow. From up here I have a grandstand view of the city and I gaze down at the long silver thread of the Clyde and the ghostly remains of abandoned shipyards as Cleggie prepares to land. This man radiates the kind of quiet un-showy confidence you so rarely find nowadays, certainly in my profession, and I barely register the moment of touchdown. Minutes later, parked at a private aviation facility away from the main passenger terminal, Cleggie is completing the paper-work for our hire car while I linger in the sunshine outside.

H has pre-booked a Mercedes saloon in the sleekest black. Inside, it feels brand new. Cleggie punches details of the Queen Elizabeth University Hospital into the sat nav and then helps me adjust my seat belt. I tell him I'll be spending the rest of the day

with my friend in the spinal unit and he's very welcome to push
off with the car and take it wherever he fancies.

Cleggie shakes his head. 'That's not the deal,' he says.

'It's not?'

'No. I'm coming to the hospital, too. I'll be nice and discreet
but I'll be there if you need me.'

'Why would I need you?'

'I'm not sure that's something we should be discussing. Hayden
was very specific. He wants me to stay close. Maybe I shouldn't
be saying this, but he's paying me very well. Mine not to reason
why.'

This is news I find far from comforting. What could possibly
go wrong up here, at the other end of the country? I'm tempted
to explore the issue further but a glance from Cleggie tells me
there's no point. This, after all, was once a man in uniform. Unlike
yours truly, he was probably born to obey orders.

At the hospital, Cleggie accompanies me to the spinal injuries
unit. I had a bodyguard once, on a shoot in Latin America where
a particularly vicious gang were trying to shake the producer down
for protection money. The money was never paid, and nobody got
hurt, but the way Cleggie is quietly shepherding me into the
building, alert for any potential threat, is beginning to remind me
of those long hot weeks in Caracas.

Inside the spinal unit I check the ward and then take Cleggie
to one side. Pavel, I tell him, is still on the last bed on the left. I
don't foresee any imminent danger from his fellow patients, all
of whom are paralysed, and the nursing staff have always struck
me as wholly benign. I will, of course, be on the lookout for false
moustaches or strange accents, but if he fancies a coffee and a bit
of a read there's a visitors' area down the corridor. If I feel the
need, I'll give him a shout.

'OK?'

He nods. I expect a smile, at the very least, but I realize he's
far from amused.

I beckon him closer. This time I'm not joking. 'What has Hayden
been telling you?' I ask.

He shakes his head and checks his watch. 'You don't want to
know,' he murmurs. 'But I got the feeling he meant it.'

                         *   *   *

Pavel, as far as I can judge, is asleep. I return to the nursing station and ask how he's been these last few hours. This is a nurse I've never met before. She has a lovely smile and I think she may be a Filipina or perhaps Malay. Either way, she seems to have all the time in the world and is very happy to chat. She calls Pavel 'Mr Sieger'.

'Nice man,' she says. 'So sad.'

'I agree.'

'Your partner?'

'My friend.'

'Oh.' She's frowning. 'But you were there when it happened? You were on the other horse, maybe?'

'Horse?'

I take a tiny step back. Pavel's been at it again. I should have anticipated this. He's either bored with the first version of the accident – the dives in Scapa Flow, the party afterwards, the moment he broke his neck by diving into the wrong end of the hotel pool – or it never happened at all.

The nurse, whose name is Blessica, is telling me about something similar that happened to her cousin back home. The horse bolts for some reason and you lose control. Fall off and land head-first and the chances are that you've broken your neck.

'Nice man,' she says again. 'Come.'

I follow her across the ward. She bends beside Pavel and blows softly in his ear. For the briefest second I find the intimacy of the gesture slightly shocking but it brings a smile to Pavel's face and that, just now, is all that matters.

Blessica's lips are still beside Pavel's ear. 'Your lovely friend,' she whispers. And then she's gone.

Pavel's head doesn't move on the whiteness of the pillow. 'It's you?'

'Me.'

'Wonderful.'

In most movie scripts, his hand would find mine. Instead, it lies limply on the sheet. Blessica has fetched a chair. I settle down beside the bed. There's a faint smell of urine but I'm not sure it comes from Pavel. There's also a smear of something pink at one corner of his mouth and I moisten a fingertip before wiping it off.

'Again,' he murmurs.

I do it a second time, and then a third, though the smear has gone.

'Kiss me,' he says. 'Please.'

I glance around. No one seems to be watching, and even if they were I'm not sure it would make any difference. I get a little closer, bend over his face, cup it in my hands, then kiss him on the lips.

'Again. Properly.'

I do his bidding. His tongue chases mine around the moistness inside his mouth. He tastes of toothpaste. Maybe peppermint.

'How have you been?'

'Still as the grave. No fuss. No bother. I'd like to say placid but that would be a fib.' He forces a smile. 'You?'

I kiss him again, a long, lingering exploration that ends, from Pavel, in a sigh that I take to be contentment. We've got all afternoon, I tell myself. All evening, if he can bear it. Physical intimacy seems the simplest form of comfort. Why ruin this moment with something as troublesome and complicated as language?

For minutes on end, we continue to kiss. Then I simply put my cheek to his and stroke his face. His unseeing eyes are open. He tells me he loves me. I'm thinking about the horse. Should I mention it? Absolutely not.

In a while, his eyes close and he seems to be asleep again. Very gently, I disengage myself. My back is killing me and when I realize that Blessica's cup of tea is for me I'm more than grateful. It's very sweet but I don't care.

'What next?' I'm nodding at Pavel. We've stepped away from the bed and I'm hoping he can't hear us.

The little Filipina doesn't know. She says his vital signs are good. Good pulse. Good BP. Strong heart.

'Always,' I murmur.

Blessica departs with the empty tea cup. I'm back beside Pavel. For the time being, we've evidently done kissing. He wants to know about me.

This interest comes as no surprise. I've been around writers all my working life and I recognize the trademark curiosity that badges every member of this strange tribe. Maybe curiosity is too posh a word. A better one might be nosiness. This is what the Pavels of this world are. Nosy. They need to find out. They need to question, to probe, to listen, to empathize, and then to make all the startling connections that will one day give birth to a book or a movie.

Some writers I know regard this bizarre alchemy as an affliction and if that's true then Pavel has probably been suffering all his life. He lives for story, for character, and for the opportunity to build that cage of circumstance we thesps call plot. That's his vocation, his calling. And now I'm at his bedside, in the bareness of his cell, I'm only too happy to collaborate.

'H thinks there are people who are trying to kill me,' I say quietly. 'Maybe that's where we might start.'

'*Kill* you?'

There's more than a flicker of interest in Pavel's face. I can see alarm there, as well, and it makes my heart leap. It means I have his full attention and just now this story of mine is exactly what he needs.

I tell him everything. I bring him up to date about Malo and Clem. I describe my adventures in Bridport – the Landfall, Danny Flannery, Dooley's steaming groin, the swimming pool, The Machine, poor broken Noodle, and finally the moment when my giddy trek through the Bridport badlands ended at the police station.

'They arrested you?'

'They did. I didn't have an option. I just went.'

'And they think you killed this boy?'

'They think I might have done.'

'And did you?'

Pavel is enjoying this. I know he is. There's a sweet complicity in the way he phrases that simple question. Our secret. No one else's. *Did you?*

'No,' I say. 'I didn't.'

'So who did?'

'I think his name's Brodie.'

'This is The Machine? The swimmer?'

'Yes. How on earth did you guess?'

'Silly question. It has to be him. Who else could it be?'

'I've no idea. That's why I came. I knew you wouldn't let me down.'

'Very wise.' He manages a nod. 'I'm here to save your life. Give me a kiss.'

We do it again. Twice. Then he breaks off.

'They'll be coming for you,' he warns.

I nod. I do my best to coax alarm into my voice. I want this story of mine to run and run. I want to hook him, to fascinate him, to enfold him in a sticky web of what-ifs, rampant speculation that will see him through the long nights to come.

'And H?' he says.

'He wants you to get writing again for him.'

'Cotehele? Is that what he wants? Swash? Buckle?'

'He doesn't know what he wants. As long as there's a decent part for me he'll sort out the funding and pay for a script.'

'You mean the French people?'

'I'm afraid they're history. H will find some other way. He always does.'

'You're serious?'

'Absolutely.'

'Then it's this, isn't it? This story of yours? It has to be.' His earlier interest has thickened into something much closer to excitement. Better and better, I think. Keep planting the clues.

'Did I mention Mateo?'

'You did. Clem's father?'

'H thinks he's talking to the kidnappers.'

'So what about the insurance people? Kidnap and Ransom? K&R?'

'Mateo's lost faith in them.'

'Of course he has. Of course. And you know why? Because he's a businessman. Businessmen think like criminals. They take risks. They draw the straightest lines. It's means and ends. And it works both ways, too. The best criminals think like businessmen. No one knows that better than H. Take the drugs trade. It's not about getting off your head. It's not about car chases and mayhem. It's about getting rich.'

I nod. I agree. Listening to Pavel, the image that keeps coming back to me is the sight of The Machine, Brodie, churning up and down that pool. Straight lines, I think. And everyone else getting out of the way. Young Brodie is determined to get rich, regardless of who he hurts in the process.

Pavel hasn't finished. Not quite. 'You know the two key words here?' he whispers. 'What shaped us all? What took society by the scruff of its skinny neck? All those centuries ago? The fence and the handshake. After the fence, you got private property. And after the handshake, you got trade. Put those two things together, you can own the entire world.'

He's exhausted. I can tell. But he's also happy. Happy for me to be here. Happy to have that gigantic brain working again. Happy to find a fully formed plot waiting at his bedside, just begging for the finishing touches.

At seven in the evening, with the orderlies wheeling in the supper trolley, he asks me very politely to leave. I think he wants to spare me the sight of him being spoon-fed and, although I'd be only too happy to do it myself, I don't blame him. His voice is weak now. He whispers that he has a great deal of thinking to do and he tells me that he's already looking forward to our next script conference.

'When?'

'Tomorrow?' He smiles. 'After I've checked my diary?'

I bend low and kiss him on the lips. Then I gently close each eye and leave.

FORTY

I collect Cleggie from the cafe along the corridor, wondering exactly how much H has paid for this kind of patience. When I warn him that we'll both be staying overnight and that we'll be back here in the morning, he doesn't seem the slightest bit perturbed. He's halfway through a fascinating book about the Battle of Stalingrad and the coffee's much better than he'd expected.

'Living the dream?'

'You bet.'

We drive into the city centre and book two rooms at a Premier Inn, leaving the Mercedes in the car park. Cleggie turns out to have a lifetime passion for Spanish food and one of the nurses has recommended a restaurant called El Pirata. The paella Valenciana, she's promised, is the best in Scotland, and according to the woman on the reception desk it's only a ten-minute walk away.

Cleggie is easy company – amusing, attentive, a master storyteller with a real gift for understatement – and by the end of the meal we've emptied the third carafe of the house white. I settle the bill and we set off under a light drizzle for the ten-minute walk back to the Premier Inn.

Crossing the road towards the hotel, Cleggie remembers that we need to pick up our respective bags from the boot of the Mercedes. The car park was already packed when we arrived from the hospital and Cleggie was lucky to find a space in the far corner. He unlocks the boot with the key fob and bends to haul out my overnight bag. As he does so I sense a movement behind us. I half-turn but it's too late. He's tall and very black. He's wearing trackie bottoms the colour of Cleggie's flying suit and a grey hoodie. He has a machete in one hand and a gun in the other, inches from my face. He's looking at me but he's talking to Cleggie.

'Shut the boot.'

'What is this?'

'I said shut the fucking boot, man.'

Cleggie holds his gaze, then shrugs. He turns back to the car and rummages deep in the boot before stepping back and slamming the lid.

'Listen . . .' he says. 'We can talk about this.'

This guy is a Somali. I'm sure about it. He has the height, the build, that intense depth of blackness you could almost polish. His eyes are wide. He's chewing what must be *khat*. He looks slightly mad.

Another figure, smaller, thinner, no more than a ghost, appears from nowhere. He, too, is holding a gun. He extends an open hand towards Cleggie.

'The key. Give me the key.' His English is good. Much better than the Somali.

Cleggie doesn't move. For longer than I like to remember, nothing happens. This is a stand-off, the four of us locked in a wordless conversation. Then Cleggie says again that we can talk about this, work something out. Money? Credit cards? His watch? A little jewellery, maybe? No problem.

'The key, man. Otherwise the lady gets cut.'

I'm staring at the machete. The Somali holds it low, dangling on the end of his skinny arm, but I don't have a moment's doubt that he could bury it in my face in less time than it would take me to scream. Maybe a bullet would be better, I think. Maybe we should negotiate.

Cleggie has decided that this maniac means it. He hands over the key. I watch the skinny guy dance round the car, open the driver's door and climb in. The lights come on, go off again. Then the wipers. The left indicator starts to flicker. Then comes a low purr and the faintest scent of diesel as he starts the engine.

The three of us are still at the rear of the Mercedes. I take a covert look round, hoping against hope that someone appears, someone fearless, someone armed to the teeth, someone who can bring this nightmare episode to a sane conclusion.

'In, man.'

The driver has got out again. He holds one of the rear doors open. The curt nod has the force of an order. This man, I decide, is the more senior of the two.

Cleggie throws him a look, then shrugs again and folds his long body into the back of the Mercedes.

It's my turn next. As the driver watches, the Somali pulls me towards the open rear door and then pushes my head low as I stoop to get in. He's looking at Cleggie.

'Move over, man.' There's a cackle of laughter from the Somali. 'You got no manners?'

I get in beside Cleggie. This thing – two black faces, two guns – is fast becoming surreal. Is it really happening? Or am I back in Pavel's world, starring in a movie that can only end badly? That last carafe, I've decided, was a big mistake.

The driver slams the door on Cleggie and me. The other Somali is already making himself comfortable in the front. Half-turned in the passenger seat, he has the gun levelled at my face. They've practised this routine before, I think. It's slick, seamless. In barely seconds we're on the way to disappearing off the face of the earth.

We drive out of the car park. The man behind the wheel is in no hurry to attract anyone's attention and we cruise slowly through the city centre. When Cleggie enquires where we might be going, there's no answer, only the barrel of the Somali's gun inches from my mouth, rock-steady. I can see the long, well-shaped finger curled around the trigger, the huge eyes in the blackness of his face, the jaws slowly working the *khat*. His eyes are slightly yellowed around the iris and I'm beginning to think he might be older than he looks. Not that it's ever going to matter.

The traffic is thinning now as we leave the city centre. From time to time the two men have a muttered conversation in a language I don't understand and as the car begins to pick up speed I realize that this might have been the way that Clem was abducted. A neatly planned ambush. A waiting car. And the absolute guar-antee of serious violence if you didn't do these crazy people's bidding. How on earth did they know where to find us? What brought them to Glasgow?

They must have known about Pavel, I conclude. The Somalis must have been waiting at the hospital. They must have followed us to the Premier Inn, found a parking spot, and settled down to wait. They'd have known we didn't have luggage when we checked in and so they knew we'd be back. Simple. So simple.

We're out in the country. The lanes are unlit, the country flat, the occasional glimpse of cows in a darkened field. The driver is evidently delighted with the Mercedes. He's driving fast, flooring the accelerator through the shallower bends, scarcely bothering to brake for a blur of oncoming pot holes. There's a rumble from the suspension as we bounce along towards the next corner, and as we lurch to the left I feel a tiny movement beside my thigh. It's Cleggie. Thrown around in the back, his body is pressed against mine and I suspect he's trying to ease something out of his pocket. I daren't look at him, daren't risk giving anything away.

The Somali doesn't like what the driver is doing with this new toy of his, the risks he's taking, and it shows in his face. He's muttering under his breath, too wary, or perhaps too junior, to risk a conversation. When I risk a sympathetic smile, trying to break the ice, it seems to make him even crazier.

'No tricks,' he yells.

Minutes later, we're on the edge of what seems to be a small town. The sight of a thirty mph sign comes as a godsend but the driver takes no notice. There's no traffic. The town looks dead. Why slow down?

I'm thinking of Clem again. By now, we've been at the mercy of these men for more than half an hour. That's long enough for that first hot rush of adrenalin to drain away, leaving nothing but the icy recognition that your life is no longer your own. That you've surrendered all control. That absolutely nothing from now on can be taken for granted. Where you're going and what might happen next is a total mystery. Pavel, I think. Shit.

The driver doesn't see the van and neither do I. It appears from nowhere, emerging from a side street. The windscreen is suddenly full of white. The Somali at the wheel hits the brakes and tries to haul the big car to the left but it's far, far too late.

We hit the van at an angle. There's a huge bang and the sheer force of the impact seems to squeeze the breath out of me. Dimly I hear a scream and realize it's me. Then I become aware of something else. The car is filling with red smoke. At first I think it's on fire and I scream even louder but then the smoke is filling my mouth, my throat, and reaching deep into my lungs. It has an oiliness that is beyond horrible. I start to cough. Then I start to choke.

Beside me, I can feel Cleggie moving. Somehow he's got the door open. His big hands slip beneath my armpits. He's out of the car now, hauling and hauling. The taste of the night air has a sweetness I can't describe. I'm lying on my back in the middle of the road and I think it's raining. I move my head in a bid to see the car. All the doors seem to be open and red smoke is pumping out, great clouds of the stuff.

Cleggie is kneeling over me. His big face is only inches away. He's asking me if I'm OK. He's telling me everything's going to be fine.

'But where are they?' I manage a nod towards the car.

'Gone,' he says.

Local residents, alerted by the bang, emerge from their houses. A burly pensioner helps the van driver out of his cab. He's bleeding from facial injuries and two women fetch water and towels to attend to him. The pensioner arrives and tells us he's in touch with the emergency services. The police and ambulance should be here shortly. I nod. I'm grateful. I'm on my feet now, hanging on to Cleggie's arm. Mercifully, everything seems to be in working order. I must phone H, I tell myself. I must tell him what's happened.

He's asleep when I ring. I end the call, then ring a second time. This time he picks up. He can tell at once that something bad has happened. I explain as best I can. Neither of us are badly hurt, just a bit shaken up. The men who took us have disappeared.

'And the police?'

'On their way.'

'Tell them nothing. OK? Cleggie was driving. It was just the pair of you in the car. Pretend the black guys don't exist. Mateo thinks he's on the edge of a deal. We can't fuck this thing up.'

Pretend the black guys don't exist? I'm staring at Cleggie. He has to know. He has to be part of this plan. I pass on H's orders. *Just you and me in the car. You at the wheel. The van driver's fault.*

Cleggie gazes at me for a moment, and then asks for the phone and gestures me closer so I can be part of this conversation.

'I've sunk at least a bottle of Chablis,' he tells H. 'The first thing they'll do is breathalyse me. Pretend none of this stuff happened? You have to be joking.'

H gives the proposition a moment's thought. Then he's back on the phone. 'These guys have legged it, yeah?'

'Yes.'

'Then tell the Filth it was just a mugging, a hijack. They were going to dump you somewhere. You got that?'

Cleggie nods, says nothing. In the distance I can hear the approaching police car, blues and twos. I get the drift. I can handle this.

The police arrive and park up. One of them starts putting out warning signs further down the road while the other checks that we and the van driver are OK. Talking to us, I know he can smell the alcohol on our breath.

'Driving, sir, were you?' he asks Cleggie.

'No.'

'Madam?'

'No.' I shake my head.

'Driving itself, then, the car?' A brief frown.

I explain as best I can. When I finish describing what happened back in the car park at the hotel, Cleggie interrupts.

'Check it out on their CCTV,' he says. 'They've got cameras. Three of them. I counted.'

The police officer looks briefly confused. By now, an ambulance has appeared and I'm watching the van driver clambering into the back. The paramedic approaches and asks whether we need medical attention. Both of us say no. The police officer returns from an inspection of the impact damage at the front of the car.

'I'd say a prayer for German engineering, if I were you.' He's not smiling. 'Let's get this mess cleaned up.'

Nice idea. One of the police officers confers with someone on the radio. He then takes our full details and suggests we phone for a taxi to take us back to Glasgow. A detective from CID will be down to the Premier Inn by noon to check the CCTV footage and take a proper statement. It will be in our best interests, he suggests, that we're still around. In the meantime, in case the CCTV doesn't provide the evidence we're after, he needs to breathalyse Cleggie.

Cleggie breathes into the proffered tube. The permitted limit for a lungful of breath is 50 micrograms per 100 millilitres. Cleggie, according to the digital read-out, clocks in at 69. The officer scribbles himself a note and then looks Cleggie in the eye.

'You're way over, sir. We'll need a blood sample, too, but that means taking you back to Glasgow. That's the nearest police station that can handle it.'

'Fine by me.' Cleggie tells me to put my mobile away. 'No need for a taxi.'

We linger at the scene of the accident for ten minutes or so while the police make arrangements for both vehicles to be towed away. Cleggie has the presence of mind to retrieve our bags from the boot. Within the hour, we're at Glasgow's central police station, where Cleggie submits to a blood test. The police surgeon grumbles that enough time has passed to bring him under the limit but there appears to be a complicated calculation they can do with both readings that will be admissible in court if the CCTV lets us down.

The officer who has brought us in from the accident scene has disappeared. As soon as we've left the police station to wait for the summoned cab, I phone H again. By now it's nearly two in the morning.

'It's me,' I say when H picks up. 'It's all fine.'

'A mugging? A hijack?'

'That's the story. We get interviewed again tomorrow morning. Keep your fingers crossed for the CCTV.'

'What?' H sounds alarmed.

I tell him not to worry. 'Say night-night to Cleggie. You owe him, believe me.'

'How come?'

'He lifted a red emergency flare from the boot when the Somalis jumped us. After he let it off you couldn't see for all the smoke. I'm betting they'd have shot us otherwise.'

I pass the phone to Cleggie. He's rubbing the back of his neck.

'Touch of whiplash, boss,' he says. 'Where do I send the bill?'

FORTY-ONE

I start to physically shake less than an hour later. We've made it back to the hotel and I'm lying in bed. I've made the mistake of rustling up a cup of coffee in my room, a poor substitute for the three miniatures of spirits a mini bar might have given me, but a modest gesture of celebration none the less. It doesn't work. Worse still, it keeps me awake. The time, according to my bedside clock, is 03.37. Every time I close my eyes and try and kid myself into sleep, the same images swim out of the darkness. The machete hanging from that skinny arm. The gun, another shade of black, in my face. And above all, the yellowing eyes of a madman whose real pleasures were doubtless yet to come.

These people stepped into our evening from nowhere. They knew everything about everything. Their mission last night was to turn my safe little life on its head and make me question everything I've ever taken for granted, and in that single ambition they succeeded beyond their wildest dreams. Thanks to the driver of a white van, I'm still alive, and I seem to have retrieved some pale version of freedom, but deep down – where it truly matters – I'm terrified. Infant junkies shooting up I can cope with. Police interviews I can cope with. Even the threat of a prison sentence seems bearable. But this is different. Like the moment I saw what had happened to Brett Dooley, I seem to have stepped into a parallel universe. All bets are off. Literally anything can happen. Extreme violence the default setting? Get used to it.

Impossible. I get up and prowl around the room, stopping beside the window on lap after lap to inch back the curtain and gaze down into that horrible car park. I linger beside the door, half-naked, listening intently at the crack for any sign of movement outside. Somewhere I read that wedging an object under the door handle might keep the demons at bay but when I test the single chair it seems a flimsy proposition. They'll be back, I know they will, and even if they never make it to the hotel they'll ambush us somewhere else. A machete is for ever, I think, and these people know no fear.

At 03.59, unforgivably, I give Cleggie a ring. His room is next door. I mutter my apologies but it turns out that he, too, is still awake. His neck, he says, is bloody painful. The rest of it – nearly dying – doesn't seem to trouble him. He'll put the kettle on. I'm welcome to pop by.

I tell him not to bother making a drink on my account and then I get dressed. Both our rooms have twin beds. Cleggie is sitting up in his, his head at an odd angle. I lie on the other, staring up at the ceiling.

'So what's this about?' he says after a while. 'Am I allowed to ask?'

The question is as crazy as the situation. Of course he's allowed to ask. We nearly died, for God's sake, and the very fact that we've been spared, that we've somehow come through, makes us comrades in arms.

I tell him everything. I don't care about H any more, about his stern instructions not to breathe a word about anything to anyone. Cleggie probably saved my life. Without the choking smoke in that car, the Somali might well have killed us both. *Merci beaucoup*, I murmur. With bells on.

At the end of the story I'm trying to describe the exotic Baptiste who I seem to have traced to a lordly pile in East Devon. Cleggie knows the area well. More to the point, he also knows the guy who owns it.

'Dominic Franklin,' he says. 'Grade-one arsehole. Runs a Spitfire.'

The Spitfire, it turns out, is the reason this man appeared on Cleggie's radar in the first place. It's a two-seat version with room for a passenger in the back and he keeps it in a compound at Exeter Airport. He once asked Cleggie whether he fancied flying punters around Torbay at £4000 a pop. Cleggie says he wasn't taken by the offer but was only too pleased to give the Spit a go in the back seat. Memories of that single flight appear to work miracles on his sore neck. The perfect lady, he murmurs. An aircraft you couldn't fail to fall in love with.

I want to know more about Dominic Franklin. Keeping a Spitfire, like keeping any kind of thoroughbred, can't be cheap. Does this man work? Does he have private means? Has he cashed in several fortunes and retired? Cleggie says he's never asked. All he knows is the man's age – late forties – and the fact that he has no manners.

This is beginning to sound a little like Hayden Prentice but when I offer the thought, Cleggie shakes his head.

'I don't know Prentice from Adam,' he says, 'but I'm really good at first impressions. I've had the pleasure of talking to him on the phone and now I've met him in the flesh. Rough diamond, definitely. But not in Franklin's league when it comes to arseholes.'

He rolls on to his side and props a pillow under his head. He wants to know about me and Prentice.

'H?' I say lightly. 'We share a son, like I just told you.'

'And anything else?'

'Not really. H has a habit of getting me into all kinds of trouble. Nothing like this but he's got lots of energy and zero patience, and he doesn't understand the word no. In a funny way I admire him. This country was built on people like him.'

'You're serious?'

'No. It's a guess. But when he's after something he's unstoppable.'

'And now?'

'He's after getting Clem back. These people have offended him. He thinks they need a lesson or two. Shame he wasn't around last night to understand the consequences.'

I close my eyes. It's happening again. A deep gust of something I can only describe as evil. How come things have got so bad so quickly? How come we got abducted in a hotel car park in the middle of a major city? In how many other ways is this insatiable monster – the narco biz – going to gobble us all up?

I put the question to Cleggie. He thinks about it for a moment or two, then shrugs.

'We used to call it going to war,' he says. 'But then it helped to have an enemy who wore a uniform.'

Thanks to the comforts of company, I manage an hour or two's broken sleep. I awake to hear Cleggie on the phone. He's being as quiet as he can, trying not to wake me up, and he seems to be talking to the police. He wants them at the hotel to review the CCTV footage as soon as possible. He's telling them that both of us, me in particular, are a bit shaken by what happened last night and would prefer to be on our way as soon as possible. It's true, I think, closing my eyes again.

Two detectives turn up shortly after breakfast. They confer with the manager and then invite us to join them in his office. He's loading last night's recording into a laptop. He fires up the DVD, lowers the blinds, and angles the screen so we can all take a look.

Cleggie has given him an approximate time, around ten p.m.

'Not late, then?' The taller of the two detectives seems surprised.

'Not at all. You'd think they'd do the decent thing and jump us in the middle of the night.'

'You're telling me they were waiting for you? That you'd become a target?'

'Not at all. I'm putting it down to recreational kidnapping.'

The phrase sparks an exchange of glances between the two detectives. I try to catch Cleggie's eye. Not too clever, please.

The manager is running through the footage. Not until 22:09 do we appear in the camera that covers the entrance from the street. I bend closer. Am I fascinated by this couple strolling along after an extremely pleasant evening in a local eatery? Yes, I am. But there's a prickle of something else here, first apprehension, and then fear as we appear on the other screens and pause beside the Mercedes. I know exactly what's coming next and I don't want to be reminded. The angle is perfect. It's very definitely us. I look away, watching the two detectives. One of them is making notes. Then comes the moment when the tall Somali materializes from the shadows. The machete and the gun are plainly visible.

'Stop it there.' One of the detectives wants to see this sequence again in slow motion.

The manager obliges. Cleggie's eyes are narrowed. He's riveted by the unfolding action on the screen.

The detective nods, asks for a third viewing, then turns to his colleague. He wants to know whether this small piece of urban theatre is opportunistic or not. Opportunistic, I gather, is code for a couple of black guys lingering with intent. The opposite, premeditation, means they're waiting for little us.

The detectives plainly can't make up their minds but as the story develops it exactly confirms what Cleggie and I have said all along. Once the car has left the car park, the manager hits the stop button. I'm looking at the time read-out. The entire episode, which I remember as half a lifetime, took exactly three minutes and two seconds. I shake my head. Cleggie puts an arm round me. I'm trembling again.

The manager tells the detectives to make themselves comfortable in his office for as long as they need. After he's left, we all settle down. Cleggie offers an account of exactly what happened. The detective records it and then produces a handwritten version for Cleggie to sign. It's a cumbersome process and it seems to take for ever.

I do exactly the same, confirming everything Cleggie has said. I make no mention of anything beyond the events of last night and the questions I'd anticipated never happen. All the detective wants to know is whether or not we were robbed, and whether we've been happy with the service we've received at the hands of the police. When Cleggie says no to the first question and yes to the second, the detective produces a card from his wallet. I had difficulties making my statement and he knows the effort of memory has upset me. I glance at the card. Victim Support.

'It's a charity,' he says. 'They'll sort you out.'

A cab takes us back to the hospital. This time I insist that Cleggie accompanies me into the spinal unit. The sight of his black flying suit creates a minor stir among the staff and he settles down with the prettiest of the nurses while I pay Pavel a visit. This time he's not asleep. I kiss him on the lips and warn him that this visit will be short.

'Really?' To my relief he doesn't seem disappointed, or even surprised.

I tell him, in full Technicolor, exactly what happened last night. He's lying flat on his back and when I've finished he moves his head so we're face-to-face.

'Lucky,' he murmurs. 'You were lucky.'

'It was beyond luck,' I tell him. 'In my little world, it was deliverance.'

'You really think so?'

'I do.'

'And now you want to go home?'

'Yes.'

'To H?'

'To his castle, yes.'

'And raise the drawbridge? Stir the boiling oil?'

'All of that.'

'But it has to be resolved, doesn't it? There has to be an ending?'

I nod. This is the old Pavel, the Pavel of the classic three-act narrative curve, the Pavel of denouement and closure and punters filing out past the popcorn machine, entranced by the movie they've just seen.

'But this is real life,' I tell him. 'And believe me, that makes a difference.'

He nods. He's thinking. 'The man you mentioned yesterday,' he says at last.

'Which one?'

'With the actress girlfriend and the big house.'

'His name's Franklin. Dominic Franklin.'

'He's rich?'

'He must be.'

'So what does he do?'

'I've no idea.'

'Then dig around. Because that's where you'll find the answer.' He closes his eyes and nods, as if he's talking to himself, which in a way I'm guessing he is. Then his eyes, as milky as ever, flutter open again.

'Come back when it's over,' he says. 'Promise me?'

Another cab takes us to the airport. I feel guilty about leaving Pavel so soon, but I know I have little choice. Glasgow is where bad things happen. We have to get out. At the airport, we skirt passenger departures and head for the VIP private aviation terminal. As we slow for the turn, I can see Cleggie's pert little airplane parked among a line of executive jets. In the back of the cab, I'm doing my best to give him a neck massage. Mercifully, I've been spared whiplash but the sense of dread, of something very bad about to happen, hasn't left me.

We're airborne within minutes. I've done my best to spot two black figures waiting for us on the tarmac when we walk out in the thin sunshine but all I can see is a fattish white man with a clipboard. Now, routing south over the outer sprawl of Glasgow, I settle down for the journey. No stowaways. No sudden presence behind me. Cleggie's checked.

We get to our cruising height. Safe, at least for now, I close my eyes. When Cleggie offers to lower the visor on my side of the cockpit I shake my head. The sun is lovely on my face. The muted whine of the engines is almost hypnotic. Within seconds, I'm asleep.

Over an hour later I feel the gentlest pressure on my thigh. It's Cleggie. He wants to show me something. 'There,' he says, pointing out of my window.

'Where?' I'm shielding my eyes against the glare of the sun.

'Down there. Trees? A lake? The big house?'

He drops the wing and suddenly I'm looking at the spread I recognize from Google Earth. It's not entirely clear how much of this land belongs to Mr Franklin but the estate looks enormous. Fields of what might be corn lap the house on two sides.

'Four hundred acres,' Cleggie says. 'Including the farm next door.'

I nod, remembering Pavel's question. 'So where did he get that kind of money?' I ask.

'Property development. At least that's what he tells us.'

'And the real story? In your opinion?'

'I've no idea. Except you'd never trust the guy. You want a closer look? Since we're here?'

Without waiting for an answer, he tightens the turn and pushes the control stick forward. My stomach comes up to meet my throat as the tiniest details in the landscape suddenly acquire an alarming size. Very low, we pull out of the dive as he circles the house below. There's a formal garden to the front of the property and, if there were fish in the ornamental pond, I'm sure we'd be able to count them.

On the second lap, I watch a figure emerge from the main entrance and stand in the sunshine at the top of the steps. He's wearing tan chinos and a pastel blue shirt. He has a mane of blond hair that may well be dyed and he flattens it against the tug of the wind as he looks up at us. A big face, the colour of the chinos. If I could lip read I fancy he's telling us – in Cleggie's phrase – to Foxtrot Oscar.

'Foxtrot Oscar?' I enquire.

'Fuck off.'

FORTY-TWO

'm back from the airfield at Dunkeswell. Cleggie has motored me to Flixcombe and pocketed a thick envelope of bank notes from a very grateful H before giving me the warmest hug and promising another outing whenever I fancy it. I watch him drive away and then step into the house. H says he's glad to see me in one piece but, as I'd anticipated, has absolutely no doubts about what has to happen next. Thank God he's had the presence of mind to summon Tony Morse back from Pompey. Another council of war, I think. That's what this kitchen was built for.

The object of our collective attention is Dominic Franklin. I come clean about my conversations with The Machine and his doting admirer, and I tell H that we owe Mateo a very large drink. Without him and his Vodafone friend I'd never have connected Baptiste and Franklin.

Tony Morse scribbles Franklin's name on a scrap of paper and disappears to make some calls. I've just told H the latest about Pavel. To my surprise, he seems genuinely upset.

'What's left for the guy?' he asks.

'Us,' I say. 'Clem. Malo. Franklin. What happened up in Glasgow. The whole drugs thing. What's happening everywhere.'

'But what can he *do*?'

'He can write about it. Turn it into a script. Do his best to amuse you.'

This possibility appears to have passed H by. Although he's patrolled the thin line between fact and widescreen fiction all his working life it hasn't occurred to him that something so fresh, so immediate, so personal could turn the key to the showbiz door and let him into a whole new world.

'You're serious?'

'Not me, him. *He*'s serious.'

'He can really do the business on all this?'

'Without a doubt.'

H studies his hands a moment, deep in thought, and then he looks up.

'How bad was it up there?'

'In Glasgow? With the Somalis?'

'Yeah.'

'It was terrible. It was beyond words. We . . . I . . . owe Cleggie everything.'

At this point, Tony returns. He has a young graduate from the university working as an intern at his office and he says she's a genius at financial analysis. She knows exactly where to go to for detailed company information and has a natural talent for connecting the key dots. Now she has a name, Dominic Franklin, we simply wait.

H wants to know how long all this might take.

Tony glances at his watch. 'She'll have a rough draft by close of play. The full Monty might take a little longer.'

H nods. Once again, he's listened to Tony and stayed his hand. Best to get our ducks in a row before we do anything rash. Only now does it occur to me to ask about Malo.

'He's gone,' H says.

'Gone?'

'I've sent him abroad again. For all our sakes. And to be fair to the boy, he volunteered.'

'For what?'

H holds my gaze. Then he extends a meaty hand and covers mine.

'You've had a shit couple of days,' he says. 'You don't need to know.'

But I do. I'm bearing scars now, and they're far from healed. I've been through an experience I wouldn't wish on anybody, not even H, and the thought of Malo ending up in the hands of the men with the machetes scares me witless. There has to be a better way, I tell H. I've had enough of being out of the loop.

H nods. He has that expression on his face that tells me he's only half-listening.

'You won't get hurt,' he insists, 'and neither will the boy. We've got this thing under control.'

'We?'

'Me and Mateo.'

'So how does that work?'

H won't tell me. He wants to know more about Cleggie.

'He was wonderful,' I say. I tell him about the emergency flare he let off in the car. For the first time this evening, H has a grin on his face.

'He did that? Nicked it out of the boot? Hid it?'

'He did.'

'Brilliant,' he says. 'You're right. Proper fucking job he's done. Moolah well spent.'

'So how much did you pay him?'

'A lot. Enough. Right peg? Right hole? Bloke like Arrows, you can't go wrong.'

Tony and I exchange glances. In H's teeming brain everyone has a nickname. Arrows, I think. Richly apposite.

I spend the rest of the day up in my bedroom. Now, I tell myself, is the moment I must try and chase the demons away. Here in Flixcombe you're safe. No one will hurt you. I resist the temptation to use the bolt on the door, get partly undressed, and slip under the covers. As I drift off to sleep I think I catch the far away bark of a shotgun. Andy, I think, out looking for something for tonight's pot.

It turns out I'm right. Half a day later, descending the stairs and padding barefoot into the kitchen, I find Jessie skinning two rabbits. A pheasant, already plucked, lies on a bloodied sheet of newsprint. H has obviously told her about Glasgow. Her sympathy feels unfeigned.

'You're right,' I agree. 'Total nightmare. You're normal and happy and quite pissed one moment. The next, some lunatic has a gun in your face. Is this what we should all get used to? Or am I just unlucky?'

Jessie rinses her hands in the sink. The water turns pink. 'Just one bit of good news,' she says.

'Tell me.'

'The Machine? Our fit friend in the leisure centre? He's gone. Haven't seen him for a couple of days.'

'And that car of his?'

'That's gone, too. No sign of it in the car park. I checked this morning.'

I nod and settle at the kitchen table. When I first met Brodie and we had the conversation in his car, I remember mentioning Pavel. I'd just come back from Glasgow and the sight of him lying there in the spinal unit hadn't left me for days. I think I'd even made a joke about The Machine taking care when he dived in. At the time this had seemed innocent enough but now I realize the implications. My phone conversation with his girlfriend Baptiste would have alarmed him. Ten minutes on Google and a call to the spinal unit would have been all it took. Better to have this crazy actress taken care of than risk her cosying up to the police.

'Thank God he's gone,' I tell Jessie. 'You can have your pool back now.'

Tony joins us. He's just been in the shower and he's swapped his suit for designer jeans and a lovely cashmere sweater. He's also been talking to his research assistant back at the office and he wants to share the results from her first trawl of the internet and the key databases.

'This stuff is complex,' Tony warns us. He's obviously been making notes during his phone conversation and he slips on a pair of half-moon glasses, peering at line after line of what look like company names.

Cleggie was right. Dominic Franklin, it appears, has made a great deal of money in property development. Sometimes, says Tony, he buys land himself, acquires planning permission and then oversees the physical build through a series of construction companies which he owns. Some of these projects are residential; others are on land zoned for commercial development. In other instances, he sells the planning permission to other developers and pockets the often huge windfall gain. Either way, Franklin's various enterprises are in rude health.

'You're telling us he's minted?' This from H.

'I'm telling you he's rich.'

'How rich?'

Tony's looking slightly pained. He tallies Franklin's assets. They include Beaufort House, a Knightsbridge townhouse overlooking Hyde Park, a newish duplex apartment beside the river in Exeter, a *finca* in the mountains of Andalucia, a five-bedroom house with Mediterranean views in Monaco, plus an ocean-going yacht in the nearby marina. Monaco, incidentally, is where Mrs Franklin has opted to live. Tax wise it makes perfect sense, he says, but we think there might be one or two other reasons. Franklin hates having his hands tied. This is a man who loves options.

I nod. The lovely Baptiste, I think.

'This stuff is kosher?' H wants to know.

'One hundred per cent,' Tony assures him. 'Franklin plays the shell game. Most of his physical assets and we're guessing most of his income is remitted overseas. It'll take Gabrielle a while to sort out the details but she thinks we're talking the Caymans, St Kitts and Nevis, Gibraltar, and Jersey. Getting inside these trusts and trying to work out the beneficial owner can take you a lifetime, which is why they exist. Mr Franklin is no friend of the Inland Revenue.'

'So where did your girl get the list of assets?'

'This stuff's open source. Mainly the *Economist* and the *Financial Times*. Franklin has a reputation for guile as well as greed. The man's a player, and that commands a degree of respect.'

H is beginning to fidget. He wants to know about this man's weaknesses, not his strengths. Tony, like me, can read him like a book.

'Two points of interest,' he says. 'Gabrielle has unearthed a chain of estate agents which also appear to belong to Franklin. He's worked the usual sorcery to disguise the ultimate ownership but Gabrielle thinks they're definitely his.'

'How many?'

'Over three dozen. Some in London, some in the Home Counties, a handful on the south coast. Always where the money is. Logically, there's no real mystery here. You're a developer. You build houses. Why not sell them, too? The fancy name is vertical integration. The only downside is all the hassle of staff and premises. Happily, Franklin has avoided all that.'

'How?'

'By basing the whole operation online. That way you get minimum exposure on the high street, which is good because the high street has become the kiss of death. Business rates, rent, utility bills. The smart guys take their operation online because the internet's free. Everyone's at it now but Franklin was one of the first to make it really work. The question you might ask is why?'

There's an exchange of glances around the table. Tony loves these occasions, playing to an audience, firing questions, savouring his own control. H says it's one of the reasons Tony's so good in court and he's probably right.

'Just tell us,' H says. 'Don't fuck about.'

'Our suspicion is he's washing money. And to make the operation worthwhile it has to be serious money, lots of money. And if that's true then it has to be drugs money.'

'Narco loot.'

'Precisely. Property is the biggest item most people ever buy. Get the right guys designing the agency software and you can wash trillions.'

'But why go to all that effort? When he's got a cracking business already?'

'Because these guys never know when to stop. They're masters of the universe. They want to play God. They want to be top of the pile, show everyone else how clever they are. Am I ringing any bells here?'

H has the grace to smile, but Tony hasn't finished.

'And you know the name he uses for the online estate agencies? *Home Free*. This, in Gabrielle's estimation, is Mr Franklin taking the piss. And I'm sure she's right.'

I'm looking at Tony. I want to know what drugs and where they might come from.

'My assumption is cocaine, and probably crack cocaine. Perhaps heroin, too. Class A definitely. That's where the market grows itself.'

Tony is looking at H. H definitely likes the sound of what he's hearing.

'But he wouldn't be hands-on, would he?' he says. 'He'd fucking sub that out.'

'Of course.'

'To who?'

'To the Plug,' I say softly, with a nod towards H. 'To the Somalis. To Larry Fab. And to young guys like The Machine.'

H leaves the kitchen to raid his cellar and reappears with a couple of bottles of Lafite. A modest celebration, he seems to be implying, might be in order. I, meanwhile, have been thinking hard about something Cleggie mentioned.

'This is a man with a Spitfire.' I'm looking at Tony. 'Am I right?'

'You are. And that's the second thing. Gabrielle says it's a Mark IX, which is apparently the one you really want. It's vanity, of course. It goes with the big yacht and the Monaco pad and the pile down the road. But Gabrielle's also found evidence that he's a genuine buff. She's been digging round some of the vintage aircraft sites and, unlike some owners, he actually pilots the thing himself. Spitfires can be like thoroughbred horses. You buy it and put it in a stable and pay all the maintenance bills and then get someone else to fly it. That's not the case with Franklin. He used to fly a Tiger Moth but these last couple of years he's done the conversion course to Spits. Now he's hands-on. Angels fifteen. Bandits everywhere. Tally fucking ho . . .'

H loves this stuff. He badly wants to get in Franklin's face, to put him in his gunsight and shoot him down. No surprises there. Our DVD of *The Battle of Britain* has practically worn out.

'Cleggie told me he's in the market for taking punters for rides,' I tell Tony. 'Is that true?'

'I don't know. This is certainly a two-seater. Gabrielle's seen the photos. But I'm not sure whether his current licence allows him to fly passengers.'

'Four thousand pounds a go? Would that be right?'

Even H blinks. '*How* much?'

I repeat the sum and I can see Tony nodding. Elsewhere in the country, other pilots are charging nearly £5000 for a fifty-minute flight, so Franklin has naturally decided to undercut the opposition.

Tony appears to have come to the end of his briefing. Gabrielle, he says, will be in touch again tomorrow, by which time she may have more to say about Mr F.

H at last looks up. On certain occasions, and now is the perfect example, he can't resist tabling a plan. You can sit around and yak for just so long. But then you have to *do* something.

'We book a flight.' He's looking at the faces round the table. 'And we think very hard about how to make that four grand work.'

FORTY-THREE

Next day I'm back in London for my three-monthly check-up. I take the Tube to Euston and walk the quarter mile to the specialist unit at UCLH. On this occasion I submit to a CT scan, which is much quicker than an MRI investigation, and after a visit to the cafe on the ground floor to get rid of the metallic taste in my mouth from the dye injection, I take the lift again to the rather bare office where my consultant holds court. He appears to warrant express treatment from the radiographers and by now the results of the scan should have arrived on his PC.

There's a brief delay while he deals with a particularly distressed patient and then I'm ushered in. I've been in this man's hands for more than a year now and after a rocky start I've grown to like him very much. He has an affability which is totally at odds with the news he so often has to impart. Even on the grimmest days he seems to have a smile on his face. He waves me into the empty chair in front of the desk and flicks quickly through my paper file. My chemo course is barely a memory. I'm naturally keen to find out whether it's worked or not and I'm wondering why he hasn't angled the screen of the PC so I can take a look at the scan.

'How do you feel?'

In truth, I feel awful, jumpy again, but I tell myself this has more to do with manic Somalis than any rogue cancer cells.

'Fine,' I say. 'Never better.'

'You mean that?' His eyes have strayed to the screen. 'No headaches? No loss of vision?'

'No.'

'Good.' He's frowning as if he doesn't believe me. 'Here's the picture.'

I peer at the screen. The X-rays have taken slices through my brain but it takes an expert to tell me what I should be looking at.

'Here.' The consultant is pointing at an island of darker grey, lagooned by white. 'It should have gone but it hasn't.'

A flurry of keystrokes take him to a much earlier MRI image. The good news is that the tumour is much smaller than it was but I sense he's disappointed.

'My fault?' I ask him. 'Or can I blame the chemo?'

'Blame the chemo. Anger can be a real tonic. Blame me. Blame anyone.'

'So what happens next?'

He's gone back to today's images. He scribbles himself a note and then consults my file again.

'No infections during the last course of treatment?'

'Nothing I noticed. Apart from all my hair falling out.'

'Good. The beret's a good look. I'd hang on to it if I were you.'

'A souvenir?'

'Alas, no. We're not quite through this yet.' There's the ghost of a frown on his face. 'This isn't going to kill you. Not in the short-ish term. But is there anything you really want to get done? Only now might be the time.'

I'm thinking very hard. I've had this news before from the same source but then he was talking about the Grim Reaper at my door. Now, my prospects appear to be a little brighter, something which gives me determination, as well as hope.

Anything I really want to get done?

'Yes,' I say. 'And thanks for the tip.'

I spend the evening back home at my apartment. In place of the crazed Somali face in the front of the Mercedes, I'm now haunted by that single image from the CT scan, the island of darkness on the map of my poor, wounded brain. Getting a terminal diagnosis and then surviving for a full year is supposed to harden you against bad news. You celebrate each new dawn, squeeze the happy essence out of every passing moment, and in the event that your longer-term prospects turn sour, you thank God for sparing you so far and count yourself lucky for the bonus weeks and months to come.

Only it doesn't quite work like that. We're engineered with an appetite for life. It's bred into us. It exists deep in our bones, our DNA. No one ever invented human beings who went happily to their grave. Even the poor souls at Auschwitz, so easily deluded by the promise of hot water and a pebble of soap, preferred Third

Reich lies to the overwhelming likelihood that their days – their
minutes – were numbered.

I nod at the bleak rightness of the thought. I plait my fingers.
I'm lying full length on the sofa, staring at the ceiling. My ceiling,
like most other ceilings in the world, is white. White is the colour
of light, of affirmation. White is the enemy of darkness. White is
where we want – need – to belong. So far, so good. Then I
remember Pavel. Is he thinking this way? Inert and immobile in
his hospital bed? Or does there come a moment of clarity when
you realize that the darkness might not, after all, be so unwelcome?
When darkness, in other words, becomes your very best friend?
To this, I realize I have no answer.

I hear a knock at the door. My first guess is H and I don't move.
But then I wonder whether it might be Malo, keyless as ever, back
from abroad. I pad down the hall and open the door. It's Evelyn,
my lovely neighbour. And she's holding a bottle of what looks
like Chianti.

'Present from Venice,' she says. 'How are we?'

I invite her in. To my shame I remember that the trip to Italy
was a celebration. After forty years with various publishing
houses, Evelyn has decided to return her editing pencil to the
jam jar and retire.

'A lady of leisure.' I give her a hug. 'What on earth will you do?'

She stays for most of the evening. We drink the Chianti and
half a bottle of Tempranillo I've found in the kitchen cupboard
that serves as my cellar. She tells me about Venice, which she'd
been very happy to explore alone, and about expeditions to various
destinations on the mainland. In Verona, she'd watched *The Barber
of Seville* in the Roman Arena. The performance, she said, hadn't
started until nine in the evening but the ancient stones were still
warm from the heat of the day and afterwards, past midnight, she'd
shared a bottle of prosecco with an Italian woman half her age on
the terrace of a nearby trattoria.

Evelyn speaks fluent Italian and has a real knack for befriending
total strangers, two talents which help make her one of life's
originals. She has a self-sufficiency, or maybe self-belief, that I've
always envied. Maybe it's something that comes from mothering
so many great books. Maybe it goes hand in hand with regular
attendance at the Catholic church down the road. Either way, I

envy her strength and her serenity and it's one of the many bless-ings of our relationship that I can tell her so.

Typically, she ignores the compliment. Instead, she wants to know about me. I've already decided to ignore what's been happening over the last week or so. She knows Malo well, and has become a bit of a fan, and I don't want to jeopardize any of that. The CT scan, on the other hand, is a different matter. To be blunt, I could use a little sympathy.

She joins me on the sofa. I very rarely cry and I have no inten-tion of doing so now but I have one or two things to get off my chest. Like every other cancer patient, I've submitted to the treat-ment and let the chemicals wreak havoc on my system. I've also believed the cautious assurances that everything may turn out for the best. Yet it hasn't. I've lost my hair, and my peace of mind, and a million other things, for nothing. I'm still going to die.

'But you may not, my lovely. Nothing is certain until it happens.'

'Really?'

'Really.' She's stroking my hand. 'Allotted span? Might that be a helpful phrase?'

Allotted span. I know exactly what she's saying. She's telling me that the whole thing is a mystery, that God decides, and that whatever happens is for the best. That's a lovely thought, and I truly appreciate her concern, but from where I'm sitting it doesn't feel that way at all. It feels raw, and horrible, and deeply unfair. Why me, for God's sake? Why not Brett Dooley? Or our mad Somalis? Or even Dominic Franklin, a man I haven't even met? Where's the fucking *justice* in all this?

It's an ugly thought and I have no intention of sharing it, but Evelyn is as intuitive as ever. In all the years we've been friends and neighbours, she's never failed to read my mind.

'It may not happen,' she says again. 'In the meantime, *carpe diem.*'

Seize the day? If only. I'm back in the consultant's office, back in a world where my life chances appear to be diminishing by the day. Was there anything I really wanted to get done, he'd asked. And now, sitting here with my lovely wise Evelyn, I realize that the answer is yes.

The closest I can get to Dominic Franklin is the number I have for Baptiste. When Evelyn has drained her final glass and left, I give Baptiste a ring. Please God, let her be at Beaufort House with her beau within touching distance.

She picks up at once. 'Enora Andressen?' She's recognized my number. 'You know what time it is?'

'Late. My apologies.'

'It's nearly fucking midnight. What is this?'

'I need to talk to Dominic.'

'*Dominic?*'

'Dominic.'

There's a long silence. I'm not supposed to know where she is, who she sleeps with, what she's up to. For a moment I think she's hung up on me, but I'm wrong.

'How did you get my name in the first place?' she asks.

'I saw you on TV. *EastEnders.* I watch the credits. It's a thespy thing. Pathetic, I know, but hey . . .'

'I used a different name. Ellen Waheen. Not Baptiste at all.'

'Yeah? Any reason?'

'That's not the point. How come you knew my real name? And how come you got my number?'

I'm picking at a loose thread in one of my cushions. Excellent questions.

'You want the truth?' I say at last. 'I can't remember.'

Another silence. Then she's back again. 'You're pissed,' she says.

'You're right. Is Dominic there?'

She says no. She says I should be careful who I phone. I know she's on the point of hanging up when the phone changes hands and I hear another voice, male, hints of a flat London accent. This is the guy I talked to before. I'm sure it is.

'Speak to me,' he says. 'Whoever you are.'

This time I make a real effort. Dominic Franklin, I think. Lord of the manor. Owner of half the world. Big in property. And huge in narcotics.

'My name is Enora Andressen,' I tell him. 'I'm a film actress. You can Google me. You may even have heard of me already.'

'You're right,' he's laughing, 'I have. What do you want?'

'You fly a Spitfire. Am I right?'

'Yeah.' He pauses. 'What's the game here? What are you after?'

I frown. I've worked hard on this. Pavel would call it back story.

'My grandfather was in the Battle of Britain,' I tell him. 'He's dead now but his birthday's coming up. Call it a celebration. Call it whatever you want. I have money. I'll pay whatever you charge.'

'That's bollocks.'

'Excuse me?'

'About your grandfather. Just tell it the way it is. You want a flight, yeah?'

'Yes.'

'No problem. A pleasure. You've got a pen there? Ring me again tomorrow on this number at half past nine. You've got a choice here. Someone else flies you and you pay him a lot of money. Or I'm in the pilot's seat and you get it for free. Your call. And apologies for my rude friend.'

I find a pen and something to write on. Then he's gone. *Carpe diem*, I think, gazing at his mobile number.

FORTY-FOUR

Cleggie gave me his card before we said goodbye and next morning, first thing, I ring the private number he scribbled on the back. When he first picks up he sounds grumpy but the moment he realizes it's me there's a real warmth in his voice. I ask him how he is.

'Bloody neck,' he says. 'Won't leave me alone.'

I want his advice. I'm in London just now but I have lots of time and a perfectly good car and I can meet him wherever might be convenient.

'You have something in mind?'

'Yes.'

'Care to tell me what?'

'No. Just bring that plane of yours. I'll give you another massage afterwards. Deal?'

We meet in the early afternoon at Blackbushe Airport, down the road from the military academy at Sandhurst. It's a lovely day, bright sunshine, just a bit of wind, and I enjoy the hour or so driving out of London. The airfield lies beside the main road. It looks like the set for the kind of period movie that features gorgeous women in floaty dresses and sleek male admirers with mischief in their eyes. I come to a halt in the main car park. Beyond the chain-link fence, just metres away, is a yellow biplane that smells of adventure and hot oil.

Cleggie is waiting in a cafe area in the terminal building. That same black flying suit. He gets to his feet and gives me a long hug. I can tell by the stiffness in his upper body that his neck is no better.

'You've brought that lovely plane of yours?'

'No, I came on my bike.'

He gets me a coffee and sits me down. We trade memories of what happened up in Glasgow the way veterans might discuss some long-ago battle. From the police, Cleggie has heard nothing.

He suspects they're far too shorthanded to waste time on a double kidnap and car theft.

'So how come the phone call?'

I'm sitting back with my coffee. Cleggie's Cessna is parked beside the yellow biplane.

'I'd like you to take me flying,' I say. 'And I'd like you to show me how to frighten someone so they start being honest with me.'

'I'm not with you.' He's frowning.

'Dual controls? One set for the pilot? One set for the passenger? Have I got that right?'

'Yes.'

'Then I'm the passenger.' I nod towards the Cessna. 'And you're going to teach me what to do.'

'I am?'

'Yes.'

He nods. He holds my gaze for a long moment, then finally he gets it. 'We're talking Spitfires? Mr Franklin?'

'Indeed.'

'And he's going to take you up?'

'That's the plan.'

Cleggie studies me a moment, then gets to his feet. 'My pleasure,' he says. 'Couldn't happen to a nicer man.'

We're in the air within minutes. Cleggie heads south-west, towards Salisbury Plain. He needs something called uncontrolled airspace to teach me a manoeuvre which will, he says, put the shits up anyone with half a brain. En route, he talks me through the essentials of flying straight and level: the lightest touch on the control column, fingertips feeling the aircraft, eyes fixed on a point I've selected some distance ahead.

'Nice and easy,' he says. 'Ignore the instruments. Just relax. Woman often make the best pilots because they're so sensitive. Don't think too hard. This stuff should come naturally.'

I assume he's kidding me. I don't feel the slightest bit relaxed but it's a relief not to be bothered by having to understand all the dials and read-outs on the dashboard, and after a while I begin to enjoy myself.

With Cleggie beside me, I feel safe in this little cocoon. I love the brightness of the light and the view is stupendous. We seem to be suspended high over the greens and yellows of southern England. Glance down and I can see a lattice of fields and country roads and tiny villages. Toy cars parked beside a church. A thin plume of smoke from a bonfire. A worm of a train slowing for a station. From time to time shreds of cloud suddenly appear and disappear and once, looking down, I spot our own shadow racing across a field of stubble, but otherwise there's absolutely no feeling of speed.

North of Salisbury, Cleggie makes contact with someone on the radio and warns them that we'll be performing aerobatics. There appears to be no conflicting traffic in the area. We have the sky to ourselves.

Cleggie takes back control and begins to climb. He says I've done well so far. A couple more sessions and we might start thinking about take-offs and landings. I tell him that's not my plan at all. I'm here to learn one thing and one thing only. How to take Dominic Franklin to a place where he might start telling me the truth.

'You're serious?'

'I am.'

'And you really think he's a player? In the drugs biz?'

'We're working on it.'

I tell him about the research that Tony Morse has commissioned, the shell companies in far-away tax havens, the smoke and mirrors he uses to get ever richer. None of this appears to surprise Cleggie.

'The man's an animal,' he says. 'Women? Money? Bricks and mortar? Shiny new toys? He can't resist it. He's Mr Ugly. Not on the outside, but on the inside. Some people are born that way and he's one of them.'

Mr Ugly. I like that.

Cleggie directs me to the altimeter. For what's about to happen, it's very important that we know exactly how high we are.

'Why?'

'Because I'm going to do something very violent to the aircraft. It'll make us black out. It won't last more than a couple of seconds but it'll give us a bit of a shake and I've a feeling that's what you may be after. You're the expert. Tell me what you think.'

I'm staring at the altimeter. It's showing eight thousand feet.

The fields below are suddenly very small. Then, without warning, Cleggie hauls back on the control column and the aircraft rears up and then falls away to the right. Violent is right. Violent is exactly the word. Blood seems to have drained from my head. A huge hand is trying to physically crush me. I can't see colours any more, no yellows, no greens, just grey. Then comes darkness and I'm struggling to even breathe. This, as promised, is terrifying. I very badly want it to stop.

Moments later, I come to. The world outside is revolving very fast. We're going round in tighter and tighter circles and we seem to be dropping like a stone. The pressure, if anything, is worse. My face feels like it's parting company with my skull. Then, abruptly, the pain stops and we're straight and level again, Cleggie is still at the controls as if nothing has happened. I'm looking out the window. The fields are much bigger.

'We call that a spin,' Cleggie says. 'In a Spitfire it can be much worse. That's because of the torque of the prop but I won't bother you with the details. What do you think?'

I think that will do very nicely indeed. How hard is it to survive?

'You mean from Franklin's point of view?'

'Of course. And maybe the plane, too.' I'm frowning. 'And me.'

'The Spit should be fine. Franklin will have a fight on his hands but it's nothing he shouldn't have practised.'

'Is that a guarantee?'

'No. In this game there are no guarantees.' He gestures at my control column. 'Your turn now.'

'*My* turn?' For some reason it hasn't occurred to me that we'll have to go through the whole nightmare a second time. 'You're serious?'

Cleggie doesn't answer. We're climbing again. Past eight thousand feet, he says, he'll talk me through exactly what I have to do. In essence it's very simple. On his command, I pull back and drop the control yoke to the right. No need for either of the pedals. Just my two hands.

'Try and get it right,' he says. 'Then we won't have to do it a third time.'

Good point. I have control. Straight and level. Miles ahead I can see an approaching ledge of cloud. I'm waiting for his cue, trying to remember the exact sequence of events. I feel a prickle of sweat, cold, on my face. Don't think too hard about what's about to happen, I tell myself. Just listen to Cleggie. And get it *right.*

'I'm going to count you down from three,' he says. 'Three . . . two . . .'

I want to take him by surprise and so I jump the gun, pulling the control column back into my lap and twisting the thingy on the top to the right. The plane reacts just like a horse might to the whip, rearing up and then spiralling away. Brilliant, I think, as the colours turn to grey and the iron corset on my body tightens and tightens, and I'm finally engulfed once again by the darkness. This time, I tell myself, it's not so bad. By the time I'm conscious again, Cleggie has regained control.

I steal a glance at the altimeter. It shows 6,780 feet.

'That was good,' he says. 'You might try a hijacking next.'

I'm back at Flixcombe by late afternoon. I've treated Cleggie to an early lunch, which is just the tonic I need because he finds it so easy to make me laugh. It takes nothing to prompt more war stories from his years in the Red Arrows and he tells them very well indeed. When I let him into our little secret, that's he's become 'Arrows' in H's fertile brain, it's his turn to laugh. He says he's flattered and I've a feeling he means it.

H knows nothing about my check-up at the hospital. He's not good around illness or injury, regarding them as marks of weakness, and on balance I prefer to keep the consultant's bleak prognosis to myself. By now, he's read everything he can lay his hands on about Spitfires.

'Why?' I ask.

'To get myself in the mood.'

'For what?'

'For my little trip with Franklin.'

Oddly enough, H has come up with the same game plan as yours truly: pay your money, get yourself in the back seat, wait until you're safely airborne, and then make life tough – in H's words – for the numpty in the front seat. H has yet to work out exactly what it takes to get a result like this but I tell him not to bother. Cleggie has wised me up about the rules that govern flying paid passengers. Very recently, the CAA have insisted that a pilot with a paying passenger in the back must have a full commercial licence. Franklin has hired a seasoned warbird pilot who's spent most of his professional life flying for British Airways to take care of this part of the business. As for friends and family, Franklin can fly them himself and stay legal.

H is frowning. Evidently this is news to him.

'You're telling me you're a mate of his?'

'I'm telling you he's offered me a flight.'

'When?'

'I've got to phone him later.'

'So what makes you so special?'

'I've no idea. Maybe he likes films that make you think.'

'Right.' He nods. 'And you're going to make it tough for the bastard?'

'I'm going to give him the fright of his life. If you don't believe me, talk to Cleggie. I saw him today. We went flying. Trust me. It's sorted.'

'What's sorted?'

'Franklin.'

H nods. He wants to know what else Cleggie has told me.

'He says Franklin's obsessed by the family tree. He thinks he's descended from John Franklin, the Arctic explorer. That's why he's renamed his pile Beaufort House. The Beaufort Sea was where Franklin was heading when he came to grief. According to Cleggie, the place means everything to him. He's owned it ten years now and spent a fortune doing it up.'

H sits back at the kitchen table. He says he's not happy with me taking a risk like this, which is nice, but I tell him this particular deal is non-negotiable. I suspect Franklin has poisoned thousands of lives and needs to confront one or two home truths.

'You're going to reform the bastard?'

'I'm going to frighten him half to death. Then we'll see.'

'You're sure about this? I don't mind paying. Four grand's small change if we put the shits up him.'

I shake my head. In a couple of minutes, I tell H, I'm going to ring Franklin on his private number. When it comes to a date for the flight, do we have a preference?

'No.' He turns away. 'Your call.'

*   *   *

H is subdued all evening. When I phone Franklin, he affects a certain rough charm. With the exception of tomorrow, he says I can have the pick of any of the next three mornings that follow. As it happens, he's in residence at Beaufort all week. After that, he's in America for a while. Best for me to ring back once I've made a decision.

Once again I consult H, and once again he leaves it to me. The sooner the better, I decide. An hour or so later, I phone Franklin again. He's not available but Baptiste is happy to take a message. Franklin must have had a word or two because she's being civil, even friendly. I tell her the day after tomorrow would be perfect for the flight.

'I'm sure that'll be fine,' she coos. 'We have so much to talk about.'

I say something inconsequential, assuming she's about to hang up, but it turns out I'm wrong.

'Dom's invited you to spend the night here,' she says.

'When?'

'Tomorrow.'

'That's very kind.' My pulse is beginning to race. 'What happens if I can't make it?'

'Then I'm afraid the flight's off. That's him speaking, not me.' She laughs. 'Your choice. Just let us know.'

FORTY-FIVE

I think long and hard about sharing the invitation with H. Part of me wants to do this thing alone. Malo is my son. I brought him up. I've spent most of my life with him. I don't have a moment's doubt that Franklin knows about Clem – knows where she is – and I want to be the one Malo thanks for getting him and Clem back together again.

But Malo and Clem aren't the only ones in harm's way. After Glasgow, I'm uncomfortably aware that I, too, have become a target. Malo has got us into very bad company and spending a night alone with the spider in the very middle of the web might not be a wise move on my part. My tumour will probably, in the end, kill me. But just now it seems equally possible that Dominic Franklin, or Brodie, or the lunatic Somalis, might get there first.

H, when I tell him about the invite the following morning, doesn't believe me.

'He wants you to spend the night before the flight there? At his place?'

'Yes.'

'Alone?'

'Yes.'

'Tonight?'

'Yes.'

'And he really thinks you'll say yes?'

'He does. And he might be right.'

H shakes his head. He says I'm crazy. He thinks I've got a death wish. Payback is fine, especially given what happened with the Somalis, but there's an art to these things. You have to stack the odds in your favour. You have to be artful, clever. You have to think time and place. Giving him a shake in his own fucking aeroplane, he says, is a demon idea. But a night alone under his own roof would be suicide.

'The place'll be full of Somalis,' he says. 'I guarantee it. He'll ship the buggers in by the thousand. There won't be enough of you to go round.'

'Then come with me,' I say.

'The pair of us, you mean? So they eat us both?'

I don't know whether he's joking but I'm not sure I care. What's important is to get airborne the following day, and to enjoy that moment when I can exact a little revenge for everything for which this man appears to be responsible. No one will die. No one will even be hurt. But I can return to Mother Earth with the knowledge that I, too, have a stake in all this, and that for a couple of seconds at least Mr Franklin – with all his power, and all his money – won't have it entirely his own way. Is this a modest ambition on my part? Yes, I suspect it is. But will it make me happy? *Mais oui.*

'If you'd prefer not to come,' I tell H, 'I'll quite understand. But don't think for a moment I'm not going.'

H says he'll give me a decision by lunchtime. I retire to my bedroom and put a call through to Pavel. He says he's pleased I phoned. He misses me badly. He says it's like having to leave a movie when you're really hooked and you want – *need* – to know how it all ends. I tell him I understand completely. A lot has happened since I last left his bedside and I take a great deal of pleasure in filling in the latest bits of the plot.

He says nothing until I've brought him completely up to date. What seems to fascinate him most is Franklin.

'Are you sure he's related to the explorer?' he asks. 'Sir John?'

'No, I'm not.'

'But he might be? Is that what we're saying?'

I'm grinning. 'We'. Good sign.

'Yes,' I tell him. 'He might, he might not. Either way it seems to matter to him.'

To my shame I know very little about Arctic exploration but Pavel is only too happy to oblige. He'd once done some work in this field for a docu-drama pitch. Sir John Franklin, he tells me, was a naval officer. A big fan of Nelson, he fought at the Battle of Copenhagen, and later at the Battle of Trafalgar. He enjoyed surviving against the odds and when peace came he turned to exploration.

Pavel's voice is very low and I'm having trouble hearing him.

'When he couldn't fight the French,' Pavel whispers, 'he headed north. Explored bits of the Arctic. Looked for the Northwest Passage. He came to grief in the end. Two ships, the *Terror* and the *Erebus*. Over a hundred men.'

'So what happened?'

'They got trapped in the ice.'

'And?'

'They all died.'

'And the ships?'

'The Canadians found them quite recently, lying on the seabed way up there in the high Arctic. Perfect condition. Pristine.'

'You dived on them?' My question is only half in jest. I'm thinking about Scapa Flow, and Pavel's strange obsession with moments of history frozen in time.

'If only,' he murmurs. 'So are you going to turn up tonight? At this man's house?'

'Yes,' I tell him. 'I am.'

This prospect appears to entrance him. I'm not quite sure what he expects to happen at Beaufort House but the sudden possibility of a historical perspective to this story of ours seems to have done him a power of good. His voice is stronger. He's back in that no-man's land between fact and fiction, between real life and fantasy, where he's done so much of his best work. There are echoes here of Cotehele, the project we've been nursing all these months, but Beaufort House, he seems to suggest, might prove infinitely more promising.

'How?' I enquire. 'Promising, how?'

'I've no idea.' He manages a soft laugh. 'But promise you'll ring back and tell me. Beaufort House? I can see it already.'

FORTY-SIX

In the end, after another lengthy discussion, H decides to come with me. In the name of prudence, he's made some phone calls to Pompey, summoned half a dozen soldiers to the colours, and asked them to drive to Flixcombe. This news is sobering. It means that he isn't at all sure about Franklin, about the way he might react if things get sticky. By now, thanks to the map in the library, H knows the area around Beaufort House by heart. There's a sawmill half a mile from the estate where the van can park up. He'll brief the guys beforehand. A phone call is all they'll need should the evening get out of hand.

'One favour, yeah?' We're in the kitchen, finishing lunch. 'Give the guy a ring. Tell him it's the two of us.'

I phone Franklin once H has gone. When I confirm I'd love to come across this evening, he seems genuinely pleased.

'You'll love it,' he says. 'It's something special, believe me.'

Something special? I tell him I don't understand.

'No worries. Trust me. Seven o'clock. Does that sound OK?'

I tell him seven o'clock's fine. Then I mention H.

'He's a good friend of mine,' I say lightly. 'Do you mind if he comes, too?'

There's a moment's silence, then he's back on the phone, as affable as ever.

'Not at all. Be great to meet you both. What size is he?'

'*Size?*'

'Yeah. Big? Small? Fat? Thin?'

I'm staring at the phone, trying to work this out. Stick with the facts, I tell myself.

'He's stocky,' I say. 'Broad in the chest. Medium height, maybe a bit shorter.'

'Perfect.' Franklin's laughing. 'Seven o'clock.'

The van from Pompey turns up in the late afternoon. These are faces I'm beginning to know very well and H meets them in a flurry of pumping handshakes on the turning circle in front of the house. They retire to the barn for a briefing and the fact that one of them is carrying a leather holdall suggests that they've arrived with weapons. Wes, for once, isn't among them.

H and I plan to leave Flixcombe around half past six. I'm wearing a really simple outfit I keep down at Flixcombe, saving it for occasions that might take me by surprise. I've put a bit of weight on thanks to the chemo and the neckline does my chest more than justice. H, who's elected for a linen jacket and black chinos, does a double take in the hall when I descend from upstairs. He's got used to the soft blonde fuzz that used to be a decent head of hair but he's never seen this dress before. He's talking to a couple of his Pompey mates and one of them gives me a whistle before H silences him with a look.

'Outstanding.' He steps across to me, his hands outstretched. 'At this rate I might have to marry you.'

We drive in convoy. H has given the map to the guys in the van and a mile or so short of Beaufort House he sticks his arm out of the window and gives them a departing wave as they peel off towards the sawmill. I've known him long enough now to recognize when he gets nervous and this is one of those occasions. He's preoccupied. He doesn't say much. He's thinking too hard.

'Don't worry.' I put my hand on his thigh. 'This is going to work. Believe me. All we have to do is get through to tomorrow. There won't be a problem.'

He shakes his head and slows for the turn into the Beaufort House estate. 'This is the guy that nearly had you killed,' he grunts. 'In case we fucking forget.'

There's a parking area to the rear of the property and discreet signs directing visitors to the main entrance, and as we follow the beautifully laid granite slabs I realize that this obligatory walk is deliberate. On foot you can't help noticing the delicate slate edging, the brimming flower beds, the lily pads on the ornamental pond and, as we round the corner of the building, the strutting male peacock on the half acre of lawn, displaying for his nearby mate.

The peacock is the giveaway, I tell H. This entire estate is a gigantic boast. Look at me. Feel the money. Admire my undoubted taste. I pause for a moment, tugging on H's arm, gazing at the view. The gardens fall away to a line of willows and what looks like a stream. Beyond the valley the land rises again and the distant ridges glow softly in the last of the sunshine. This is a million miles from a sagging tent in West Bay, I tell him. Take a good look. Remember. Because drugs money probably paid for this.

'You're right.' H is limping slightly. 'It paid for my place, too.'

A flight of stone steps goes up to the front door. It looks freshly painted, black gloss, and there's a period bell tug recessed into the wall for visitors.

I ring twice. We wait. Finally the door opens. The last time I saw Dominic Franklin he was standing on these same steps, staring up at Cleggie and me doing an overhead circuit of the estate. Now, I'm looking at a middle-aged man in a heavy double-breasted jacket with fall-away wings, edgings in gold braid, and elaborate epaulettes on both shoulders. On the left breast of the jacket is a star-shaped decoration of some kind, not small. Beneath the jacket is a pair of creamy breeches with a line of buttons above the knee. Lightly muscled legs are clad in white hose and the patent leather shoes are topped with a large silver buckle.

The legs come smartly to attention. The apparition offers a courtly bow, and off comes the tricorn hat.

H takes half a step backwards. He can't take his eyes off the sword, worn on the same side as the decoration.

'What's this?' he says. 'And who the fuck are you?'

'Sir John Franklin,' he says in a flat London accent. 'At your service.'

We step inside. This isn't a house at all, it's a stage set. Dominating the entrance hall is a huge polar bear. Erect on its back legs, it must stand eight feet tall. The eyes are beady and the mouth is half-open. Remarkable.

Another figure has appeared, a woman this time. I recognize Baptiste but only from her face. She's wearing a full-length dress in lovely greys and blues with an explosion of velvet bow at the breast. The flatness of the broad-brimmed straw hat is lightly ribboned, also in blue, and she extends a gloved hand in greeting.

'Lady Jane,' Franklin says. 'My second wife.'

'Delighted to make your acquaintance,' I tell her.

'On the contrary, my dear. The pleasure is entirely mine.'

Franklin is beaming, delighted that I've slipped so easily into role. He's shorter than I imagined, having seen him from Cleggie's aircraft. His face is heavily tanned, a shade that marries well with the powdered wig and the tricorn hat, and when he escorts us towards the sweep of the staircase there's just the hint of a limp.

'You know Greenhithe? On the Thames?' He's paused beside a framed watercolour hung on the panelling at the foot of the stairs. 'HMS *Terror*. I commissioned the artist especially. A fair likeness, might you agree?'

I'm gazing at a two-masted sailing vessel with a huge bowsprit. A crowd of spectators on the foreshore are waving their hats in the air and the occasion has the feel of a joyous farewell. Other boats are decorated with bunting and the crew of HMS *Terror* are two-deep on deck.

'A hundred and twenty men,' Franklin says gravely. 'All to perish.'

I nod. I express my sincerest sympathies. I've known this world of make-believe all my working life and it's a pleasure to accept such an unexpected challenge. For an amateur, Franklin's performance is far from shameful. He can't do much about his accent but he's happy to play the role for all it's worth. Baptiste, I suspect, may have helped.

I mount the staircase, following our host. H trails behind me, looking lost. Every next step is another picture, another scene, another face, and Franklin pauses beside each with a word of explanation. A ship's engineer in full uniform. A storm off the Orkneys. HMS *Erebus* in a pencil sketch on a flat, grey sea. A flight of geese against a flaring sunset. The expedition's first iceberg, a menacing tower of bluey white, lapped by wavelets. On the landing above, also panelled, we pause beside another image. This time it's a photo, an underwater shot taken with the help of a powerful lamp. The water is soupy, thick with tiny particles, but in the throw of the light I can see planking, even individual nails.

'My flagship at fifteen fathoms,' Franklin announces. 'All that remains, I'm afraid.'

'They found your ship?'

'They did, ma'am. And I thank them for their efforts. Does one shed a tear? So much effort? So many prospects? So much suffering? So much grief? Let time and history be our judge. Come . . .'

H is staring at the photo. Franklin's little party piece has sparked a snort of derision but he can't tear himself away. He wants to know what he's looking at. He wants to know what this thing *is*.

'I think it's Franklin's ship,' I tell him. 'Pavel told me the Canadians found the wreck a couple of years ago. Up in the Arctic.'

H nods. 'Bloody hell,' he grunts. Despite everything, I think he's impressed.

Baptiste shepherds us onwards. Franklin is waiting outside an open door. With a flourish, he invites us to step in and make ourselves at home. This will be our bedroom, our quarters. We have half an hour to dress. Dinner will be served downstairs.

'Dress?' H is lost again, much to Franklin's amusement. He indicates the two sets of costumes on the big four-poster bed.

'The dress,' he says, 'is for Eleanor, my first wife. And the uniform is for you, Captain Dannett. The last European to see us alive. You'll have much to tell us. And believe me, we'll hang on your every last word.'

He offers H what might be a smile and then, with another little bow, he's gone. I'm already inspecting my costume, holding it up against myself in the big full-length mirror. The empire line dress, in fine white lawn, is cut low and gathered tight under my breasts. On top I'm to wear a loose gown, framing the bareness of my neck and shoulders. Nice, I think. I glance round at H. He's staring at the rough woollen jersey, the greasy peaked cap, the stiff serge of the jacket. He seems to be in pain again, a sure sign of tension.

'I'm not wearing that,' he says.

'You must.' I kiss him on the lips. 'You're Captain Dannett. I expect you're a fisherman of some kind, or maybe a whaler. Make it up. The more extravagant the better. No one minds. It's a game. It's fun.'

H shakes his head. He didn't come to this poncey museum to be humiliated. He's not doing it.

I shrug. Franklin, wittingly or otherwise, has already stolen a march on H, literally upstaging his fellow drug baron. Whether or not he knows that H is Malo's dad isn't at all clear, though privately I suspect he must. What awaits us downstairs is also anyone's guess but already the evening has acquired a dimension – and, to be frank a promise – that I'd never anticipated.

I ask H to help me with Eleanor Franklin's dress. He's trying very hard not to look at my breasts but failing completely.

'If you're thinking Antibes,' I murmur, 'that was a very long time ago. A girl puts weight on, especially after chemo.'

'Lovely,' H says. I think he's perking up.

The dress fits perfectly. I do a couple of twirls for H's benefit and then kiss him again.

'Be Captain Dannett,' I suggest. 'Just for me.'

H is looking at the bed. I suspect he's wondering whether this might be the moment to negotiate the sleeping arrangements and I'm glad when he resists the temptation.

He takes off his jacket, peels off the black polo neck and steps out of his chinos. Like me, he could lose a few pounds. I hand him the trousers. It turns out they're made of canvas and even have the kind of stains you might acquire hunting something big and bloody out at sea. He struggles to button them round the waist but the pullover and the jacket are a looser fit.

He checks himself out in the mirror and I catch just a flicker of approval before he turns back to me and pulls a face. 'I'm boiling already,' he says. 'This stuff was made for the fucking Arctic.'

'Then take the jacket off, once we're downstairs.'

'Yeah? You think he might do that?'

'Who?'

'Captain Dannett.' He pulls me closer. 'You might have to owe me. You know that, don't you?'

I look him in the eyes. His face is inches away. 'You never talk to a lady like that, my dear. Especially not me. What if my husband were to get wind?'

'He's fucking dead, love.' H is grinning now. 'I read it in a book, so it must be true.'

FORTY-SEVEN

We dine downstairs. The room is enormous, wood everywhere, high ceiling, thick velvet drapes at every window. The middle of a long refectory table has been set for four. I've no idea whether the serving staff, or indeed the people in the kitchen, belong to the house but I realize that none of this stuff matters. What's far more important is that we preserve the fiction that costume and language has conferred on us.

We eat three courses of rich food, including cuts of meat that look like venison but aren't, and all the time between mouthfuls we make-believe that we're an Arctic explorer and his two wives and the gruff, slightly sweaty whaler who was the last white man to lay eyes on the fearless Sir John. This little party game spares us all the embarrassments that attend the reason we're really here and, by the time we're drunk enough to risk a home truth or two, we've definitely got to know each other.

By now, I'm expecting H, as it were, to break the ice and bring us back to real life, but it's Baptiste who interrupts the flow of period banter with a compliment I haven't been expecting.

I've been aware of her eyes on me all evening. She reaches across the table and takes my hand.

'I meant it about *Arpeggio*,' she says. 'I thought you were fabulous. Such a great performance. Friends of mine think you're wasted on the arts movie circuit.'

By now, I know I'm drunk. I nod. I'm wondering whether to respond as the first Mrs Franklin but decide against it. Enough is enough.

'That's kind,' I say. 'But I owe everything to the arts movie circuit. It lets you take risks. Mainstream makes you rich. My kind of movies keep you sane. Does that make sense?'

'Big time.' She's stroking my hand now. 'Such a pleasure to have you both here.'

For one giddy moment, H thought he was back in a real

conversation. Now, watching me and Baptiste, he's not so sure. He turns to Franklin, who still appears to be Sir John.

'Tell me about our Clemmie,' H says. 'What have you done with her?'

Baptiste stops stroking my hand. Franklin's looking slightly pained. There's a tiny hand bell beside his place setting and he pushes his chair back before picking it up. Within seconds, one of the women in period costume who've been waiting table appears. She's carrying a folded sheet of paper.

'For Eleanor, if you please.' Franklin nods at me.

I spread the sheet of paper on the table. Five verses of a poem or perhaps a song.

'*Lady Jane's Lament*,' Franklin explains, 'penned after my demise. As my first wife you were a poet of some distinction. Sadly you were taken by tuberculosis while I, my dear, finally succumbed to the ice. Hence this lament from Lady Jane. Would you do me the honour? Please?'

Another of the waiting staff has appeared, a youth this time, no more than Malo's age. He's dressed in what Evelyn once described as 'fustian' – heavy cloth woven from cotton, deeply practical. He has a guitar in one hand and a stool in the other. He settles on the stool, strums a chord or two, then looks inquiringly at Franklin.

'Ready?' Franklin's looking at me.

I'm trying to get the measure of the first verse.

We were homeward bound one night on the deep
Swinging in my hammock I fell asleep
I dreamed a dream and thought it true
Concerning Franklin and his gallant crew.

I look up at the youth. 'Just play the tune once,' I tell him.

He readily obliges. It's catchy and it's simple and before he even gets to the end I know there isn't going to be a problem. I have a good singing voice, especially with a couple of drinks inside me.

I glance at Franklin.

'Off you go.' He raises a finger. 'Three . . . two . . . one . . .'

The guitarist starts to play. I come in after the intro. I sing the first verse, my feet tapping, and then the rest of the lament. There's applause round the table for us both and I get up to give the guitarist a hug. The moment I'm back in my seat, reaching for my glass, Baptiste is all over me again.

'So where's Clemmie?' H is looking Franklin in the eye. 'And don't change the fucking subject this time.'

Franklin proffers the decanter of port, recharges my glass, helps himself, and then passes it to H. H doesn't move. He's barely touched his glass all evening. Crunch time, I think. Rather later than expected but here nonetheless.

'Your Clem is fine,' Franklin murmurs. 'She's perfectly safe.'

'You know where she is, don't you?'

'Of course.'

'And you've been talking to Mateo? Her dad?'

'I've been helping things along.'

'What does that mean?'

'It means my Somali friends have brokered an agreement. This was always their negotiation, not mine.'

H nods. This is what he's always suspected, that the Somalis made the money at the sharp end while Franklin stayed in the background, washing it, mainly by turning it into bricks and mortar.

'You're telling me you've fallen out with them?' H isn't smiling. 'Bit of a tiff?'

'They can be difficult people. In your day you were spared.'

'In Pompey, you mean?'

'Yes. In my book that makes you lucky. Wesley Kane was an exception. Most of the guys you relied on were white.'

'You know about Wes?'

'Everyone knows about Wes. The man's a legend. That makes you twice lucky.'

I withdraw my hand from Baptiste and settle back in my chair. I have a question here. 'Two Somalis nearly killed me up in Glasgow. How much did you know about that?'

'Not much. Until afterwards.'

'And you?' I direct the question at Baptiste. She's looking pained. It's obvious she wants no part of this conversation. 'Was it Brodie?' I ask her. 'Was it his idea? Did he think I'd talk to the police? Mention his name?'

She holds my gaze. Seconds tick by. Then she looks at her hands and nods. 'Brodie,' she agrees.

'He sent the Somalis up there?'

'He talked to them. Explained what was at stake. The rest was down to them.'

'Business hates uncertainty,' Franklin says quietly. 'Everyone knows that. Brodie had everything nailed down. He's an operator, that boy. He never drops a stitch. Everyone rates him. Especially the Somalis.'

'But he knew about my friend up in Glasgow. And he must have told the Somalis.'

'He did.'

'Which is why they came for me.'

'I expect so.'

'*Expect so?*' I'm suddenly very angry. 'You know. You *have* to know. The word I've heard is wholesale. That must put you at the top of the tree, because in the end you're the man in charge. I doubt you'll ever get your hands dirty. There's no way you're ever going to be in Bridport or Brixton or anywhere else for that matter. But you know the way it works, you know about the shit that goes in one end, and you love the money that comes out the other, and it must be very wonderful living here with your port decanter and your peacocks and knowing that the machine, the operation, the laundromat will just keep churning on. Am I getting just the teeniest bit warm here? Or should I blame the port?'

This is very definitely not the demure Eleanor I've been assigned in the evening's script but I don't care. Sir John, with his fancy costume, and his archly wooden dialogue, has made me vengeful. Glasgow, I think. The Premier Inn car park. The Landfall down in Bridport. Brett Dooley. Noodle. Kids chained to sofas and crap television in case they stray outside and come home with a habit. The glue's dripping out of what we used to call society and every-thing's falling apart. But how, exactly, do I voice this? How do I concentrate a mind like Franklin's and make him understand the damage he's done? And even if I could do this, if I was clever and articulate enough, would he even begin to care?

'Icebergs,' I tell him. 'Think icebergs, Sir John. The bit you can see on top and everything else that you can't. It killed you up there in the Arctic. And now it's killing us. All that shit you're selling. County lines. Kids out of control. Whatever it takes to make a profit. It's killing what's best in us. Slowly, oh so slowly. And it fucking hurts.'

H is studying me with something close to respect. Given his background, and everything that happened down in Pompey, he'll never be blame-free, but the man across the dining table in the tricorn hat has taken the drugs game into another dimension and everyone around this table knows it. Dominic Franklin can't fail to get richer. Neither does he intend to stop trying.

Baptiste beckons me closer across the table. I assume she wants to offer some form of apology on behalf of the Somalis but I'm wrong.

'I'd really like to fuck you,' she murmurs. 'You think that might be nice?'

I don't react. H is shaking his head. Franklin breaks the gathering silence. Malo, he says, was the one who took the deal to the Somalis in the first place.

'What deal?' I can't believe my ears.

'Deal?' Franklin is toying with his glass. 'Maybe business proposition might be closer. Clemmie's father is a rich man. He also carries kidnap insurance. The Somalis loved it. Why not borrow this rich kid's lovely girlfriend for a couple of days and then sell her back?'

'To whom?'

'To Clemmie's father, my dear. Or perhaps the insurance company. Twenty per cent of a million dollars? In real money, I make that two hundred grand. Not bad, eh?'

'But who gets the money? Who gets the two hundred?' I'm lost.

'That enterprising son of yours. Except it all went wrong. The guy with the dreadlocks and the teardrop tattoo? You know who I'm talking about? Your son took him for a friend, or perhaps a business partner, and that was foolish on his part. No way would he ever see any kind of commission. Not a penny. Neither, it began to occur to him, would he ever see the lovely Clemenza again. Which is when, I suspect, he began to panic.'

H nods. He seems to know most of this already. Unforgiveable.

'So what's going on?' I turn to H. 'You said you sent the boy abroad. Why? Why did you do that?'

H shakes his head. Looks pained. He doesn't want this conversation. He's in denial.

'Well?' I'm staring at Franklin now. 'What's my son been up to? Are we talking Bridport? Is that where it happened?'

Nothing. I'm looking at Baptiste. My last chance.

'You'd know.' I can hear my voice rising and rising. 'You're thick with Brodie and Brodie knows everything because Brodie's made that way. So what happened?'

Baptiste slips out of her chair and comes round the table. Moments later her tongue's in my ear. 'Come upstairs,' she whispers, 'then we can talk about it.'

Her hand has slipped into mine. She's trying to ease me back from the table. H is aware of her every move.

'Leave her alone.' He's looking up at Baptiste. 'I'll sort it.'

I don't give him a chance because something's suddenly hit me. It's come with the kind of force that good screenwriters, Pavel among them, reserve for the final reel. Malo is here in this house. Clem, too. Maybe at the back of the property. Maybe upstairs. Maybe they're banged up together. Maybe not. But that's exactly the kind of trick a man like this would pull, a little curtsey from the ultimate control freak after the dressing-up and the after-dinner musical entertainment. Here they are. Your precious babies. The rabbits from the hat. My pleasure.

I'm on my feet again. Whatever else happens, I need to deny Franklin that pleasure. He's robbed us already, helping himself to our lifeblood, to our kith and kin, to our peace of mind. If anyone lays hands on Malo and Clem in this house it's going to be me.

I ask Baptiste where I might find a toilet. For one agonizing second I think she's going to come with me but when I shake my head and ask for directions she sits down again. Down the corridor towards the kitchens. First door on the left.

I don't bother with the loo. I weave past and try the next door on the left but it's locked. At the far end of the corridor I can hear a fall of water from the kitchen. Between me and the kitchen is yet another door. This time, it opens. I peer inside, aware of a blast of chill air. Then comes laughter from the kitchen and the sound of footsteps. Alarmed, I slip inside the room and close the door behind me. In the pitch darkness I wait for the footsteps to approach. When nothing happens, my fingers locate a switch on the wall. The room is very cold, close to freezing.

By now, the evening has become surreal: too much alcohol, too much make-believe, and then the sudden, hot spark of anger that triggered my little outburst. I meant every word, and then some, but in truth I've slipped my moorings. I'm not sure where I am, or even who I am, and unlike Pavel I'm hopelessly under-equipped to cope. Anything can happen. And probably will.

My imagination, for once, has ceased to be a friend. I turn on the light, praying that this isn't the moment I discover the stiffened remains of my precious son and his lovely girlfriend, but mercifully I'm spared. Instead, I'm looking at what must be a cold store.

Shelves are laden with various perishables. There are boxes of butter and margarine, piles of fresh salad veggies, vacuum packs of bacon and other meats. But what really takes my eye are two headless animals, unskinned, hanging from meat hooks against the left-hand wall. They have hooves, like deer, but their pelts are thicker, hairier. Someone has run a knife up their bellies and disembowelled them but they still, visibly, belong in the wild. A knife – almost of the length of a machete – lies in a plastic bowl on the floor. The bowl is smeared with what I take to be dried blood. I've taken a step closer when the door opens silently behind me.

I sense the movement, the stir of cold air, and spin groggily around. It's Franklin. And he's closing the door.

I don't bother with excuses about getting lost. No point.

'Where are they?' I manage.

'Where are who?'

'My son. Malo. Clem.'

'You think they're here? In this house?'

'I know they are.'

'Really?' Franklin's smiling now. 'How sweet.'

Sweet does it for me. I bend for the knife and turn to face him, fighting for my balance. The smile has widened. The knife is evidently a further source of amusement.

'You know what they are?' He nods at the animals.

I shake my head, hold his gaze, the blade of the big knife steady in my hand. I don't care about his fucking animals, about his fancy dress, about his Spitfire, about the view his wife enjoys from their grand Monaco apartment, about all the money he's made. I just want my son and his girlfriend back.

'Caribou,' he says softly. 'They're caribou. I laid hands on a breeding pair a while back but it hasn't worked. They need it to be colder. Thousands live up in the Canadian high Arctic. Sir John used to survive on them.' He nods at the animal on the left. 'We had a couple of fillets from that one at dinner just now. *Un vrai hommage, n'est-ce pas?*'

I'm staring at him, amazed. Mr Ugly speaking French? In a passable accent? *Impossible.*

'You think I'm a yob, don't you?' He's read my mind.

'That would be unfair to yobs.'

'What, then? What do you think?'

'I think what I thought back then at the table. These last few weeks, believe it or not, I've learned a thing or two, seen stuff even you would find hard to believe. Your business is obscene. It eats people whole and spits them out.'

'My business?'

'Drugs. Bad. Smack. You name it. Any fucking thing that will bring you a profit. Noodle? A psycho called Brett Dooley? Larry Fab? I doubt any of these people mean anything to you because you've never got your hands dirty, and that just makes it worse because the real obscenity is here, in this house. Everything you've bought, everything you've hung on the wall, every car you've parked outside is paid for by drugs money. People bleed to stock your cellar, to have your Spitfire serviced, to improve your view, and all of that to feed your grotesque ego.'

Franklin doesn't say anything. Then comes that hideous smile again. 'And your friend H? Does he get this brave little speech as well?'

I shake my head. I'm not going to play this game any more. I've said what I've said. I'm done. All that matters, I tell him, is Malo and Clem.

There's a long silence between us. Then Franklin shrugs and says I can have free run of the entire house, every room, every cupboard, every outhouse. Either now or tomorrow morning. My choice. In the meantime, we might return to the dinner table and behave like civilized people.

Mention of civilized people does it for me. I take a step towards him, tightening my grip on the knife.

'One question,' I say. 'Just one. Do you know where they are? Malo and Clem?'

'Yes.' He half-turns and reaches for the door handle. 'And so does your friend.'

'Friend?'

'H.'

Our eyes lock. Franklin is within range now but he's making
no effort to defend himself. A single thrust, a downward stab,
and I can bring this whole miserable business to an end. The
police won't be amused, and neither will Tony Morse, but at least
I'll have extracted just an ounce or two of payback. The likes of
Dominic Franklin, I realize dimly, are more right than they'll ever
know. Life, in the end, is all about money. In for a penny, in for
a pound.

Now, I think. Allotted span, I think. Pretend you're a Somali.
Pretend you're in a Mercedes that's just crashed. Pretend you
need to settle accounts once and for all. Seize the moment. *Carpe
diem.* Just do it.

Franklin at last understands I'm serious. He takes a tiny step
towards me, reaching for the knife, and as he does so the door
behind him bursts open and there are suddenly three of us in the
chilly gloom. H has a talent for reducing complex situations to a
line of the simplest dialogue. He pushes Franklin aside and twists
the knife from my hand.

'You're welcome to kill the bastard,' he grunts. 'But spare me
the fucking paperwork afterwards.'

FORTY-EIGHT

We're out in the corridor. Franklin has disappeared.

'You OK?' H is looking at me.

I nod, say nothing. My anger has gone and I'm exhausted. I'm also very drunk.

H steers me towards the door that leads out to the hall and the staircase. I know already that the staircase is going to be a challenge and I'm praying that our hostess isn't on hand to witness the car crash that's about to happen. H knows it's going to be tough, too, and the moment we get to the bottom stair, wincing with pain, he half carries me up in a cascade of soft cotton-lined lawn, lightly scented with Coco Chanel. As we leave the ground floor, and picture after picture drifts past in a blur of icebergs and impending catastrophe, I plant a sloppy kiss on the moistness of his cheek. He's saved me from killing Dominic Franklin and – even more importantly – he's saved me from that bloody woman. He's also lied to me, not just once but a trillion times.

'This has to stop,' I tell him.

'What?'

'The lying. You treat me like an infant. I'm better than that. And so are you.'

We make it upstairs. H opens the bedroom door with his foot and carries me across to the safety of the four poster. There's a brass bolt on the inside of the door and he slips it across. When he returns to the bed I hoist myself half-upright and try to get him into focus. Shouldn't we summon the Pompey crew?

'No point.' H shakes his head. 'There's no way anything's going to happen.'

'How do you know?'

H smiles down at me. Then he pats the bulge in the pocket of Captain Dannett's serge trousers.

'What's that?'

H produces a gun. I recognize the Glock automatic Malo had stolen.

'Franklin knows you've got it?'

'Of course. And he knows I'll use it, too. If you think he's just like me, you're wrong. The guy was never on the street. He's never done the business. He's always kept his distance. Just now that makes him there for the taking. And he's bright enough to understand that.'

I nod. Distance, I think. This is exactly what I've just been raving about in the chill room. At least I got that bit right.

'And Malo?' I mutter.

H settles on the bed and takes a closer look at me. 'You're sure you want to know? It's not the funniest story. The boy was a dickhead. Even he admits it.'

'I have to know. Just tell me.'

H nods, then sheds the jacket and lets it fall to the floor. Malo and Clemmie, he says, had got into the habit of riding down to Flixcombe once the weather cheered up in late spring. Some evenings, they'd take the Harley into Bridport and trouble a pub or two.

I nod wearily but at the mention of the Landfall, my mind is suddenly pin-sharp. I can picture this happening. Clem doesn't drink. She'd park the beast outside the pub and unzip her leather jacket, feeding the locals' curiosity. Malo would sort out the drinks. They were young. They were beautiful. They were exotic. They obviously had money. And this combination would open countless conversational doors.

'They made friends with the locals?' I've closed my eyes. 'Is that what you're telling me?'

'They did. Big time.'

'And some of them were selling?'

'Of course.'

'Anyone in particular? Anyone I might know?'

'The kid on the beach. Whatever his name was.'

I nod. Noodle.

'Cocaine, was it?'

'Yes. At least that's what our boy owned up to.'

'Really?'

I hear a grunt from H, then I drift away. Time seems to pass. Maybe I've been asleep. I open my eyes. My hands are tidily folded over my belly and H has been kind enough to prop my head on a couple of pillows.

From the bed, I have a perfect view of a framed pen-and-ink sketch of a sailing boat trapped in ice. This is the same vessel that left Greenhithe all those years ago, but the crew crowding the decks seem to have disappeared. There's nothing except the ship, the bare rigging and a wilderness of ice. This bleak image, it occurs to me, serves as the perfect metaphor for H's unfolding story. A shipwreck in the making. Lives at stake. And fates possibly worse than death.

'The crew ate each other,' I tell H. 'Pavel told me that. The Eskimos knew about it at the time and Canadian scientists have been working on bones they recovered. Human bones. With saw marks. So maybe we were lucky tonight. What do you think?'

H laughs softly. He's sitting on the edge of the bed. He half-turns and reaches down before stroking my face. The Glock still lies on the counterpane.

'Malo?' he says. 'You still want to know what happened?'

My nod draws another smile from H. The boy Noodle, he says, came up with a couple of deals that our son described as 'outstanding'. Clemmie wouldn't touch the stuff but that made no difference to Malo. Through Noodle, he met another dealer, younger, much more together.

'Brodie,' I murmur. 'The Machine.'

'That's right. They spent some time together, had a drink or two, talked business.'

'This is to do with cocaine?'

'Big time. And it was about Clemmie, as well. You can hear him, can't you? He worshipped the girl but he loved to show her off, too. Fabulous to look at. Drove the biggest fucking bike in town. Rich daddio. Great connections back home.'

'Meaning Colombia?'

'Right.'

'Meaning cocaine?'

'Of course. This Brodie's not stupid. A couple of nights in the pub with Malo and he's looking at the deal of his dreams, hundreds of kilos of the marching powder at a silly price, all thanks to this loved-up bloke who never knew when to stop drinking.'

'And Clem? She knew about all this?'

'She knew lots. She was there. She was listening. She was probably the only one sober enough to realize what a twat Malo could be. All he had to do, our boy, is plant an idea and that's exactly what he did.'

'Deliberately?'

'Yes. He wanted to play the big man in town. The girl, the bike, the connections, it was all there. People like Brodie can spot an opportunity at a thousand yards. It was there for the taking. Franklin was right. In the end Malo even *suggested* the fucking idea. He knew about the kidnap insurance Mateo carried. There was money to be made.'

There for the taking. The simplicity of the proposition suddenly hits me.

'You mean Clem, don't you? You mean *she* was there for the taking?'

'Of course. Brodie put the boy in touch with Mr Dreadlocks. Malo wanted twenty per cent to help make it happen. Brodie knocks out a plan and the Somalis do the rest. The next thing Malo knows is a phone call from a number he doesn't recognize and a shot of his lovely girlfriend's favourite tattoo. Game, set and fucking match to Mr Dreadlocks. Malo was out of his depth from the start. He wanted to be the next Mister Big and he didn't have a prayer.'

'He probably wanted to be you,' I point out.

'Yeah? Well, I've met the dreadlocks guy. And believe me, he's terrifying.'

I close my eyes again. My head is beginning to thump, not a good sign, but I want to know more. And I know how to get it. My hand finds H's on the counterpane.

'Undress me, please. Start at the bottom and work up.'

H does my bidding. I ask him about Mateo.

'He fell into the hands of the insurance people. We all did. That meant O'Keefe. Me and Mateo weren't impressed, Mateo especially. He wanted to talk to these people himself, do his own deal. By the time O'Keefe got Clemmie back she'd be drawing a pension.'

'So how did Mateo make contact?'

'He got a number. It arrived on his phone from a burner. It was Brodie's number but he'd no idea who sent it.'

'Malo,' I whisper. 'Had to be.'

'Of course. And that's when things started to shift a bit. Mateo and Brodie got together. The Somalis love Brodie because he delivers, and so does the idiot downstairs.'

'But Baptiste is all over Brodie. Does Franklin know that?'

'I've no idea. No offence, but I get the impression that woman is all over everyone. Maybe that's what turns Franklin on. Everyone to his own, eh?'

I'm smiling. H is making a very good job of removing my cotton hose. I can feel his thick fingers, remarkably deft, working under the layer of lawn. On his command, I ease my bum up to let him slip the hose off. My legs are now naked under the dress. He stops when he gets to my knickers.

At this point, he's telling me everything he learned from Mateo. Clemmie's dad had discovered that his kidnapped daughter was being held in a remote Spanish *finca* in the mountains above Granada. The estate, complete with swimming pool and fully equipped gym, turned out to belong to Franklin. Clemmie has been there since she was intercepted by the Somalis in a backstreet in Beckenham, bundled into the back of a van and driven on to a cross-Channel ferry. Her Harley has now been dismembered and bits of it are for sale on a spare-parts site registered to a company on a Luton trading estate.

'And Malo? Our lovely son?'

'I needed to get him out of the way. Once the deal had been agreed and Mateo knew that Clemmie was safe at the *finca* he was happy to talk to Franklin and make that happen. The boy was all over the place. You must have seen it yourself. He wanted to become a big player in the narco-biz and he fucked up. Call it convalescence. Call it what you like. But he was safer with Clemmie.'

'And he's OK now? Malo?'

'He says he's been spoiled rotten. Franklin flew a chef down who knows a thing or two about Colombian cuisine. The boy says we ought to try *lechona casera*. It's a kind of pork thing. The chef gave him a recipe.'

'You've been *talking* to him? Malo?'

'Yes.'

'And the deal?'

'Done. Brodie and Dreadlocks get two million US of the marching powder for free. That's street value, of course. Wholesale it's way, way cheaper which should keep the insurance people happy. The Somalis think it's fucking Christmas and you know what? They're right.'

I nod. Sick, I think. But great business.

H is examining the top of my dress. In search of a button or two his fingers brush my breasts. His eyes find mine.

'What do you think?'

'The buttons are at the back.'

'You wanna turn over?'

'I do.'

I make the move, my face flat on the pillow while H works on the line of buttons. Then comes the lightest knock on the door. H freezes. I lift my head from the pillow.

Another knock, louder. Then someone tries the handle.

'*C'est moi. Vous êtes la dedans?*' It's Baptiste.

'Tell her to fuck off.' H's mouth is very close to my ear.

'*Qu'est-ce que vous voulez?*' I ask.

'*Toi, chérie. Et ton copain. Ca fait trois. Parfait.*'

I tell H she wants a threesome. H is horrified.

'No fucking way.'

This is an impasse. For whatever reason, Baptiste has started to sing. It's the *Lament* again and she's word perfect. Dimly I remember that Franklin has ordered a helicopter for tomorrow to fly her to Stansted. She's off abroad for a while, so maybe this is some kind of farewell treat. Bizarre, I think. Then I have an idea. I twist my head and look up at H. Second thoughts.

'Maybe your guys in the van?' I whisper.

'You mean the Pompey blokes? Because of her?'

'Yes. That's why they came, isn't it? To dig us out if things got sticky?'

H shakes his head. The thought of Pompey's finest discovering their boss in fear of a beautiful woman offering sex doesn't appeal at all. She'll get bored and go away, he says. We'll just ignore her.

And so we do. H sorts the last of the buttons and I turn over and extend my hands and let him pull me up until I'm in a sitting position. Then my feet find the rug on the floor and, with H's help, I stand up.

He treats me like the child I've become. He makes me put my arms in the air while he reaches down, gathers the dress, and slips it over my head. Naked apart from my knickers, I'm aware of his eyes on my body.

'You're beautiful,' he says. 'More beautiful now than then.'

'Then?'

'Antibes.'

'Ah . . .' I smile at him. 'Malo.'

Baptiste appears to have given up. After a snort of frustration, I listen to her footsteps padding away down the corridor outside. I collapse backwards on to the bed.

'I was drunk last time,' I mumble. 'This is becoming a habit.'

H is looking down at me. 'You need looking after,' he says.

He begins to get undressed. I take a final look at the picture on the wall. For a moment I swear I can hear the Arctic wind keening around the bare masts of that doomed ship, half-wrecked already, and then my eyes close and I'm gone.

Some time later, I'm aware of the sigh of the mattress as H climbs in. My hand finds his under the sheets, and I give it a squeeze.

'You're a good man,' I tell him. 'Despite everything.'

FORTY-NINE

We're down for breakfast by half past eight. My head is pounding and even the sight of a rack of toast makes my stomach heave. There's no sign of either Baptiste or Franklin and it appears from the table setting that we shall be eating alone. A single ship's biscuit on a bone-white plate is the only reminder of last night's performance. I look hard for weevils but see nothing untoward. Our revels now are ended. And despite a growing urge to throw up, I'm glad.

Water helps. I drink two glasses, one after the other, and decline the offer of devilled kidneys. H, unlike me, seems to have emerged from last night unscathed. I'm very grateful for last night and I tell him so. If I was a pain, I add, I'm afraid he has to put up with it. One of us has to have a conscience and it happens to be me.

'Conscience?' The word appears to mystify him.

'Noodle,' I tell him. His body sprawled on those wet pebbles is the one image I can't seem to shake. It even eclipses the thought of a Somali machete.

H calls for more toast and another jug of coffee. There's still no sign of our hosts but very faintly I think I can hear the clatter of an approaching helicopter. It gets louder and louder until it seems to be directly above the house. Baptiste, I think, off to Stansted. Last night's rejection must have hurt. She's not even bothering to say goodbye.

Abruptly the noise stops and I assume the helicopter must have landed. H, still waiting for the toast and coffee, pushes back his chair and walks across to one of the tall windows that look out on to the front lawn and the ornamental gardens. The landing pad must be elsewhere because there's no sign of a helicopter and H is about to return to the table when something catches his eye.

'Fuck me . . .' I hear him mutter. Then he's gone.

I sit alone at the table. The coffee arrives. I eye the fresh toast and decide not to tempt fate. Then I hear voices. One of them belongs to H. Another to Franklin. But it's the third voice, lighter, that makes me blink. It's a woman. She sounds young. She's laughing.

A door opens behind me. I turn in my chair. First into the room is Franklin. He's wearing jeans and an old T-shirt and a pair of sandals and this time he's playing the magician for real. He stands aside, one arm outstretched. The rabbit from the hat.

Clem.

I get up, overwhelmed. I put my arms round her. She looks wonderful. She glows with health and sunshine and good living. And she's not alone. Behind her, uncharacteristically quiet, is Malo. He gets a hug, too, maybe longer. I tug them both towards the table. I want them to sit down, to have a slice of toast, to drink coffee. I want us all to be together, to be normal again. The last couple of weeks barely happened. And so here we are.

H joins us. Franklin, with admirable tact, has disappeared. This, it turns out, is the real point of the invitation. Not to spend an entire evening celebrating a long-ago explorer who blew his chances and lost all those men but to welcome back the most important, the most wilful and the most reckless man in my life.

'I'm sorry, Mum,' Malo says.

'You bad, bad boy.' I'm crying now. I give him another hug. 'Tell me everything.'

He doesn't, of course. I get a mumbled account of life in the Sierra Nevada, of days around the pool and chilly nights eyeing the barbecue pit. He's learned a little Spanish from his new friend in the kitchen at Franklin's *finca* and he's been trying it out on Clem ever since. I nod. I'm aware of a new body language between them. They were always physically close, closer than I dreamed Malo could tolerate, but just now they seem inseparable. Clem has obviously forgiven my son his many transgressions.

I must do the same, H tells me, once they've gone upstairs for a shower. The deal is done. The police remain out of the loop. Brodie and Franklin will doubtless get richer by the minute, but just now that's none of our business. The boy and Clemmie are home safe. And that's all that matters.

It's at this point that Franklin joins us again. He appears to have forgotten my attempt to kill him. The chopper, he tells us, will be taking Clemenza to London where Mateo is waiting to greet her. In the meantime, the Spitfire is at my disposal. Exeter Airport is a forty-minute drive away. We could be airborne by mid-morning.

I shake my head and make my excuses. I got a great deal off my chest last night and this man knows exactly how I feel about the life he's chosen for himself, and for others. My son and his lovely girlfriend are back in one piece. And – possibly more important – I'm not at all sure my stomach could handle another gut-wrenching spin from God knows what height.

This news appears to come as no surprise to Franklin. He's already mentioned this morning's expedition to Malo and said there might be the possibility of a spare seat.

'And?'

'He jumped at it.'

Listening, H can only shake his head. The boy – our boy – has given us nothing but grief for what feels like an eternity. He's tried to play the apprentice drug baron and failed completely. He's forced H into corners of Brixton he never wants to smell again, and he's left me on the receiving end of a possible prison sentence. Yet here we are, as silly and complicit as ever. Relief is too small a word. Love might be better.

'This shit can't go on.' H is beaming. 'There has to be a better way.'

At the end of the week, at H's insistence, Cleggie flies me to Glasgow again. By now I've decided to try to learn to fly. The medical might be tricky, and the statutory tests will have to await the next CT scan, but in the meantime Cleggie is only too happy to let me handle the straight and level bits as we head north. He even talks me through the slow descent to the grey smudge that is Glasgow, and only takes over once the runway is in sight.

We get a cab to the hospital. When Cleggie offers to accompany me into the spinal injuries unit, I shake my head. Franklin has given me an assurance that my problems with the Somalis are over. They, like Brodie, are too busy celebrating the deal they've pulled off.

Pavel, when I finally make it to his bedside and stoop to kiss him, is very pleased I've come. There's a little colour in his face, which is a surprise, and when I ask why, he nods at one of the windows across the ward. The window faces due south and at certain times in the afternoon the sun comes streaming in. The nursing staff, aware of his love of sunshine, have been wheeling him over to the open window on a regular basis and the result is a modest tan.

'Not just outside but inside.' Pavel's smile is another transformation. Wonderful.

I settle down and tell him everything. He especially likes the costume games and role-playing at Beaufort House. When I do my best to describe the way the house looks inside – so many caps doffed to Sir John and his doomed expedition – he seems transfixed. People should do more of this, he tells me. We need to get out of our tiny selves. We need to think hard about being someone else. This kind of make-believe isn't just free, it isn't just fun, it can be a liberation.

'From what?' I ask him.

He ponders this question for a while. Finally he says we all need to shed a layer or two, free ourselves from the dead weight of being who we are, turn life on its head and take a proper look. On the face of it, this sounds like a charter for some far-out loony cult, but it's impossible to be with someone in Pavel's state and not realize why it might be so important.

It also reminds me of another development. 'You remember my dealings with the police? Over the boy who ended up on the beach?'

'Noodle.' He nods. 'So what's happened?'

'The post-mortem showed death by drowning. No other damage.'

'And the tox? They did the tox?'

'They did. Heroin and crack cocaine.'

'Supplied by you?'

'Helped along by me. NFA.' I'm smiling. 'No further action.'

Pavel is deep in thought again. He remembers every detail of the various accounts I've shared with him.

'Brodie,' he says finally. 'He saw you in the car park that night. He checked the tent on the beach. The boy was out of it. He weighs nothing. He's light as a feather. Brodie carries him into the sea and holds him under.' He offers a nod of approval. 'As a way to go, not at all bad.' His eyes find mine again. 'You agree?'

I do.

'Something else.' I edge the chair a little closer. 'H wants you to turn all this into a movie. He's fallen out of love with Cotehele and he doesn't want a period piece any more. He wants the real thing, real life. This is on our doorstep. You can be you, H can be H, Malo can spend all the money, and I can be me. How does that sound?'

Pavel takes a while to consider the idea. Finally he closes his eyes. 'Perfect,' he whispers. 'Because real life is one of those propositions you have to take on trust.' He summons the flicker of a smile. 'Sight unseen.'